VOICES

To Holly—
In admiration of
your gifts of voice &
words — enjoy the music!

4-22-
"Launch Day"

ROBERT YEHLING

Open Books Press
Bloomington, Indiana

Published by Open Books Press, USA

www.OpenBooksPress.com
info@OpenBooksPress.com

An imprint of Pen & Publish, Inc.
www.PenandPublish.com
Bloomington, Indiana
(314) 827-6567

Print ISBN: 978-1-941799-49-9
eBook ISBN: 978-1-941799-61-1

Library of Congress Control Number: 2017904946

Cover Design: Shane P. Brisson

In memory of my first music editor, *Blade-Tribune* editor and author Bill Missett (1939–2016). Thank you for opening my world to concert reviews, musician interviews, and your collection of ten thousand albums that forever changed my relationship to music.

PART ONE

"With our music, we are trying to play into the souls of people."

—Jimi Hendrix

1

AUGUST 15, 1997

CHEERS, SMOKE, AND ELECTRICITY ENGULFED TWENTY thousand fans, their delirium a rogue wave about to consume the singer before he could exit stage left into rock godhood. Hoisted matches and lit cigarette lighters burned through a supercharged haze of sweat, herb, diffused light, and pyrotechnic exhaust. The singer slumped against his microphone stand as blue and yellow floodlights swept the stage, capturing and releasing his equally disheveled band mates beneath their glare.

Tom beamed at the ecstatic fans. Those he could see in the first ten rows anyway; beyond that, the thunderous roar emerged from darkness. Three Super Troupers, magnificent light beacons conceived when rock concerts evolved from hall and ballroom shows and free concerts in Golden Gate Park into arena and stadium extravaganzas, allowing him glimpses of the back rows and upper tiers. Exhaustion dripped from his hair and face, another three-hour, non-stop, lights-out set catching its final breath.

The last set. *This is really it.* Sadness grappled with joy in a heart that spun and yielded a quarter-century of lyrical and melodic gold, many of those tunes becoming fixtures on "classic rock" playlists from New York to Sydney, to use the new term.

"One more show! One more show!" The thunderous chant seemed to merge all voices and hearts and dreams and wishes of Fever and rock fans globally.

In the front row, a buxom blonde's piercing blue eyes swelled to lunar size. "Tommy T! Come home with me!" Her screams disconnected her from the reason she was at the show; to spend a rare night with her husband, on whose shoulders she sat, away from their triplets. She hoisted a placard: "My Fever Burns Forever." Fat, multicolored letters roller-coastered up and down the poster, circa 1968. "I'm yours—*RIGHT NOW!*"

She clamped her legs against her husband's neck, her half-tattered Guns N' Roses t-shirt falling off one shoulder, and began gyrating like a Tahitian dancer on fire. She symbolized all those delicious on-the-road teases, always available, but as Tom mused while leaning on the mic stand, *verboten* since his bachelorhood and the Sixties ended together. How many offers had since streamed through? Hundreds? Thousands? They came in all forms: marriage proposals at concerts . . . suggestive notes sent to the dressing room . . . undergarments thrown onstage, phone numbers pinned to them . . . hotel lobbies filled with hopeful suitors . . . wee-hours knocks on doors from girls posing as maids, clerks, or room-service waiters . . . whispers into roadies' ears . . . invitations to "ride home with us" . . . chance meetings on the streets. For all the heat that rock musicians took for seducing women from center stage, all of it warranted, there was another side: the women fueled by a charismatic singer delivering their music directly into their deepest inner desires, the pheromones of stardom, music, dancing and wine a lethal concoction.

Center stage. Lead vocalists represented the freedom, youth and sensuality of music, their moves, energy and egos the central fuel of the live concert. Tom Timoreaux, the legendary Tommy T, was a modern-day minstrel, his lyrics and emotional power providing a tour de force few had seen before. *Gather ye, townfolk.* His voice was the most written and talked about in rock, his mighty three-octave range so distinct that, from his first dance hall gigs, he earned the nickname every singer secretly coveted: The Voice. He was treasured by fans; they felt he was one of them. No doubt about that. Which is why, before every concert, he hung out front stage before the lights went down, turning routine meet-and-greets into small tailgate parties.

He shielded his eyes from the Super Troupers and surveyed his fellow revelers. If the bouncing woman leaned any further forward, she and her man would crash into him at the head of the runway. Her pendulous bosom swung in a goodbye wave of sorts, recalling a funny little literary aside Fugs' raconteur Ed Sanders once sang about Emily Dickinson's hidden desire to free her swaying breasts.

The fans kept cheering, trying to push the end further from sight, hold back the inevitable, how every fan feels near the end of a great concert. Only this really *was* the end. His tears gave the sea of faces an ethereal, collective beauty, as though every grin and smile ever directed at the band were coalescing right here, right now. He'd anticipated this moment for all eighty stops on the Fever's farewell tour, running a speech in his head numerous times. He imagined over and over the final cheers, the moment rock gods never consider during their season of immortality, but all aging singers must face.

He could feel it now, the opening of his weary bones and muscles to receive the welcoming news of *being done.* Time to get back to Megan, their toddler, to normal fatherhood in a normal family. Still, how do you stop giving fans the music they—and you—love? How do you step away? How do you replace the nightly euphoria and its magical ability to rub out exhaustion, the problems of the world? How do you stop being the ringmaster night after night after sold-out night?

How do you say goodbye?

"When a place goes mad! When a place goes mad! When a place goes mad!" Fans swayed and chanted, their voices hoarse and legs buckling from a frenzy of dancing, singing and celebrating, the moment converging into a bone-shaking final throwdown. Toss in a mountainside, bonfire, and barrel of wine, take it back two millennia, and those dynamic frontmen of old, Dionysus and Bacchus, would've stoked the flames with their adoring maenads and goblets of fermented grapes.

Tom walked back to center stage, glanced at his foot pedals, and looked stage left, where Chester Craven slung his guitar around, ready for more. Since day one, he had glanced to his left and saw Chester, no matter which dives, bars, clubs, honky-tonks, juke joints, theaters, parks, halls, plazas, bandshells, amphitheaters, campuses, arenas and stadiums they played. Every band has a rock, the team captain and musical director, the anchor without whom it doesn't happen. Chester even looked like an anchor.

Another crowd eruption: "When a place goes mad! When a place goes mad!"

Chester's handlebar moustache drooped like a tired walrus as sweat leaked through his headband. He wiped the back of his hand against his eyes while gripping his guitar neck like a plucked chicken. "Let's give 'em a little more, Tommy. They ain't ready to go."

Tom cupped the mic. "We've already done three encores, man."

"They want the night. They ain't leavin'. What we doing tomorrow, anyway?"

Chester glanced back. Will Halsey twirled his drumsticks gamely despite arms limp as wet noodles, a towel draped over his shoulders. Treg Arbanne smiled from his keyboards, absorbing every cheer for a career well played. He'd never imagined lasting a year in the band, let alone staying on the road until he turned gray. Now that the appointed hour was at hand, he couldn't wait to retire. Not bad for forty-five. Vacations could now become temporary addresses. On his other side, Raylene Quarles stood with skirted leg and bare arm cocked, her fingertips poised like talons. All night, as with every night, her throaty backing vocals and thunderous riffs rose from a deep, ancient place inside, summoned from the scrapes, wounds, ecstasies, tragedies, incurred prejudices, abuses, love given and received, struggles, joys and sadness of a life. Her life.

Her legs wobbled. Tom turned back to Chester. "Do we have anything left?"

"We'll survive, brother." Chester shrugged at the man who'd lured him from the hollows of the Cumberland Gap to the flower power scene, and transformed his life from turning wrenches on tractors and combines into authoring some of the greatest guitar solos and phrasings ever laid down on vinyl . . . and CD. "We'd better come up with somethin' quick, y'all."

Here they are for the last time, ladies and gentlemen: the Fever. Named after the smoldering Peggy Lee song, their bluesy, seductive, psychedelia-infused rock, and guitar-driven, keyboard-enriched jamming fanned by Chester's cat-quick riffs—part blues, part rockabilly, part surf guitar, true thunder of the gods—created a sound fast, thick and smooth, unlike any. "The ballsiest, grittiest, most diverse band on Earth," a scribe for the mightiest rock magazine in the land once wrote. "Nothing can stop them."

Except time.

"When a place goes mad! When a place goes mad! When a place goes mad!"

The arena threatened to come unhinged as Chester cupped Tom's ear. "You really want to walk off now?"

A dozen roses landed at Tom's feet. He swooped them up and handed them to Raylene, who sniffed deeply and blew a kiss to the crowd.

"When a place goes mad! When a place goes mad!"

Tom grasped the mic as though it was a silver cord about to snap and send him tumbling through space. *God bless David Bowie.* So certain was he about calling it quits, a decision the band shared after years of postponing solo projects or film scores for *one more album, one more tour* . . . now, he couldn't leave.

He tapped a foot pedal and hard-strummed a power chord. "OK, people! It's your night!"

More cheers. More foot pounding. More hoisted lighters, matches, posters and girls, who threw more kisses. A bra whizzed past his head.

"Tommy T! Tommy T! Tommy T!"

"What can I say?" The planned goodbye speech evaporated from his tongue faster than rain in Death Valley. *This* was the goodbye speech, music and cheering, the best farewell imaginable.

A lithe, graceful woman walked on stage, draped in scarves that reached to the hem of her short, elegant black party dress, accompanied by a squirmy toddler. Recognition, wild cheers: "Mystical Megan! Mystical Megan! Mystical Megan!"

Megan Timoreaux waved while the toddler peered into the crowd, her tiny body vibrating as though she'd just feasted on prime Halloween pickings. She jumped up and down, trying to break her mother's grip so she could play with the happy people. Some kids might turn and run the other way. Not this one. Megan's hand tightened.

They reached center stage, the toddler fighting Megan's grip all the way. Tom peered again into the emerald eyes that first enraptured him during a Boston Tea Party gig. He had spotted the fetching lady in a Red Sox cap shooting 16mm film, and asked her backstage. In the ensuing decades, they dodged the highway of crumbled relationships that littered the rock and roll landscape, roughly equivalent to scaling Mt. Everest in running shoes.

"Mystical Megan! Mystical Megan!"

Tom swept up the toddler and grabbed the microphone. "Thank you for the great ride, people! You've given us so love, so much beyond our dreams. I hope we've given you back some nights and songs to remember. We hope you carry our music in your hearts, just as we'll carry the memories of playing for you in ours."

Jeremiah Denton, reporting for the king of rock magazines, turned to his wife. Like most in the crowd, tears filled her eyes. "That's why these fans are goin' home and spinnin' Fever records until he's been dead a hundred years," he said, his voice gravelly as sandpaper. "Gonna miss that sumbitch something' fierce."

Tom turned to the band. "West!" Then he threw up two fingers: *Two trips around the refrain.* He walked across the stage, the microphone in one hand, his feisty baby girl in the other. "Megan, Christine, and I are heading out, heading for the sunset, heading . . ."

"To the west of the west!" fans scream-sang.

Chester and Treg cut loose, Treg pounding out the melody relentlessly. Tom loped up the runway for the final time as Christine squirmed like a prisoner seeing her chance to make a break. The voice rose again, the voice that entertained two generations in a blood sport with a typical two-year half-life:

> *We're heading to the west, we're heading to the west,*
> *We're heading to the west of the west!*
> *Where the stories of gold will be forever told,*
> *Out here, in the west of the west.*

As Tom sang, Christine made her break, sliding down his hip. She started to dance, gawky arms and legs jutting wildly, hair flying off her shoulders, finding the beat, ignited by a boundless spirit, the purity of music, the purity of being a kid.

> *So let's jump in my car and let's aim for the sun,*
> *We're heading to the west of the west!*
> *Where our hearts and dreams meet Highway 101*
> *Out here in the west of the west.*

Tom watched her, the love, the absolute joy of being *Daddy*, filling him. Christine was *gone*, lost in her spirit, her dance. After losing little Annalisa, he and Megan had agreed not to raise their miracle baby on a road littered with prematurely extinguished flames—Jim, Janis, Jimi, John, Otis . . . Jerry. Time to lay down the mic and be Daddy.

Chester and Treg ascended on the final chord. Raylene summoned the song's underbelly, and Will smacked his kit as hard as his shaking arms could thump.

> *I'll see you in the west of the Wesssssssssssst . . .*

Women and girls bounced and danced in place. Complete strangers slapped high-fives, hugged and twirled each other through the aisles. *It's our night!* The yellow-shirted security crew, the bouncers, choked down their football players' instincts to hit someone, many jamming in place. These final, chaotic moments of a show always provided the emotional fuel for the Fever to move on and play the next night. After twenty-five hundred such nights, the tanks had finally emptied.

The houselights popped on. Tom shielded his eyes, waved to the crowd, and glanced at Christine. She jumped up and down, her wiry arms and legs twitching, ready for more. "One day," he yelled, "I hope to see you again in some shape or form."

Christine watched her daddy bow and throw kisses. She stepped in front of him, stared out at the crowd, smiled, made her own bows and threw her own kisses until he dragged her offstage.

2

PRESENT DAY . . .

TOM POUNDED THE FLOOR, GRABBED THE SQUARE NAIL PINNED between his teeth, and pounded again. A year of sawing, hammering and pounding, preceded by twenty years of dreams and sketches, was down to a few nails. Almost done. Almost finished.

Sweat streaked his stubbled face as the sharp scent of sawdust and fresh-cut wood filled his nostrils. He squinted through the studio's wall-length window into the late afternoon sun and the face of Sierra Blanca, the nation's southernmost glacier, golden eagles circling overhead like feathered benefactors. He viewed the mountain as he imagined the Anasazi would, that tribe of pre-Columbian mystics so mysterious that they vanished from civilization after spotting the Crab Nebula overhead. *Poof!* Exit stage right, perhaps into a portal, more likely absorbed into other tribes; no historian has figured it out. *A good way to go.*

He rubbed his hands, trying to get the achiness out, acquired from months of sawing and hammering the studio into being, and intensified by playing again. More and more nights, he strummed, fiddled and noodled until Megan stumbled into the unfinished studio at some fog-inducing hour. Hence the sore hands. He'd first dreamed of building the studio while playing surf gigs, sketching ideas out in drafting class. He held the dream through countless bar and surf stomp shows that got him to San Francisco, to his musical destiny, sweatbox shows you can't believe you played in front of all ten or twenty people, but now, in retrospect, took on the nobility of paying your dues. It took a while, but his dream of a state-of-the-art home studio had come true.

He stared at the new floor, absorbed and wrung out. The yellow yew floorboards radiated the room's sunlit warmth. It still baffled him how different woods amplified, muted and enriched sound. No one knew their properties better than woodworkers and old guitar makers like Chester, who'd found the yew in an otherwise burned-out church near his farm, the slats still carrying the voices of worshippers singing ethereal Southern gospels. It reminded him of what he'd first asked Chester while they coveted guitars beyond their meager Haight-Ashbury cash reserve stashed inside a Salvation Army sofa: "What difference does it make whether the belly is hard rock maple, cherry, swamp ash, basswood, or mahogany? Sound is sound." Chester had no answer. The resulting curiosity gnawed at him until he became a fine luthier after the Fever hung it up.

A sharp, sudden motion flashed by the window. A roadrunner began feasting on prime Sacramento Mountain fare, a foot-long alligator lizard snatched from the flagstone surrounding Megan's garden. Tom watched the spectacle while slugging down mud-thick coffee, some real campfire sludge. He walked slowly into the adjoining shop, a space so claustrophobic that Thoreau would think his Walden Pond cabin a McMansion by comparison. He pulled the last two yew planks, cut them to size, brought them into the studio, and returned one final time to the rhythmic routine that defined his past six months: hours of sawing and hammering, a shower, and some tired guitar strums.

Those strums triggered the return of an old friend, enchanting and sultry, adorned in a red dress and stilettos: his Muse, lyrical lover through hundreds of recorded songs and thousands buried in file cabinets and old four-, eight-, and sixteen-track tape. She'd roared out of nowhere, aroused from a sleep Ichabod Crane would appreciate. She ushered him forward with her "come hither" wiles, flashing her newest lines, lifting her hem, showing off her curvaceous hooks:

> *Can you see the way*
> *She stared so deep into his eyes*
> *Dissolving his disguise,*
> *Making him realize*
> *That within the poet's heart there lies . . .*

The lyrics were seductive enough, but the tune still craved form, shaping . . .

> *Making . . . realize . . . poet's heart . . .*

He settled the planks into place as he sang the refrain over and over, fishing for the next line, the next word, the right key and chord sequence. He hummed the melody assembling in his head, sang some more, and positioned the last loose floorboard. He gripped the hammer while stretching out the new melody, testing how high the riff could climb before its wings melted and the whole damned thing crashed to earth, pulling an Icarus on him.

> *. . . That in the poet's heart there lies . . .*

No, no, no, not "the poet." *Her* poet's eyes . . . personal, *grab the heart* . . . what lies beyond them?

> *A place beyond his need to hide*
> *Where whispers kiss those hard-fought dreams . . .*

That works. He moved the last nail an inch forward and pounded it home.

"You're really done, aren't you?"

Tom dropped the rag. "You scared the hell out of me. When did you sneak in here?"

"You still scared of cute and adorable me?"

"When I need to be."

Megan smiled broadly. "You always were smart." Soft, cautious footsteps brushed the air and wood behind her. "Looks like Steppenwolf came with."

Behind her, Steppenwolf found a sun-splashed spot, his activity of choice over a dozen lazy years. He stretched out his ample black and white body and began licking his feline parts while staring indignantly at his human subjects. Tom shook his head. "He reminds me of more than a few lead vocalists, the ones with L.S.D."

Megan glanced at him skeptically. "Uh, honey, that would have included you a time or two way back when."

"Not that. Lead Singer Disease."

She laughed as Steppenwolf's self-absorption carried on. "Where do you hear this stuff? Musicians, carpenters and the one-liners you guys come up with . . ."

Her locks curled and cascaded from her shoulders, the strawberry-blonde mane known to fans finally graying. She slid his arm over her breasts and surveyed his work. "I hope I don't lose you to this studio any more than I did while you built it, baby."

"Won't happen."

She chuckled. "*Right.* Tell that to someone else who hasn't had to drag you off your guitar and into bed the past two months." She repositioned his hand over her breast and rubbed his fingers, both hand and breast benefitting. "What were you singing just now? Sounded like another Tommy T tune for wooing a green-eyed girl."

Once upon a time, in a meadow . . . on a blanket she laid onto the grass. On the day their lives grew wings.

He slid his arms to her waist. "I can re-woo you any time you'd like."

"Now would work." She licked his lips.

They kissed softly in the empty space soon to be filled with instruments, speakers, monitors, mics, and the boys, en route to see if they could recapture what they left on their final stage. He ran his lips along the soft lines bracketing her eyes and then her queen-of-hearts mouth, reminded again of his luck. So many men chased their vanished youth forever, hopping from one crib to the next, missing the chance to entwine so completely with another that every day felt like an eternal youth's journey to the intersection of the human and divine, where matched souls went to roost, possible for most, attained by few.

Megan drew his face onto a shoulder well defined by yoga, her source of exertion and endorphins in the decade since her knee caved at the finish line of a marathon. She didn't have to crawl across, like the Ironman girl years before on *Wide World of Sports*, the crawl of fame that introduced the world to the craziest of endeavors, but when a knee feels like mashed potatoes, it's over. "You've got some serious stubble."

"Lost track finishing the studio, baby. You know how it is. Makes me feel like a frontiersman."

"Earth to frontiersman Tom Timoreaux: it's the twenty-first century."

"It happens. Handel didn't eat, drink or leave his room for three days while writing *The Messiah*. Keats wouldn't leave his favorite pub until he'd written his latest poem on a bar napkin . . . sometimes getting locked inside so he could work until the barkeep came back to share morning coffee with him. I'm easy by comparison."

"And Handel and Keats lived *when*?"

"Dedication to craftsmanship is timeless."

"More like obsession."

Tom smirked. "You know how it is."

She rolled her eyes. "Don't I . . ."

He rubbed her firm yoga mom belly and kissed her forehead, taking her in, borne by a desire and enthusiasm still very much around. Could anything, he wondered, surpass being in your sixties with the woman who joined you to usher out *the Sixties*? If anyone better flew the 'Sixty is the New Forty' flag . . . Silly, really, the mythical green light he and other Boomers gave themselves to recycle youth and romp through it a little longer, a phase those in past generations outgrew by thirty . . . a phase five decades alive and counting.

"I have to get in the kitchen and finish dinner. We'll celebrate—later." She skimmed his stubble with her fingernails and squeezed his side. "*After* you shave." She walked away. Steppenwolf flashed Tom a typically disinterested glance and followed her, willing to nuzzle and butter her up, anything for food.

Tom grabbed a tattered rag, a hundred uses beyond its lifespan, and flicked sawdust off the nearby wall. Within a week, the gang would drive up the hill and baptize the studio properly, among them the grandson of old Harlem hornblower Ulysses Washington, a possible replacement for Treg, his late, great keyboardist. *Playing with someone's grandson . . .*

He rubbed his achy hands. Never did the imagined vespers of eternal youth flee a room more quickly.

3

H E EMERGED FROM A WELCOME SHOWER, THE LOVE CHILD OF
steam and air. He wrapped a towel around his waist, grabbed a brush,
and faced a long walnut bureau that once belonged to an American
Revolution ancestor of Megan's. He looked into the oval mirror and its thick,
slightly smoky glass, and combed gray locks that flopped midway down his
sun-leathered neck, hair ignored while building the studio, hair that once
expressed freedom, openness, dissent.

A light-brown arm wrapped in bracelets encircled his waist. "Ahhh, a
freshly shaven face and brushed hair. One of the seven wonders around here
anymore."

"Now that the studio's finished . . ."

She stroked his hair. "Don't worry . . . you'll always look like the kid
brother to everyone else in your scene."

"*My* scene?"

Megan laughed. "You *are* from the scene before me."

"I'm only five years older than you. What's five years?"

"An era. You're Dick Dale, the Stones, Jefferson Airplane, Hendrix, Cream,
and Janis. Ten Years After. Steppenwolf. I'm more Joni Mitchell, Carole King,
Santana, Zeppelin, and Wings. Thin Lizzy. The Eagles."

Tom rolled his eyes. "You watched Hendrix get started in London,
sweetheart. That's my timeline. Besides, it's all semantics."

Megan shrugged. "I was sixteen. Just remember that I'm the kid in this
house when Christine's not here." She softly rubbed a face on which time
had indeed rendered a kind hand. His eyes crouched alertly within their
sockets like buckskinned hunters, anchored by soft, wise pouches, a night owl.
His thinning eyebrows rode a prominent forehead above a nose that jutted
like a roosting eagle. Everything about his face spoke of strength, foresight,
fortitude. She'd first made love with a striking singer, but had fallen in love
with the brain, heart and voice within. "I'm glad you made health a priority,"
she whispered against his neck. "Unlike many of your peers . . ."

"My peers." Tom shook his head as he cupped her hand. "If only they'd lived long enough to give us everything they could have done, what with their passion, all that unwritten, unplayed music . . . we'll never know."

"Lights that burned too brightly. And blindly."

He thought of Jim Morrison, the Lizard King, a bookworm with a memory as deep as his voice. He'd never forget a night in Laurel Canyon perfumed with eucalyptus and night-blooming jasmine as purple and red bougainvillea exploded off palms and trellises. He and Chester walked into a rousing party to find JDM expounding on Artaud, Rimbaud, Brecht, Voltaire, Collette and Rabelais, libertines and creative masterminds all. While partygoers soared into various states from the acid-spiked punch, Tom reclined on a cushion and listened to Morrison recite one excerpt after another, his eidetic recall kicking in. He recited like he sang, becoming the poem or piece of writing, his identity discarded like husked birdseed, as shamanistic as any fur-wrapped ancient sage. Maybe he *was* the Dionysius of the times, as his keyboard player claimed, the darkly handsome bad boy entertaining the masses while mini-skirted, beaded and high-booted maenads surrounded him. Sadly, though, his creativity succumbed to self-abuse, his blazing light extinguished in a Parisian bathtub.

Then there was Tom's own reckoning, the night he spun out on acid mid-show, confused fans in the Matrix wondering what he was babbling about as a combination of purple microdot and rear-wall projection blobs turned his head into a rapidly spinning gyre. It was the week after Maria ripped his heart out of his chest and vanished to Italy with it and their baby, Annalisa, in tow. Her tempest shipwrecked him and everything he considered loving about the Love Generation. Her shadow haunted him now as then, the five-year-old screaming "Daddy!" while being whisked overseas . . . then, later, hearing that she was dead.

A month later, sick of life, sensing his impending death from sorrow and substances—if not his own hand—he walked into a yoga studio. Not an ordinary thing in 1968, but neither were the circumstances. "I need to do something; can you help me out?" he asked the wide-eyed assistant, a flexible-bodied San Francisco State co-ed already sporting a "you had me at 'do'" smile.

"I can't believe you're in our studio!" she squealed. "I've seen a ton of your shows. You guys are so far out!" She grabbed a photo she'd taken and developed of Tom, Chester, and Raylene playing Longshoreman's Hall, pulled it out of its frame, and thrust it at him. "You sign, and I'll be your yoga teacher. It will change your life."

He signed the photo solemnly, as if it were a lifetime contract. In a sense, it was.

She guided him onto a yoga mat. "Touch your ankles or feet with your fingers."

When he bent over, his back popped. His arms and fingers stretched hard before they came to rest, just below his knees. Even with the approximate wingspan of a condor, he couldn't get within a foot of touching his toes.

But he liked something about it. He came back the next day, sore as hell but oddly refreshed. Then the next. A vow entered his head as weeks and months passed and the fog began to lift: *I will not die from excess. Or Maria.* Once health found its way back in, he protected it like a father guarding his daughter's first date night. Talk about being scared straight.

He wrapped his arm beneath Megan's breasts and gazed at her through the mirror that once reflected the freckled face of John Adams' kid cousin. She carried life as lightly as a feather pillow, a poise he never quite felt. Losing two parents, and a baby girl you loved more than your next breath, tended to shift your inner security plates. Her hair framed an angular face and cheekbones as prominent as mesas, ancestral souvenirs from the Abenaki squaw who once appealed greatly to a lonely Boston revolutionary. They fell in love and lived harmoniously within Abenaki customs, imparting the best of his and her cultures to their children.

He slid his hand over the pendant dangling between her breasts, the half-woman, half-lion turquoise bust of Sekhmet, the Egyptian lion-headed goddess. He brushed his lips against her ear . . .

> *Her heart was something new,*
> *A beat from far away,*
> *Sweeping out a broken soul*
> *Her heart was something new.*

"The song that broke a million hearts." She unclasped the towel from his waist. "I will be more than happy to re-live our first weekend."

The towel tumbled to the floor. She stepped over it, her now untied kimono sliding from her body as she did. "Bath water's running. Care to join me?"

His stomach grumbled. "And dinner?"

"Dinner can wait."

Dinner caught cold. Megan's legs popped above the bubbles and stretched onto his upper torso as she leaned forward and washed every inch of his chest and abdomen, her periwinkle anklet gleaming in the candlelight behind his shoulder. Dvorak's 7th symphony, that immortal testament of love, flowed from four wireless speakers Tom had cornered into the wainscoted walls, the last step of renovating the master bathroom around a turn-of-the-last-century, standalone tub Megan found at an estate sale. Thick candles burned on the corner shelves, their flames dancing like the eyes of Shiva, reflecting in Megan's eyes, gleaming.

She rubbed his stomach with her fingertips, a healer's touch, circling his skin, caressing him with fingertips, bubbles and kisses until he was both relaxed and aroused. She stood and straddled him, arching her back while she moved up and down, engulfed in her hunger, their love, joined to the man who sang about that love, but like so few others in the business, delivered fully at home, too. She rocked back and forth, ever so slowly, deeply, the nectar of their communion filling her soul. The bathwater sloshed back and forth, swamping a row of scented candles she'd streamed along the lip of the tub. She swept her hips in slow, engulfing circles, ecstasy rippling through her body, all their years of rapturous days and nights ushering from the depths of her cells and soul. They coalesced in her quickening movements, carrying her above and then down into the lavender bubbles, locked to him, propelled by the love they poured into each other anew. Such a beautiful place, this bridge joining sacred and physical, each feeding the other, a bridge built with the well-laid stones of cherishing, treasuring, and coveting. His eyes closed, the outside world suborned by heaven and earth mingling with limbs and love and shortened breath and plaintive hearts and every poem ever written about love rising and cresting and gushing into just—about—

Her fingernails clawed his arms. She closed her eyes, bit her lip, threw her head back, held off as long as possible to absorb this *feeling* . . .

the essence of holy creation . . .

no other moment before this . . .

mattered except to lead to . . .

what's happening . . .

right now.

Megan grasped the tub and arched back. Water splashed over the rim as a low cry arose from her womb, her body awash in its deepest release. She moaned into his ear as they quaked in shared ecstasy, spirits merging, drawing ever closer to that most exquisite state, *Antakarana.* The bridge to the divine.

The phone buzzed. It buzzed again, piercing their reverie. "Why did you bring your phone in here?" Tom asked. "Let it go."

"In case it's Christine, baby." The words stumbled from her mouth. "She's supposed to call tonight. I can't help it. You know, mothers . . ."

"Daughterus Interruptus."

"Not the first time."

Megan swung her legs over the rim. She wrapped a towel around her waist and stood still, slowly regaining control of her shaking legs. She grabbed her phone and shuffled into the bedroom. "Coming back?"

She glanced over a shoulder covered with suds. "Of course. We haven't had dessert yet." Then, a moment later: "Hello?"

He took a deep breath and slid beneath the bubbles.

4

"BAD NEWS, TOMMY." SNIFFLES. SOBS.

Tom white-knuckled the phone, hoping a call like this would never come. With each passing day until the gang arrived, his hope of a healthy reunion grew. That's what you did when yesterday's youthful rock and roll stars became today's elders. You hoped they could still get up there and throw down some music.

"Raylene, what did they tell you?"

"Diabetes is bad. I have to go in or else . . . I may lose my leg below the knee. Soon. Still might."

Tom raked his hair. "You get a second opinion?"

"Umm-hmmm. And a third. Same diagnosis, Tommy." More crying.

"How did it get—"

He knew the answer before the question left his lips. "Too much good cookin' and sweets, honey. Not enough workin' out. My daddy had it, too.."

The phone filled with her sobs, this strong, robust woman broken down to her core because a body organ couldn't process a substance. What a tragic bitch this thing called life could be. Worse, he knew her sobs had as much to do with what she would miss as the disease that didn't miss her.

"Your weight was down when we worked with those Bronx kids. You were eating well, doing all the right things . . ."

A sigh. "A few pounds and years ago, sugar."

Tom glared through the bedroom window as moonrise illuminated the last patch of snow on Sierra Blanca's summit, pines and aspens spanning the slope like angel's wings. Now the angel seemed dark, eerie as a fractured dream or a midnight interloper, poised to sweep away another Fever member. He shook his head, black holes and old ghosts lashing at his soul like barbed tongues, those same visions and ghosts that nearly ended him when Annalisa was torn away. What next? Megan plopped onto their round nest of a bed, her eyebrows arching, then knitting together when she noticed gloom swiping the smile off his face. She grabbed her kimono, pulled the twin dragon panels together, tied them off below her waist, and draped her arm over his shoulder.

"Damn! Can they save it, Raylene?"

"Save what?" Megan mouthed.

Tom cupped the phone. "Her leg. Her diabetes worsened."

"Maybe. If I get on it right now. That's the thing—*right now*. I thought I would lose some weight out there playing and it wouldn't come to this. Except it did."

More sobs.

Megan rubbed his shoulders and walked out of the room, her eyes filling. Soon, the delayed dinner's aroma wafted into the room, salmon seasoned with what smelled like half the Silk Road. He waved it away.

Raylene's predicament landed hard, like a boulder crushing a tree. She was the anchor. She kept such perfect time that Tom sometimes watched her swaying body mid-song, one with instrument and music, as accurate as a metronome. She was every bit the shining light of a childhood spent among talented, drunken jazz and Dixie bluesmen in honky-tonks, juke joints and chitlin' clubs, the daughter of a traveling string man—basses, banjos, guitars, you name it—and a mother who kept everyone's shit together and their mouths fed. Raylene's brilliant, hard-hitting, understated style rose straight from those sweltering stages and hard life lessons.

Now, no one would see her fingers dance on strings again. No one would again feel the bass runs that flowed from her soul, her riffs as mighty as the town heavy you never screwed with, as vibrant as unstoppable hearts.

He fought off tears. "You got someone taking you in?"

"My ex is on his way."

"Your ex?"

A tired chuckle clipped her sobs. "Why not? No harm, no foul in it, Tommy. I ain't lookin'. He gives me some lovin' without me having to jump back into the dating game—scariest thing in the world, Tommy, dating—glad you'll never know. You can talk to the ex, fight with 'em, love on 'em . . . then send 'em home."

"Sounds like a grandkid."

"Yeah, he's about the right emotional age to be one." They shared a badly needed laugh, her honeyed chuckles soothing the moment. "Honey, you do realize you're gonna need to replace me."

"I am getting that." So much for Jason Robiski's simple, hit-and-run tour fantasy, the simplistic, almost whimsical hope most label owners and promoters hold for reunions. Only it's never simple. Case in point . . . "But that's for another day."

"Sugar, now is a perfect time for that talk."

He pictured her thick right brow cocking over her moon-shaped eye, the way it always did when she got serious.

"We can always get a bass player . . . see how your treatment goes. We're not going out for six weeks, and not at all if we can't play. Ulysses' grandson can play bass organ to hold us over until you're—"

"—Tommy, there is no *until*. Not now. Not later. Not at all."

"I know. I don't want to know, but I know."

Now the so-called reunion tour would depart the mountain ridge without two of its five faces. Treg was gone, and now Raylene . . . why bother?

Tom flashed to the night he first saw Raylene play in an old Beat bar in North Beach, how she sat in with a jazz troupe and played a cheap jug bass like a guitar stood upright. Impressive. When he and Chester approached her, she told them, "I can hold a beat for any band with a tub, jug, or string bass. Four, five, or six strings. Don't matter."

"Those words can get you hired—if you're not full of shit," he'd said.

"Hardly." She poured her coal-black eyes into his for the first time. "What you cats got happenin'?"

Ever since that night, she'd stared down bouts of darkness and someone else's imposed limits on her, then flicked them away like minor nuisances. Sustained greatness has that power. How do you replace that? You don't. You can't. As a female musician in flower power San Francisco, a curious rarity in a scene where men were cool hippies and women were their old ladies and women's lib was still a dream, though approaching fast, you didn't necessarily show your ass unless your name was Grace or Janis. Yet, when you hit town with swing jazz, delta and mudbug blues in your blood, the aunts and uncles of rock, you could throw your hips as much as you want . . . and she loved to throw her hips. Then she taught him to throw his, molding him into an electrifying live performer, not merely a singer-guitarist who stood frozen at the mic like a nervous folkie. She'd pulled off the impossible for a black girl from Plaquemines Parish: earning a music scholarship in San Francisco while opportunities were fleeting at best. She, like Tom a year before, stumbled into a psychedelic vibe as potent with possibility and optimism and new ideas as anything she'd seen back home . . . and far more colorful. *The dawning of the Age of Aquarius.* A thousand bands spread the spirit in lyrics more poetic and music more diverse than anything ever known in popular music, blending blues, jazz, folk, and rock and roll into a mind-bending experience with distortion, fuzz, lights, and sonic voyages. The credit often went elsewhere—Negro girls need not apply—but she just wanted to play, move, and play some more. She anchored the sound like few others, richly deserving her spot in the Rock & Roll Hall of Fame.

Raylene and Tom first met at that North Beach club a few months after Tom rotated home from his Army stint, a stop in Vietnam pre-empted when Maria learned she was pregnant, the outcome of nineteen-year-olds not paying attention. Chester had made his peculiar journey from Tennessee to San Francisco on the back of a Grim Reaper chopper, hitching a lift on the fledgling club's first ride out west. They found in Raylene an unassailable toughness, the perfect counterpart to the kindness and sweetness that flowed from her bottomless soul. Honey to a bee. There was always a strong men's scene around Raylene. A month later, they celebrated his twentieth birthday with the first Fever show, a six-song set on a rain-drenched afternoon in Golden Gate Park, the free concert feeding the growing onslaught of utopia-laced brothers and sisters. Maria and the baby, Annalisa, stood side stage, his musical and natural families together . . .

"You go somewhere, Tommy?"

Tom rubbed his forehead. "Yeah . . . to a happier time. I can't think of any bassists, Raylene—I've never *had* to. Shit. I'll just keep the new kid on bass organ, like I said."

"No need. I've been working it out. Wouldn't leave you hanging."

"I should have figured."

"Remember that kid, maybe eighteen at the time, when you were here right after 9/11?"

"Not off hand . . . we worked with a lot of kids." An understatement: their five irregularly scheduled blues rock clinics had brought in a couple thousand fledglings.

"He sessioned here for years, went to Europe, became a hit in every ensemble he played in."

A picture began to form from the thin mist of lost time. "Lightning fingers, could play anyone's songs? Yeah, I remember. Roger or Ricardo something or other, right?"

"Rogelio. Rogelio Matias."

"That's it . . . Rogelio. What about him?"

"Well, some friends came back from Venice a year ago, goin' on and on and on *and on* about 'rock star,' how this cat played violoncello like lead guitar in churches Botticelli would've known about. When I learned who they were talkin' about, made me feel good. Well, Tommy, he's home, and everyone's fighting over him. Producers call me all the time—like I have any say, right?— to see if I can persuade him to session with their artists. They're all up in my business. Should just be his agent."

Intriguing. "But how does playing in front of a few hundred or thousand people in a church or symphony hall translate to ten thousand rock fans?"

"Rogelio loves rock," Raylene said, her voice rising. "He knows half our catalog. He loves it. Cat is so good he makes my best runs feel like crawls of shame."

Tom laughed for several seconds, touched by her black humor. And the need to just laugh. "I doubt it."

"Don't. He's the real deal. He can make all of you better . . . and younger."

Younger. It had to sound fresh, feel young, rekindle the crowd. The smartest reunion bands roll back out with a younger musician or two, some by choice, some because of what Tom was facing—a band whittling down from natural attrition.

But she was right. "He busy right now?" Tom asked.

She laughed heartily, loud and full, a laugh that could overturn depression like a tornado flipping a car. Damn, he'd miss that. They needed to record her laugh for future generations. "He's got session work lined up till your future grandkids are senile . . . but last month, after you told me about this thing we—or you and Jason Robiski, I should say—are doing, I told Rogelio I'd throw in a word if my results came back bad." She sighed. "I gave him the boxed set. He's got those songs down. He's been rummaging in my tapes and the other albums since. Not sure when the cat sleeps."

He didn't want to ask the question forming at his lips, the question sheathed in sadness, the question that would change the direction of the band. What choice did he have? "When can he fly out here?"

"Probably a week. He's finishing a couple of tracks."

"Then tell him we will see him in the next couple weeks, whatever he needs. No guarantees on our end, though. He's gotta fit with the program."

"Done." She sighed. "You're going to forget I ever played with you soon enough when Rogelio starts cutting loose."

Megan returned to the room, saw the strained look on Tom's face, and began rubbing his neck, her long fingers stroking softly, easing a brewing migraine. "Yeah . . . I don't think so."

"Then it's settled." He heard her pause, catch her breath. "Speaking of the fountain of youth, how's baby girl doing?"

"Great. She's home in two weeks, after school ends."

"When the boys are there? You crazy, man, turning Christine loose among that crew?"

"Say what?"

She chuckled. "You two getting along?"

"Yeah. She was up here for Easter; we had a good time, really felt comfortable around each other. It's been gradually improving the last year or so. I think she just had to be in L.A. for a while to see me as—"

"—Or maybe you needed to recognize her as a woman hurt by you not telling her about Annalisa. Girls do not like surprises like that . . . ever. Ask your wife sometime."

"Yeah."

Tom glared at Sierra Blanca, now a mottled yellow. Thin clouds veiled a summit, his view framed by the window and its tied-off Turkish curtains, the material's rich, theatrical blues and crimsons both dramatic and haunting. "After she's up here, she's going back to L.A. to paint her murals. She landed a bookstore gig, also a couple of walls in the city. Doing her thing. Doing it well."

"Well, that happens when you teach your kids to find their own path and to submit to no one." A cough. "Speaking of baby girl and her other little talent . . ."

He felt it coming. "Don't go there . . ."

"You ain't singing my harmony parts by yourself, Tommy."

"Backup singers are out there, though nothing close to you."

"She's right under your roof."

"I don't think so."

"Baby girl can *groove*. Ask her to jump in. Give her a summer vacation she won't forget, Tommy. Do you both some good."

He exhaled deeply. "That seems like a stretch. A desperate stretch."

"Think about it. She grew up with the music, Megan told me she's singing up a storm in L.A . . ."

"Ka-ra-oke," he enunciated derisively. "And a few stand-ins at friends' bar gigs. Not exactly a tour."

"For God's sakes, Tommy, listen to me and listen to me good. She can sing . . . and she *moves*. Remember the Donnas show we took her to, the way the band gave her shout-outs when she took over the aisle with her dancing? Remember that?"

Webster Hall opened inside his eyes—gawky teenager scoots to the aisle, talks the bouncers into letting her dance, then unleashes . . . "Maybe."

"Give her a try," Raylene said. "You're adjusting half the band anyway."

It did make some sense. What didn't add up, though, was standing side-by-side onstage. At least not in his gut. He could already sense her exasperation if it didn't play out in a way that worked for her, taste the bitterness of another dismissal . . . nothing he wanted to experience again. They may not last two weeks. Or if they could be adults about it . . .

"We'll figure it out," he said softly.

"Do it, Tommy. When have I dropped bad advice on you? If my judgment were as clear on men as it was about the band, I'd have saved myself a lot of heartache. Was I wrong about suggesting I sing more our last couple years, so we could save your voice?"

"Right on the money."

"*Ummm-hmmm.* And was I wrong to suggest right away that Chester move from being a back-porch bumpkin into a showman?" He'd traveled this road many times. No use arguing. "You already have two new faces in Tommy's music camp. What's a third?"

Muffled yelling. "Shit. My ex is honkin'. Still driving his pimpmobile, hip-hop thumping out the ass end, can't even come up to get me. Says the elevator and my cane works fine. Still thinks he's twenty, cattin' around in Harlem like he does, Superfly or Shaft or some such. He ain't no twenty. Hair's whiter than the president's ass. Gotta go."

You couldn't bottle or create her sassy humor, which could defuse a bomb. "Call us when you know more."

"I will, sugar. I love you and Megan with all this old girl's heart. Speaking of which, let me shout at your lovely lady a minute."

"Get well, Raylene. Let us know what you need. Whatever it takes."

He handed the phone to Megan, walked to the window, and peered into the skybound field of stars, big and sparkling, ancient suns, spirits of sons and daughters . . . how would the sky ever open itself up enough to contain Raylene's spirit? His heart plopped into the gnashing pit that opens when a loved one's life force ebbs, someone with whom you've gone to battle, sat up until the wee hours, talking and dreaming. They watched how Marty and Janis shouldered each other through the tribulations of being young phenoms in the Summer of Love, Jefferson Airplane's honey-voiced pilot acting as a big brother, an emotional sanctuary. Tom and Raylene adopted that as their approach after a night of kissing that they left where it belonged... in that night.

Tom shook his head. Why sail again without the anchor?

5

THE WHEELS OF A REUNION BEGAN TURNING INNOCENTLY. TOM had called the band on Robiski's request to green-light a new boxed set of the Fever's eight best-selling CDs. His appetite stoked by strong sales and glowing reviews, surprising in that the Fever hadn't charted in two decades, Robiski talked them into streaming the farewell concert, followed by a DVD re-release. Tom and Chester decided to add bonus footage—the full final encore of the final show, ten minutes of "West of the West" capped by toddler Christine bowing to the crowd. *The Fever: Final Stand*, bulleted to Number 2 and went viral online.

No one anticipated the response, not even the pathologically optimistic Robiski. In a giga-blink, while the freaks and foxes of the Love Generation bounced grandkids on their knees, or told older grandkids or still-at-home adult children to quit immersing in video games, Fever songs became popular again. The new legion of teens and young adults found what they were hunting for, a sound with equally provocative servings of musical and lyrical meat, to offset the over-produced pap that clogged most airwaves with sonic constipation. As record execs kept pumping out pop silage, an entire subculture of teens and college students did exactly what literature professors beg fresh minds to do—root through the classics.

Good music was good music, right? *The Fever: Final Stand* bulleted into the top five of all major charts within two weeks and stayed for ten more, through the holidays. Rumors, innuendos, and hearsay then cranked up on radio stations, TV shows, social media, and music blogs. DJs, writers, industry executives, and even a few musicians chatted up a possible Fever reunion. No one in the band knew anything about it.

As winter loosened its grip, the rumors heated up. With *Final Stand* holding in the charts and video clips piling up view numbers like the national debt, how could the band make good with this new audience, most of which had never read liner notes or heard what needle on vinyl sounds like? The only time they'd played live in twenty years was to trot out "West of the West,"

"She Flew Away," and "When A Place Goes Mad" during the hall of fame induction gig a decade before. They didn't flirt with fans or tease them with pop-up reunions or benefits. They retired — full stop — just like The Band after its Last Waltz.

As far as Robiski was concerned, it didn't matter. The old fans would pay *beaucoup* to see them. The kids would come. These very real scenarios—not projections, but viable scenarios—were marbling through his head one day when he asked Tom, "So, knowing everyone likes something new, you guys writing again?"

"Sort of. I'm tinkering with some things. Chester's been writing . . . mostly reworking Appalachian folk songs and blues he's dug up, you know, his little love affair with the roots."

"A different roots than what I think of."

Tom chuckled. "Yeah, not exactly Wyclef Jean and Lauren Hill, but roots just the same. Chester's pretty proud of his." *Where was Robiski going with this?* "Why would you—or we—be worried about something new?"

"Do-do-dooh-dooh-dooh-dooh-dooh-do . . ." Robiski mumbled. "*Deliverance*, huh? Does Chester know what century it is?"

Tom shook his head. How one shocking scene in one movie released before Robiski was born could be the tag for all things backwoods . . . He pictured Robiski in his thousand-dollar threads, standing knee deep in one of Chester's pigsties, coloring in the picture, laughing beneath his breath. *City boys* . . . "It's great music. Listen to it sometime. You're avoiding my question."

"Sure, Tom. I'll put it on the gramophone next time I grill up some roadkill."

"You know, Jason, you're part of what ails our country."

"What's that?"

"Everyone should know how the other half lives. That alone would solve part of the mess we're in."

A pause on the other end. "I'd really like you guys to consider playing again. You'd make a huge fan base happy. Maybe even yourselves. And a few new songs wouldn't hurt."

"We *are* playing again—the boxed set."

"You know what I mean. A tour. Get the gang back together for a one-shot deal, a handful of key cities. Twenty, twenty-five, thirty stops max. Have some fun this summer."

"With Treg gone? And Raylene struggling? I don't think so, Jason."

"Your music is back. You've dragged in Millennials and kids, too, judging from sales and airplay on *college* radio stations now, for Chrissakes. Plus, that grandkid of Ulysses Washington's, X, is some find."

That was becoming clear—and the kid wasn't even up the mountain yet. After Ulysses convinced Tom to try him out, Tom sent X files of about a hundred songs, twenty of which X sent back, the keyboards rearranged in ways that were both distinctly Fever and definitely *not* Treg's style. He couldn't wait to plug the kid into the band.

While grinding on the here-and-now, and what might be possible with X jumping aboard, Tom sensed more passion in Robiski's pitch, a palpable excitement beyond filling the bank with more Fever proceeds. The young guy was good, just like his old man . . . and the late Don Robiski merely achieved industry immortality with the way he shepherded the Fever to superstardom and kept them on everyone's radar for more than two decades.

"Megan says you're writing more than *tinkering* . . ." Robiski paused for an overly long moment, "so throw in something fresh, a four-minute reason or two to fall in love with you all over again, and I'll get you the keys to the summer. Mark my words."

"Optimistic as ever."

"Why our label is where we are . . ."

"By the way, Jason, how's that *signora* you've been escaping to?"

More and more, Robiski junketed overseas and brought home stories of his Italian woman. Apparently, she'd achieved what no woman had before, tacking down the notorious lady's man whose dating legacy could fill *Us Weekly*. "She's great. I'm happier every day."

"That's becoming evident. Then you've found the right woman. But so am I."

"What?"

"Happier every day. Retirement has that effect."

"Megan tells me you can't string together three relaxing moments in a row. You can't sit still."

"Damn, Jason, my wife your newest confidant? There a spy in my own house?"

A laugh. "She *is* a great source of intel."

Few industry executives held more clout than Robiski. Or touch. Since the Fever's finale, when he was learning the ropes at his father's side, he'd consistently anticipated the next sound or sub-genre, and then discovered the bands, solo artists, session musicians and songwriters to deliver the goods. It was a different ball game now, more constricted, more cutthroat and unfair to new acts than when Don Robiski brought the Fever to stardom. In rock music's prime, a highly promising band could count on a three- or four-album deal to make a mark; now, they gave you one. *Song*. What could be more cutthroat? It took a special ear to find success against such needle-in-a-haystack odds, but

Robiski's was that ear, golden, impeccable. He'd absorbed the old man's A&R and business genes well, along with his love of good music. If you didn't love good music, in all its forms, how were you supposed to find it?

Three days later, after polling the band, Tom called Robiski. "What the fuck; we'll do a little tour. But we need six weeks minimum, at my place, to see if we can still put two and two together and sound younger than a hundred ten. Agreed?"

"Yes," Robiski said. "And no one will know. No leaks."

"I'm not the one who needs that reminder."

Sure enough, two weeks later, the first story hit *Billboard:* "The Fever Reuniting: Tour? Studio? Or Both?"

"That didn't come from me," Robiski protested.

But it did. Since then, phone calls, texts, and emails besieged Tom. So did doubts. Would Chester take one more spin? Would Raylene's health hold? What could pry Will from his Mendocino redwood forest treehouse setting, or get him out of the offshore kelp beds where he caught his daily dinner? How to replace Treg? You don't. Yet, when his eyes closed and the Fever played inside, the thought of performing again felt good. *Maybe so.* If he could dust off the fretboards and cobwebs, and sing the songs decently, they might again hear cheers, and thrill teens dying their hair blue as much as rekindling old times for grandparents whose hair *was* blue.

His doubts slowly began to dissolve. Soon, they felt like matchsticks in a tsunami, that tsunami being the buzz of Fever fans, of the entertainment world.

Now, weeks later, the boys were on their way, minus Treg. And Raylene. *Maybe* was about to become *let's see.*

6

"How do we forget songs we've played a couple thousand times? You never think you're going to lose it, never think you're going to slow down. Then one day you wake up, and you've *slowed down*."

"You haven't lost a damned thing, brother," Chester said. "We haven't played in a long time. Chill and have some fun."

"Give it some time," Will said. He fiddled with the guitar he'd borrowed from Tom for their "attunement" session, though it felt more like the first day of boot camp.

Chester kept plucking. "I ain't gonna worry about it. I'm gonna enjoy breaking in this spankin' new studio. Even folks at home roll their eyes like I'm on a damned fool's errand, trying this. Right down to Chandra and her baby blues. But this old coon dog needs something new to bark about. You can only recycle the old times to a point."

"Maybe that's what I should become, our on-stage storyteller," Tom said. He rubbed his throat, achy from his first full days of singing since walking off stage. "I sure as hell don't seem to be able to *sing* these songs, so might as well try a more Lou Reed approach. Would fit my new range."

Chester grumbled. "Lou Reed, my ass. I gotta get my fat ass in shape, you gotta get your pipes in shape. Same difference."

He plucked a string of notes into blossoms ready to burst, his fingering tender as teatime with a century-old belle. The young Chester, the rebel rocker who sent concertgoers home with uproarious final solos that could last ten minutes, could never sit still long enough to tease out acoustic honey like this. It reminded Tom of what older musicians often told their fans and the press: "We're better musicians than we were then. How could we not be? We've been at it for thirty, forty years. Not three." Really, who's going to tell Jimmy Page or Keith Richard that they're lesser musicians just because they don't jump all over the stage anymore?

Will adjusted his guitar to open tuning. He knew little about the instrument until the first years after the Fever stepped away, when Denise persuaded him to play more guitar and less drums at home for the sake of her eardrums. And their domestic bliss. He became hooked. "We're gonna get there," he said. "We hit it out of the park on our final tour, left to a lot of cheers. That's what we'll walk into—a lot of cheers. Let's get our shit together, and let the fans decide if we're any good. Check that; the fans *will* decide. These days, we're going to know as fast as you can hit 'send.'"

Chester pulled a well-chewed toothpick out of his mouth. "That's right, Tommy. We all need to stop fussing. We'll find our groove, and when the new kids get up here, we'll put a little sumpin' sumpin' together."

Tom slid the capo up his guitar neck, gobbling up two frets. "Let's hope we make it that far." He grabbed his two-liter growler, and chugged the liquid amber fiesta inside.

Chester caught the local brewery name on the growler label. Misty Mountain Hops. "Can't beat that," Chester said. He strummed a few bars of its namesake.

"There's the point I'm trying to make," Will said.

Chester's forehead furrowed as he strummed. "What point? You're confusin' me, brother."

"When Tom said 'Misty Mountain,' you started strumming. You know how it works: the songs will be in our fans' heads every second before, during, and after. If we miss notes, they're not going to care. We might, but they won't. They'll be thrilled to hear us live again. We'll feed off that energy and get our groove back in no time."

"You sound as optimistic as Robiski," Tom said.

"Damn straight," Chester said. "So let's do what we do—have some fun."

Tom started "Rainy Day," keeping the mellow tone Chester had set. As he played from old memory, he wrestled with another reckoning: No longer were they wide-eyed kids living on sodas, beers, tacos, chips, candy bars, and the odd hot meal strewn across a van. They'd moved people in amazing ways, from hard rockers to their parents, from blue-collar workers to the sons and daughters of presidents. And rumor had it, a certain sax player in the Oval Office. A writing teacher in California once handed his classroom of very unpoetic high school students the lyrics to "Alchemy," "When I Become the President," "Aching for a Change," and "West of the West", in a futile attempt to connect them to poetic meter. It worked. "Two poets, two songwriters, a musician, four authors, and a journalist emerged from those knuckleheads," the teacher later wrote Tom. "And a classroom of Fever fans."

Tom noodled through the first four bars of "Elder Chief," a favorite though they only played it live a few times. He glanced at Will, recalling how he rolled it out at the drummer's surprise thirtieth birthday party. He'd never forget how much Will's dad loved it, the older guy in the peasant shirt, clip-on earrings, headband, and beads on, the man drawing younger partygoers around him like he was Wavy Gravy, or a Grand Poobah of Haight & Ashbury. In reality, the World War II veteran considered marijuana the gateway drug to heroin, and the Sixties the beginning of America's descent from greatness. But for a day, for his kid, the retired officer acted like his kid.

Now, *they* were the old men.

Robiski, Will, and Chester were all right: time to take these songs down the hill one final time. So what if they weren't strapping rock gods anymore? A grin broke across his face, his concerns easing. No matter what, it would be fun. And if they rocked the worlds of audiences coast to coast? Icing on the cake.

Tom fired up the sound system for the first time with other musicians in the room. He tested the vocal and guitar mics, and loped across the silent, polished mahogany planks of the stage. His heart jumped. No matter how long, no matter how many stages, he felt like the sun feels at dawn whenever he rifled off those first power chords, spreading rays of sound throughout the studio, Cat Stevens' immortal ode to the morning filling his brain like beautiful birdsong. On the other side, Chester checked the wireless transmitter on his hip and flipped on his '59 Gibson Les Paul, a stick he only broke out for gigs that mattered. Will put his guitar away, straddled the drum stool, and twirled his sticks.

He counted them in: "A one—a two—a three—off we go."

Chester's guitar quickly crackled with the lightning riffs that made "West of the West" one of rock and roll's great anthems. With each note, chord switch, and flood of sweet sound, the electricity zipped through them, the current of creativity so native to who they were: men who could find a million other things to do, but when it came down to it, they played music and uplifted audiences like few others. As they drove into the classic concert closer, Chester soloed, Tom followed on bass, and Will thundered away. Every time they cycled through the refrain, they felt tighter, cleaner. They kicked over to a half-dozen different songs long since mashed into their muscle memories, now flowing out as a makeshift medley. They jammed for an hour, time and space stepping aside . . . always a good sign. Tunes that opened as clunky as rattletrap trucks bouncing on washboard mountainside roads finished like nights in eider down beneath buttery summer skies.

Megan and Chandra strolled through the studio door as free-flowing as sunshine on the run, ponytails flopping on their backs, their bare feet and shorts completing the picture of two fetching girls who never bothered to grow up all the way. At least on the outside. Chandra walked up to Chester, a beer in her hand, and squeezed his sides. He was still well-padded, but slowly shrinking after a month of what felt like forced labor in the gym, a first for him, but conditioning she insisted upon after they decided to tour again. "I'm not losing you to a heart attack onstage." So once a day, he left the cave-like comforts of the guitar-building shop and trudged into the gym. A man does that when he wants to keep up with a woman twenty years younger. The younger, toned grizzly bear she married was beginning to show again, like a ship peeling off its outer visage as it emerged through the fog. "You know what this means?" she asked after the effects of the gym became apparent. "I find you irresistible again."

"Words like that'll land you in the bedroom," Chester said, squeezing Chandra's round, strong thigh. She'd gained maybe twenty pounds over the years, the natural padding of life and biscuits and gravy, but her every curve formed a landscape he'd never tire of admiring, the inner and outer gorgeousness of a woman that spoke of all the reasons to be happy. After Savannah died, some women thought they could make him happy; others wanted him to be their emotional rescues. She reminded him of what it was to be happy, and reminded him daily when he awoke and looked into her sleeping face or smiling eyes. A woman like that comes along, you've just struck gold.

She turned to Megan. "Chester doesn't have any idea of how much his losing weight is doing for us, how much better he feels now than the porch potato he'd become. But I don't get the 'men play, women work' thing he's been sticking me with since we got here."

"A Sixties thing," Megan chuckled. "They always need to act like they're in charge, you know."

"Showing his ass . . ."

"Alphas beating their chests." Megan's chuckle bridged into full laughter.

Chester looked up while retuning. "Ladies, how's our food comin' along?"

"Why are you like this, honey?" Chandra rolled her eyes, shook her head, her kidding now mingling with the joy of seeing her grizzly play Fever music again. A California girl can only take so many back hollow songs forged alongside moonshine stills and tailgate parties in the middle of the woods before curling into a corner, slapping on earbuds, and drowning out the day. "He doesn't say this stuff when we're home."

Will glanced up and smiled. "Why would he? He has no chance with you alone." Megan rolled her eyes at Chester, then pat-slapped Tom's face, tapping him into a conversation he had nothing to do with. "What the—"

"The way you guys revert when you're together. You remind me of a little-spoken truth about the *luuuuuhve* generation. All those beautiful girls with flowers in their hair and love in their eyes had to clean up after you and buy groceries or scavenge for food—or hit the daily Digger feeds in the Panhandle—because money was so scarce or unwanted. Or both." Megan glanced at Chandra, struggling hard to suppress a laugh. "We women raised your babies, kept you together as best we could, and made your food. Not exactly free love." She noticed plumes of opposition in Tom's pupils. "Well, *you* were good with your little one, honey, no doubt. But you boys made your women stay off the road, away from the studio, so you could what you do on the road . . ."

Tom looked up, wondering from what vent her sentiment had escaped. "Must be something you heard. Never that way with you, sweetheart."

"The way it was." She patted Tom's cheek. "But true—never that way with me."

Chester turned to Will. "Listen to them, comparing hippies to rednecks."

Will threw up his arms. "I'm sitting this one out, Chester. You're on your own." He laughed his way through studio and hallway, laughed all the way to the refrigerator, laughed until he chugged that first deeply satisfying beer after a solid start.

In the studio, Chester shook his head, put aside his guitar, and began kneading Chandra's shoulders. She relaxed into his hands. "Think I was that way, little girl?"

Chandra's eyebrows collapsed on her forehead. "*Little girl?* Answer me this, *big boy*: why do some of your friends back home marry their women, prod them to gain weight and wear oversized t-shirts, cut off their gorgeous hair *and* put away their makeup? That from the Sixties, too?"

"Not my way."

"We would've never gotten past 'hello' if it were."

"Yet you're stirrin' it up on me, Tommy, and San Francisco."

Megan shooed Chester and Tom toward the stage. Will followed, beer in hand. "Let's shut these boys up and *serve* them. When the others get here, they'll be dining buffet."

They strode out, arm in arm, their laughter lingering like a jet's contrail. Chester rolled around the wad in his cheek, turned, and nailed the coffee can spittoon he'd set up stage left. "She drives me nuts, but she makes my world. I love that crazy surfer girl. Life without her ain't life. She keeps me young."

Tom nodded thoughtfully. "She *is* young, Chester."

A few minutes later, Chandra carried out a tray of fish tacos. "Enjoy. You're on your own next time."

"We'll see about that, girlfriend," Chester said. He down-strummed in D, the ensuing wall of tenored sound hitting Chandra like a shock wave.

"Now that we've done our work, fed your bellies, isn't it time you gentlemen played again?" Megan rubbed Steppenwolf as he assumed the position that, she chuckled, men covet like no other—deep in the girl's arms, not a care in the world beyond the next meal or shadow to chase.

After eating, Tom adjusted his mic and turned to Will and Chester. "You guys ready to show these feisty women how we *work* for our food? Count us in—"

> *The sky's electric, the land is sad*
> *Oh currents above, what has happened here?*
> *Let's spread our wings, it's time to rock*
> *Into the spirit of a place gone mad—*

They played through a few verses and repeated the refrain, again tightening the sound with each pass, before Chester zipped into a finger-splitting solo, glued to every note. Every lead guitarist catches fire with one of their band's particular songs. "Night Train" always turned Slash into a ramp-jumping, power chord–breathing hellion, and "The Ocean" seemed to do it for Jimmy Page. "When A Place Goes Mad" was Chester's catnip. After a few minutes in his personal parallel reality, he connected with Tom's voice at mid-range, just like old times. Tom strained for the half-octave lift to close, his vocals reaching, reaching . . .

And falling short.

Chester circled around and met him again—no luck. He held steady and dropped the key down a notch as Tom took the tune home, his voice crisp and melodic but a peg lower than the recorded version.

Megan and Chandra halted the dance they'd broken into, Megan holding Chandra while looking over her shoulder. "I'd buy a ticket if I wasn't the chick who married the singer . . ."

Tom shook his head. "Whose voice is misfiring . . ."

"Whose voice sounds wonderful." Megan brushed her hair out of her face. "You sound great. It's the first time you've belted it out in ages. You're fine."

"We'll see."

His brain insisted his voice was still there, he felt the music rising through his heart and into his pipes, ready to ascend the summit of the song, but his upper range only reached middle camp. He was pitch perfect, in-tune, on key, but too low.

"You're good, brother," Chester said. "Your falsetto is lower; whose isn't? Look at Jagger. McCartney. Prince before it ended for him. Chrissie Hynde and Blondie, for Chrissakes. Some can't sing worth a damn anymore, but fans still listen and take what you give and their brains fill in the rest. Problem fixed. Just go easy on your falsettos and vibratos right now. Don't do them. No screams. Save them for the tour."

Tom cleared his throat. Chester was right, very right, but it was hardly consoling. Where was *the voice?* What would audiences think if he marched songs three-quarters of the way up the ladder—and fell off? They'd ship him to the Golden Throat Retirement Home on a chorus of boos and catcalls, that's what. He shuffled the microphone and kicked the stage floor. "Let's try something else, middle range."

"Mystical Dreamer," Will suggested.

"That'll do." Tom winked at Megan, the star of the tune, the woman who found her place as the First Lady of Fever Fans when the song properly announced the band on the national stage by bulleting to number one a few months after their honeymoon. She never complained about her ensuing nickname, Mystical Megan, although she would've chosen almost anything else. "Let's cut to the chase. Second verse, refrain."

Chester fiddled for the chords, but couldn't connect them. "Lemme see the sheet."

Tom knelt down and rummaged through a tall stack of lyrics, chords, and notes scribbled on legal pads, notebooks, and even a cocktail napkin. They'd had twenty-five years of touring, and another twenty of sitting, to put down formal compositions, but they'd never bothered. If Marty Balin could scratch out the definitive '0s ballad "Miracles" on lined paper in India after *darshan* with Sai Baba—even sketching his shaggy dog, Willy, in the corner—then they could scribble on whatever was available. A paper stack sat next to Tom, broken into two piles, the guts of twenty albums and hundreds of unreleased or partially written songs. With more in the office file cabinet.

He found the chords and notes to "Mystical Dreamer," scratched on *Creem* letterhead above their lyrics. What a magazine. *Creem* was the musicians' choice in music journalism's golden age, the Seventies. Guitar bands, prog rock, heavy metal, blues infusion, arenas and stadiums . . . *Creem's* fleet of writers, as devoted to their craft as musicians, dug into the tunes, performers, and surrounding ecosystems alike. The joy of being featured in so many issues brought a smile to his face. It was pure pulp music writing, everything on an even keel, dishing out high praise one moment and trashing a band, album, or performance the next. *Rolling Stone, BAM, Crawdaddy, Melody Maker, Circus, Billboard, Fusion, Uncut,* and *ZigZag* spread the word. *Creem* dug in from there.

While interviewing Tom during the band's first major tour, a warm-up swing for a well-known headliner, the writer asked about how he and Megan were navigating a scene booby-trapped with groupies, all-nighters, drugs, and other marriage detonators. Before answering the writer's question, Tom asked for a piece of paper. "I've got a song right here," he said, tapping his forehead. "Let's see if I can tease it out."

Out came the *Creem* letterhead. For the next thirty minutes, Tom wrote out "Mystical Dreamer," humming as he threw down lyrics, Megan and the stunned interviewer looking on. So fluid was the connection between idea, soul, brain, and pen, so pure the feeling, so refined the songwriting, he dropped the song as effortlessly as maple syrup on tapping day. "Here is how I feel."

The writer had never seen a song written in front of his face, chords, lyrics, and all. Noodling backstage on guitars, making up pieces of future songs as they went along? Sure. But *channeling* a song from thin air, from verse to refrain, bridge, hook, line, and sinker? "Holy shit," the journalist wrote, in awe of witnessing the song's creation—and how it sounded when Tom tested it on guitar.

Thanks in part to *Creem's* extended feature, "Mystical Dreamer" smashed through the charts. The writer promptly dubbed Megan "Mystical Megan," to honor the song's inspiration. A half-million readers caught on. So did the nickname.

Tom handed the yellowed letterhead to Chester, who grabbed his granny glasses and followed the chicken-scratched chord changes. Within a few minutes, familiar progressions built up to a soaring refrain that could make a dreamer out of anybody.

> *Into our hearts, our sacred hearts*
> *The mystical dreamer blesses us*
> *With her flowing blonde-haired love,*
> *This vision of pure soul,*
> *I stand here before all you folks*
> *To sing her song tonight,*
> *A song that wrapped me in her wings,*
> *The mystical dreamer's ode . . .*

". . . Shit." Tom croaked like an aging bullfrog.

Will cut the drum fill short. "You're good."

Tom kicked the stage, frustrated to be like a stadium missing its upper deck. He looked at Will and Chester. "We're going to have to re-evaluate how we approach this. I'm missing Raylene *a lot* right now."

Chester shrugged his shoulders, completely unfazed. "Do what she said, Tommy—check out Christine. Maybe she solves the problem, maybe she doesn't. She can take the high range parts."

Chester hooked Tom into a bearish arm as Megan and Chandra caught their breaths, sweaty from dancing, always a challenge in a mountain ridge studio at eight thousand feet. Chester nodded to them. "I'll bet a dollar to a holler they'll get up here to get us through this session."

"Ahhh, what the hell . . . Ladies?" Tom grabbed two microphone stands and hooked them up.

"Tell me where to sing," Chandra said. "I know some, but . . ."

"Just stay with me," Tom said. "When I give you a thumb's up, go higher than I'm going. Here are the lyrics."

Chandra clucked like a teen as she scanned the next four songs. "I never imagined being in a rock-and-roll band."

"Say what?" Chester guffawed a loud, long guffaw, seized by his funny bone. "I know sure as hell you imagined it, just like every other California girl. Either being in a band or hooking up with one of 'em."

"You don't stop, do you?"

Chester laughed. "Havin' fun, baby." He turned to Tom, the smile leaving his face. "So let's cut the riff-raff and have some fun, superstar."

Megan and Chandra filled the higher range more or less. Meanwhile, Tom and Chester performed selective surgery on a pair of tunes with high notes. Chester found places to replace Tom's old falsettos with solos, and Tom tracked where a bass run could heighten his voice, where a keyboard solo might do the trick, where he could drop down. Who said this was going to be a piece of cake? Robiski. *Note to self: kick his ass.*

They improvised, sensing and feeling the other's rhythm, intuiting how each would play, carving out solutions on the fly. However, some songs were impossible to change, especially those Raylene amplified. They demanded a woman's voice.

He shrugged. "When Christine gets here, we'll give her a try."

Will smiled and clapped his sticks together. "Good on you," he said.

"I happily turn over the mic when she gets here," Chandra added. A smirk billowed from her lips as she wrapped the tails of her shawl just above her small diamond navel stud. She looked at Megan and winked. "We played together. Dream fulfilled."

Tom held up his bass like a drink at a toast. He turned to Chester. "Here's to all sorts of possibilities . . . or directions this could go."

7

VENICE, CA

THE STENCH OF CHEAP WINE HOVERED AS THE ONSHORE BREEZE continued to slumber. Daylight's first rays etched palm trees that filled the skyline. Christine stepped over a pale man and dark woman sleeping cheek to dirty cheek on a doubled-over piece of carpet. She pulled a disheveled blanket from their nearby shopping cart, covered them from the cool, moist air, and glanced upward, into the palms. *Without divine grace, mom, and dad, I could be here, too.* She closed her eyes and silently renewed her own resolve to move forward, always. What other direction was there?

The passed-out homeless couple wasn't exactly what tobacco mogul Abbot Kinney envisioned when he conceived the canals, amusements, palm trees, and boardwalk of his utopian playground, Venice-by-the-Sea, nor when Charlie Chaplin waddled along the boardwalk as The Tramp. Yet, it spoke to Venice's greatest asset, in her eyes: a collective soul that invited everyone in, the people caring for each other as they could, creating a sanctuary of sorts.

She passed a narrow throughway of gingerbread cottages, clapboard houses, and other dwellings that, like the rest of coastal Southern California, was reminiscent of the simple beach town that preceded SoCal's race to vacation resort prominence. The homes were draped in bougainvillea, wild roses, century plants, night-blooming jasmine, and palms. She loped along the sidewalk like an athletic runway model, elegant and determined. At the end, an off-white house built in Chaplin's heyday crouched behind its grapevine-covered archway. She passed beneath the arch and walked along the brick sidewalk, the curious little girl in a Brothers Grimm story. She reached the door and pounded the knocker, shaped like a treble clef.

Deep, sleepy dark eyes set in a light-brown face, framed by bed-tussled black hair, peered through the window, the face of a Mediterranean priestess, as though Elvira or Morticia Addams suddenly sported a tan.

The door swung open. "Hey sweetie! Didn't anyone ever tell you that real artists and musicians don't get up till noon?"

Daphne swept Christine into her ample arms, all lavender scent and terrycloth and breasts and curves. "It's been too long."

"Right?" Christine smiled. They exchanged cheek kisses. "A lot going on. Like my final finals."

"So happy to see you." Her dark priestess eyes sparkled with light.

Christine smiled faintly. They chattered while Daphne cleared off a table filled with bills, gallery business, and sketches. Christine took her hand and squeezed. "I need to talk to you about something; hope it's not too early."

"It is, but . . ."

"Sorry. Got used to getting up for Danny's morning surfs. Inner alarm clocks don't just disappear when the dude does."

Daphne flashed a faint smile. "No worries; last night wasn't exactly a thrill ride. I read, tinkered with a painting, and sketched. Look at my table. How exciting." She rolled her eyes, slowly. "That's my thrill anymore. Unless I can find a gallery opening or a friend's gig, or someone wants to scoop up this increasingly *round* babe."

"Yeah, my nights are quiet, too . . ."

"What happened with Danny?"

"He split to Baja a few months ago—you know, surf came up. I guess it's still up, because I haven't seen him since. Either he didn't come back, or didn't want me to know he was back. Guess I wasn't enough beach blanket bimbo for him. Just as well." She flicked an unseen fly off her shoulder.

Sadness seeped into Daphne's black pearl eyes. "I'm so sorry."

"I'm over it." Christine shrugged her shoulders, though tears crept into her eyes for the umpteenth time in the past three months. When would it stop? Would people stop coldly rejecting each other if they had to feel it, too? "I didn't like going on surf trips, anyways. I'm not much of a beach ornament or camp mom."

She blinked away her tears, but the low burn kindled in her belly. How she let herself fall in love, only to become the token woman on a desolate Baja California beach, still baffled her. Her heart ached for Danny's love as the guys surfed, checked out *senoritas,* ate chips or fish tacos, drank *cervezas,* and told inflated big-wave stories. None of which involved her . . . except that Danny insisted she ride along. *How can I be OK with that?* She protested the way his friends peered at her, the way he eventually viewed her as hot wallpaper in his world. Apparently, her protests were too much. He never understood how blowing off her feelings turned off her desire, either. Which fed their final argument: "You don't like having sex with me anymore," he'd said.

"I love having sex with you . . . but not with you always mentally off on another trip or another chick or wherever your brain goes when you're being so, um, *mechanical* with me. And definitely not on the beach with your crew listening in."

"Then how about you never go on a trip with us again?"

Those were the last words he spoke to her. Not easy to overcome.

"Let me get you some coffee, tea . . ." Daphne's thick arms spread out, her hair cascading down her shoulders to touch voluminous breasts partially exposed by her low-cut, full-length black gown.

"Black tea would be great. Caffeine's my BFF. Late night last night."

Daphne hummed through the kitchen, and walked in with a steaming mug. "What's the story with this Danny?"

Christine swiped her eyes. "He wanted me to be his beach ornament. He couldn't stop counting at one . . . ornament." She blinked rapidly and squeezed Daphne's hand. "I was in love with him . . ."

"Honey, that's probably what scared him off." Daphne sipped. "We can both sing the blues. Plenty to go around."

"That's why I wanted to talk to you . . ."

"My men? Relationships?" That brought out Daphne's full-bodied laugh, as full as a choir of angels in sheer mirth, one of her many treasures that drew Christine in, created this friendship between the generations. "Yeah, I can tell you about relationships . . ."

"Not relationships." Christine sniffled again and chuckled. "Blues. Singing."

"Oh."

As Christine sipped, she regarded Daphne's gown again. How would the design and black satin look when modified into a short dress with long sleeves? "It's cool how you make longer gowns and dresses look sexy," Christine said.

"A necessity, honey. Forty or fifty pounds ago, I too paraded around this place in skirts and shorts, like you."

Christine smiled. Nice to have *someone* notice again, even if Daphne was closer in age to her parents. She swept her hand along the table's centerpiece, a coal black sculpture, a Daphne creation of two entwined lovers, he fawning at her, she staring upward, her mouth open, eyes at half-mast. Behind the sculpture, a quartet of paintings hung on the living room walls, positioned in cardinal directions. *Shiva's Dance: One Second*, the placard read. It was quite a second: On the east wall, two people faced each other, meditating, their feet pressed together; to the south, lava poured into an oceanic belly. The north wall fended off a mountaintop blizzard, while waves peeled onto the western wall. Anyone who believed in love should see these, Christine thought.

She warmed her hands on the mug. "So, you're like the only person I know who would have any perspective . . . even though I kind of said yes already."

"Yes to what?" Daphne fiddled with the Celtic cross jutting from her gown.

Christine put one knee on the chair and stretched her other leg. Soreness lingered from a full night dancing with her girls, a night that ended when everyone left with their boyfriends or new finds. The slow-cutting knife inside her heart jabbed for the thousandth time. Would be nice to be around some unconditional parent love again . . .

"Are you with me, sweetie?" Daphne peered at her, the vapor from the tea veiling her eyes ever so slightly, softly. "Well . . . ?"

"My dad called and invited me to sing in his band."

"Really? How cool! Few times we've gone out to the bars . . . you can sing." She shrugged her shoulders.

Christine nodded. "That's just messing around . . . karaoke. Popping onstage when my friends' bands are playing."

"What does your dad have going on? What kind of music?"

"Rock and blues. Classic, though he's writing again. Thing is, if I do this, I'll be spending the next month in New Mexico—and I've got commissions lined up here for the next six months. I'm looking forward to visiting home, but I get claustrophobic after a week or two. Lots of reasons not to do this."

"Where in New Mexico?"

"In the mountains, above the White Sands . . . know where Ruidoso is?"

Daphne nodded. "Gotcha, girl. I'd have done anything to live in that area once upon a time."

Christine slid into her chair. "Really? I can't *even* picture you living in the mountains." She chuckled, trying to imagine Daphne chopping logs and pulling splinters from her meticulously manicured fingers.

"You'd be surprised. After I stopped playing, I wanted to head for the hills, but everywhere we visited, my old man—he wasn't my ex, *yet*—" she bit the word "—said he wouldn't leave the ocean. Then one day, out of the blue, he bailed for the Olympic Peninsula where it rains every day. Coldest rain forest I've ever seen. Go figure."

"But you stayed."

"He asked me to come, but half-heartedly. I think he was ready to become what I always saw in him, what I secretly feared would knock us out . . . a hermit in the woods. I love the man, but I won't live with him there. We do best in short spurts."

Daphne studied Christine's eyes, the same deep green as the rainforest where, in a week, she would be tucked away with her ex in his cabin, enjoying bountiful lovemaking without obligation—what do you do when you don't want anyone new? Then she would head home before they got sick of each other. Prime time rarely topped a week.

She shook off the warm tingle rising in her womb. "Is your dad's band one I might've heard before?"

"You and millions of others."

Her thin eyebrows steepled. "Since you've never told me about your family, who we talking about here?"

"The Fever."

Daphne's next breath fled the scene. She felt like a moonwalker lacking an air hose. "*The* Fever?"

Christine bit back a chuckle. "My parents said to tell you hello."

"How the hell didn't I make that connection? On facial expressions alone?" Daphne gazed at her living room paintings, one wall at a time, visiting the stations. "I'll be damned."

Christine fiddled with her hands. "Everything OK?"

"Sure . . . just stunned, honey." Daphne pursed her lips, sealing what they could say *about the part of your father's life you'll never hear from me.* She cupped her mug. "You never know, do you?"

Christine smiled, her curiosity growing. "I guess not."

Daphne studied her face further. "Yeah, I can see Tommy and Megan in you . . . how could I have missed it?"

"Why would you have looked in the first place?"

"Good question." Daphne rubbed her eyes and forehead. "You think you've seen everything . . . and you *do* know how big they were, right?"

A nod. "But he never made a big deal about it. And they were done when I was really young. That's my oldest memory: dancing onstage with Dad."

"How could you forget since it became one of rock's most famous photos? Sweetheart, that's *the world's* lingering memory of your dad and the Fever." Daphne flipped her hair over a reddening cheek, her eyes flashing. "Kind of nice to have Saturday morning coffee with the baby girl I've been friends with for two years, without a clue about where she came from . . ."

They broke into laughs, Christine at the absurdity of her Venice bestie knowing her dad, Daphne at never putting it together. Though now, studying her through a somewhat yellowed map in her memory, how *did* she not see it?

"If this is something the boys want to do, well, knowing your dad, it'll be good. He wouldn't bother otherwise." Daphne planted her hands on Christine's arms, her eyes blazing like polestars. "I'd say check it out, and stick with them if you're a good fit. You'll always have mural and urban art work around here, with your talent." She took a deep breath and squeezed Christine's shoulders. "So all these rumors about a Fever reunion tour are true?"

Christine nodded.

"Thousands of singers would crave your spot on stage—"

"If I do it."

"If you do it . . ." Daphne shook her head in disbelief. "If nothing else, you'll have quite the calling card if you want to keep singing. And the association isn't going to hurt your visual arts presence, either."

"Well, I'm not relying on my pedigree for that."

"Honey, house rule number one of succeeding: who you know matters as much as what you know. I'd name-drop him like the candy man on Halloween if it were me."

Christine let out a nervous chuckle, which dwindled to silence. Then, "I'm not sure about being onstage with him."

"Why not? He might be your dad, but he's also *Tommy T!" What could possibly hold you back?* "Are you two on the outs or something?"

"Hmmmmm . . . we had issues—"

"—And what teen or young adult girl doesn't with their dad?—"

"—but I think we're good again. I love my dad, but he's like . . . my *dad*."

Daphne stroked her hair. "Which is why you should go for it; you'll have someone who knows the ropes and will keep an eye on you . . . let's just say the rock and roll road is full of Dannys."

"It's about the secret he kept from me until way too late."

Beads of sweat suddenly sprouted onto Daphne's forehead. "What secret?"

The question swept through Christine like a shudder in a dark forest, Daphne's face and the portraits behind her fading, fogged in . . .

"Tell her, Tom! Tell her what happened to Annie . . . Christine has a right to know," Megan pleaded. "Just let her know."

Christine, awoken by the most uncustomary sound in the house—a pitched argument between her parents—tucked further behind the corner, out of view.

"No! What does that have to do with us right now?"

Had he *ever* yelled at Megan? She wondered. He sounded like another person, a tyrant, a complete dick, one she would never try to know. She froze, petrified as the Mesozoic Era. She curled her legs beneath her, curiosity displacing her fear just enough to hold her ear to the wall.

"I love you, baby, but you won't talk to me that way, not now, not ever—especially when it's *your* problem!" Megan shouted, almost as loudly. "You *do not* want Christine to find out any other way. You're on your own if you don't tell her what she should've known from day one."

"Then I'm on my own," he said, his voice calm, yet hard as a closed door. "She doesn't need to know."

"Then you can explain to her why today was so nice until you remembered it would have been Annie's birthday and plunged into this bottomless pit where no one gets out, including your wife. It almost ended us before Christine was born, remember? You really want to keep going there, honey?"

"She'll never know."

"*Wrong.*"

Christine pounded her bedroom wall with her head and cried herself to sleep. The next morning, when Megan asked Tom to tell her about Annalisa, he refused. Megan then broke the news, which sent Christine out of the house in tears.

A month later, high school diploma in hand, sick over his exclusion of her—*don't you think I'd want to know I had a sister, even if she was like dead?*—she fled to L.A. She waitressed at a West Hollywood hole in the wall, and buried herself in work, partying, and tears. Then she met Trish, who became her anchor, alternately her friend, mother, roommate, confidant, and comforter. A year later, they enrolled at UCLA, remained roommates, and turned their affections toward yoga, dancing, the arts, and men . . .

Christine shook her head. "I still can't believe he hid that from me. Like, *why?*"

"Losing a child is something you don't get over, honey," Daphne said. "Most men wall off pain like this, and this was as painful as it gets. He just didn't want to expose you to that." She shrugged her shoulders. "I don't for sure, but as a woman who had two stillborn babies, I'd consider that possibility."

"Mom told me she vanished, then died." Tears filled Christine's eyes. "It hurts to even think my dad went through that kind of hell, but like, why keep it from *me*? The one person besides Mom who would've done anything to comfort him?"

Daphne's stomach dropped beneath the floorboards. "That's a good question. Part of it's a man thing. But regardless, losing a kid is not in God's order of things."

Christine ran a hand through her hair, her fingers stopping to unravel a small knot along the way. "I stopped trusting him. I mean, I felt like a bitch about it, but I also didn't know my dad when he was like this. He writes all these incredibly beautiful and emotional songs, touches everyone's hearts in that way—"

"—He's definitely the one percent of the one percent," Daphne said softly.

"But why can't that guy not be able to open up to *tell his daughter*—"

"Most men don't come back all the way from what he went through, let alone talk about it. But yes, that was a mistake."

She took a deep breath, held it for a few extra seconds, and then exhaled. "We've figured some things out in the past six months, and part of me wants to dive back in. But I don't know if I can . . ."

"Let it come to you. Let him come to you." Daphne stared out the kitchen window at a back yard lush with fan and coconut palms, bougainvillea and plants with leaves the size of small children, and wrapped her hands around her mug. "Who knows? Touring together might help you both."

Daphne glanced up at the clock. "Want to cruise the boardwalk?"

"Yeah. I want to show you the mural in the bookstore. It's almost done."

"I'd love to see it." Daphne began to relax as Christine's face finally softened. "Any way I can be there for you . . . but I *will* push your tight little ass forward if you don't give this thing with your dad a chance."

Christine chuckled and wiped her eyes. "That's cool how you know my dad, though. Should've figured as much, your band and his playing at the same time . . . how did you become friends?"

Despite Daphne's best efforts, her cheeks began reddening. "Without the Fever, I never would've met your dad. My life as I know it would not exist." She winked at Christine, now rippling with curiosity. "He helped me start my career. We go way back."

She smiled broadly. "Right on."

She walked to the kitchen window, turned her back, grabbed a tissue, stared at the sunlit plants, and closed her eyes. "There are a few things about your dad I'd like to tell you . . ." *And some will never know . . .* "If you'll excuse me so I can get dressed."

Daphne changed into black jeans and a long-sleeved blouse, the shoulders of which she pulled down. She always felt younger with Christine, though in her eyes, only her shoulders qualified as sexy anymore. She looked into the mirror. *Girl, how could you* not *know she was his kid? And isn't she the right age—*

They burrowed in the sand, arms and bodies pressed together, tops cast aside, lonely denizens of the rock and roll circus about to consummate the sparks that had flown during the half-dozen times their tours had intersected over the summer, their friendship conflating into a place neither imagined.

She wrapped an arm around his neck and looked squarely into his eyes. They were shifty, conflicted, canoes in a hurricane, what a man feels when he's been unmoored from the love of his life for almost a year and doesn't know where to turn next. What an honorable man, Daphne thought, as honorable as his songs . . . this beautiful man who would never be able to love her completely. She knew it.

They kissed languorously. He looked down at her messy black curls and flushed face, her eyes pleading for her long-held love to receive its reward. "I can't go further, Daphne," he said. "I just can't."

There it was. Every burning fiber from her soul to aroused nipples wanted to push forward, but she didn't. She had some honor and dignity to keep, too. Never lead a wounded man, or woman, into a place both will deeply regret. "You still love Megan," she whispered, wishing it were she. "Think about going home now, Tommy."

"I'm with you... what about you?"

She brushed tears from her eyes and cheeks and kissed his chest, then lay her head into it. "I want you forever . . . but you're not mine to have."

He cupped her breasts in his hands, stroking them with fingertips and nails, as he'd done the few other times they escaped to the beach. "I don't know if she'll want me home, but . . ." he paused and took a deep breath, "you're right—I'm not completely over her."

They grabbed their shirts, wiped off the sand, and walked hand-in-hand to the boardwalk. Daphne hailed a cab and accompanied Tom to Hollywood and the Hyatt House to shield him from the lingering groupies who spotted him. After seeing him off a final kiss, she cabbed tearfully back to Venice, deeply hurt, without anger. Or regret. How do you regret loving someone, really loving them, when they reach your deepest spirit and honor every last thing about you?

A year later, their marriage reconciled, Tom and Megan called Daphne. "We have a baby girl!" Tom exclaimed. Added Megan, who took the phone at her birthing center bed, "I'll never ask what happened between you and him. Whatever it was, thank you so much. The Tommy I loved came home to me."

"You good, Daphne? You're like a million miles away."

She twirled the jade broach on her chest, looked at Christine, took a moment to focus. "Memories, honey."

"Did you know you've been standing here for like a minute since you got dressed, off somewhere . . ."

"He did wonders for me." She hoped her voice didn't rise suspiciously.

"OK..."

"By giving me the confidence to believe I was good. 'West of the West' gave me the idea to bail from Minneapolis after high school—as in, *the next day*. We drove to L.A. in my boyfriend's Camaro, summer of '72, 'School's Out' and 'Summer Breeze' playing every ten minutes on the radio . . . what a summer! The Fever, Zeppelin, Hot Tuna, Deep Purple, the Stones, Allman Brothers, Neil Young, Ten Years After, the James Gang, Humble Pie,

Mountain, Black Oak Arkansas, Grand Funk . . . Joni Mitchell, the Eagles, the whole Laurel Canyon crew." She paused to revel in the memories. "People can go on about Sixties music all they want, and should—it threw open the floodgates to what was possible in rock and roll, folk, hard blues, all of it—but for live guitar music, kick-ass rock and roll, I'll take the summers of '72 and '73. They were the best, your dad, Chester, and that motley crew at the top. He was a powerful performer. And that voice . . ."

"So when did you meet him?"

"A few years later. Punk was firing up in L.A. I loved the Germs, the Dickies, *loved* X, and of course the Runaways—note for note badass girls. That was my energy, my anger, and I wanted in. I started by nailing flyers about singing to telephone poles and taping them to streetlights, then a guy walked by and heard me singing to myself and *voila!* I was in a band. Someone spots you, you take the steps they tell you to take, and off you go. Then you carve your own way. That's how this business works . . . or worked.

"When I met Tommy, I told him about my new band. When he realized I wasn't just another groupie after him . . . sorry, honey," she laughed as disgust swept across Christine's face like a haboob. "He hooked us up with our first gigs. I dedicated our first album to the Fever, even though I think your dad likes punk about as much as I liked my parents' Perry Como records."

"Who?"

"Never mind."

"The only Perry I know of is Perry Farrell. And Perry Ellis."

"Right?" Daphne laughed at herself. "Point is, unlike your parents, my parents preferred pedestrian, vanilla *Leave it to Beaver* shit."

"*Leave it to Beaver?*"

"Forget it."

She could see Daphne as a punk rocker, amping up the Viper Room, the Roxy, the Starwood, and other old haunts. Her wild hairstyles, Goth eyes and nails, black hair and priceless expressions, every emotion a story unto itself on her face, would've commanded center stage, right down to a good kick to a front-row maniac's face with her heel. Or boot. She thought of her dad in that scene . . .

Not. "What are you laughing about?" Daphne asked.

"Nothing . . ." She kept laughing.

Still, it was beyond weird listening to her wax over Tom. *What's up with that?* Her instinct clawed against her hesitation to push forward, finally prevailing. "After our blowout, when I wasn't talking to Dad, I asked Mom if they had ever separated or been with anyone else. Yes and yes . . . before I was born."

Daphne tried hard not to stare down China through her chestnut floor. "Yes, but they never stopped loving each other. Each saw someone briefly, but it reminded them of what they were missing. They worked it out, and their reward was a miracle . . . you."

Christine squeezed Daphne's hand, fighting back tears uncorked from a half-dozen entangled feelings, never having heard herself described like that. *A miracle.* Wow. "Let's go down to the beach."

8

V ENICE BEACH CRANKED INTO HIGH GEAR. JUGGLERS, FIRE-
breathers, portrait painters, tarot card readers, trinket merchants, bun-
flashing inline skaters, acrobats, self-proclaimed prophets, unicycle
riders, tattoo artists and human billboards, pot shop hawkers, and other
characters with more stories than possessions rolled out their three-ringed
lives onto the boardwalk. Palm trees, big sun, soft sand, and a crystalline ocean
painted the day, hooked by the Malibu coastline to the north. The only thing
missing from Cirque du Venice was the big top.

As they walked, a few passersby stopped Daphne, asking about her
sculptures and paintings, or the theme of the next major exhibit at the
Appoggiatura. She'd named her gallery after her favorite word, Italian for
"grace note," the high point in an operatic solo. One gray-bearded, heavily
tattooed man stopped them and asked when she was going to perform again.
"Honey, this chick was smart enough to get out before my voice wrinkled
like the rest of me." She then hugged him, kissed his cheek, and signed an
autograph.

She turned to Christine, laughing. "I get asked the same shit as your dad.
Only on a much more local scale."

It reminded Christine of the time Tom took her to Haight-Ashbury,
womb and incubator to the Love Generation. People flew out of nowhere,
reminiscing about a past they never completely left. In their excitement to
meet the rock star, they failed to see what Tom wanted that day: to share a
major thoroughfare in his life with his daughter. "Always the hard part," he
told her. "They think they know you, they all kind of know a piece of you
through your songs, but you don't know them."

"What did he tell you he does in those situations?" Daphne asked.

"Just like he did that day. He thanks them for listening, maybe tells a
quick little story, and keeps walking."

"Same thing he taught me."

Christine studied the bearded, pocked, glittered, scarred, delicate, rough, wrinkled, downtrodden faces of the Venetian homeless as they walked past. She turned to Daphne. "I like walking around these people and even though half of them are toasted or burned out, they feel more real to me than most," she said. "They don't want to be messed with, yet they've been nothing but hassled. Now, they're broken. Any kindness will do, but everyone's like too afraid or up to their necks in themselves to talk to them."

Daphne nodded as she watched the piano man tickle the ivories on his boardwalk stage, his bird's nest beard contrasting sharply with his beautiful composition and shirt aswirl in a dozen colors. If ever a song captured a specific scene better than that old Venetian minstrel, Jim Morrison, did with "Strange Days," then she had yet to hear it. She whistled the tune, mashing it with "Moonlight Drive," imagining Jim skipping on the boardwalk as the elements of the two magnificent tunes marbled through his beautiful, mercurial, brilliant, universal mind. "This is a true outpost of humanity," she said. "That's what turns me on about this place."

Christine peeled off her sandals. Were it possible, she'd never wear shoes. A true throwback, Daphne thought, possessed by adventure, as bohemian as black lights and paisley shirts, yet far too driven to drift about in a pharmaceutical haze. "You're Flower Child Three-Point-Oh, if there is such a thing," Daphne said.

"Look at that dude—" Christine pointed to a gray-haired man mumbling to himself, broken glasses tilted sideways, and an overstuffed duffel bag twisting his torso. "Know what he does every day?"

"I should know, I'm down here enough, but no. What?"

"Calculus. Vector math. Rocket science stuff."

"What?"

Christine smiled broadly, thinking of the man's disdain with interaction of any kind, like a displaced sadhu. Questions formed in Daphne's eyes. "Really. He goes into The Mad Cow, gets a coffee, pulls out his index cards, and does his math." She glanced at an ocean shimmering in sharp spring light. "They're like sidetracked spirits. They need someone to remind them of how beautiful they are inside."

Daphne smiled, her body warming with Christine's words. "Honey, I'll bet God took a long nap after creating you."

A skater approached, awash in the music pouring through her earbuds. Her lengthy legs grew in detail, stretching long and lean toward the pavement beneath her pea-sized shorts, her path holding steady, eyes and mind oblivious to all surroundings, probably lost in The Weeknd or Ariana Grande, heading straight, closer . . .

"Hey—what the hell!"

Christine jerked Daphne away from a certain collision. The girl skated away, oblivious that she nearly caused a three-woman crash.

Moments later, another teenager approached. Her polka-dot knee socks partially covered her spindly legs, a look as random as a Jackson Pollock splash party. "Gotta love that," Daphne said.

The girl blinked once, twice. "Oh . . . my . . . God! You were like the queen of the scene! I love your songs!"

"Thanks, hun . . . a long time ago . . ."

"The old music is way better anyway. I just bought this." From her oversized shoulder bag, she pulled a copy of *Entertaining Bacchus,* Daphne's poetry collection of the many phases of men and women dancing around and around, seeking ways into each other. She handed Daphne a pen. "Can you sign it?" Daphne obliged, throwing in an inscription about the girl's courage in being herself. "Thank you." The girl held her book in both hands and shook it a few times. "I'm so honored."

The girl stayed put, not knowing when to break away. Christine smiled at her. "Want to join us? I need an opinion on something I'm finishing up."

"Sure . . ."

They walked into the bookstore, and directly to the back wall, where Daphne's teenaged fan noticed the mural. She turned to Christine. "You did this?"

"Yeah."

The bookstore was testament to the way bookstores used to be—clerks engaging with customers, free tea and coffee, a mother reading to her sprawled-out five-year-old in the children's stacks, and staff reviews of favorite new titles handwritten and placed like bookmarks within the chosen books. The day independent bookstores die, Christine thought, is the day to throw in the towel on all hope for an intelligent society.

The three central characters on the wall's mural were easy to recognize: Charlie Chaplin as The Tramp, waddling on the original Venice Pier; Jim Morrison, writing on the beach; and the femme fatale of L.A. punk belting out to frothing fans. Above the trio hovered the ghosted outline of Venice's founding father, Abbot Kinney. She saw a couple places to touch up the edges on his panel, maybe add a few stars, swirls, and clouds to highlight the vast spatial dimension of creativity represented on the wall.

Daphne locked in on the punker's panel. Such an understated heroine of the scene, a brilliant woman whose lyrics connected like few others to the gnawing in her soul, the yearning in her heart. "She's what it's all about," Daphne said, her voice barely above a whisper. "Where did you get the inspiration for this mural?"

"The Mahabharata."

"The what?" Daphne folded her arms. "How can you know about *The Mahabharata?*"

"Been into it since I started realizing yoga is more than *asanas*, postures. And even longer."

"How's that?"

"My parents took me to Delhi, Varanasi, Bangkok, and Phuket when I was fifteen, and that's when I first read it. We went to the Golden Palace. That ruled. They have *Mahabharata* scenes painted on the outer walls. That's when I decided I wanted to paint murals. Then we boated to Phuket and snorkeled, went to the tiny islands, ate food and drinks served by cute boys, one in particular . . ."

Daphne laughed softly. "Who might that be?"

Christine closed her eyes and feasted for the millionth time, or thereabouts, on lychee fruit, mango drinks, fresh-caught fish, and the hands of the beautiful local with the ten-letter first name she sometimes remembered, his fingers and lips igniting her, the first time she'd felt like *that* inside, the sun and his hands running up and down her legs, all following her first kiss, straight to paradise halfway around the world.

"You still with me?" Daphne started laughing.

Christine looked at Daphne, then their accomplice, still glued to her study of the mural, oblivious to the conversation. Christine shrugged her shoulders.

They left the store and walked past a man dressed as a tree. They exchanged looks, said goodbye to the girl, and finished walking the next few minutes to the end of the boardwalk and the palm-covered bar packed with drinking, dancing, and loud talking. "A bit of fun to be had." Daphne grabbed Christine's hand. "Let's check it out."

On a tiny corner stage, a man contorted himself into a hundred contrived emotions while butchering an Usher song. "Only one thing worse than mangling Usher," Daphne said. "Nothing. Nothing is worse."

Christine looked at the stage. Her head and chest tingled. She'd tried karaoke on a dare from Trish. Now, she was hooked. Songs rifled through her brain like a prom queen's hands running department store racks. She immediately stood in line with a half-dozen other contestants and sang a few scales to warm up. Everyone fancied themselves a star. Why not? How you ever going to get anywhere if you decide early on that someone else gets to be the star? One thing she'd learned about being in L.A.—never let them know you're unsure. Which, come to think of it, were Tom's words.

Twenty minutes later, after one good performance and a few hatchet jobs, she walked onstage and shook her hair out, then took off her hoodie and sandals. A dainty butterfly tattoo rode along one of her exposed hipbones. Daphne chuckled, her take on Christine as a throwback reaffirmed, men now creeping closer to the stage like bees drawn to honey.

She dropped her head, ran her hands through her hair, breathed deeply, and muttered her typical benediction before she started any new music or art event: "May someone out there feel better because You moved through my voice."

"We got us a hot one!" the emcee screamed.

Christine looked at the older, grayer crowd and performed a folk song and a rocker. The audience loved her, raving about her chops and her dancing. "Great songs, power, lots of emotion, on key, the way you dance . . . wow, baby girl!" Daphne exclaimed afterward.

"I think it's just because it's like the second time you saw me."

"Really? Do I look like the sugar-coating type?"

She didn't answer.

A few minutes later, the bar owner called Christine and two others, a thirtysomething woman and a man in his fifties, to the stage. "Let's let our finalists battle it out, then we'll choose a winner. Youngest first. One song."

Christine twirled the microphone in her hand. Move slowly at first, let it build . . . *that's the one. Perfect song, perfect place.* The machine bellowed the snare drum open to a generation's ode, Alice's trip into, within and beyond San Francisco wonderland. The song that wins singing contests if you can handle the vibrato. Christine *became* the song, so graceful and urgent, her voice seducing and ensnaring. She roared ahead, solid and sustained, whirling in place, lost in the song, incanting the hook line over and over while spinning into dizziness. The power within her grew, not the heady power of taking over a situation, but the soulful power of throwing down some of your life's hidden potential and encouraging it to come out of its hiding place.

She admonished the crowd to feed their heads, and then slowly lifted her own, belting as she tilted her head back, her throat exposed to the heavens, her voice anchored to her chest and belly, the crowd a blur, hair spilling across her face, cheers and cat calls filling the bar.

She stopped—then launched into something no one had ever heard before:

> *Higher and higher my heart flies,*
> *Above the rainbow skies of love,*
> *The fire in my eyes*
> *Longs for and gives rise*
> *To the deep space of your heart,*
> *So climb with me*

> *Right out of your skin,*
> *So climb with me*
> *Why don't you climb with me*
> *Your love is my gypsy's prayer,*
> *Your love is my gypsy's prayer.*

Never had she tried her own lyrics before more than a mirror. She repeated the last line another half-dozen times, in sync with her approach to the anthem with which she started, before twirling to a stop.

She held her breath, not an easy feat while trying to catch it at the same time.

The audience glanced at each other, stunned, unsure of what they just saw. Finally, after enough sideways glances to feed a convention of conspiracy theorists, applause broke out, full and mighty, spiked with loud whistling. *What a feeling!* "Let's hear it for Christine!" the emcee yelled. Louder cheers. *What a rush!* He turned to her. "What was that last song?"

"Something I've been working on at the beach. Nothing really."

He glanced at the cheering patrons. "Tell them that."

Christine grasped her first-place trophy, a *weissbier* glass shaped like a microphone, and two free drink coupons as they reached the boardwalk. Daphne looked at her, still trying to absorb the stunning performance that belonged on something far greater than a corner bar's karaoke stage. "That last tune . . ."

She shrugged her shoulders. "'Gypsy's Prayer'? It's this poem I've tried to work out but it keeps coming out more like song lyrics."

"They *are* song lyrics. Great melody, too. It's a song, not a poem."

A disheveled, middle-aged man nearly stumbled into Daphne while trying to woo her with a card trick. He fanned the cards, which fluttered to the ground. She gave him a dollar for his trouble, then turned to Christine. "You asked what I thought about you singing with your dad? You just answered your own question."

A cold, sudden wind goosebumped Christine's skin, the leading edge of an encroaching late-season storm still somewhere over the horizon. She grabbed the hoodie from around her waist and put it on. "It's still going to be weird singing with him."

"Anyone would play with those guys in a heartbeat," Daphne said. "This Fever reunion, if it clicks, will take you places . . . you have no idea. Tours usually do, especially reunion tours. Just do us both a solid."

"What's that?"

"Keep your head, watch your back . . . and teach your song to them."

Christine chuckled. "I don't know. I doubt they'll be into the singer's kid pushing beach poems on them."

"I beg to differ. Knowing your dad, Chester, and Will, they're not going to settle for singing greatest hits to aged baby boomers every night. They'd rather eat iron. They swore they'd never be rocking chair legacy rockers. They're going to need new energy and new songs. When they hear yours, well . . ."

They sat on the beach, talking of tours and galleries and sculptures and boys and men and families until the sun claimed them and called it a day.

9

CHRISTINE SHOOK HER HEAD, UNSURE IF SHE COULD MATCH UP to his wishes. "Honey, I need you a half-octave above whatever I sing, sometimes a full octave," Tom reiterated. "Let your voice go; cut it loose; blend within mine unless I tell you to take lead."

Simple enough instructions . . . if you've been headlining for twenty years. "I'm getting there, Dad, but I'm afraid I'll sing too loud for people to hear you, and then I'll mess up these harmonies."

Tom adjusted her microphone stand and walked to the sound room, lowered her levels slightly, returned onstage and blew into the mics, testing them. "Just focus on syncing with my voice and working on the high notes, the higher registers. We'll be in great shape in no time and I'll be done having a heart attack about vocals."

Will counted in the band. Within a few verses, Christine found a groove, her voice soaring to heights he could no longer reach, like a sprinter who can't own those final ten meters anymore. While singing, he listened to how she crowned his voice without eclipsing it, one note directly above another. How did she grasp that subtle touch within a few songs? And her range! She could ride rock bottom, her low notes no more than a shade higher than his, and then fly a full octave over his head. He never possessed such a wide natural range, Rock & Roll Hall of Fame career and a hundred million record sales be damned.

After a few minutes, Tom twirled his hand in the air. *Bring it home.* X raced on both keyboard decks, his right hand creating its own harmonicsphere with Christine and a fast-strumming Chester, his left holding bottom notes with Rogelio and Will.

Christine hooked her hand into Tom's. Thrilled by the songs, being home on the ridge, singing with seasoned pros and not karaoke clubs with the same sob stories that kept Bukowski and his barfly pen busy for years, she danced in tight circles, stops, and hops, emulating a young Tommy T performing "Street Party" on scratchy YouTube videos:

The fun is on the streets,
The sun is on the streets,
Just grab a girl, give her a twirl,
Let's party in the streets,
Let's party in the streets,
Let's party in the streets . . .

The band began to find rhythm with each other. Rogelio and X were comfortable enough to riff in the spaces between chord progressions they'd just learned, their musical prowess leaving Tom and Chester scratching their whiskered chins. What luck! Their constant urge to jam extemporaneously reminded Tom of their extended jams during the Seventies, the decade of the endless solo, along with X, the way his hands journeyed on the keyboard, somehow tossing riffs of progressive rock, jazz, and blues into almost every number. X was becoming intrigued by where he could take the music, using Christine as well as Tom for the vocal drive. "Like that *power* and expression, girl," he said, his admiration rising. "You sound strong."

"Thanks," she said softly. "When you're used to singing at hella loud bars with shitty speakers, power is good."

X leaned over his keyboard. "Hey, I saw you with a notebook the other morning."

"My journal?"

"What's in it?"

"Just things I jotted down at the beach. More poems than lyrics . . . I don't know."

"Any melodies down on paper?"

"Just in my head."

"Works for me."

She twirled her long spiral earring as they studied each other. "Why do you want to know?"

"Maybe I can help you put one or two to music." He smiled, his white teeth gleaming, made more striking by his coal-black face.

"They aren't really . . ." She eyed the delicious physical specimen before her. *Where is he going here?* He must have an angle; don't they all? But there was something else . . . *where have I seen him before? I've caught this dude somewhere* . . . in L.A.? Had to be L.A. "You said something about being in a band . . ."

"A blip on the screen. Fifteen seconds of fame. Make it five. That's it."

X, X-Man, The X-Man . . . L.A. One night, two shows, two or three years ago. "I know who you are."

"Really? I probably would have remembered a woman who looks like you."

"Nice . . . let me drop that in my journal." She chuckled. "My girl in L.A., Trish, has both Crescendo CDs. I've got one somewhere. We saw you on the Strip, the Viper Room. Maybe the Whisky . . . we did everything but sweep Sunset some nights."

"Damn!" X laughed. "Our big tour. Two weeks on the West Coast. So *you're* the ones who boosted our sales."

She looked him over, head to toe, a little more directly and confidently. What a beautiful man. "Someone had to, right?"

"Crescendo . . ." X brushed his hand through the air. "Let's do this next tune. I'll ride with you on the keyboards."

Christine twirled her hair into a bun. She couldn't remember the last time she'd played with her hair so much, being this nervous for this long; three days is a marathon to an exposed nerve. Time to get comfortable, soon. Why sing all summer just to stress?

Tom looked over. "What you have in mind, X?"

"'Rainy Day Stomp'. . . with a little extra gas." X and Christine exchanged glances while Rogelio grabbed his twelve-string bass. "Swing-your-booty-all-night blues." He winked at a smiling Christine.

Tom pawed the stage with his foot as he grinned. "Well, X, don't forget to take one of the world's best axemen on the ride. Might want him along."

Chester's face dropped, jowls first, eyes squinting at X. *Cocky little shit.* Then he burst into laughter at the nonsense careening through his head; *who thought we'd be jamming like kids in a garage band now—and getting ready to see our fans again?* Life did some squirrely, tough things to you. Then, when you least expected it, delivered a bucket of gold that drained right into your heart.

Over the next hour, "Rainy Day Stomp" became "Street Party" became "When I Become the President," one song blending into the next, the band tightening around their gold-throated legend and their new vocalist. "I'm used to singing two or three songs, not like ten," Christine said after boosting Tom's vocals in "Her Heart Was Something New." The song always warmed her bones, the story of a love affair that, midway through its third decade, created her. She flashed back to the night she taught the song to Danny, curled up on a nameless Baja California beach, warmed by a fire, sand, desert winds, and each other. Happier times.

She closed her eyes, dismissing his unwelcome intrusion into her thoughts by imagining the summer ahead. If this worked, they would be playing halls and arenas, while he'd be doing whatever—and, likely, whomever—he pleased on his paddle toward oblivion. *Who's riding the best wave now, Danny?*

Megan walked in with a glass of wine and a bucket of beers. She handed Christine the cabernet while the others grasped for their beverages like parched wanderers. "I never knew you could sing like that, all the range," she said.

Christine shrugged her shoulders. Her lips lifted up from the rim of the glass. "You haven't heard me in a long time, like probably before I moved to L.A."

"True."

Chester grabbed a towel and buffed the belly of his exquisite Brazilian rosewood guitar. After twenty years of building guitars in the backwoods, learning the finer properties of woods from all six wooded continents, and then suffering through a small fortune of errors, he had created his very own Stradivarius. He got the idea from Jack Casady, the man with the flying fingers and time-keeping eyebrows, who after decades of flying with the Airplane and weaving blues and acoustic gold with Hot Tuna, emerged late in his career with a signature bass that left fans as riveted as they were over the music. "She can sing, for damned sure. We got lucky with all these guys, Megan."

"You guys ready to call it a day?" Tom kicked a piece of duct tape that had stuck to his foot. He turned toward X and Christine, who had walked over. "I have another idea. Why don't you take X and Rogelio, go into our entertainment room and watch some old videos and 'You Tubes'? See what we were."

X chuckled. "They had video then?"

"These dudes were *stars!*"

X gawked as a youthful Tommy T prowling the stage, a tiger possessed, preying on "When A Place Goes Mad" as much as singing it. His movements wrapped perfectly around the emotion of each word and note, his timing automatic. Chester darted in and out, his head bouncing to every note, his brown bear frame exerting pure force and power, like a burly caveman on the hunt. Put a headband on him, silhouette him against a strobe light, and you see a young Ted Nugent was in the house. Only Chester played with more style and touch, his musical range much greater.

The converted 16mm film bounced, flickered, faded, zoomed, and jump-cut to bizarre camera switches and emphasis on the wrong musicians, the cameramen not timing the band's switches and solos . . . catching Raylene standing still during Chester's lead . . . zooming in on Treg's impassive face though his *hands* lit up the keys . . .

Christine watched her future dad roar through songs extended well beyond the recorded versions. She could watch it a thousand more times, always weird to see him in this time warp, knowing she would one day come from him. It was like reaching into the PC past—pre-Christine—and touching your own face.

She turned to Rogelio. "Dad's lucky to have this footage. He told me that bands then were lucky to get anything on tape."

Rogelio smiled and tugged at the three chains dropping from his neck, gifts from patrons in Italian and Austrian churches and halls. Too cool, Christine thought.

"My mom and her boyfriend loved watching concerts on TV," he said. "When I was small, re-runs of *Soul Train* were our weekend ride." He chuckled to himself.

X and Christine laughed. "For me as a little kid, it was MTV and my fantasy girls, Martha Quinn and Downtown Julie Brown," X said. "I went crazy over Martha. I met her a couple years ago at a producers party, took Ulysses with me. He told Martha all about it; they laughed their asses off."

"Like Mary Ann on *Gilligan's Island*," Chester said, walking into the room, beer in hand. "Girl-next-door types appeal to me. Married one."

"Like who?" Christine asked.

"Mary Ann."

"Mary Ann . . . never heard of her."

Chester grumbled and started to walk away from the flat screen, but turned as he heard Treg rifle through a keyboard sequence, a calm wizard uncorking a hard-line blizzard. "Good playing, brother," X said softly. "Dude was a wizard."

"Yes he was. He and Raylene were our anchors; they kept the rest of us from ruining ourselves . . . me the most," Chester said. "Miss Treg. Always will. You can have your great keyboardists, you can bring in new blood, but you can't replace style and mastery. You don't replace signature sounds." He tipped his bottle to the screen.

A moment later on tape, Tommy T swooped in front of the stage and pressed the crowd into its own collective hearts: "*When a place goes mad! When a place goes mad! When a place goes mad!*" Rhythm. Electricity. Magic. He glued his energy and presence to fans the way a good backwoods church sermon grabs you by the heart—and the throat, and sometimes elsewhere—and never lets go.

Christine caught herself looking at X, maybe ten seconds after the last time. "So X, you've been around awhile, right?"

He smiled broadly. "A *little* while . . ." If she could guess his age, she could have it; he wasn't volunteering numbers.

"Where do women fit into the rock world? I've always been curious what a dude like you would think."

"Babes *are* music. They drive music. What are dudes always singing about?"

"What about on stage? Rock chicks performing on stage?"

"A few make it, mainly singers, but it's still kind of a man's game."

"Not quite my question, but . . ."

"Any band that has a really good woman—or women—is automatically fun to watch in all the right ways. Totally down with it . . . but it doesn't happen that often."

"We can sing and play instruments, too, you know? What about Chrissie Hynde? Joan Jett? Lita Ford? Alicia Keys? Or Lady Gaga? Gale Dorsey, Bowie's bassist a few years ago? What about Dad and Uncle Chester's old bassist, Raylene? She's probably responsible for thousands and thousands of girls—and boys—playing music."

X nodded. "I hear you, girl. But check the *tunes*. Eighty percent are man-meets-woman, man-pursues-woman, man-conquers-or-gets-shafted-by-woman. Played a million ways, a million twists on the lyrics . . . eighty percent."

"What about when a *wo*-man leads the band?"

"You sing about dudes and problems, right? Pain, longing, rejection and grief. But it still comes down to men and women, girls and dudes."

She thought about it for a moment. "OK, I hear you, though not like in the division of gender way you broke it down. I've been writing about love—lost, found, dreamed, turned on, turned off, healed, destroyed . . . learning to love yourself after you pick your heart off the ground."

"I rest my case."

Rogelio swung his leg off the reclining leather chair before it consumed him for the night, and leaned forward. His eyes felt soft, puffy, after nearly a week of constant jamming and fitful sleep at an altitude meant for comets. "No wonder that whole generation followed your dad like some crazy little army," he said. "He owned not only the stage, but everything on it! And everyone in the crowd. No wonder he is who he is."

Christine chuckled. "He wasn't my dad then." *But he was someone's.* "It's still weird seeing him the same age as I am now . . ."

Rogelio looked at the wall. Next to the flat screen, in its mounted glory, hung the magazine cover photo that drove stakes through the hearts of Fever fans—Tom's final teary-eyed bow, and a pint-sized Christine bowing next to him. "What a great memory," Rogelio said. "Remember that concert at all?"

She shrugged. *Might as well get used to the question.* "Just dancing on stage. I guess that's why I like singing in bars, or watching people look at my murals. Something about being on stage."

X moved next to her. She felt his heat, his energy. "I like giving people a rush, feel good about themselves," she said, her words rasped by vocal cord and general exhaustion. She smiled, and took a half-step back. "That felt good, X, but no ideas, 'kay?"

"No ideas," he said, his smile blocking a few choice ideas from spewing out.

Rogelio walked over to a voluminous bookcase built into the front wall, the precious, long-gathered treasure trove of one Thomas Timoreaux, Rock Legend turned Bibliophile. The collection could pass for a small bookstore, its hundreds of volumes spanning a thousand years of time, pieces Tom and Megan picked up during Fever tours. Wherever they played, in whatever town or city they huddled, they searched bookstores, fairs, and auctions for local authors, modern and antiquarian treasures. The greatest piece was an ancient Persian manuscript, lit from above and below, encased in glass: the legacy of the Pandava brothers, *The Mahabharata*. The scribe was as elegant as lace with his penmanship, his illustrations, the work. A visual masterpiece. They'd bought it from a dying Iranian collector, through Swiss friends, partly to satisfy Christine's fascination with the story after their trip to Thailand— and her new love for illustration panels.

"Seen *that* in a musician's house before?" X asked as Rogelio carefully traced the air above the case with his finger, trying to imagine the hand that produced such meticulous work, every line, tone, shade, object perfectly rendered. What an exalted place, where creation flourishes and time stands still in music, singing, baseball, anything that balances craftsmanship and artistry. Even the universe must have exploded with a creative, timeless surge; that's what it felt like in the zone, like a universe expanding from a single note. Imagine drawing such perfection through colors and sweeps of line.

"Why are you surprised?" Megan laughed as she walked in. Christine realized she was again in X's arms, and stepped to the side. "We couldn't believe our luck; these manuscripts are out there, but not this pristine at this age."

X thought of saying that back to her, but stopped himself.

Megan turned to Rogelio. "I see that you appreciate the love, tears, sweat, weeks, and months that went into the manuscript. I can always tell those who don't value learning by the lack of books, art, and music in their houses."

"I never thought of it like that," X said.

"True. Books. Music. Art. Having one is essential to survival, as far as I'm concerned. Two, you're curious. All three, you'll never stop learning."

Megan lifted Christine's fallen shoulder strap onto its original perch. "I want you guys to know that you're doing wonders for Tom, Chester, and Will. They're blown away by how quickly you're learning. They can't believe the possibilities ahead, all because you're here. Thanks for making me a road widow—again." She chuckled and rubbed Christine's cheek. "You started finding a groove with your dad today, sweetheart."

Christine managed a weary grin. "I wouldn't get too excited yet, Mom."

On the flat screen, Tommy T swayed, his eyes lifting upward, proclaiming his love, the love of his life, the love that shaped and formed him all over again . . .

> *I know that she's my lady*
> *Her love—deep sunlit face . . .*

"That's what you're up against on this tour. Memories," Megan said, hooking her arm into Rogelio's. "The memories people have. They've simmered for twenty years, and now, for the really hardcore fans, memories will more or less overlay your actual performances. Unless you blow them away with a new approach. Tom, Chester, and Will are playing against their younger selves, in a sense."

10

CHRISTINE SLIPPED OUT THE DOOR, NOTEBOOK IN HAND. SHE proceeded along a rock chip pathway, passing X, midway through his first outdoor breath of the day. "Want to go for a walk? I'll show you my little lookout."

Ten minutes later, X followed in a hoodie, shorts, and sneakers, straight out of Harlem. As they walked, he tried hard to keep focused on the pinons, scratchweed, Jerusalem artichokes, purple thistle, and cactus Megan had planted alongside an assortment of buildings on the property: his guest cottage, Megan's studio, Tom's main wood shop, a canning kitchen, and a large storage shed. The place looked more like a hacienda or communal living setup than a single-family home. Probably was communal at some point, X thought, with the Timoreaux's Sixties roots and all. Aspens ran up the adjoining ridgeline, slim, tall and regal, their newly hatched leaves shimmering in the morning breeze.

"Shit! These things have teeth!" Blood rose from his forearm as he pulled away from a hungry purple thistle.

She looked back. "You OK?" She noticed how X's eyes darted from her legs to the biting plant. "Hike like you hopefully drive: Eyes on both sides of the road," she chuckled.

He pulled out the barbs that stuck, tried to shake the sting out of his arm, and resumed his study of her taut legs, from low-cut hiking shoes to the hem of her shorts, high on her thighs. Legs were his thing, the end-all and be-all of the healthy, sexy, vital woman. They expressed so much: fitness. Sexiness. Strength. Style. *Personality.* The way you move through the crowd, the way you move through life. You can learn so much about a person by how their legs bend, stride, dance. The pride of countless runways, shorelines, and straightaways. *Not Just Knee Deep* is right, George Clinton.

"I'm glad you like what you see so much." Christine tapped her notebook, eyebrow cocked, her hand on tilted hip. "I brought you up here to talk about something. Let's get to my lookout, the wilderness."

They welcomed this rare downtime. For the past three weeks, Tom and Chester had run rehearsals like football training camp, playing a set, breaking it down, working on the weaker songs or parts. The routine reminded X of the two-a-day drills he loathed during his running back days with the Harlem Bulldogs, though this came with far more laughs, much better beer, and less physical punishment. Sometimes, they even split apart, the instrumentalists going one way, Tom and Christine the other. They worked on when they would sing solo or together, when she would shadow his vocals, when she would crown them. "It seems like he's shaping the vocals around your good, his bad," X told her, looking her in the eye, hand on shoulder . . . comforting. "Pay attention to what he's doing."

She sang until her throat hurt. She studied lyrics until her eyes collapsed into sponges, often with X or Rogelio playing acoustic guitar so she could nail the registers and melodies. She then headed for the outlook, a towel and notebook under her arm, practiced yoga, and meditated. The sun and swales of pines and aspens carried her into a blissful inner state once known to the Apache at the same outlook, where women and girls followed golden eagles while grinding pine nuts and acorns. Refreshed, she turned her walk back down the hill into a deer's dance, with a few gypsy twirls thrown in.

Now she walked briskly, leading X along, following a narrow deer trace. She moved up and down the ditches and hills deftly, her steps solid on red clay made slippery by a late-night thunderstorm that threw its typical petulant temper, arriving in a full force of lightning, rain, wind, and anger, and wringing itself out within twenty minutes.

"You got this hike down," X panted. He wiped his forehead.

"If you roll easily, breathe with every other step, you're good." She heard his wheezes, not uncomfortable yet, but getting there. When she turned, he was stretched to the sky, arms overhead, gulping the somewhat limited oxygen. "Need to catch your breath? You're a mile and a half above sea level. You might need a minute."

He waved his hand. *Keep going.* He couldn't speak it.

Christine swept her arms upward, the morning vibrating through her chest as she breathed. "You don't see views like this very often in the city, you know, mountains piled on mountains." She slithered her arms like an awakening genie. "I think we can *feel* these mountains."

X's constricted lungs sought breath. "Honey, I can . . . definitely . . . feel them."

She laughed. "C'mon, flatlander." She grabbed his hand and led him through a field of broken scree and stone, fragments of a long-buried volcano. Nearby creeks flowed with runoff from spring rains and a melting snowfield that started a few hundred feet above, winter receding around them. She had traction on every step, while X continued to slip, his treadless kicks no match for the trail.

Thirty minutes later, they reached a long, flat rock. She motioned him to join her as she put down her notebook. "I'm curious about something."

X lifted his arms and forced a smile through his collapsed breath. He raised his index finger. *Give me a minute.*

A hummingbird hovered five feet in front of her, its wings buzzing. "I never seen a bird do that," X said. The hummingbird hovered for another second, considered darting over to X, and flew away swiftly.

She cupped X's hand between her own. "Can I ask you something?"

"Go . . ."

"Is there a problem with you and Chester?"

"No . . . why?"

"I just sense a vibe, some edginess . . . not in the music, but how you guys don't really talk about anything."

"Besides music? What else is there? I hardly know him."

She nodded and rubbed his hand. "I get that. But . . . I don't know . . . something a little uncomfortable . . ."

Damn. She's got radar to go with her sonar. "I don't get how the dude rolls."

"Do tell."

He did. The growing divide with Chester concerned him; he'd begun to wonder if he would be the first casualty of this patchwork reassembling of the Fever. If you can't get along with the co-captain of the ship, you're screwed. But it wasn't over music; he knew the songs well, having spent the spring learning them before flying out. That didn't explain why Chester grumbled at him, nagged him to stretch a riff, shrink another, play slower, play faster, get with the program. Just riding his ass. Maybe the condescending looks were passed down instinctively, the memory-fed residue of forebears who went to their gated family graves still pissed about the Emancipation Proclamation. He felt the sad saga in his bones every time he played thick, heavy blues, the music drawn from gospel hymns the people sang to survive whips, thirst, gnarled fingers, the hard bites of cotton plants, wrenched backs, and crushed spirits.

X put his free hand on Christine's extended leg, which she curled towards his hand. "Here's the question I'm trying to figure out: why does Chester act like I'm on the chitlin' circuit? When I do my thing for more than a few seconds, he gives me this *look* . . . I mean, that's a look no black man wants to see—"

"—*Hello!!!*" Christine released his hand, shock and a dash of anger intersecting at the furrow between her eyebrows. "Where are you *going* here?"

He remained silent.

She looked at the treetops, from which a mother hawk flew to forage for brood food, and turned to him. "X, listen carefully to me. Uncle Chester might look like the poster child for the Confederacy, with the beard and scraggly hair and flop hat and shit, but there's nothing racist or bigoted about him. That would've caused a problem; his late wife was white—and Cherokee—and African-American."

The darkness receded from X's eyes. "Say what?"

"He had to put up with some nasty words from people who were supposed to be his neighbors and friends, for years . . . until she died . . ."

"When? How"

"A couple years before I was born. Cancer. He nearly lost it after that."

"Drugs? Booze?"

"Along with his mind." She nodded, the sun dappling her face. "The band took a hiatus, because Dad refused to replace him, even temporarily. How do you replace the co-captain? Then Uncle Chester met Chandra during a tour stop in L.A. a few years later, like a little after I was born, they fell in love . . . she saved him."

"Chandra . . . I had no idea. I see her with him and think, 'That's one lucky old dude, get to spend the rest of your life with a girl a generation younger.'"

She patted his hand and rubbed her fingertips along a forearm of steel cable, her body tingling its approval. "He's a redneck in some ways, no doubt. So what? Look where he's from, the Cumberland Gap. He's really funny when he gets up in people's business with his banter. Sometimes, I laugh so hard I have to pee. Sometimes, I don't quite make it to the bathroom. He's awesome."

X considered diving into the Jerusalem artichoke bush next to their rock. "Well I got that one wrong. Gotta figure out the dude's vibe, where he's coming from."

"Please do, because Uncle Chester loves the way you play." She squinted into the sun, which silhouetted X's shaved head like a corona. A gust of wind swept her hair off her face. Despite the conversation, the friction between X and Chester, she felt herself drawing closer to him, eroding the promises made to Trish and Daphne in L.A. to stay clear of men for a while, but when did an ascending heart ever listen to reason? "They're so happy you and Rogelio believe in them enough to put your studio careers on hold. It means everything. You remind Uncle Chester of how he used to command a stage with his guitar, and it frustrates him, so he sometimes pushes you."

"That's a good way to look at it."

"That's how he does look at it, big guy. He's chiseling you into the perfect keyboardist for this band."

X dragged his fingers to her proud, pointed chin, and stroked upward to her cheeks, golden and glowing as the day in front of them. She moved her face into his hand. His fingertips traced her skin, soft despite constant sun exposure that Christine did nothing to reduce, unlike many of the alabaster-skinned girls in L.A., who lived by the creed of black and white: black clothes. White skin.

She lifted her head onto his shoulder, a stone pillow clothed in chestnut flesh. As her breath warmed his skin, he tried to reconcile this very beautiful L.A. woman, a worthy reflection of the great Doors song, actually *growing up* on this mountain ridge. She was nothing like the local folk. Since arriving, he'd eaten dust from locals busting up and down the washboard road in their F-350s, and dealt with more tobacco-chewing, swill-talking, bearded John Deere cap-wearing, Blue Collar TV-watching good ol' boys than in the forty years preceding his trip up the hill. Many were decent people, but they never showed that side behind stares that lingered and sneers that followed like a posse. And you knew, you just *knew,* that stuffed deer and elk heads hung above their mantels or across from their front doors. "Meet George. He's a twelve-point."

"What'd you get him with?"

"A thirty-thirty First shot."

"How'd he taste?"

"Damn good."

She slid his hand to her thigh, leaned over, and kissed him. He squeezed her side slightly, sending a shiver from head to toe. *Soft touch . . . listens . . . willing to try to see it my way . . . likes me for who I am . . . such men really do exist!*

She backed off, reluctantly, and grabbed a large water bottle from a diagonal fracture in the granite outcropping. "It's melted snow from the streams up top," she said, calmly, hoping her speeding heart would get the message. "I left it here yesterday." After drinking the ice-cold water and stretching her legs, she pulled off her boots and socks, and cracked open her notebook. "Look through this and see if anything grabs you."

He grabbed the book. "You share these with a lot of people?"

"You're the first . . . well, the second. My friend Daphne has seen some of them. She's an old punk rock singer. A local legend, actually."

X raised his eyebrows, then opened the notebook. She cupped her knees to her chest and stared into the colors, cloud swirls, and land mass that coalesced into Sierra Blanca and the surrounding sky. She thought of an invisible breath whispering those swirls into existence, spirit and nature dancing together, as visceral and ephemeral as wind itself. *A-ho.* She rubbed a chunk of rose quartz, envisioning Mescalero Apache women chanting simple homilies of their relationship to Great Spirit, most of them passed down orally and then lost, the tragic fate of virtually all conquered cultures.

X read her lyrical poems, or poetic lyrics—hard to tell, the way she wrote. He noted the keys she wrote at the beginning, new chords in places where you'd expect a switch, and closed his eyes, giving each piece the full floor in his mind. She watched his fingers tap out her chords on keys of air, imagining a day she could join creative forces with this strong, beautiful man. "These are strong lyrics, good twists and turns. Anyone can relate," he said. "And you got ear, girl; most of these chord switches work."

"What do you like?"

"Most of it." X dog-eared another page. He tried to jostle the words into different beats, but the only order that worked was the way she laid it down. Her lyrics reminded him of Ulysses' era, Tom and Chester's musical teeth-cutting years, when lyric writing was an art form. Got Bob Dylan the Nobel Prize for Literature, didn't it?

She grabbed his hand and kissed it, holding her lips in place for a few extra seconds. "So, do any of these work?"

"Sing them, so I can hear the melody lines, but yeah . . . a few pieces."

"Awesome!"

She spread her towel onto the lookout, a promontory of solid granite, and curled her legs to one side. X flipped to a page near the front. "What about 'Bring It Out?'"

"A girl shaking it to her sweet delight. You've heard a million of them."

"Well, then you pick one. Wait." X stopped midway through the notebook, the breeze kicking up and rustling its pages. "This 'Black Kiss' . . . haunting."

"Yeah, it's kind of intense."

He nodded. "Can you sing it?"

She cleared her throat and looked toward the sky, trying to work in Tom's adjustment for more staying power on her high notes as she dug into the song:

> *What did I ever do to you*
> *To drive you away like this?*
> *It doesn't make a bit of sense*
> *For me to get black kissed,*
> *All because I didn't follow*
> *The script you penned for me.*

"Sad," X said softly.

"My move-on song." Her fingertips traced his cheek, wondering if she was far enough beyond Danny to move into something new. The last thing she needed was to encumber him with the shards and shadows of a guy whose greatest love was the next big swell . . . and in the end, whatever *wahine* happened to be with him. "You never know how deep you're in until it ends, and it hurts to even think about the person," she said.

He stared at the mountains, stoic and majestic in their silence. "Here's something songwriters know—the more emotion, the better. The more life takes you down, or up, the better you can tell the story. Take your great blues singers. Billie Holiday, Nina Simone, and Dinah Washington weren't exactly chilling." He tapped his heart. "Missy Elliott? Mary J. Blige? Beyoncé ? Lauren Hill? Best songs hit hardest."

"I don't want to have to die inside to write a song."

"I hear you, Christine, but there's something about those little deaths. They wake us up. That's when you reach inside, no matter how badly you got your heart kicked, if you want to move on. I see it in 'Black Kiss.'"

"Moving on?"

"No. Reaching in and pulling out the loser behind this song."

Surprise galloped through her eyes, surprise at the depth of his response. "It's just an ending in my life that took up an entire song."

"Which happens with forced endings—and having to get our shit back together when we think we can't."

"Now that you put it that way, I definitely felt a rush, like an 'a-ha' moment, when I was writing it."

"You connected with the your deep truth. You know what I'm talking about."

In that moment, X reminded her of something a date once said when she chided him for being a wise ass: "You have to be the first of those words for the second to happen." There was no second date. Still, X resembled that joke, light to the point of jocularity in rehearsals, but filled with a quiet wisdom all the same. She kissed his shoulder, her heart retaking the lead in the pheromone battle within. "Can you look at another one? I won a contest with it. I'll sing it."

A few minutes later, every bit as consumed as in the Venice beach bar, she ran out the parting line, "Your love is my gypsy's prayer . . . your love is my gypsy's prayer . . ."

Silence. Then: "You shittin' me? You wrote that?"

She curled her fingers like a debutante holding tea cups. "Beneath the palm trees of Venice."

"*That*, sweet lady, is rock solid gold. We're practicing that one."

"I'm so happy you like it—"

"Which leads me to lesson number one: guard these songs with your life. No one but the band should know about them right now . . . *no one*. And get these babies down onto sheet music and copyrighted. We can all help you."

She smiled, her face glowing. "One more question . . ."

"Bring it."

The way she asked wasn't a question. She leaned into him, found his lips, and lingered for a few seconds. He followed her lead, unsure whether to proceed, the roaring tide inside him crashing into the harsh rocks of her still-frazzled heart. Not to mention a decade's age difference between them. Plus, how smart was it to go after the band leader's daughter, at his place, after she'd just been shipwrecked? He backed off, but she leaned in. They kissed once more. "You sure about this?" he asked.

"I think so." She peered into his eyes, her own swelling. "Yeah, I like this."

She felt him growing against her body, growing against his waning willpower. It felt so good to be valued for her songs, and wanted by this Adonis of a man. Pushed by the urge to explore his every muscle, she pushed him gently onto the rock, laying atop him, feeling his warmth . . . and the resistance of his hands. She knew he was right, playing it smart, not about to piss off Tom . . . not willing to hurt her.

She rolled off and kissed him one final time, fighting off her own screaming body, closer than it had been to fulfillment in months. She kissed her finger and brushed his lip. "To be continued."

11

"WHAT YOU WANT TO PLAY?" ROGELIO ASKED.

X pushed down repeatedly on a single key, trying to dislodge it. "Black Kiss.'"

Christine walked behind the keyboards and wrapped her arms around him. "No matter what becomes of this tour, X, you're totally worth being here." She kissed the top of his head. "I didn't know a man would ever make me feel good again."

"Yeah, sugar, well that goes both ways."

She walked to the back corner of the studio, thinking of the past few days locked in X's clutches in his guest cottage. She grabbed a few cushions, disrupting Steppenwolf's sprawled slumber. He hissed at her, and then chased a ray of sunlight down the hall. Megan had gone psychedelic retro with the corner, furnishing it with a lava lamp, low-cut sectional, three-foot hookah pipe they'd bought in Marrakech, Matchbox cars of Volkswagen vans and mini-buses, and framed prints: a peace sign, Jimi Hendrix adorned by a rainbow aura of guitars, and a sixteen-year-old Megan in her shortest, wildest Swinging London miniskirt. It may as well have been a beach wrap covering her bikini panties. And nothing further. On the opposite wall, the polar opposite: a comical, menacing black light poster. An ogre emerged from a rock canyon, growling his take on Psalms 23:4: "Though I walk through the valley of the shadow of death, I will fear no evil, *because I'm the meanest son of a bitch in the valley.*" Once upon a time, it resided on the bedroom walls of half the teenagers in America, so it seemed.

Welcome to Timoreaux '66.

Rogelio tuned his bass while slinging a guitar on his shoulder. X continued to remove tiny sand flecks from the keys, the result of a rainy sandstorm, or a sandblasted rainstorm. Take your choice. A wicked thunderstorm had injected part of the White Sands Missile Range into the jet stream, carried it over the Sacramento Mountains, and sandblasted the ridge with rain and wind. No matter how closed the doors and windows, the sand clung like glue. Afterwards, residents brushed the grit out of their hair and teeth, and hundreds of cars needed new paint jobs. And keyboard keys stuck.

After X cleaned off the deck well enough to play, they ran though "Black Kiss" over and over again, Christine settling into the arrangement the other two had developed. They tried different keys and time signatures, exploring every possibility, only to end close to where they began—the basic chords in her notebook.

After that, they broke out another song X had dog-eared, "Holy Child Blues." It was even more haunting than "Black Kiss," a struggle, someone else's struggle this time, echoed in Christine's vocal plunge . . .

> *They say you're a menace to society*
> *A subject full of rage,*
> *You barely reach the judge's chest*
> *They're jailing you today*
> *For making a very big mistake*
> *How could you ever know?*
> *Your momma's sick, your daddy's dead*
> *You sold a little blow*
> *To feed yourself, to clothe your sis*
> *Your intentions all so pure*
> *For inside that twisted angry mask*
> *A soul shines bright and pure*

Rogelio's wailing slide guitar merged with X's lower-note work. Teardrops all but formed on Rogelio's strings to match those from Megan, peeking around the corner. After fine-tuning the bridge, Rogelio switched to violin and played the tears into a miserable, achy night on a Lower East Side stoop. There, Christine and Tom once met the girl whose vacant stare and pain-wracked face inspired the song. As Rogelio lifted out of the pit, Christine stepped into the finale of the holy child's flawed story:

> *You've helped so many inmates read,*
> *They're gonna set you free,*
> *A few months more you'll be nineteen*
> *Done time for you and me,*
> *They'll tell us out there on the streets,*
> *You're a scourge to society*
> *They had to send you up the creek*
> *To appease their propriety*

> *Oh holy child, dear holy child*
> *I hope you find your way,*
> *You're free so go make yourself strong*
> *And cast your light again,*
> *Upon the beauty of your soul*
> *I hope you find your way,*
> *I hope you find your way . . .*

The song reminded X of a dozen old friends who'd lost their way. She sang it so sweetly, sadly, *haunting*. You couldn't easily pull away from its grip.

Tom walked into the studio, a beer in one hand, the other tapping his leg, getting the timing down. "What was that? Can you play it again?"

"Sure."

For the next ten minutes, the trio jammed. Midway through, Will ducked behind his drum kit and played lightly, locking in the beat. Christine pranced across the stage, closing her eyes, a butterfly spawning into a tigress while singing her commitment and solemn wish to the girl on the stoop.

Tom glanced over to Chester, Chandra and Megan, their astonished expressions reflecting how he felt. "Where did you come up with *that?*" Tom asked. He turned to X and Rogelio. "You brew this up with her?"

"It's hers all the way, man," Rogelio said. "We just helped her work it out."

Chandra turned to Rogelio as the goose bumps on her arms finally started to recede. "That violin, honey . . . my Lord."

"My Lord, is right," Megan said. "How many instruments *do* you play?"

"Seven."

Tom engulfed Megan in his arms. "He's our one-man orchestra. We're just learning that about him."

"I like variety," Rogelio joked as he wiped down the violin's blood-red belly.

Tom rubbed his stubbly beard, incurring a sharp, quick sneer from Megan, and turned to Christine. "You good with us trying out this song?"

"Good with it . . . uh, *yeahhh*." She almost strangled the microphone with excitement.

"After you copyright it." He winked at X. "I'll show you how."

"The younger crowd will eat it up," Will said. "I think our core audience will get into it, too."

Chester shook his head. "You got a gift, little girl," he said. "Hang onto it—and whatever else you got stored in that notebook of yours." He glanced at X, who had walked up to her.

"See what I mean?" X whispered. "They've got you."

"How about that other song, X," Chester said. "Gypsy something . . ."

X looked at Christine. "Baby?"

"Sure. If you guys want to play it," she replied, oblivious to the flash of eyes between Tom and Megan.

Rogelio plucked them into "Gypsy's Prayer." By mid-song, Christine held her audience of eight spellbound. Her talent, carved from zero stage experience beyond school plays and recitals, and wherever she was singing in L.A., reminded Tom of the early days in San Francisco. He'd try out anything and everything, seeing if it would fly. Everything seemed possible in that revolutionary era, almost every approach and instrument tried and utilized, styles, melodies, genres, sub-genres, and lyrics forming and reforming like the earth trying out new plates. The collective consciousness of a generation resulted, fueled by music of expression, words of change and the flat-earthed, suburban "I Like Ike" mindset that craved the white-bread normalcy of a world no longer at war.

As she sang, she reminded him of his purpose, his essence, what he came into this world to leave behind: finding someone to whom to give whatever wisdom you learned, , the very best of what you did in your place in space.

Christine twirled to a close. She opened her eyes to find Megan and Tom holding back tears. She'd stayed away six long years, stonewalling him yet wanting his support, not wanting to fall again into his open wound that would not heal. Deathly afraid of it, in fact. Finally, when it became too hard to stay away, she wanted a reset, to the way they'd communicated before, with hugs, whispers, and talks, good laughs over stupid jokes, kisses on the cheek, hikes in the mountains. To get there, she needed to move past the whole Annalisa thing. Deep down, where pain and desire to heal are at their most raw, where the next step forward can break either way, how could she really know how he felt? Why wouldn't he say?

She smiled as the room blurred with her tears. She knew she'd again connected with the part of him she missed most of all, the feeling of being warmly snuggled by the most loving but protective bear on the planet.

Later, Christine dragged herself into the den, exhausted by eight hours of sessions. She rolled onto the sofa, stretched her legs across X's waist, and curled her feet toward the roaring fire. Her toe rings and hummingbird earrings glimmered against the flames.

She sank into his chest, although it felt strange, even borderline awkward, to cuddle with both parents in the room. She'd not done it since high school. Of the boys she'd dated since, the only one who visited overnight was Danny, the weekend he met Tom and Megan, and they'd been fighting, so contact was scarce. She saw a cute protectiveness in the way Tom and Megan eyed her, entirely obvious while thinking themselves discreet. Annoying, but cute.

"You sounded great in there," Tom finally said, his mind whirling at the warp speed known to all fathers when their baby girls meet men.

She bounced her legs lightly on X. He tried to slide away, but she stopped him with a scissors hold. *Get used to it, folks.* "It's like less work and more fun every day, Dad," she said, her throbbing muscles screaming *bullshit.*

Chester held up the turkey leg on which he'd been chomping, his other arm draped around Chandra, who studied the flames dancing near her feet, browner after three weeks in the mountain sun. With drumstick in hand, Chester looked like the grand poobah among the prehistoric artists of Chauvet. "I got an *i-deaaaah* for this tour." The word stalled like a flatlining Piper Cub. "We get a song going, you kids take it over, and we'll head backstage to drink beers with friends. Might even come out and stand sidestage to watch. Fans won't know the difference."

Tom leaned forward, skewered a cube of cheese from a tray, and popped it into his mouth. Only the toothpick emerged. "Remember when we had those back-to-back hits in '81 or '82, our cheesy songs, and our hardcore fans stood and rocked except for those two tracks—and the radio listeners stood for *only* those two?"

"You mean listeners like me who rocked their teen brains out to those two songs?" Chandra asked.

Tom nodded. "I feel like that right now, in a different way. You three have songs that might catch with the kids. One for sure will. We have our songs. It's going to be interesting how this works if we give them a new thing or two. . . honey?"

Christine was fast asleep, her eyes open. "She's exhausted, Tommy," Chester said. "Hard worker. Driven. Reminds me of her daddy."

Chandra moved to the floor, one arm on Megan's knee, the other on Chester's, tucking her legs beneath her willowy, long-sleeved, short-cut dress. "I haven't seen that look in a long time," Megan said.

"Just reminiscing." Despite her growing hips, Chandra still filled a dress well, her gliding stride and swinging beach walk arms revealing her coastal roots. She looked at X. "It's the same dress I wore when Chester and I met, backstage . . . San Diego . . ."

Chester smiled. "The Distorts Arena. Sound bounced off them tinny walls. A friend saw us play there a few times had it right: you get back-row seats against the wall, turn your back to the stage, and listen. Swore it sounded better."

Chandra turned to X while lightly poking Chester's ribs. "I talked a bouncer into letting me go backstage by convincing him I was Chester's niece."

Chester grumbled. "They bought it. Look on their faces the next time I saw Chandra was what it's all about—'Thought she was your niece?' 'That's what you get for thinking; let her backstage.'"

She shrugged her shoulders. "I did what I had to do. And I was older than I looked."

"I took some serious shit. They all thought you was sixteen."

"And you complained . . . not at all. Crazy me fell in love with you on the spot."

"You helped me escape from a marriage that would've killed me." She looked up to Chester, still awake with eyes barely open. "I still wish you'd scooped me up a few years before. Would've saved a lot of trouble."

"You were sixteen a few years before."

"Would that have stopped you?" She turned to X. "Know what I did when my ex and I drove to our honeymoon cabin in the mountains outside L.A.?"

"Is that a question?"

"I popped the wedding video into the VCR, and watched it over and over and over, seeing if I'd really made the decision I'd just made."

"Didn't see that coming," X said softly.

"I couldn't believe I'd fucked up like that. I stayed almost three years, but he ended it by pushing me into a wall. He'd pushed or slapped me three times before, and I'd warned him. I wrote a note, walked out, and haven't seen him since. When I met Chester, I was finally able to feel safe, to get over that man." She smiled sadly. "But he'll never really be distant enough."

Rogelio leaned forward, overwhelmed by the urge to lighten the moment. "A touring rock star isn't the greatest guarantee of a long, healthy relationship, you know . . ."

"He was *ready* for this beach girl. Every time they played in San Diego, Orange County or L.A., I showed up. At first, I sent notes backstage and Chester ignored me. Then, he started sending a roadie to get me. Finally, he just left backstage passes." She turned to Chester and rubbed his knee. "Nothing happened for a while, and you never rushed me and always made me feel comfortable."

He drew his hand across her chest. "You were my angel, my redemption. I knew what had walked into my life; wasn't gonna screw that up like I'd screwed up everything else since Savannah died."

She hooked her arm around his calf, noting its growing tightness, their long walks and hikes before and after rehearsals steering him towards a fitness level that she'd worried had passed him by. "Finally, the Fever and my favorite guitarist rolled through during another tour. Maybe our tenth get-together. We became inseparable."

"Now that's a story," X said.

"One that never gets old. Hell, I run a tractor and a canning kitchen now, not quite what I imagined when surfing every day after school, one of the only chicks out there. But I don't have to punch a clock, either, because God blessed this man with an amazing talent."

Rogelio shook his head. "From a surfboard to a tractor . . ."

Chester grumbled. "How it is, Stradivarius. She knew what she wanted and pursued until I got my head out of my ass. That's my story—"

He thrust his chest outward like a strutting peacock as Chandra pummeled him with a pillow. "You inscrutable lovable redneck!"

Chester absorbed the soft beating and pulled himself up. "Ever wonder how a Cumberland Gap hillbilly met a San Francisco kid and became best friends, for, what . . ."

"Awhile," Tom said.

Chester scratched his beard and looked at Rogelio and X. "A bedtime campfire story for you boys." He turned to Tom. "Remember when we first walked up to that backwoods church and peeped in on that gospel revival?"

Tom smiled. "The day I fell in love with music. The way the people sang their praises, their feelings . . . I felt and heard their voices every time I sat inside or outside that church. The floorboards of that church are now in my studio."

X and Rogelio glanced at each other. "No shit?" Rogelio asked.

Chester folded his arms and chuckled. "Right from that church."

"How . . . did you do that?" Rogelio asked.

"About five years ago, the church burned down. Chester drove there from his farm and checked it out . . ."

"The church was ashes to ashes, but the floor was still intact. Planks looked good," Chester said. "Century-old yellow yew. Out of Washington, cut and sent back home by wagons. A preacher's uncle so-and-so settled out there, lined up the wood. Can't find it anymore."

Tom nodded. "The wood gave the church great acoustics, as you've probably noticed. So Chester called me, and we stripped out the lumber and shipped it here."

"And our first kisses happened on them floorboards," Chester said.

"Where you going here?" X asked.

Chester's eyes gleamed. "Yessir, with each other."

"TMI . . ." Christine mumbled. She immediately fell back asleep.

"No, really, we were twelve and hiking with a couple girls," Chester said. "Tommy got Wilma Bickett. Great kisser." He glanced at Tom. "The girl missed you when you left—till she found the real kisser . . . me. A few years later, me and Wilma snuck into the church with some new records and listened to folks you didn't listen to in church—Howlin' Wolf, Elvis, Chuck Berry, Memphis Minnie, Jerry Lee, Etta, Big Mama Thornton, on and on . . . and we made out, and . . ."

"And?" Rogelio asked.

"We got busted. Wilma's daddy lost his shit, called me the devil's right-hand. He even accused me of violatin' her, mean-ass old gar. Never happened. Never did nothing but kiss her. I was *twelve*. Old man sent Wilma off to boarding school or an out-of-state relative. I don't know which. Never saw her again."

Chandra patted his heart. "Sounds like something's still there, big boy."

"Always is with the first kiss."

"That's messed up with the preacher . . . and the dad," Rogelio said.

"Damn right, and I would've been more screwed up had it not been for my old teenage buddy here calling from Frisco." Chester turned to Tom. "He invited me to come out, check the new scene." He glanced at Christine, who had twisted herself into X's chest and shoulders. "Just out of high school—space shots, psychedelic rock, Janis and Grace, 'Nam, hair, long beautiful hair . . . everyone feelin' something big. Love Generation, Age of Aquarius, the Beautiful People . . . call it what you want. Funny we have a high-and-mighty name for it—the Summer of Love—when shit, ain't that what every summer should be?"

Chester slid his hands along Chandra's slumped, sleeping shoulders, settling on her tummy. "I ended up stayin' until we'd become what the homefolk, God bless 'em, warned me explicitly would ruin our souls, send us to eternal damnation . . . hippie pinko rock stars."

His laugh echoed through the wee hours, while the fire flickered itself to sleep.

12

TOM JUMPED ON STAGE AND CLAPPED HIS HANDS, NEARLY dislodging the papers tucked beneath his arm. Boom mics descended from the ceiling like rock climbing ropes, flanked by a simple stage lighting system, which would now wait another spring to host the house concerts he long coveted. Four other mics surrounded the drum kit, including a pair pointed into Will's bass drums, and for his backing vocal turns, a swing mic affixed to his high hat cymbals. "I'm used to sitting in a soundproof room, headphones feeding me tracks," Rogelio said. "Not playing live soundstage. But I see your point. Hope your mixing board brings out our best."

"It will. Our very own bootleg album," Tom chuckled.

"Now *that* was a cottage industry, though it pissed us off when we saw those guys selling bootlegs of our shows, terrible soundboard recordings of us," Will said.

"My granddaddy made collecting bootlegs his pride and joy. Even got a few with him on them," X said.

Chester folded his arms and gave his beard a firm scratch. "Bootlegs and moonshine, maybe some friends or a girl, made me many a good night." A grin grew across his face as one of those good nights swept through like a waft of jasmine.

"Sounds like a good Southern album title. Or a book," Will said.

Tom shrugged his shoulders. "It was great for the fans, bad for us." The crackly, tinny soundboard-recorded albums, sold in arena parking lots or flea markets, leaked royalties out of the band's spigot. The industry was hatched by disgruntled or unscrupulous sound engineers running soundboards in concert, preying on the naïveté of virtual kids making records and becoming stars while knowing nothing about the business. For many musicians, those times were a financial bloodletting. "Two percent is what you get; you aren't putting up the money to press this!" one label owner yelled at Tom, who walked out—before Don Robiski took charge and stomped out any further bootleg albums. His action instantly converted Fever bootlegs into hundred-dollar gold pieces on the collectible market.

Chester shook his head as finished tuning one guitar, set it on its rack, and grabbed another. "Bootleggin's a mess, unmixed tracks and noise flyin' everywhere, but at least it's a concert set, some order to it. Not like downloading separate tunes. Took me a decade to get used to CDs. Then DVDs. Just give me a scratchy old album and the liner notes, a turntable, my quad speaker system and some headphones. Followed by every song on the album, in order, as the band intended."

Tom smiled. "Then you'll be happy to hear what Robiski emailed me this morning: he wants to re-release a few albums on vinyl, with some newer cuts."

Chester closed his eyes, nodded, and mashed his lips together like a content bulldog. "Now the kid is talking."

As everyone moved onto the stage, Tom awaited them with handouts. "Robiski also emailed this. He's flying in from Venice; he'll be here day after tomorrow."

Rogelio's eyes bolted open. "Tour dates!"

"In the flesh," Tom said. "It's really real . . ."

They stood before him, dates followed by cities and venues: the first tour dates with his name on them in twenty years. "Around the hamster wheel in sixty days. Thirty dates," he said softly. "Welcome to the big top."

X looked up, surprised. "This is a good schedule. A good reunion run for you."

Chester tapped the itinerary. "All good rock and roll cities."

"Without a doubt," Will said. "New York. San Francisco. Atlanta. Denver. Cleveland. Seattle. L.A. St. Louis. Chicago. New Orleans. San Diego. Stadiums, arenas, amphitheaters, Red Rocks, a couple concert halls, festivals . . . all here."

Chester ran his finger down the list. "Don't recognize but a few of these venues."

"They all have corporate names now. Sponsors," Rogelio said. "I'll bet you played in most of them."

Chester's face compressed into a whiskered prune. "I get the naming crap, they need the money, but it takes something off the fastball, if you know what I mean."

"We had a love affair with some of these places, Rogelio. So did our fans," Tom said, reading down the list. "The Fabulous Forum, Ice Palace, Deer Creek, Fiddler's Green, Red Rocks, Boston Garden, Cow Palace, Shea Stadium, Madison Square Garden, The Big A, Tanglewood . . . not the Purina Dog Chow Arena, or XYZ sponsored by ABC Center. Let's see if we've earned our chance to play the"—Tom ran his finger down the list—"Getmethere Airlines Arena. Or whatnot." The words tasted like spoiled food.

Tom taped set lists on the lip of the stage, beneath his and Chester's foot pedals, atop X's piano and alongside Will's snare drum, then checked the mic levels. X and Christine walked over from the kitschy corner, where they'd been tucked in a beanbag chair while Christine repaired an old macramé owl. She slid off her sandals, ready to take the stage, a morning of hiking with X and making love on the outlook still humming through her body..

She knelt down and read the set list. Tom, Chester, and Will broke it into groups. The stock hits were first: "Mystical Dreamer," "West of the West," "Street Party," "Her Heart Was Something New," "She Flew Away," "I Know She's My Lady," "Quantrill's Revenge," "When A Place Goes Mad," and "When I Become the President." Then came the jams, "Chester's Rag" leading the way, his excuse to cut loose with Rogelio and X for ten or fifteen minutes, or a half-hour, as he famously did when guitar jams *were* rock and roll. Also in that group was "Rainy Day Dance," a musical bacchanal that triggered wild dancing from aisles to rafters. Deep cuts for hardcore fans followed: "Your Song Never Ceases," "Lama in a Tea House," "Blood Moon," "Harmony Rising," "Midnight Madness," "Spirit Mischief," and "Stones & Blood." Below that were even deeper tracks, from an archival back alley: "Fury of the Gods," "Cumberland Crumble," "Healing Woman's Sutra," and "Moonshine Blues." At the bottom, Tom wrote, "Holy Child Blues—Gypsy's Prayer—Black Kiss*"

"What's the asterisk?" Christine asked.

"It means we figure out how to work them in," Tom said. "But we work them in."

"We've been learning your material while you and X have been *hiking*," Will said, leaning over his cymbals. "These songs work well."

She smiled nervously. "Well enough to be on the set list?"

Will laughed. "They're on there, right?"

In six weeks, they'd run through and whittled down nearly a hundred candidate songs, along with a short acoustic set Tom, Chester, and Will planned if any off-day opportunities popped up. Robiski had received inquiries from smaller venues looking for more intimate sets, which all three liked. The few times Christine, X, or Rogelio grumbled about the song load, Tom reminded them how the Stones sometimes worked through *four* hundred cuts before settling on the twenty to twenty-five that made up their road shows. "Are they always the same songs, every night?" Christine asked.

"For us, no, we're doing something else," Tom said.

She flipped on her mic switch and tapped it. Levels were good. "Like what?"

"Like we need to be ready to play every song we've been practicing. You never know what I'll throw on a set list . . . we did it before, we'll do it now."

"And we'll know when?"

"At sound check the day before we play it. That way, we get two passes before going live."

"Ummm, yeah, well . . . I'm not much for surprises, Dad."

"A sad indictment of constantly being hooked up and connected with every moment on the face of the earth," Tom said, shaking his head, wondering how anyone, let alone many in an entire generation, could dismiss such things from their lives as surprise, anticipation, spontaneity, adapting to a sudden change. Or a switched song. "Well, sweetheart, you'll just have to experience surprise again. We'll do this the back-in-the-day way. Playing what we want to play, throwing in the hits, taking requests."

She rolled her eyes. "Like . . . OK." She cupped her hand over the mic and ran through her scales as X piled notes into the morning, melodious and layered, reminding Tom of the Three Dog Night keyboardist who blistered the ivories when he wasn't serving up three-part harmonies to the singers. Tom had considered hiring him when Treg came down with pneumonia, as much to give the big Fever fan a break from pop with a week of hard blues and straightforward rock. However, Treg only missed two dates, they rescheduled, and the backup plan faded into one of entertainment's million footnotes that could have been.

"Amazing, isn't he, Dad?" Christine muttered, her voice level but the glow in her cheeks and eyes anything but.

"Yeah. Excellent," Tom said softly. "My brother Ulysses did a good thing by sending him." His eyes narrowed, growing sharper. She knew the look. "But, on the other side, I hope you know, sweetheart, musicians aren't always the most reliable partners. Especially when they're on the same tour as you."

"You and Mom did OK . . ." She blushed from equal parts embarrassment and irritation. "We're just two grown adults enjoying each other, Dad."

He squeezed her hand. "You look to me like you're into each other, you really care. And you're every bit a grown woman, without a doubt. But I never want to see my baby girl hurt again. Danny did a number on you. I'm not sure how I'd react if it happened again, no matter how old you are."

Christine started to protest but something stopped her, the thought of how much she missed his protectiveness, concern, presence. "I'm being careful with it." Not really, but good for him to hear it.

"If you two are still tight after we finish this tour, then great for you both. Tours are a bitch on relationships. I've seen all too many go to their graves somewhere on the road; a lot of things happen out there. But right now, please don't let your attention to him, or him, distract you from why you're here." Yet, as he watched her twirl her wrist bangles, wouldn't it be easier if she and X stuck together on a road whose temptations could become roadside bombs for newcomers like Christine?

"Don't worry; I'm keeping one foot dry." She folded her arms and smiled with tightened lips. "When I commit to something, like singing for you, I don't stop until it's finished. Ever. And it comes first."

She glared at Tom for an extra few seconds, burning her comments into his consciousness, as Megan peered from around the corner. "Sounds like someone I married."

Christine grabbed her mic as X transitioned into a sweeping, magical composition she'd never heard before. Rogelio stopped, his hair curling over one eye, a look that reminded Tom of the black Irish cat fronting Thin Lizzy, bass at his side, X's composition reminding him of the festive atmosphere of Germany in the winter, *Christkindlmarkts* and *tannenbaum* and chestnuts roasting in his heart. "Do you know what he's playing, Rogelio?" she asked.

"Sure do. 'It's Schneesturm'. . . . Snowstorm. Happens to be my favorite Schubert piece." Rogelio quickly racked his bass, grabbed his violin and tuned. "I've got to jump in on this one. You want to give yourself a musical gift, Christine?"

"Yeah."

"Sit next to him, watch his hands, close your eyes, and feel."

"I'm not going to disturb him."

"You won't. Look at him. He's completely *gone*, playing the snowstorm, probably deep inside it."

She sat on the bench. X never noticed as his fingers piled up sonic snowdrifts before flurrying into soft notes. After the delicate pitter-patter, he raced into the heart of the storm, his hands crisscrossing keys faster than Christine could follow, faster than fingers are supposed to move. Rogelio's violin teased out the shifting, swirling wind for a good five minutes, until X brought the *schneesturm* to a screeching halt. The cloaked forest and village before his closed eyes fell into silence. So did the studio.

"Damn, that was something," Chester said. "Something else." He turned to Tom. "Next time you see Ulysses, thank him for me for sending this kid our way." He stepped back to the keyboard riser, put one hand on Christine's back, and threw his free arm around X. "No matter what you think about me and my redneck ways, son, you're my new keyboard player and I ain't gonna lose you. You're family."

"Told you," Christine whispered, pecking X's cheek, as Chester walked away.

"Yes you did."

How nice to be validated by a guy, she thought. He validated her so often, that at first, she didn't trust it. How do you trust a man's words when the last one either dismissed or berated you, or twisted your own words against you? As days became weeks, she began to trust X because he never wavered in validating her. It didn't take much, just a "you're right," or "what a great idea, honey," or "I like your way better," but the language was unknown to too many men. Thankfully, not the solid black hunk of a man whom she kissed again before walking back to the mic.

Tom adjusted the soundboard levels. "Let's see what we can do after X just reminded us of how much talent we lack, boys." He glanced at Chester and Will.

Will chuckled as he counted in "Street Party," revving up a hundred thousand imaginary screaming fans with the call and response format they'd developed to replace Tom's old single-vocal delivery, mainly to give Christine an immediate platform:

> TOM: *The fun is on the streets,*
> CHRISTINE: *The sun is on the streets,*
> TOM: *Just grab a girl, give her a twirl,*
> CHRISTINE: *Let's party in the streets,*
> TOM: *Let's party in the streets,*
> BOTH: *Go party in the streets . . .*

They carried on for over two hours, throwing in duets, runs, and solos, Tom and Chester setting up each other, X catapulting into each song on the set list with equal conviction, his rich higher-level runs and bass chords enabling Rogelio to tease out darker currents and subtleties of the songs, their bottom notes. They moved from one song to the next, their act tightening, polishing, the glitches starting to lessen.

As the set neared its end, and he began to feel that old invincibility again, Chester slung his guitar to his side and rubbed his wrist. "Damn carpal tunnel."

"You're playing like you're twenty-five," Tom said.

"My wrist don't appreciate it," he grumbled. "Hurts like hell. Price you pay."

"That's why we have the young studs," Will said. "And the coach's daughter."

Chandra walked up and rubbed Chester's wrist, one of those rubdowns that comes more often as the years move on. *The end* looked the same to every great guitarist with diminishing stamina and once blazing speed, like trying to drag race in a clunky sedan. You know you were fast, but suddenly, you can't get there nearly as quickly. Frustrating, Tom thought, since there was no shortage to the variety and complexity of music they could play. Don't you get better as you get older? That didn't matter to Father Rheumatoid. What did matter was playing fast, complex riffs with hands and wrists that covet the nearest rocking chair. Chester handled his mortality like everyone else—by rather wanting to chew nails. Who thought they'd grow old? With Roger Daltrey's generational anthem leading the call, aging wasn't a big topic on the streets or communes. Dying before you got old was.

Tom turned to Will and Chester. "Let's go listen to some of these songs."

Chester unhooked his guitar strap. "Lemme get a beer."

X stepped out from his keyboard, slung a towel over his shoulder, wiped his sweaty face and bulging arms, and caught Tom's eye. "Can I talk to you first?"

"Sure."

After a spring of jet stream winds and thunderstorms, summer foaled itself as serenely as an alpine lake in July. The scene felt to X like a Chinese brush painting: all blues, thin wisps of cloud, lush green woods, snow-fed streams shimmering below the turnaround, woven meticulously together like a deified tone poem. Down the driveway, a red-tailed fox watched warily, ready to scurry into the bushes at first flinch.

"'Snowstorm' was fabulous," Tom said. "Haven't heard that in ages."

"A classical pianist played it at my cousin's birthday party at an old cigar factory in Tampa. My cousin's friend converted the place into an art and music studio—great little setup. Classical's not my thing, but I look at it a different way . . . their era's blues and rock stars, jazz men, horn blowers with ivory keys, dude."

Tom thought of the scraggly-haired busts and portraits of the European maestros, their intense faces, how they careened through tempestuous lives, no different than the life arcs of many rockers. He thought of an old mashup someone did during prog rock's heyday, mashing Rick Wakeman, Keith Emerson, Jon Lord, Richard Wright, Tony Banks, Ray Manzarek, John Paul Jones, and Ken Hensley into a composite photo with Beethoven, Mozart, Liszt, Schubert, Chopin, Scriabin, Vivaldi, and Handel. The rock stars of their centuries. "You've got a point," he said.

He rubbed his strumming hand as a bird landed on the driveway, its final mistake. In one splendid, spitfire motion, the fox seized its helpless prey and scurried behind a cluster of alligator junipers. Seconds later, a handful of feathers blew onto the dirt road.

X shook his head. "No mercy." He thought about making small talk, but no sense in stalling. "As you know, Tom, me and Christine are more than bandmates."

"I see that." Tom smiled warily. "Interesting turn of events."

"We've been collaborating on her songs . . ."

"Among other things."

He bypassed the comment. "Her writing is *the shit*, Tom, some really good stuff, and I'm telling you, the keys and melodies we're practicing the three songs in are very close to what she originally wrote. The same, really. We didn't change much. Ask to check out her notebooks. Quite a few other possibilities in there."

X focused on the spot where the fox pounced on the bird, considering how quickly and finally one's life can change—or end—when erring. It happened twice on the streets when he was a teen, saw it happen *right in front of his face*, enough to keep him away from gangs, searching for his gateway out of the trashcan alleys of Harlem. Music provided it. Feathers and echoes of final desperate squawks echoed in his ear as Tom coughed. "So let me ask—"

"Why her? Why Christine?"

"That's a good place to start."

"Two lonely people on the road, caring about each other."

"Kind of a country-song answer," Tom chuckled. He looked at X, the straight shooter Ulysses said he'd be, and how much happier Christine seemed. X might be black, and Christine white—or golden tan, after all the sun from her constant hiking—but that didn't bother him. Neither did their being together—except that it was happening before a tour, where chemistry between the band members needed to be uniform. New loves tend to tip that equation. This saga of taking new love on the road sometimes twisted into a tale as dark and harrowing as a Poe soul-grinder, or Stephen King or Anne Rice horrorfest.

"You're putting a smile on Christine's face, much appreciated, but she's our daughter and we don't want to see her hurt. And she's coming off being hurt. I thought the tour would give her something else to focus on."

"I catch you, Tom."

"So can you assure me you'll focus on performing first, and her second?"

Without hesitation, X said, "That's my role this summer."

Tom shuffled nervously. "I'm her dad, I can't help it. It's what dads do, the ones that care anyway. That unfortunate boy in L.A . . ."

"She told me."

"It took some pleading to get her up here, and even then, until I talked her into singing with us, she was only staying two weeks." He waited for the words to sink in. "Have fun with her, enjoy each other, but don't break her heart, man." The sharp, pointed light slowly receded from his eyes.

"I will never do anything to make you question bringing me on," X said.

"Then we're good. Let's keep it that way."

"If the vibe gets weird with Christine, we're done. Right away. You have my word."

"Thank you. You really are just as Ulysses described." He patted X's shoulder.

They returned to the control room. Will was replaying vocal tracks for Christine, who looked up at X, saw the relieved look on his face, and exhaled. She eyed Tom quizzically. "What?" Tom asked.

"Dads . . ." She both chuckled at and admired his chivalry, how it never goes away, she being twenty-five, he reverting to protective fatherhood. "Can't flip off that oversight switch, can you?" Something sweet and loving about it, comforting. Still, he'd never burdened her teen years like most other dads on the ridge, the obnoxious, smothering type whose implied (or implicit) threats left puddles beneath boys' pant legs at the front door, causing many to run, never to be seen again.

Tom pulled up a chair next to Christine. "Will, can you cue up 'Mystical Dreamer'? Let's see if it sounds like it did when we played it."

It did. Her voice touched that place where dreamer and visionary merge, a presence filled with soft, yearning power. "Singing inside out, driving it with your emotions," Tom said as they listened. "You found this song's heartbeat, but take it a step further. *Become* the mystical dreamer. *Become* every note and word. Allow the melody to guide you. Do that, sweetheart, and you'll soon command this and every other song you sing." He rubbed her hands. "Own these songs like you own the hair on your head."

"Comparing it to her prized possession? That'll work," X laughed.

Christine smacked X's shoulder, then sat silently as Tom and Will replayed 'Mystical Dreamer' twice more, breaking down the song. Tom turned back to Christine. "Just remind yourself that you're singing with a band that's been through this. We've got your back. Take chances; make these songs great again with your own signature."

She glanced at X, then Will, back at Tom. "When will it all come together?"

"Maybe opening night, maybe a couple weeks into the tour, maybe a month down the road . . . you'll know. We'll know. A feeling comes over you . . . trust me, sweetheart, you'll know."

She thought of the buzz that swept through her at the Venice bar while performing "Gypsy's Prayer." She also remembered Daphne's shout-out from the crowd: "*That's it, kid! You connected! You became your song!*" *The feeling.*

Tom chugged a beer next to the soundboard, while Will grabbed another. "You're also singing for our fans, Christine," Tom continued. "Once those lights go down, your sole focus is the fans—and keeping tight with the music, of course. Give it up for them. Take this batch of songs, and feed them."

Christine glanced at X, who was listening to another track on headphones, then back to Tom. "It really always was about the fans with you guys, wasn't it?"

He raised his beer. "That, and trying to play the perfect set. Our nightly motivators for twenty-five years."

Will cued up another track. "Right before I take the stage, I remember how I felt at my favorite shows." He fidgeted with the digital soundboard as Tom watched. "How you feel when a piece of music *permeates* you, I mean, fucking takes over and changes how you feel about yourself or look at the world. Takes them out of their own lives and problems for a few precious hours."

Tom adjusted the high levels and flicked a wayward fly off the board. "We want to entertain and touch souls at the same time. They paid for that. If we don't touch or entertain people, then why are we out there?"

13

POTATO HILLS AND LETTUCE BEDS SURROUNDED FLAGSTONE grotto and thick pine logs that Tom halved into benches following a wicked windstorm a winter ago that felled a hundred-foot giant no fire could touch. Though several had tried. The metamorphosis of earth from slate, quartz, and ice and snow patches to summer food source attested to the potency of Megan's green thumb. Endless clusters of pinon sharply scented the night.

Christine curled her toes beneath the main bench, the multi-shaded core a subtle story of the abundance, fires and droughts of the pine's two-century life. Next to the bench, a recycling waterfall pattered into its surrounding stream, moistening the collection of succulents and cacti. The light-gray Carrara marble sign at the base of the waterfall, its inscription rendered in classic Latin lettering, caught her eye:

> *Da mi basia mille, deinde centum,*
> *Dein mille altera, dein secunda centum,*
> *Deinde usque altera mille, deinde centum.*
> *Dein, cum milia multa fecerimus,*
> *Conturbabimus illa, ne sciamus . . .*

Megan walked up and sat. "One of the greatest love poems ever written. Would you like to know what it means?"

Christine chuckled. "Sure. I can tell from the lettering it's even too old for Dad to have written."

> *"Kiss me now a thousand times, a hundred more,*
> *and then a hundred and a thousand more again,*
> *till with so many hundred thousand kisses*
> *you and I shall both lose count . . ."*

"Oh my. Who wrote this?"

"Catullus. Rome's most love-crazy poet," Megan said. "A senator's wife filled him with love, though he only saw her a handful of times. This is my idea of how love writes itself when you're filled with it."

Christine nodded and read over the sign again. "Yeah, that would work for me."

"So speaking of working, how are you doing with the band? Your dad?"

"As long as it's fun, and stays fun, I'm down." Her newly curled hair flopped to her stomach as she leaned forward. "Who wouldn't want this?"

Tom walked up, kissed her warmly, and turned to Christine. "We need a few minutes if you have it, sweetheart."

Christine twirled her hair nervously at his dead-serious-dad look. "What now?"

"Annalisa."

Her dead sister. The sibling she never knew. The lurking phantom . . . the damage it had caused. And the secrets. How could a man as open as Tom willfully keep from her the prior existence of *her sister?* It was like finding out you're adopted, then confronting your parents who tell you, "No, you're ours," then running into your real mother on the boardwalk. Total betrayal. She'd forgiven him and drawn closer, the singing and reunion stirring her heart. But forget? Never. What other unspoken bombshells were there? When things like this happened, you could never be fully sure.

As Tom and Megan talked briefly, she thought of the last six years without him . . . you don't get those back. Something really bad happened to make her sister dead, for sure, and it waylaid him, but *why make me feel unworthy?* She'd not only lost the rock in her life, but wanted nothing to do with him.

Her attitude began to soften when Trish and a few other co-eds shared tough stories about their uncaring and—in one case—abusive fathers. As she listened, the difference in temperaments and depth of relationship between their fathers and Tom grew apparent. She recalled how he juggled a crazy schedule to sit at the dinner table whenever he could. He even made the ultimate fatherly sacrifice, stopping while the Fever was still smoking hot. How many could leave the nightly elixir of live crowds, adulation, girls, and playing songs you love, keeping adolescence afloat *ad infinitum?* There were far too few stand-up fathers in the circus. Instead, all too many kids rarely saw their dads, if at all, and endured the occasional sordid stories of fathers behaving badly on tour.

She needed to throw off the blindfold. Which she finally did.

Tom and Megan returned and sat on either side of Christine. Megan rubbed his hand as though summoning Aladdin from the bottom of the bottle. "I'm ready to talk about your sister," he said softly. "I'm sorry it's happening six or seven years late."

"Or twenty-five."

"Fair enough. You have every right to be pissed." He glanced at Megan, who blinked, intentionally. *Press on.* "We handled it terribly. Me especially. You should've known from the day you were born. I guess I wanted to protect you from . . ."

"Your pain?" Her eyes followed the word from mouth to sky.

"Sure."

"But I didn't have pain about it, Dad . . . and she *was* my sister."

"All true. I guess I didn't want you to see me hurting from a daughter that—" he snapped his fingers. "You don't get over it. Not completely."

"I get that, Dad, and it sucks that it happened to you. Of all people . . . that's just unfair in ways I'll never understand." She slid her bare toes beneath a soft dirt patch, the ground cooling. "But it's no excuse to hide it from me. I mean, why *wouldn't* I have the right to know about my sister, or any other children you have out there?"

Tom clenched his fists and pushed them into his legs. "Well, there are no others."

"I wouldn't care, as long as I knew they existed."

Megan chuckled, partly to break the ice. "I might beg to differ." She leaned in front of Tom and grabbed Christine's hand. "We made a huge mistake, honey. We wanted a life for you without any more darkness than you'd be exposed to, anyway, and your dad thought it would bother you to know about Annalisa. And I supported him. A terrible mistake, incredibly stupid and selfish on our part, but never meant to hurt you."

"And the argument you had that night?"

"Almost ended our marriage." His eyes gripped the ground. "We had it rough for a while."

Megan coughed and started sniffling, the memory raw, timeless. "We had to fight for us. We *had* to get through it, knowing that we may or may not have you with us."

"Well, I know you split apart one other time. Right before you conceived me. Something else you never bothered to mention."

"Well, on that one, not sure why you needed to know," Megan said, her voice soft but firm. "What happened between your dad and me before you were born, we'd like to keep between us."

"Fine."

"Who told you?" Tom asked.

"Daphne."

He laughed somewhat harshly. "Of course."

"Did you date other people while you were apart?"

Megan gave Tom a sideways glance, then returned to Christine. "Since you asked, yes, we each dated others briefly, without any consequence other than to remind us of how good we were—are—together."

"That's a pretty big consequence," Christine said softly.

Megan nodded. "And the best."

Christine turned to Tom, her eyebrows creased, intent. "So what was she like, Dad? My sister?"

Tom exhaled deeply, thankful that Daphne didn't drift further into the conversation, outside of the little dust devil she stirred up. "For our brief time together, she meant everything to me, her free spirit, warmth, the way her dark hair blew when the winds swept through Golden Gate Park . . ."

Christine wedged in closer. "Sounds a little like me. Except for the dark hair."

"A little like you." He stroked her hair softly. "She liked studying objects more, like a little scientist. I imagined her becoming an historian or curator of some kind, maybe even a naturalist. Or archaeologist. She loved to learn the names of trees and plants, and dance. She loved to dance."

Christine soaked it in. *Wow.* "What an awesome older sister to have."

"She would have treasured you."

He then told her of meeting Maria in Haight-Ashbury while she was a foreign exchange student, having Annalisa six months after being deployed, and being called back to fatherhood. All before turning twenty. He told her how, as Annalisa became a little girl, Maria's fits of anger escalated. "They were like pop-up storms; you never knew they were coming. She'd be laughing one minute, chewing off my face the next." Then, just after Annalisa's fifth birthday, how Maria grabbed her and rushed back to her native Italy. A year later, a note, postmarked Verona: "Annalisa died of pneumonia."

"I couldn't believe for a long time Annalisa was gone. Finally . . ." He wrung his hands like they were stinging dishrags. "I had to figure out how to move on. Without music, I would've died, too."

Christine saw an underlying sadness in his eyes, a somber dark-blue light, present in every loving parent who survives a child. Part of Annalisa's spirit remained calcified in his soul, going nowhere, her freckled nose just out of view, the itch in his bosom impossible to scratch. A ghost.

"Thanks for telling me." She hugged him and stretched her arms into the night.

14

"I HAVE A SIMPLE QUESTION, TOM."

"Yeah?"

"Could you possibly hide any further from civilization?"

Tom looked at his passenger while fighting off a late afternoon glare that would blind the sun. "Paradise, my friend. Furnished with nature, silence, a place to think and be yourself."

He and Robiski drove past an abandoned church parking lot. Will's RV sat in its resting place, attached to hook-ups for visitors whose rigs couldn't climb the steep ridgeback road. As they rounded the bend and climbed toward the skyline, Robiski rolled down his window, clasped the rooftop, and inhaled mountain sunshine, junipers, and pinons. He brushed his immaculate locks, every brownish-gray hair in place. "It's like living in the jet stream."

"You get used to it. Eventually."

Robiski wheezed. "Well, had I been here for your month-long love fest, I would be able to breathe by now."

Tom chuckled, as amused by Robiski's new look as by his remark. Where had the scruffy, manic, unkempt ball of lunatic fire gone? Who was this *GQ* walk-in? He even *looked* like a refined man, not merely the privileged son of a recording legend. When Don Robiski's oversized heart collapsed from carrying and realizing the wildest dreams of the Fever and dozens of other acts, Tom assumed Jason would continue his *trustafarian* life, paid for by Don's royalties from the Fever and the other bands. This man did not resemble the stubbly-faced nomad at Don's funeral a decade ago who hadn't seen soap or razor in two weeks.

Rather than coasting on coattails, Robiski took charge and rebooted the label for the twenty-first century. He always loved studios, concerts, hanging out with performers, parties that stretched into the next morning. What Tom did not know was that he also enjoyed the record business. His bands never played less than forty shows when promoting a release. He adhered to the old man's credo: tour to sell, and keep your fans hungry for more. They would blitz the digital and streaming sites, drive sales through the roof.

Robiski glanced back and forth, taking in life thousands of miles from the sinking city he'd just left. The car bounced atop washboard riffles, rattling his teeth. "Can't you just grade this son-of-a-bitch? Grading vehicles do exist."

"We have electricity, Robiski. We've discovered that."

"One speculates. One wonders."

Tom rested his forearm on the wheel. "Glad you're here for some music, instead of spending all your time in Venice. I was beginning to wonder if we'd ever see you again, or if you'd bought a little shop on Murano, started blowing glass, and settling in your own little sea with your lady." A radiant glow lit Robiski's cheeks. "She must be taking good care of you."

He raced up the one straight section in the mountain road, then hit the brake and guided his jacked-up jeep through a quick S-curve. The road grew steeper. Robiski held onto the roof, shaking his head as he peered at Sierra Blanca. "So this explains it."

"This explains what?"

"This remote place. Why it's been so damned hard to get you to green-light a tour."

A shadow roughly the size of a prehistoric raptor swooped over the road and soared above an aspen glade like an F-16 going vertical. The source, a golden eagle, fanned out thirty feet above, all wingspan and wonder. Tom stopped. The bird arced and banked into one turn, then another. "*That's* why I don't come down the hill more than I have to."

"Yeah. I get it. Not my thing—too remote, probably too redneck—but I get it."

The eagle rose in front of a growling thunderhead before carrying its hunt to another ridge, the brazen deity commanding the sky. Tom passed an aspen stand from which he had dragged a half-dozen vehicles after they'd slid on ice, and accelerated up the final ascent until they came upon the house and side buildings of his hacienda, encircled by the driveway. Robiski slid his sunglasses over his eyes. "So this is it—where the most-talked-about comeback tour in years is being hatched."

"*Reunion* tour. In and out. Thirty gigs is all."

"If only people knew . . ." Robiski shook his head. "Semantics."

Five minutes later, greetings flowed like New Year's champagne. Christine walked onto the front porch, her hair pulled back, sweaty in half-top and leotard, a stretching strap in her hands. Robiski looked at her, then at X and Rogelio, wondering how two New York musicians kept their hands off the California girl during their extended isolation. Must feel like boxers in training camp, he thought. "Have you ever grown up nicely," Robiski said, giving Christine a European one-two on her cheeks.

"So awesome to see you, Jason! Just finished yoga, heading up the hill. Back soon—"

She began her ascent up the back hill, X's eyes following her. Robiski turned to Tom. "She could be your secret weapon, you know. If she sings as good as she looks, then she's going to connect with younger crowds. And they're the downloaders."

"This our manager?" Rogelio whispered to Chester, sizing up Robiski's suit. "Dude looks like he just got off the plane from Rome, those threads."

"Pretty much did," Chester said. "He's our producer, co-conspirator, manager, your best friend this summer, son. No matter what you think—and I think he needs a roll in a back hollow bog m'self—he's the best. Just like his daddy. Wish my lazy old bloodhound had his nose for trends and hits. Would eat from the woods every day. He gets 'er done."

As they stepped inside, Megan walked up, hugged Robiski deeply, and handed him a beer. She kissed his cheek and took his bag. "I've got one of the back rooms ready, Jason. Make yourself comfortable. Dinner's in an hour."

"These guys sounding as good as I keep hearing?" He knew he'd get a straight answer from Megan, bypassing Tom's nitpickiness or Chester's backwoods bluster.

"They might surprise you."

So much for a straight answer.

For the next few days, Tom and Chester rolled tapes for Robiski when they weren't rehearsing and working out song combinations and medleys, the precursors to the official set lists. As Tom explained a few musical alterations they made to factor in Christine, X, and Rogelio, Robiski rifled through potential opportunities like a prodigy busting out vector math. Christine struck him at first like other blonde diva-types, but when she sang, he thought of Annie Haslem, the Renaissance frontwoman with the divine four-octave pipes. He thought of Country Girl, who vaulted from an Oklahoma pig farm to become America's Sweetheart in one television season, remaining on top more than a decade later because the angels found someone who would appreciate a heavenly singing voice—and happened to look like an angel herself. Christine wasn't polished, he thought, but Tom could take care of that—and a tour has a way of polishing its actors. Especially when the world is watching. Under the blaring Klieg lights of the global stage, you get your shit together quickly, or go down in a flaming flurry.

"Your love is my gypsy's prayer . . . your love is my gypsy's prayer." He sang it over and over, tapping his foot. He looked at Tom and Chester. "Smart to appeal to Christine's strengths, *signores*. Chasing the younger crowd . . ."

"*Signores* . . . you've gone rogue on us," Tom said. "But Christine wrote it. And 'Holy Child Blues.' We're just her backup band."

Robiski looked up from the liner notes of *For the Children We Bring Forth*, the band's third album and its second platinum, following *The Fever* and *Mystical Dreamer*. "Shitting me?"

"Shit you not." Tom shrugged. "This is the 'It Is What It Is' tour. Everyone chips in, adds music, throws in a backup vocal once in a while. It worked before. It'll work now."

"Can you give me a dozen songs with this crew, Tom? Have you recorded that much?"

"Need to clean them up, but yeah. Why?"

"Anything on video?"

"Sure . . . *whyyy?*"

"A few hard heads in St. Louis, Cleveland, and Pittsburgh want to hear how you sound and see you before they book us. Plus, want a radio blast—and online clips if you have video."

"We've got both, Jason, but isn't a hundred-and-whatnot million album sales enough for a booking?" Tom asked. "Am I missing something?"

"No one has a memory in this business anymore, Tom. And no one believes a band can dust off after this many years away—not to mention showing up with new music. If they don't like it, fine—believe me, phone's ringing off the hook. And they can answer to irate Fever fans in their cities. They'll miss out on a helluva greatest hits tour."

"We're not doing a greatest hits tour. Don't forget, Robiski: That's why we walked while our peers tried to remain relevant with old stuff alone."

"So you do have new music . . ." Robiski smiled. "I knew I'd drag it out of you."

"Besides Christine's songs? A couple things . . . but not as polished as hers."

Chester scratched his beard as he joined them. "Now y'all see why I'm happy feedin' my horses, ridin' around on the tractor, turnin' wood into guitars, or playin' with my porch band. Let us worry about the music, Jason, you worry about the gigs, and when we play near my place, I'll give you a real Southern treat—a mud bog."

Robiski scratched his head. "A what?"

"Cars playing in the mud." Chester chuckled, his diminishing jowls jingling. "Come to my place, and we'll set you up with a nice beater truck or car, find a mud hole . . ."

Robiski waved him off. "Just give me a dozen songs, and . . ." He gave Chester a once-over from head to toe. "Good on you for cutting weight, Chester. Looking in fine form."

"The wife told me last thing she wanted to see on stage was her grandfather."

"Speaking of which, how is your beautiful and wise California lady?"

"Great. Just headed back home to check on things. She'll be out in San Francisco."

As Robiski and Chester continued their banter, Tom tuned his guitar to Rogelio's bass. For the next two hours, the band funneled into place six weeks of sessions, jams, doubts, songwriting bursts, collaborations, solos, style, age and cultural differences, and everything else that happens when six playing styles draw together. They closed with the second song of their debut album:

> *I came upon a little bird,*
> *So gentle and so pure,*
> *I brought her in and told her that*
> *My love would help her cure*
> *The daunting little mystery*
> *Of who she really was,*
> *We knew her mother, there was no doubt*
> *Her father was the question mark.*

While Tom plucked an acoustic guitar, Christine sang the final line a half-octave higher than originally recorded, capped by a cat-quick Rogelio note pattern that took his bass to its high point, like a heavy bird discovering how well he can fly if only he believes.

Robiski watched with slackened jaw, peering straight ahead, stunned by lyrics he hadn't heard since childhood, lyrics that meant nothing before but slammed into his heart now, trying to regather parts of himself as they were blowing away. Will put down his sticks and swung his vocal mic to the side. "That work for you, Jason?"

"Give me a second." Robiski peered at Tom, studying him in a way he'd never studied the man before, his eyes, long nose, how he showed plenty of joy but little other expression unless excited, and then his body language opened up like Christmas on Parade. *No way. Not possible.* His heart skipped. *Except that it was.*

"Speechless, Robiski?" Chester asked.

"That's one way to put it."

Tom and Christine commiserated over her vocal parts, Tom pointing out subtle nuances, particular notes to hold for a second longer, or shorter, letting a note build and billow by sustaining it, "something you can do freely in concert, as long as your band is clued in," he said quietly. "And your backup singer, of course."

Christine playfully slapped him, and looked at Robiski. "He's being nice, Jason. He'll get over it."

"You two are quite the duo," Robiski said. "Leave it to you to come up with something for the drop-off in your range, Tom. Though you sound pretty damned good . . . far better than most of the croakers who still think they sound like they used to."

He started chuckling. "And that's funny *how?*" Christine asked.

"Just thinking of the few promoters who are giving me shit about dropping a grizzled greatest hits package on them. They have no idea."

"We kinda like it that way," Chester said. "Always have."

Robiski chuckled. "Time to get out of Sleepy Hollow and onto those forty dates . . . maybe more."

Tom turned away from Christine. "I thought it was thirty. That was our deal . . ."

Robiski threw up his arms like a traffic cop. "Easy, Tom. Give this some breathing room. I'm mulling through three dozen existing invites to play in stadiums, smaller cities and venues, unplugged, even halls in Europe, a couple of castles . . ."

"If we have thirty dates, and three dozen invites, you can choose the best and throw out six," Tom said.

Robiski smirked, took off his blazer, and laid it on a chair. "That's three dozen invites *in addition to* the thirty already booked dates, Tom."

"Hot damn," Chester said.

Then Will: "What castles?"

Robiski rolled up the sleeves of his snappy white linen shirt, and smiled. "One in France, one in Germany, the Hohensalzburg for an acoustic set . . . where Mozart performed as a kid, where they filmed the *Sound of Music.*" He glanced at Christine, X, and Rogelio. "Trust me: you want to play one, just for the experience, though from what I understand, you, Rogelio, probably know the feeling."

"There's nothing like it, no doubt," Rogelio nodded. "Those walls have centuries of music in them. And lives. And wars. Music seeps out the best."

Excited story-swapping about European holidays ensued, and then: "OK, Jason. Ten more *good* dates," Tom said. "All here in the US of A. Maybe we can go overseas for a few gigs after this . . . including a castle. Would love that! And a London club, something small."

"I was thinking O2 Arena. Even getting on a Wembley bill. Something's brewing in the late summer, a benefit, if I can get you on there. If it happens. Or if your schedule will allow."

"I'm thinking a club, you know, a back-to-the-beginning thing. But any of us would take Wembley in a second."

Robiski nodded and grinned, his shining eyes revealing a card he'd wanted to play later. "How many gigs did you *really* line up, son?" Chester asked.

"Forty, and holding, since you can't decide if you want to do forty-one shows. Or fifty. It could be seventy-five, just from new requests. The list is growing."

"So much for thirty. Jason, we haven't played a lick to a live audience . . ." Tom paced back and forth, uncomfortable with that simple truth. "That scares me, all this demand without a peep from us in twenty years. We might suck eggs and they might head for the exits."

"Or you might be the hottest seat in the land—and the hottest act," Robiski said. "Now you know why I want some tunes and video clips. Recorded here. To preview you."

Robiski started to walk away, glancing at Tom, glancing again over his shoulder, fidgety in a way the others hadn't seen in him. "If you'll excuse me, I'm going to let my *signora* know I haven't asphyxiated in the nosebleed seats up here. Yet." He shook his head. "Do me a favor, guys. Mix your set and give me a recording. And some video clips."

"Why do you still think this, *mi amore?* We have discussed. It is not possible."

"Anything is possible. I don't know for sure—yet—I'm probably just dreaming."

"It is silly . . ." She spoke slowly, the wee hours crackling through her voice, enunciating the double consonant by splitting it, *sil-lee,* trying again to grasp his outlandish idea. It was like gathering all the planets that spun from your orbit a lifetime ago, globe-sized pieces of your soul that got lost and stayed lost and you went on without them, diminished but surviving. Then suddenly, they circle around from a forgotten galaxy, trying to return to your orbit. Only your orbit has been shrunken over the years by the unbearable task of daily survival . . .

Robiski stared out the guest room window. Remnants of a meteor shower earlier in the night whisked through the sky, then vanished into dark matter. Could she see any of the shooting stars through the milky haze on her rooftop, a far different atmosphere than the harsh dryness of this mountain air just down the hill from the troposphere?

He'd settle for sea level. Better yet, below it, sinking further into her arms as they and Venice descended into the sea. "*Bellissima*, I've wondered about this the past few months. I see too many things, too many coincidences—your eyes, your cheeks, how you laugh, the way you walk, that long almost model's stride . . ."

"I don't know . . ." Her voice resigned like an argument that had long worn itself out. "But I am feeling on top of life. Maybe you want this so much for me that your mind is making the story for you?"

"That's probably the sanest thing that's been said about this. You're right, probably a crazy thought, like you said last time I brought it up." The words left his mouth, but his speeding heart and the large weight in his belly couldn't disagree more.

"*Mio bellissimo uomo,*" she uttered. He could forever draw daily sustenance from the way she said "my beautiful man," her voice soft, her accent adding a smoky sensuality not unlike the leading ladies of Antonioni, Fellini, and other creators of the golden era of Italian film. As he spoke, he wanted to slip through the phone and crawl into her voice. "Is your band ready?"

"Next Saturday, go online at midnight your time. We're streaming the first concert. See what you think. See what keeps me up at night."

"Besides me."

He chuckled. "I wouldn't compare the two."

"I will watch. *Graci, mi amore.* You make me very happy. Every day, happier."

He once ran from such comments, viewing them warily as lures, handcuffs on his freewheeling, free-loving style. Tender imprisonments, those comments. No longer. *Whatever your magic, bella signora . . .* "I hope we're just getting started, sweetheart."

PART TWO

From the poet's scroll there spilled
A tale old as light,
A tale wrapped in many forms
A tale told at night . . .
Concerning the future world he said
Let's leave it in the past,
Leave it with your wayward thoughts
And take me to your soul . . .

—Tom Timoreaux, *Poet's Song*

15

THE FAMILY TIMOREAUX MEANDERED THROUGH A THICKENING sea of wild makeup, tie-dyed shirts, beaded necklaces and tops, ponytails, granny dresses, velvet and leather vests and skirts, tattoos of every imaginable design-origin-symbol-totem-meaning, bell bottoms, berets, holy jeans, and t-shirts pressed with the logos of iconic bands and current causes. Incense, barbecued chicken and corn blended with exhaled herb and vape sticks, the pungent mixture reminding him of the old 4 p.m. Digger feeds two blocks down from where they were walking. A half-century before, Haight Street hosted starry-eyed teens and committed elders in their twenties and thirties as they embraced an expanded idea of Love and created music, community, art, activism, environmental concern, and heightened awareness. Rock music was elevated as a social and political vehicle, while the two magical summers of love implanted seeds that, for many, never stopped growing.

For one glorious Sunday afternoon in June each year, the half-mile stretch between two gems among parks, Buena Vista, and Golden Gate, reverted to hints of its past. A few original Haight-Ashbury shops still existed, window merchandised hookah pipes, Wes Wilson and Rick Griffin poster art, Moby Grape or Jefferson Airplane t-shirts, and Jerry Garcia top hats. Many teens and Millennials embraced hippie couture, fashion, and music anew, some concluding, albeit reluctantly, that their parents and grandparents might really have been hip at one time. Take the soaked, exhausted couple comforting each other at Woodstock, now the paternal and matronly grandparents next door, yet the very faces of the coolest era of them all. An admixture of social cliffhangers, nostalgia freaks, bookworms, the homeless, and curious roamed the district now, along with faux hippies or old hippies hoping to reclaim an era now relegated to the music and stories of those who made those times.

Tom took in the sea of people as Marilyn McCoo's scintillating voice proclaimed it to be the Age of Aquarius from a vendor's wireless speaker. He stretched his arms, hitting a solid object. "That was my jaw, Ali," Megan said.

"Sorry." He kissed her jaw.

"I'll get you back." She slapped his butt. "At a time and place of my choosing."

They arrived in character. His leather vest and jeans framed a multicolored shirt, its concentric swirls resembling a projection wall. Her black skirt, tights, and calf-high boots matched her billowy blouse and purple sash. They strode past vendors hawking t-shirts, CDs, magazines, street rags, and literary journals, Tibetan prayer flags and tinksha bells, hats, vests, a wide variety of foods, daypacks, beads, necklaces with peace signs and spiritual symbols from a dozen indigenous cultures, candles, and other wares.

Nearly fifty thousand people joined them. Some recognized Tom, walking up, shaking hands or kissing his cheek, getting a photo, and saying a few quick, appreciative words. When The Fever made it, he couldn't walk down his own street without well-wishers accosting him. He loved accommodating fans, but sometimes, when you want to take your wife to dinner, or walk in the park, you want one-on-one time. It can be an elusive shadow when carrying a bull's-eye of fame on your back.

Not today, though. Connection was the whole idea.

"Michael!" Tom reached out his hand.

"Tom! Holy shit! Tommy T and Mystical Megan return to the Garden!"

They exchanged warm hugs, the warmest coming from Michael Strauss, whose thick beard framed a deeply wrinkled face, the roadmap of a full life. "I heard you were playing; how long's it been?"

"Twenty years," Tom said. "Damn, it's good to see you."

A purple serape draped from Michael's arms. He looked like a high priest extending blessings as he spread his arms wide. "And you, Megan, symbol of elegance, grace, and beauty, stunning as ever. You people know you're supposed to age, look like the rest of us?"

"We haven't grown up yet," Megan chuckled. "So wonderful to see you, Michael." She squeezed his hand and kissed his cheek.

Michael glanced at Christine. "Who is this beautiful lady?" She stopped twirling her earrings long enough to glare at the wild-eyed, silver-haired man, who could pass for a raver photoshopped into grandfatherhood.

"Meet our daughter, Christine."

"Your daughter . . ." Michael took Christine's hand and kissed it. "Wow. Last time I saw you, sweetheart, you were knee high to an ant. And that was in a magazine photo."

Christine grinned out of deferential respect, the kind of grin you give your parents' friends to support their friendship rather than your own impressions. Though the man could charm in his crusty, loose-talking hippie dude way.

"Michael was a leading underground journalist, Christine," Megan said. "A very good one. One of the real revealers, inconvenient as it was for those in charge at the time. Did you know, Michael, that some of your articles made it to Boston, got reprinted in the *Avatar, Boston Free Press,* and some mimeographed handouts at Wellesley, and impacted a few co-eds, including *moi*?"

"Really? Well, you Wellesley girls were all the rage, honey. Your sisters even made me happy the year I ran the Boston Marathon, the way they lined up halfway through and screamed away. Gave me all the mojo I needed to finish. Should have seen all the gray, bald runners drifting to the right side and obliging the girls holding up "Kiss Me!" signs. I saw one co-ed panning for gold."

"I slapped those girls' hands twice myself," Megan said. "The best feeling in a race, running by my school, my sisters in education. Then my knees gave out and I had to stop running."

Megan's comment soared by Christine. "Panning for gold?" she asked.

Michael chuckled. "Yeah. She carried a sign saying, 'Let's Make YOUR Baby!'"

"I stood in that line in '69 and '70," Megan said. "Then a rocker swept me away." She hooked her arm inside Tom's.

"And you became Mystical Megan . . ." Michael's voice drifted, dreamlike.

Christine shook her head. "Mom, what's the big deal about Mystical Megan?"

"Her background is far-out," Michael replied.

Christine noticed Tom and Megan becoming antsy, and folded her arms. "I have a minute if you do."

Megan shot a glance at Michael, turned to Tom, and shook her head. "Fine." She ran through her year of high school in London, half of it spent on Carnaby Street during Swinging London's preening glory, hoarding every possible pound and shilling to buy the mind-blowing designs of Mary Quant, hang with "the wildly fun" *Blow Up* crowd, and listen to the Kinks, the Cream, and the Who. Her complete absorption into the scene followed, the colors, dreaminess and expressiveness, the music, art, and fashion. She mingled at showings, crashed parties, danced until dawn, talked with budding musicians, philosophers, writers, dancers, costume designers, and stage directors, shared a few nights with a student from the Lake District ("*not* mentioned in my letters home," she chuckled), and found her calling. "My favorite boutique, Granny Takes a Trip, had this motto above the front door that pretty much became me: *One should either be a work of art or wear a work of art.*

"I was far away from my family and friends, and as an American girl, I got a lot of attention," she said. "Then another American blew through and changed music. Forever."

"Who?" Christine asked.

"Hendrix," Michael replied.

"Yes." Her eyes drifted back to that rainy January night in a packed, low-roofed nightclub. "We dropped into Bag O'Nails, one of our favorite dives. We heard everyone was coming. Paul McCartney was wearing a new moustache, his *Sergeant Pepper*'s moustache. Paul . . ." Megan batted her eyes and puckered her lips.

"Nice, Mom."

She waved Christine off. "But the best was the black guitarist dressed like a colonist in a headband. He tried a song he'd been recording all day. 'Cuse me, while I . . ." Megan blew a kiss into the heavens. "He brought the house down. My girls and followed him to 7½ Club. He probably thought we were stalkers, a fox force. My crush on rock musicians began then and there."

"Which explains the Hendrix poster in your throwback corner," Christine said.

Megan laughed. "It explains a lot of things."

Christine tried to picture Megan as a sixteen-year-old, wearing thigh-high boots, hair draped down her back, the eclectic, mod styles covering her long, sleek body. "So you switched from being a swinging London hottie to a wife?" She snapped her fingers. "Like that?"

"Well, that was three years later. I met your dad in Boston, right after my girls and I got back from Woodstock. I told them a couple weeks later, after he took me to the mountains, I'd end up marrying him. They still remind me about it."

Megan turned to Michael. "Enough about me. What wisdom are you pontificating these days?"

Michael handed her a hardbound anthology of *The Oracle*, the bible of the Summer of Love. "You'd be amazed at how many we still sell at these fairs. And today's a big day, because the radio has been talking about you all week." He turned to Christine. "That was a great interview the other day, young lady, with the top-rated young talk show host in the city? And the girl's not even thirty."

Tom took the book from Megan and rubbed its embossed cover. "It's yours," Michael said. "My gift. How long you in town?"

"A week. Warm-up gigs. Make sure we can still stand."

Michael jotted down his mobile number. "Here. Call me. Let's catch up."

After exchanging farewell hugs, they stepped into a throng that meandered as aimlessly as a drugged anthill. Joy, happiness, and old friends created an electric atmosphere, smiles and excited discussions popping up on all sides.

"Tom? Tommy T? I'd know that voice anywhere. Classic. How are you, man?"

A man with a gray ponytail approached, his face leathered and pocked by hard drinking, decades of California sun, and as many wrong turns as right. Maybe more.

"Good. Good, thanks." Tom didn't recognize him. "Really appreciate you coming out today. We're all going to have some fun." He shook the fan's outstretched hand.

"Great to see you back." The man's words lisped in the gap formerly occupied by his front teeth. "Old times are the only times. *Our* times are coming back. They're coming back. Times they are a-changin'. Look at this tour . . ."

The *Twilight Zone* theme rippled through Tom. "Thank you."

The man left with an extra jig in his step. "Dude was bugging," Christine said.

Tom chuckled. "Stuck in a time warp, for sure."

"You handled him well, honey," Megan said.

He turned to Christine. "Remember what we talked about the last time we were up here, honey? It's all about saying 'thank you.' Leave them feeling good, like you gave them personal attention. They've given us a great life, our music means something to them, so we can smile and give them a few kind words." He looked at his watch. "I've never understood musicians icing their fans. Let's get to the stage."

After walking for another minute, Tom pointed to a Victorian, its upper gables dressed in blue, the lower floors white. The paint job resembled the bi-colored popsicles he bought every afternoon when the ice cream truck rolled into the neighborhood, crackly carnival music blaring. "Want to hear a funny Chester story that happened in that pad?"

Christine looked at the bronze plates next to the door. "It's a vintage clothing store on one floor and an architect's office and lawyer's office on another, Dad. Not quite sure anything funny *can* happen here."

"It used to be something else." Christine shrugged her shoulders as Tom pressed on. It was useless to slow his roll at, essentially, his college reunion. "A few months after Chester came back for good, we met Raylene, got on the Matrix and Fillmore stages as a warm-up act . . . me with my surf and acid rock, Chester playing blues like he was kicking the devil's ass himself."

"I could see that."

"We managed to get more gigs. We sometimes had to practice and play with borrowed equipment. A lot of places weren't letting bands play electric, and we were just learning how. At least we had the Matrix; we could always plug in there." He pointed to the building. "That's where this place comes in."

"How so?"

"Chester needed to learn how to play electric. I plugged him in, up there, and told him to strum, *hard*. His hair's probably still on that ceiling. Half of mine is. The sound blast about scalped us."

Christine cocked her eyebrow. "I would've kicked your ass, Dad." She threw her fists out in rapid succession, then cranked off a quick side kick, disturbing the air three inches from his ribs. "Boom-boom-done."

"Well, that didn't happen, but a funny thing: Chester figured out chord and key changes for our couple of songs. And he could really play . . . almost immediately became one of the top two, three guitarists in the city.."

They reached the end of Haight Street, where a huge flatbed truck blocked the road. A vendor sold t-shirts with multi-colored blotches and blown-out, blown-up psychedelic lettering splashed across the front. Above the lettering, a singer swung his microphone stand and one leg toward an invisible audience. Megan nudged him as Christine studied the shirt. "Honey, is that you?"

Christine mouthed the stem of her sunglasses like a cigarette piece. "It *is* you . . . except let's see you make that move right now without losing your hamstring."

Tom smirked. "That's your job now."

She positioned her sunglasses onto her nose and face. "I'm down with that."

"Look at the art on that shirt, the poster art." His tone softened into a degree of reverence. "Wes Wilson, Bonnie MacLean, Stanley Mouse, Rick Griffin, Alton Kelly—the Murph the Surf cartoon guy . . . they created an art form with their posters, handbills, and album covers, the rollercoaster lettering, the colors . . ." While Christine worked out which styles the poster artists cobbled together—*art nouveau, Dada, elements of Victorian art*—Tom grabbed three shirts and handed the man eighty dollars, double the asking price.

The vendor promptly handed back the money. "Tom, you, Chester, and your whole bunch helped make the greatest scene we've ever had. Every time I hear a Fever song, I want to go back there. Thanks for coming home and keeping the music alive."

"Thanks for being alive, now, to hear us play again."

A few minutes later, they reached a chain-link fence that separated the massive crowd from the flatbed truck. After six months of uncertainty, six weeks of rehearsals, and trying to work three new faces into the mix, it was time to play.

Tom glanced at the flatbed, its top strewn with equipment, power lines, and roadies scrambling back and forth. The back line was in place—speakers, amps, and Will's drum riser and kit. Roadies jumped onto X's accompanying riser to position his keyboards, electric piano, and Hammond organ. They plugged three stand-up mics, Chester's guitars, and Rogelio's bass into amps on a beat-up, knotted piece of wood accustomed to hauling cinder blocks and landscaping tools. When a tech sound-checked Chester's amps with his signature arrow guitar, huge cheers erupted.

They entered the roped-off area and walked to a small trailer behind the flatbed. Inside stood at least fifteen roadies, techs, soundmen, and stagehands. "We used to get a flatbed, park it on the Panhandle, and play," Tom said. "No permits, little advance notice, no tickets. The Panhandle was packed. Great times."

A moment later, a huge pair of arms wrapped around Tom's stomach, squeezing every bit of breath from his lungs. A three-hundred-pound biker with a salt-and-pepper Fu Manchu held him with tattooed arms the approximate size of oak limbs. "For God's sake, Dudley, grab me a little tighter next time!" he gasped. Dudley lifted him six inches off the ground, turned him around, and engulfed him in a warm, deep hug.

"Damn, Tommy boy—good to see you, my man!"

A bear of a voice clawed through the gravel, grit, and raw throaty edges of five thousand gigs he'd overseen and a thousand bars he'd shut down. Dudley leaned past Tom, grabbed Megan's outstretched hand in his own, and embraced her warmly. "As always, the finest lady to walk our streets. Why again did you settle for *him*?"

She kissed Dudley on his stubbled cheek. A ripe, earthen scent emanated from the vested biker, a road smell, the scent of a man without a ring on his finger, who would be going home to no one, a recent development after thirty years of being married. Sadness scratched her heart.

Dudley glanced at Christine, stopped, looked again. "Who's this beautiful lady?"

Tom folded his arms and laughed. "Our other vocalist."

"Honey, you're just about the hot—"

"It's his *daughter*, Dudley, you dirty-minded no-good sumbitch." Chester walked up and slapped Dudley on his meaty back. "How the hell are you?"

Dudley turned to Tom. "Your daughter? The little girl bowed with you end of the last tour?" He eyed Christine from boot tip to sunglasses. "You're her?"

Christine smiled and laughed. She couldn't help it; old men were so uncomfortably *cute* when they wanted to sneak a peek but couldn't. "That would be me."

"I'll be . . . you just never know." Dudley shook his head and slapped Chester's shoulder. "Goddamn, Chester. Could've let me know before I made an ass out of myself. Wondered if you'd ever drag your ass away from your moonshine stills. I mean, your farm. Glad to see you here."

"What stills?"

"Can't bullshit a bullshitter, sparky."

He turned back to Christine. "Since you don't really know me, but I know you as the little girl you once were, lemme tell you about this road crew I run for you guys." He pointed to Tom. "As my man Tom's daughter, you just became *my* daughter for the tour. Anyone on this team screws with you—anyway, anyhow—they deal with me."

Christine's face was a full, round question mark. "I appreciate that . . . I think?"

"He's to be appreciated," Tom said. "Dudley's like a stake-out. You never know he's there, but when something goes down, there he is to handle it—*right there.*"

Christine tugged down the hem of her dress to mid-thigh and started pacing, chatting, pulling overly chewed gum out of her mouth. Tom's belly rumbled as he watched her pace some more, twirl her hair a few times, text someone, check her lipstick and eye makeup, glance around like a cat chasing shadows, and pace some more.

"Nervous thing," Dudley said.

"Me, too," Tom replied.

"A big day for all of you."

"For all of *us*. Fever family's back together. Let's keep it that way this summer."

The tech conducted final sound checks and roadies checked instruments, moved drinks, and finished taping down cords, with a smiling Dudley double-checking their checks as he taped down the set lists. When he finished, he huddled the crew together. "Five minutes till showtime, people. All good?"

"Ready to roll," one of the roadies said.

"Looks good to me, too." He glanced at three bare-chested roadies standing next to the soundman and lighting engineer, a woman. "Oh yeah, in case you boys are interested in entertaining or sampling the nightlife on tour, see the smoking hot vocalist there?" He pointed to Christine.

"How can you *not*?" a roadie replied, his torso ripped from years of lifting amps, cabinets, and instruments. A sweep of hair bounced on his shoulders.

"Tom's daughter. That smoking hot vocalist. For this tour, she's *my* daughter."

"OK?"

"Which means lose all thoughts of chatting her up . . . now." He looked around the circle. "Touch her, move beyond a nice conversation, and you're fired. Which will be the easiest part of your final day. We clear, men?"

One roadie snickered. "Our final day . . . on the job? On earth?"

He glared at the mouthy roadie, and then dismissed the crew.

At the base of the stage stair, Chester held court among the daughters, wives, and girlfriends of the accounted-for roadies. "What you telling them, you bag of air?" Dudley asked as he walked past.

"Everything they want to hear." Chester brushed his hand dismissively. "Go tend to your business . . ."

X walked around the corner behind stage and saw Christine for the first time since she took off with Tom and Megan shortly after waking him up with an arousing San Francisco welcome. "You dress up for me, baby?"

"Just for you." She smiled nervously. "And fifty thousand others."

They waited for Rogelio and Tom to emerge from a small construction trailer, where they checked transmission bugs with broadcast engineers. Everyone with a computer and Wi-Fi, from San Francisco to Perth, would be able to see the streamcast shortly. Pre-event messaging had been intense. As Tom held the door open for air, the possibility felt overwhelming, like everything else within the technologically interconnected world, a world only McLuhan *really* believed possible when the Haight was a symbol of a free, beautiful future and psychedelic rock was king.

"We're set," the webcast producer said. His slumped eyes, dark-framed glasses and disheveled black beard reflected a night life of fighting it out with gamers the world over. His Linkin Park t-shirt swam on him, and his lengthy shorts ended at calves inked with matching lion tattoos that added the appearance of muscle to legs otherwise lacking them.

The producer pulled Tom aside, interrupting his reverie. "I just want to tell you that one of my grandparents liked your early music. My parents liked it all. The fondest memories of my childhood—hearing your songs." He extended his hand. "I'm excited to be part of this day."

Christine popped her head inside. She'd changed again, into a long-sleeve shirt that blossomed at her broad shoulders before screeching to a halt a few inches above her navel. Her skirt clung onto her hipbones. "Time to go, Dad."

The festival coordinator, another old salt from the psychedelic mines, led everyone to the gathering area, tapped Tom, Chester, and Will on their shoulders, thanked them, walked to center stage, and grabbed the mic. "It's been too long, San Francisco, but are you ready to catch The Fever?"

Never had a cornier line elicited louder cheers.

16

T HE THREE ORIGINAL FEVER MEMBERS TOOK THE STAGE,
acoustic guitars in hand, leaving the younger half of the band fidgeting
at the steps. "This is a hit-and-run. In and out," Tom said, and then
turned and waved to the crowd.

"Whoa-ohh!" He yelled into the microphone stand he carried across
the flatbed truck but was drowned by the thunderous cheers. "Whoa-ohh!
Whoa-ohh!" He pranced back and forth like a wired cheetah, waving, his
guitar slung to his side, hair dancing in its curls beneath his flop hat, his smile
one of sheer excitement and joy. "San Francisco!"

He pumped the mic stand up and down, marching in place, singing in
five-second bursts to warm his voice, commanding the audience's attention.
"Can you believe it's been this long?"

The crowd exploded. Two bouquets of roses landed at his feet. Will
counted them in, Tom twirled the mic stand like a majorette, and off to the
races they went.

> When I become the President
> I'll knock down all the walls
> I'll crush the mighty force that dares
> To make you live outside
> The power of your open minds,
> Inside their disregard for truth . . .

The three strummed side-by-side. The sea of people swayed, turning
Haight Street into an oscillating wave. Many sang along to the tune that
accompanied the summer of '72, and suggested again an urgent situation.
Tom stared into the eyes of a young girl riding on her grandfather's shoulders
three rows back. He smiled broadly, pointed the mic stand towards her, and
waved. The grandfather tried to wave back, but thought better and held on to
the girl's legs.

> *My country, oh sacred country*
> *With abundance and ability*
> *To choose our path,*
> *To choose our voice,*
> *To choose our brothers*
> *To choose our call*
> *To respect them all*
> *Let's stand up for America,*
> *Let's stand up for all souls.*

"I love you Chester!" a thirty-something woman in the front row screamed. "Come to me!" Her eyes lit up like a crazed teenager's.

Chester chuckled and nodded to Tom, who closed out the song.

The crowd roared as if it were riding shotgun in a hurricane.

Tom cupped the microphone. "Remember the flatbed gigs a thousand years ago?"

"I remember!" a woman screamed.

He pointed to her. "So you're the one who drove us all home!"

Hoots and laughs. Chester switched to his trademark Stratocaster aimed the arrow-shaped guitar at the crowd, and fired off a fusillade of power chords to welcome the three newest members onto stage. Rogelio walked from side to side, cool as every cruising feline, his fingers plucking, jamming with Chester. X saddled up in front of his Hammond. "What the hell?" a front-row fan yelled, already infatuated with Rogelio. Apparently, he reminded her of a Brit who once strutted and tomcatted across the stage, playing songs of demons and wizards, easy living, traveling through time. Sadly, he loved the needle, too, and it swept him away on the neap tide of rock casualties.

Christine followed, wireless mic in hand. Howls and cheers rained onto the stage as she made her way to Tom, kissed his cheek, and opened right up:

> *The fun is on the streets,*
> *The sun is on the streets,*
> *Just grab your girl, give her a twirl*
> *Let's party in the streets*
> *Let's cut loose every way we can*
> *Tomorrow's not arrived,*
> *We owe it to ourselves to rock*
> *It's good to be alive . . .*
> *Let's GO!*

As Christine high-kicked, Haight Street morphed into a raucous dance floor. She pranced back and forth and joined him, their harmonies more Jefferson Airplane than Tom Petty, fetchingly off-center. You never know how it really turns out until you play live. During "Mystical Dreamer," she covered Tom's high range, squatted front stage, and while bouncing in place on her legs, serenaded a trio of co-ed skateboarders who'd raced down the hill to see what the noise was about. Behind her, a videographer barked into his headset, "Hey dude . . . The girl's off the hook. Bass player, too. Keyboardist . . . all good shots. Then Tom and Chester . . . how do we get all this?"

"I'll get another camera sidestage," the producer replied.

"And get me one more behind the drum kit."

Within two songs, Tom's greatest worry had vanished. Fans would *not* find the music fossilized. Not on this day. His smile was that of a proud father's as Christine seized the crowd. He'd taken Raylene's advice, brought her onstage—as he once promised Megan, God and country he would never do — and uncorked a slumbering genie. *Lord have mercy.*

The band regaled the crowd with classics, rotating jams and solos by Chester, Rogelio, Will, and X, with Tom sometimes joining in. They glanced at each other constantly, watching the lead instrument, eyes closing to feel and hear the music, guiding and adjusting to each other. How great it was to actually *hear* music again through the wedge monitors, Tom thought, his ears finally healed after a quarter-century of sustained hundred-decibel pressure. Between songs, he slipped in band anecdotes while the others re-tuned or switched instruments, faces young and old passing joints and pipes and pointing smartphones at him, shooting photos and videos.

After a three-song mini-burst, the band switching and blending with a smoothness that surprised Tom, he brought the music down to a low bass beat by Rogelio. "As you can see, we have some new faces," he said. "You know the guy my left—we lived in a flat right back there"—he pointed to the blue and white Victorian, Christine noticed—"and walked down this street long ago, dreaming of forming a little band to entertain our community of brothers and sisters. Our co-captain, Chester Craven!"

Big cheers. Chester saluted with a furious chord burst. "Behind me, we dragged this man out of his redwood treehouse in Mendocino to rattle his skins and your hides. Will Halsey!" Will stood up, twirled his sticks, and tossed them into the crowd. As a scramble for the prized souvenirs ensued, he flung another half-dozen sticks.

"We're not all here—Treg and Raylene couldn't be with us, and Raylene sends her love . . ." More cheers. "For the first time with The Fever, on keyboards from Harlem, the real X man, Xavier Washington." X bowed and rifled off an organ shot that whistled through space. "On bass and a whole lot more, the man they know as Rock Star in Europe . . . Rogelio Mejias." Rogelio pranced along the stage, grinding out a riff you could feel in your bones.

"And joining us on vocals—Christine Timoreaux!"

"Owwwww!" a man yelled.

Christine followed Rogelio across stage, sexy and assured, wrapping her arms around him when they got to stage right, kissing his cheek, then skipping back to X's keyboard and kissed him, her heart surging with enough adrenaline and endorphins to feed an Olympic team. She leaned against X's Hammond as he played. Tom cut in:

> *We first connected in the park*
> *I sang into her eyes*
> *She danced and laughed and pranced and then*
> *Got quiet as I sang,*

"Oh my God!" A volunteer roadie grabbed his smartphone while tapping the beat alongside Megan and Chandra. He dialed and got a quick answer. "Honey! You're not going to believe this!"

He held the phone toward center stage, toward Tom, and turned to Megan. "I proposed to my wife with this song on the radio—we were in the backseat. Right there, mid-song, while making love, I asked her to marry me . . . during this song . . . I can't believe they're playing this!"

Megan smiled broadly. What a great gift, music, how it dissolves time and space and brings us to our deepest memories. Wrap up a memory in a song, and it will always be a part of life. The man danced again in that beautiful night as he continued talking to his wife, every other word an exclamation, every punctuation an endearment. Whoever these people were, they deserved it all. His happiness spread through her heart.

Tom followed Megan's eyes to the roadie, who held his phone toward the closest speaker stack. Tom turned to Chester and Rogelio, circled his finger in the air—one more instrumental round—and shuffled over. "Is it someone special?" he asked.

"My wife," the stunned man said. "We got engaged to this song . . ."

"Got it." Tom grabbed the man's phone without hanging up, and returned to center stage. He wrapped his arm around Christine, who had danced up to join him, cupped the phone against his mic, and sang.

> *Her eyes caress the sky, her hair*
> *Takes flight upon the breeze,*
> *Her body merges into mine*
> *I know that she's my lady . . .*

They halted as X and Chester stretched the heartstrings of the song. As the crowd screamed, he said into the phone, "Your husband's idea; he really loves you," then handed it to Christine, who returned the phone to the man. He shook his head, tears creasing his cheeks. "What a beautiful thing your dad did."

"True, but she's lucky to have you," Christine said. "Girls fantasize about guys that do what you just did." She kissed his cheek and stepped over to Megan, as exuberant as the star of a *quincenera*. "I'm like blown away, Mom! This is awesome!"

"Honey, you're fantastic!"

"Truly amazing," the man said.

As Christine swiveled back toward center stage, Chandra cupped Megan's ear. "I knew she could sing," she yelled, barely audible, "but the performing . . ."

Megan chuckled. "Ever since she was a baby. We just haven't seen it in a while."

Chester jacked up "Quantrill's Revenge," leaving Tom to belt out the finale at full tilt. He took a few bows, and tried to speak, but was engulfed by crowd noise.

After a raucous minute, the noise subsided. "We're playing in the city this week—then hitting the road. Listen to the radio stations for where we'll be." He looked at Robiski, who had appeared side-stage. "Hope to see you out there. Good night!"

The band filed off stage, trailed by the streamcast cameras. They gathered behind the flatbed, guzzling beers and bottled water to give the crowd a couple minutes to further shred their vocal cords. "It's like watching a movie you once starred in," Will said, wiping his eyes with his wristband. "Now it's colorized."

"Pretty much so," Robiski said. "We already crashed the server once on the streamcast, all the people trying to see it. You got your message 'round the world."

Tom stuck his thumbs inside his belt loop. "This was a great start."

A roadie handed Chester a guitar last played publicly at the grand finale, and he revved up "West of the West." Tom sang, Christine danced behind Chester and his slithery smooth slide work, and Will fired off machine-gun drum volleys. X and Rogelio held the madness in place, smiling like festive thieves who God dropped into the best possible gig of the summer.

The crowd was still singing "West of the West" when they slipped into Dudley's SUV and raced off to the Cliff House to break oysters and celebrate where the west of the west dipped into the sea.

17

SOMETHING ABOUT THE WAY HE MOVED . . . THE SHADOW
flashing through her furthest memory like a distant comet. The way he
talked to the audience, told stories, his voice. The way he blew kisses,
smile wide as the world . . . *in his arms.* How he sang the slower songs like
lullabies . . . .

It cannot be possible. She squinted at the streamcast half a world away. *Not
possible at all.* Then he spoke again, walked again . . . that stride, that voice. *Not
possible . . . except it is.* Fragments of a lost time skipped through her mind like
meteorites bouncing off the atmosphere. How do you—how do you deal—
how does this happen?

She studied his face, his tone. His words. She closed her eyes, welcoming
back the rhythm of his voice, the warmth bubbling up. . . *painting pictures on
his cheeks . . . dancing beneath trees that smell like medicine . . . castles of sand . . .
staring at the sky, turning over, rubbing noses like a couple of cats . . .*

> *. . . How do I say to the little bird,*
> *"I'm here no matter what"?*
> *Papa! Papa! Come back to me!*

She wiped her eyes as she stared. The song wasn't about a bird at all.
It's about me.

She pushed her graying curls aside and rubbed a jaw aching from a solid
hour of grinding. Tears stung her eyes. He smiled into the camera, at the
crowd and his bandmates. Into her bosom.

It was something new, something to behold. And it all started when she
gave Jason a vaporetto ride along the Canal Grande while taking Paolo's shift
during his latest bout with illness.

And now this.

> *One day I know she will return*
> *From the roost where she took flight,*

She'll be a full-fledged carrier
Of the heart and of the light . . .

"Papa."

She thought of Jason's call from the ridge before the band decamped for San Francisco. *Mi natale.* He had finished by saying, "I feel like I should have said something from the moment I first suspected, but how did I know? How could I? The whole idea that, out of seven billion people in the world; completely outrageous. I never even gave it a thought, until I . . . couldn't stop noticing similarities. I'm still not positive."

He didn't need to be. *She* was positive now.

Papa.

The word had vanished within, along with her childhood. Now both ghost and lie were exposed, the ghost that had haunted her, the lie she was just learning *was* a lie, the ghost that, as the years rolled on, sabotaged whenever she had a chance with a man.

On screen, he smiled as he sang. A beautiful, tall blonde girl danced and sang with him. *Does he know? About me? Did Jason say anything?*

The gorgeous girl kept perfect time, her legs long, hands expressive . . . *like my own.* It hit her flush: his daughter. His *other* daughter. Robiski had told her about the new singer, but she hadn't connected the dots. *Why would I? Nothing to connect.* Until there was.

The concert ended—for the third time. She'd risen early for the live streamcast, then watched it twice more. She grabbed her tea, paced the floor, threw her negligee onto the bed and plopped down, the soft Adriatic breeze cooling her body. She rubbed her eyes, remembering the vaporetto shift for Paolo. It started in a couple hours. After months of relative health, his illness was back. *Worry about Paolo—forget this fantasy about your Papa.* As she gnashed against her deeper sense of reason, another thought scratched the surface, wedged the door with its foot, seeped through: *Maybe one day, Paolo can be healthy enough to meet the grandfather who just . . . appeared.*

She closed her eyes and imagined Tom stroking her face while serenading her with songs and stories before the sweet, kind, long-haired people. They'd shared everything a father can share with his little girl. They laughed a lot. How is fighting possible if you laugh a lot, and sing and tell stories? *Who would want to leave such a place, Mama?* A crackly old movie played in her memory, of a little girl twirling in a park. Then a face flew in, a dark, violent face, shattered the movie, grabbed her by the wrist.

Mama! The End.

Maybe not.

Light thick as milk poured through the windows, dissolving a jittery daybreak dream of pursuing a jet and not grabbing the wing fast enough. Her eyes burned, her slumber disrupted by his face, the streamcast face, popping in and out of the dream. She reached for his hand on the plane . . . only to grab her mama's and fly the other way, every time.

She eyed the mirror and shuddered at the puffy-eyed mess before her. Thank God for sunglasses, mascara, and hats. She clicked on her DVR and replayed the streamcast yet again, rewinding, jump-cutting, focusing, panning, and zooming into every minute. She watched his long stride, deep-set eyes, and joy-streaked smile, delivering songs that made you think as well as feel. *Singing songs and telling stories until I fall asleep . . .*

She glanced at her bedside clock, embedded in the belly of a blue and ivory urn. An hour until shift. The canals were getting busy with tourists. Paolo's detail covered the Grand Canal, the islands—Burano and Murano—and the Lido, so not as boring as running the inner canals. She stared at her ceiling's painted stars and galactic swirls, a vision of expanding the world while controlling its ability to touch her at the same time. There were so many other things to do besides ferrying tourists—the vegetable market at Rialto Bridge, cataloging artifacts at the Accademia, sun-worshipping at the Lido with a foot-high gelato, or heading downstairs to the shop and helping Poppa Maurizio push out shoe repair orders. He'd given her half-ownership of the three-story building and business after his beloved wife, Gratia, passed. He didn't want to impose, but Annalisa insisted they be close. He originally bought the building primarily for the cobbler shop, and she rented the top-floor flat. Now, she co-owned it, her first ownership of any kind after bouncing from place to place with Maria and the mess of an adult life that followed.

She opened her butterfly windowpanes to inhale the sun-kissed Adriatic, its scent primordial as first life. Her hair cascaded from olive shoulders, the sun backlighting her like a corona. She pulled one of Robiski's long-sleeved shirts from a hanger and pressed it to her nose, recalling a night making love at 2 a.m. in a gondola tinted by foggy mist and deep-blue lights dancing on the canal. She dropped his shirt and buttoned her blouse slowly, noticing its tighter fit across her shoulders and how it loosened near her tummy. The weight loss plan was working. The Jason Robiski weight loss plan. Now, when she hit the streets, she saw more smiles, sideways glances, comments from colleagues, a gelato salesman even side-saddling over a stand in Sirmione to woo her, not a half-mile from the villa where her favorite among Roman poets, Catullus, wrote his sweet, desperate missives to the Senator's wife that infatuated him but he could not see.

Now this news from San Francisco.

She brushed her hair quickly, marveling at how the extra six inches made her look healthier and younger. It took some getting used to, since she'd pruned her hair like the Vatican landscape right through her twenties and thirties. She'd started letting it grow, but when Jason commented on how brave he thought women were for growing long hair into their later years, she canceled all future hair appointments. He treated her like gold, and the more of herself she could share, the better.

Since finding Robiski, she'd also redecorated the flat into a place a man would want to visit, rather than, say, a spinster's hovel. She saved and starved for nearly every item, her barren wallet clashing with her Michelin taste, her home subsequently populated by a few cherished items rather than a mountain of clutter. Urns of different colors and shapes ran along the kitchen counter, some two millennia old, from her digs in the Peloponnesian Plain with the Accademia's archaeological teams. Loose-leaf tea filled the urns, concocted from her rooftop garden of rose petals, chamomile, spearmint, lavender, and a half dozen others. "Start a tea business," Maurizio told her once. "You have more teas than I have shoes."

Her urns reflected her obsession with Ancient Greece. From a large *oinochoe* of a Medeian warrior, she scooped oolong tea pellets into an infuser. The stove creaked like a rusty bicycle chain as it heated up the water. Next to the *oinochoe* stood a *lekythos*, a gift from the archaeological minister after the year-long dig ended, her only extended foray outside Italy, a wondrous year for her and Paolo. On the *lekythos*, a teacher and student sat in a garden, the typical Ancient Greek classroom, reading from a scroll. The student wore a rosemary head wreath for mental stimulation. She mouthed the words on the scroll: "Long life to whoever is in love and death to whoever is ignorant of love. Death twice over to whoever forbids being in love." Every time you run out of reasons why the Greeks were by far the most brilliant civilization for their spot in time, you find another.

The timeless magic of urns was enthralling. She told stories of unearthed urns to Accademia visitors, some from the short digs she and Paolo joined in Santorini, Mykonos, and Lesbos, and the Plains of Marathon. One *oinochoe's journey* involved plenty of trading. "A prized possession," Maurizio said when he gave it to her. "Ours since Marco Polo acquired it for spices." His eyes glinted like a magician's. "Marco had to pay back the Doge Lorenzo Tiepolo for helping to finance his journeys. He sold it to our family. So the story goes."

One more thing to do before work. She filled her mug and headed for the bedroom, and tapped her fingers on her phone. It was 2 a.m. in California. *Answer . . .*

"Aaaahllo." The voice croaked.

"*Buona sera, mi amore.* You are sleeping?"

"Just, beautiful," Robiski said. "Long party in the city."

"I saw my Papa."

A nervous chuckle. "So you watched. You think it's him?"

"*Si*, but I do not know what to think. What to do."

He cleared his throat. "Be amazed, for starters. I sure am."

"It seems crazy, *si?*"

"Very. If it weren't happening to you, to us, I'd never believe it. And tell someone they were full of shit for suggesting it.."

"His smiles, eyes, long walk . . . the way he tells a story . . ."

Robiski chuckled. "He has his own way, for sure."

"It started with him reading and telling bedtime stories to me." She wiped her eyes. "Did you know he had a daughter?"

"Besides Christine?"

"*Si.*"

"Yes. He's talked about you. A lot." The whole sordid tale raced back to Robiski, the horror Annalisa must have experienced, forced to live in a place she'd never seen . . . "I don't think he ever gave up hope of seeing you again, even after he was told you—"

"—were dead," she said softly.

"That is *not* what I was about to say." He decided to stop as the pieces of a dark, dark puzzle came together . . . Hard to fathom. Telling father and daughter the other was dead. *Who the hell would do that?*

She felt his discomfort, his shock over it all, guessing that his stuttering was his attempt to make sense of the cruelty dealt her. Who lies and tells a little girl her father is dead? *Maria è il male cazzo cagna!* Crushing. Shameful. Spirit-killer. It's one thing to be a bitch to a man you don't love anymore, but *this?*

Tears flooded her eyes. "I don't know how to feel, *mi amore.*"

Robiski measured his words against the torrent trying to rush from his head. "What I know for sure, from Tom, is that his daughter disappeared, and he poured his pain over losing you into the music. A lot of that music became very famous, because he put so much of his heart into it. He kept doing that for many years, becoming at one point the most popular rock star in the world, until Christine was born. Then he quit playing. Now, he and his band are back, and I'm the lucky man who manages them."

She grabbed a tissue with her free hand. "Why is he playing again?"

"I talked to him and Chester—the guitar player. I asked them to do one more tour. They didn't want to at first, but they finally took me up on it."

The burly, bearded man onstage. "Uncle Chester?"

A long pause. "*Uncle* Chester?"

"Papa's brother. He is still there? I loved Uncle Chester, *mi amore!*"

"I'll be damned . . . Who else calls him Uncle Chester? Christine."

Christine probably lived the life Tom originally dreamed for her, she thought. Her stomach crumbled like a ruined wall. "Uncle Chester lived with us. He put me on his knee when he played music. He talked funny."

"You remember that?" Robiski chuckled. "But then again, who forgets *that* accent? Nothing's changed. He still talks funny. I can't understand him half the time."

Robiski prattled on about the new tour as she clicked link after link, absorbing what she could of Tom's career before ferrying tourists the rest of the day. She clicked onto both fan and media sites: "One of the most diverse singer-songwriters ever"; "this is what it sounds like when souls and hearts are put to words"; "a living legend"; "The Voice of Rock & Roll"; and "too humble to let rock star worshipping affect him." Then this, from a female critic: "He makes love to twenty thousand every night, and then gives you a long, tender kiss goodnight . . . night after night after twenty years of nights. Like a Catullus poem."

Catullus. His immortal description sat above her bed, her dreamcatcher, her hope of one day catching a heartful man, feeling again a lover's lilting sigh . . .

> *Da mi basia mille, deinde centum,*
> *Dein mille altera, dein secunda centum . . .*

She glanced at the computer clock. "*Mi amore,* I have to go. I am driving for Paolo today."

"Still sick?"

"*Si* . . . he worries me."

"Anything you want me to tell Tom?"

She smiled from a place she never imagined opening again. "Tell Poppa I am here. And let us talk. Soon."

18

A CRACKERBOX HALL NAMED FOR AN INCONSEQUENTIAL president seemed an unlikely spot for a generation of bands to launch legendary careers. However, the Fillmore's compact atmosphere was perfect for night after night of trance dancing, trippy light shows, and mind-bending wall projections and blobs matched only by the variety and originality of the music. The lineups were fluid, diverse, reflective of the community. Jazz trumpeter Dizzy Gillespie might join a garage band on Monday, country icon Johnny Cash could pair with Country Joe on Tuesday, The Ike & Tina Revue may shake it up with The Blue Cheer or Thirteenth Floor Elevators on Wednesday, Steve Miller and Quicksilver Messenger Service could soar into guitar nirvana on Thursday, followed by a Santana and Moby Grape on Friday night, or the Grateful Dead or Jefferson Airplane turning Saturday night on its head. It was the era of variety shows, on stage and TV alike; the San Francisco rock shows and their colorful, noisy lineups advanced that mantel like few others, with a poet, comedian, small troupe, magician, jazz musician, or mime often opening.

The Fillmore packed them in. As he looked around the refurbished hall, Tom recalled the nightly sweatbox of dancing and tripping to performances that, as the Fillmore grew teeth and Bill Graham grew power after taking Jefferson Airplane worldwide, became most local artists' best shot of getting picked up by a label. In L.A., you played the Whisky, Starwood, or Troubadour. In Nashville, it was the original home of the Grand Ole Opry, the Ryman. The City drew its next smoky breath inside the Fillmore.

Tom stood center stage, absorbing memories. Above him, chandeliers twinkled in the lights, a nod to the Fillmore's ballroom past. His eyes followed the main floor and balcony toward the cave-like walls. Favorite moments collided within, future legends mixing it up with bands that never made it but were just as good. How about the wake-up call The Cream delivered? Or Santana rolling out of the Fillmore and into one of the most famous sets ever played, at Woodstock? Or shortly before Woodstock, when The Fever first scorched the stage with "West of the West"?

Chester took the stage. "This will always be our touchstone, this and the Boston Tea Party." Tom glanced around the stage. "The others coming?"

"In a minute." Chester looked around the hall, slowly, his eyes crawling over the cozy venue like they were sluicing gold. "Damned good times, the Fillmore." He cupped his hand over his eyes, blinded by the front light bank. "You back there, Damian? Need some sound checks."

"Right here."

Chester stuck a finger in his ear and rubbed furiously. "Tell y'all right now, this ain't happenin' with the earpiece. Feels like a damned tick's in there."

"You'll get used to it," Damian said. "Saves your hearing."

"My hearing's fine."

"Maybe now, but not after plugging in night after night."

Damian started fidgeting with the soundboard buttons, knobs, and levels. The board looked like the business side of Mission Control, with enough controls to run a Mars mission. The soundman smiled sheepishly. "Earpieces and dead-sound stages are the saving grace of . . . well, your era."

Chester grumbled. "What about *feeling* it? Through my monitors?"

"We can do that, but normally, it's dead sound. Everything goes through earpieces now." Damian chuckled.

Tom tapped on the boxy fixture at his feet. "We want these wedge monitors on, man. These aren't here for show."

"Here then." Chester ripped out the earpiece and unclipped its receiver.

"OK," Damien said, nodding disagreeably, "but I'm keeping the stage volume down, to make sure you guys can still hear later on."

"I've got my life to get the ringing out of my ears," Chester said. "Crank that volume up and don't worry about us, young 'un."

"Damned punk kid," Chester grumbled as he watched Damian. "Earpiece . . ."

X leaned over his keyboards. "Hey, Damian knows his shit. I worked with him before. He's the real deal. Just looking out for you."

"And Dudley's the one who hired him," Tom said. He spotted Will and Rogelio working out a song behind the stage. "You ready? Get the singer out here."

"You are the singer."

"The other singer."

For five nights, The Fever operated on their Ridge rehearsal schedule, practicing for an hour every afternoon before playing two- to three-hour sets at night. One difference: sellout crowds saw their sets now. They ran through fifty different songs in the first four nights, switching out five numbers per shows, looking for the right sequence, the right feel and fit, the songs that would tour best. Many bands did their shuffling in rehearsals, but how do you really know what moves a crowd unless you *try moving the crowd?* Christine and Tom fine-tuned their deliveries, positions on stage and vocal combinations while allowing plenty of room for spontaneous moves and vocal runs.

Every night, the intersection of Fillmore and Geary came to life with cars, chilly latecomers, and scalpers, bartering with the passion of bazaar stall owners in Istanbul. Early crowds were decidedly older, many wearing clothes and beads dragged out of boxes, attics, or storage sheds. Or time capsules. By mid-week, younger faces became more prevalent as word got out that The Fever might not be as geriatric as their history suggested.

After each show, the band broke down the performance and further shaped their traveling show. Shaping the show was everything: You can have the best music in the world, but if the songs don't flow together smoothly, and your singer can't sync his or her personality to the band's style and music, the show fizzles. Rock history is loaded with great road bands that never broke album sales records—J. Geils and Rainbow came to mind—while some of the greatest studio bands eventually chose not to play live at all for large parts of their careers. Meet The Beatles.

With fifty songs in play, three of Christine's among them, and another twenty cuts on deck, they moved into the final Fillmore tune-up gig with a game plan: three to five song changes from one gig to another. It used to be how they toured, but in today's pre-scripted, tightly choreographed live scene, such spontaneity was far from the norm. "Fans can post set lists on their social media all they want," Tom told Christine, "but they'll never get it right."

"Not sure what the big deal is, Dad," Christine shrugged.

"When you see gigs, do you like already knowing what a band's going to play?"

"Well, I know most of the songs that are coming."

"But not all."

"No."

"Way it should be. Surprise me. Blow me away. But don't tell me."

Forty-eight hours earlier, Robiski and Megan stood amidst a checkerboard of industrial buildings that cemented South San Francisco's status as the city's oil-stained, unwashed stepbrother, the one you shyly admit to having when he shows up for Christmas dinner. Only to find out he's a success. They studied a pair of stages, the first a construction site unto itself: three-story catwalks, railings, boards, ramps, and risers, built for a band that liked to move. A projection screen stretched the entire width of the stage, with light banks jutting from shelves built to fit the amp stacks.

Foreman Fred Garrison pointed to the upper catwalk, no wider than a single-track deer trail with a railing. "Your thoughts, Jason? Mrs. Timoreaux?"

"Maybe a little more length on the runway ramp," Megan said.

"The ramp above the stage looks good," Robiski added.

"Any particular reason on the runway, ma'am?" Garrison practically barked his question.

Robiski narrowed his eyes. "You need one, Fred?"

The singer's wife and manager prevailed on that point, but both knew that Garrison understood his stages. Behind the gruff, "I'm going to poke your eyes out if you look at me wrong" face was a former Marine—infantry and proud of it—upon which dozens of new and old acts relied. His crew's fierce dedication and excellence offset their raunchy banter. "Snot, the original rubber cement," one cracked as he squeezed a tube of rubber cement dry, drawing a chuckle from Robiski while Megan pleaded for God to sprinkle some culture into the conversation. Fueled by their freely traded jokes, and a hard deadline, Garrison's team moved fast, taking less than a month on the original stage. When stadium promoters started asking for Fever dates, surprising everyone, Robiski realized he had no choice but to beef up the arena structure.

Megan worked out the adjustments visually. "Fred, I think maybe a foot wider for the catwalks, risers, and ramps, and extend the front and side ramps a few more feet."

"We can do that." That came from the other side of Garrison, the one that made him great. He might fight, bitch, and moan about a suggested change, but once he worked it out, or someone else showed him a good solution, he moved forward.

Garrison looked up at the catwalk as a worker hammered down boards, a sheen on his bare back from the effort. "Andrews, can you come down here? Bring Donatelli with you. And the blueprints." He turned to his visitors. "This is gonna cost you some seats to future shows and a little face time with the band, Robiski."

"Not a problem." Robiski shook Garrison's hand, flinched, and shook out the pain from the foreman's Master Sergeant grip. "Can you wrap this up and get on the road by late Friday night, up to Portland and loaded in for Sunday's show while my band is high-tailing after the Fillmore run?"

"Done and done. We'll work 'round the clock, but yeah. Like humping a big ridge overnight."

"Not touching that one," Megan said, hands and fingers splayed like a girl drying out wet fingernails.

Robiski pulled out his phone and checked his calendar. "Let's do six o'clock Friday night, Fred—you, your wives or dates, and the band. I'll let 'em know." Robiski whistled to gain the crew's attention. "Five hundred pieces of fresh lettuce to each of you if it's on the truck and out of here by Friday night. Three days from now."

Garrison folded his arms and addressed his crew. "And dinner. And a concert. We're invited. It'll be a big blow-out."

"You gone over any of this with Dudley yet, Fred?"

"He and a couple others came over last week and looked at everything. He's seen the blueprints, knows what they'll be working with."

Garrison smiled, revealing a few missing teeth. Robiski and Megan weren't sure if he lost them through neglect, in combat, or from a hard right in an alley brawl. "Tell you what, Robiski, Mrs. Timoreaux. When the crowd sees our stage, they won't be talking about smoke and firecrackers and other pyrotechnic shit people throw out there. They're gonna be saying, 'Now *that's* a rock stage. Built for *that* band.'"

"A couple of *that*'s make a masterpiece, yes Fred?" Megan cocked an eyebrow as she hugged Garrison, and then walked across the warehouse to the other stage. It was smaller, more intimate, adorned by velvet curtains, drapes, mirrors, and four screens for the nostalgic four-minute film they would show when the house lights went down each night. The film was down to the final cut in their Presidio studio, studio space and production time furnished by a local moviemaking mogul, a huge Fever fan. It seemed half of San Francisco was working to get the band on the road.

As Robiski caught up, a bespectacled woman with short black hair approached from a side office, her heels clicking the floor. Her left arm featured a striking half-sleeve tattoo of a mermaid, her sailor lover, and a seascape. She looked like the love child of a *Mad Men* secretary and a goth clubber. "Jason, you have a call." She held out the phone.

"No calls right now, Michelle." He glanced at the legs that once set off every siren in his body, accented further by the three-inch heels and black summer dress. She glanced over her shoulder and chuckled. When you grow up as an ugly duckling before Aphrodite furnishes your adolescence with an hourglass figure and new facial beauty, you appreciate every doting look that comes your way. But more importantly to Robiski, she thrived on the work. She had the perfect temperament. She could squeeze the last fine detail or concession out of any promoter.

Michelle's eyes opened wider than fisheye lenses, her thick eyebrows arching well over her frames. "It's Annalisa. She's pretty insistent."

She handed the phone to Robiski, her long black fingernails releasing their catch, and noticed the surprised look crossing Megan's face. "I always wondered who could tame him," Michelle said, glancing at Megan, "and now I know." She turned back to Robiski. "You two are going beyond serious, aren't you?"

"Yeah, yeah, yeah. Give me the phone. Don't we have a promoter to crunch numbers with? What about that asshole in Memphis who's been trying to get these guys for a penny?" He took the phone. "Hi baby. . . what's up?"

"*Buon giorno, mi amore.* I miss you."

"Should I give you some privacy?" Megan asked softly.

He turned the phone against his leg. "For a minute. Thanks." He pictured Annalisa on the rooftop veranda, a prosecco in hand, soaking up the sun, wearing only bikini bottoms. Something sweet and childlike about European sunbathing, respectful and innocent, minus the puritan fear of the body's innate beauty. Refreshing. "I miss you, too."

"Jason, I am sorry to bother you, but have you told my Papa yet?"

"Honey, I'm on the other side of San Francisco . . . I haven't seen him but twenty minutes this week."

"*Mi pare de capire.* I understand. But tell him soon?" He felt her edge, urgent, like a train heading into a tunnel without quite knowing what's on the other side.

"Sweetheart, as soon as I get time with him."

Megan ran her eyes over the curtains backing the smaller stage, listening more intently despite herself, her curiosity redlining. Michelle noticed the look on her face, pulled off her glasses, and walked over. "He's been a different man since he met this girl. Much happier."

"I've seen," Megan said. "He didn't party much when he was with us on the Ridge, and seemed to relax when he wasn't going over songs and mixtapes with Tom, Will and Chester . . . relaxing is new for him."

"I can get on it . . . I will get on it," Robiski said, his eyes glued to a point on the wall.

Annalisa's voice dropped. "I start to call him—and hang up. I write twenty emails—and erase all. I usually do everything by myself, but I cannot do this. It is hard."

Robiski felt like a man holding a keg of dynamite, the once lengthy fuse now a fingernail away from igniting. He heard a skepticism seeping into her voice, a dark-toned questioning bordering on hopelessness lodged deep inside, now inching out. The hopelessness of being fatherless.

"I'll take care of this right away."

"*Graci, mi amore.* I know how difficult this is."

"Let that now become my problem."

After a few loving missives, he gave the phone to Michelle. "Honey, call Tom right away. Tell him we need some time. Alone. As soon as possible." He rifled through the calendar on his smartphone. He paused for a moment, his forehead beading. "And please, no more calls until we get done here."

Michelle tapped the schedule on her phone. "They're still rehearsing."

"Text him then."

Michelle texted as she walked away, her thumbs speeding like two roadrunners zipping through a coyote bar. "Will you please tell me what's going on?" Megan asked, her tone furtive, her brain battling her heart.

Uncertainty skipped in Robiski's eyes. "I really can't before I talk to Tom."

"Maybe you should." Her voice was firm, intent.

He thought for a moment, and then nodded tentatively, her look one that would skin him before letting this slide. "Only if you agree to let me handle it. Not a word to anyone. Including your husband — until I see him first."

"That serious, Jason?"

"Oh, yeah." He paused. "We agreed?"

"I suppose, though I don't know what I'm agreeing to."

"It's a yes or no question, Megan."

She rolled her eyes. "Yes."

Jason put his arm around her shoulder. "The lady on the phone—the lady I've fallen in love with—is Tom's daughter."

Her hand flew to her hip, exasperation and relief rushing side by side. "Really?" A playful sarcasm tinged her voice. "How, when our daughter is right here and X is very much her new man?"

"His other daughter. Annalisa."

She started to respond, but the air wouldn't leave her lungs.

19

THE HOUSE LIGHTS DROPPED. THE WALK FROM THE DRESSING room apartment felt like descending a treehouse as they funneled down a thin, steep flight of creaky stairs into the corridor. They left behind a table filled with gourmet food for Fred Garrison and his exhausted but elated construction crew and their families, taking a break before hitting the road to Portland with the new stage.

Tom turned to Christine as the cheering escalated. "No matter how many years you play, you never get tired of the noise when the lights go down. What a feeling. As intoxicating as any I've known. Makes me want to turn that love and energy right back on them."

Christine eyed the paisley rug at center stage, bent over, stretched her legs, and unzipped her boots. "Goin' barefoot, sweetheart?" Chester asked.

"Whenever possible, Uncle Chester. I like to touch the earth."

He thought the little girl next to him, now a woman comfortable doing her thing, as bohemian and committed as any hippie he ever knew. "Whatever works." He looked down reverently at his boots.

"Let's do the medley, and then bring out the gang," Tom said.

"Works for me." Chester noticed a funny look in Tom's eyes, spacy, oddly distant, the look of a man separated from his moorings. "You OK, brother?"

"Fine. Let's do the medley."

Chester put his hand on Tom's shoulder and peered deeply into eyes he'd read for a half-century. "What's going on?"

"Blown away, man. Let's play, then I'll tell you."

X rubbed Christine's face, kissed her quickly, and waited for Tom and Chester. "You two talking about changing the set—already?" he asked.

Tom shook his head, trying hard to regain focus. "Get used to it. We're gonna be spontaneous, make switches on the fly. Consider this practice." He glanced into the crowd, reminding himself of what mattered for the next couple of hours. "We're going to open with our acoustic medley." He glanced at Rogelio, who was fiddling with a key on his alto sax. "Bring the orchestra with you."

"Sure you don't want to tell me what's up?" Chester asked.

"Not right now." Tom's eyes glistened. "But it's good. As good as it gets."

"Look, brother: your co-captain ain't going up till I know what's got your goat."

"We've got a crowd waiting."

"They've waited twenty years; what's another minute?"

"Fine." Tom put his hand on Chester's shoulder. "Robiski knows my daughter."

Chester glanced at Christine as she zipped through a quick sequence of yoga postures. "Well, no shit. . . the kid's lookin' like a pretzel at the moment."

"Not her. Annalisa. He knows Annalisa."

Chester nearly swallowed a cheekful of tobacco juice, his reaction much the same as Tom's a few minutes earlier.

"What do you mean, you know Annalisa?" Tom's stare nearly sheared the stubble off Robiski's face. "She's been dead forty years, more . . ."

Robiski glanced around the dressing room, really a small apartment. It was loaded with period posters, photos, and memorabilia, steeped in history and mystique. The cultural history of two generations peered from the walls, a phantom rock opera for anyone who knew the songs, the soundtrack that made the Fillmore. A posterized Jimi Hendrix looked down from center stage at Monterey, the sorcerer and his flaming guitar. "Tell me what the hell's going on," Tom said.

"Annalisa lives in Venice. Italy."

Tom grabbed his heart mid-leap and reeled in, guarding himself, not willing to risk new belief only to face more heartbreak. That is, if he didn't suffer a heart attack. Funny, how we hope beyond hope, and then, when that thing for which we hope arises, we have trouble believing it. "C'mon, Jason. Italy's full of Annalisas . . ."

Robiski took a deep breath. "How many Annalisas were born in San Francisco around the time of the summer of love and have a grandfather who probably was around to make shoes for Vivaldi?"

"Maurizio?" One of the nicest, most loving men he'd ever known. "I don't get it. I was told she was dead . . ."

"Far from it."

"When Megan and I went over to look for her, five or six years in a row while she still would have been a girl, and then a couple times after, we didn't find Annalisas in town registries for Verona or Padua, where Maria is from. I couldn't find Maurizio, either; he would've pointed me in the right direction. So I had to assume Maria was right, she was gone . . .

"Well, *this* Annalisa favors you, tall, same eyes." Robiski glanced toward the kitchen, where Christine rubbed X's shoulders with one hand while sipping an energy drink. "Her hair is darker. The Italian in her."

Tom stared ahead, frozen. Here it was, sudden as a sneak attack, the news he wanted to believe, and poured forty years of life into hoping. Then burying. Then hoping against hope. Then burying again, so he wouldn't lose the other daughter.

Megan walked into the room and sat next to Tom. "Jason, you're sure . . ." she said, leaving no hint of his earlier revelation.

Robiski saw the protective way she clasped Tom's hand. "Very." He blinked. "I'm seeing her. Have been for around eight months."

Tom's eyes sharpened. "You're *seeing her*?" His mind whirled in foggy bewilderment. "How did you not know the second you met her?"

"Why would I know? Why would it enter my mind? Why would I even consider it as a possibility?" Robiski spoke softly. "My dad told me a long time ago what you thought you knew—that she was dead. Why would I make the connection? Even though, now that we know, I laugh at myself over why I *didn't* see a few things?"

"When did you begin to wonder, Jason?" Megan asked.

"When we were talking about how she dreamed of going to California, not too long ago, and she told me she couldn't wait to get *back*. Then she told me about her first few years, what she remembered of them."

"And her? What does she know?"

"That you're alive and well. She watched the streamcast the other day. She knows some of your songs, has for years, but she'd never connected them with you. How could she? She was in the same boat as you. She thought you were gone, too."

Tom shook his head. "I don't know, man. Anyone could know Google me and see. . . people take advantage. It happens."

"No bullshit here," Robiski said. "We're not talking about a third cousin twice removed, digging for gold. She's your kid, sure as we're talking in St. Francis' blessed city, and now that she knows, is driving me bonkers trying to connect with you."

"She wants to talk? I mean . . . I haven't been a father to her since—"

"The only malice she feels is toward her mother—and, soon, me, if I don't put you in touch."

Robiski looked at the wall clock, a timepiece built into the belly of a red Stratocaster, its twelve-hour symbols logos of classic Fillmore house bands. "Time to get on stage." He took Megan's hand, and then Tom's. "Reach out to her. Soon."

Tom ground his teeth over the surging tidal wave that, instead of punching his heart and gut for the thousandth time, released a joy he had wished for, over and over, until it seemed pointless to wish anymore. It felt like two tidal flows colliding, the dark tide finally receding, something new and light and powerful rushing in its place. He wanted to rush to the bathroom. He peeled off his headband and wiped his eyes. "OK, how do I see her? You've got us scheduled for months."

"We can make something happen." Robiski scribbled her phone number and email address. "She wants this as much as you, Tom."

Tom looked at the number. There it was, twelve digits, a number he'd spent four decades trying to find.

How am I going to play?

Christine tied a jewel-studded waist scarf Daphne had overnighted, part of the wardrobe she was assembling: spicy dresses, skirts, tops, scarves, and belts procured from San Francisco vintage stores with Megan and Trish, who flew up for the first three Fillmore gigs before scooting back to L.A. to start her own career as a costume designer for a film studio. "What were you guys talking about up there?"

"You didn't hear from the kitchen?" Robiski asked.

"Nooo . . ."

"Amazing; I thought we were loud."

She rolled her eyes. "You were whispering, eyes all over the place, like amateur spies trying to look cool while sharing intel. Or old people keeping it from the kids."

"I can't tell you. Your dad will. He needs you on stage now."

She cocked her hip. "Jason?" Her fingers tapped her hipbones.

Stubborn as the old man. "Not my place, Christine. Talk to your dad."

While Christine waited, her curiosity piqued, an old anger simmered—*Dad's holding another fucking secret, right when we're getting right!* The Fever founders took the stage to concussive applause as she tried to fight off the deep burn inside. "We used to play here, a hundred years and a couple thousand light shows ago . . ." Tom began.

"I remember!" a woman screamed.

"Glad you do, sugar!" Chester replied to more cheers. He glanced at the others, he alone knowing the reason Tom was pacing too frenetically to settle into their soft set. He and Will nodded at each other, and put their acoustic guitars in the racks. "We're gonna scratch the Kumbaya circle and rock you all night long," Chester told the fans.

He grabbed his guitar, pointed it skyward, and cracked his first volley. X swept his hands and arms across his keyboards like an octopus on a feeding frenzy, the latest to benefit from Athenian engineer Ctesibius, who invented the organ around the time Buddha was finding enlightenment in Bodhgaya. Chester kept pace, flashing to the summer night when Carlos Santana and Michael Shrieve first played "Soul Sacrifice," Woodstock's most famous guitar-percussion speed trap and drum solo. He strummed while X drew notes from his Hammond B3 so sweet they seeped into your marrow.

Fans danced where they stood, the only way to move on the packed floor. Tom strummed along, wondering how he was going to tell Christine, how the news would affect her. How do you tell someone whose long-dead sister was very much alive and in contact?

After X finished, Tom and Christine strutted to center stage, Christine bouncing five feet from the front row guests. She twirled as Tom swayed back and forth, he matching X's keyboard flights note for note on guitar, she running up and down the tune's three-octave range. She danced across stage in loops, naturally and playfully, every boy and man in the house eye-mapping her legs, her face, her moves.

> *Give her a twirl*
> *Make her your girl*
> *Throw down your soul*
> *Rock and rolllll!*

Chester's solo cut the crowd loose. Women bounced on men's shoulders while their sons or grandsons played air guitars. Rogelio rode counterpoint behind Will's steady time keeping, his runs and fills pure medieval lightning as he pranced back and forth. X handled high melody, allowing Rogelio to duel Chester with devilish licks while Tom grounded the riff, a unique twist where the guitarist anchors the bass player. His vocals were crisp and sure, often ceding the high road to Christine. He knew he sounded good because of how pure the music felt leaving his mouth. And because he pictured himself singing directly to Annalisa through the eyes of the infatuated women in the front rows.

After they took "Party on the Streets" home, Tom leaned over. "For the rest of tonight, and every other night, Christine, keep doing what you're doing." He kissed her on the cheek and motioned to Dudley, crouched alongside Will. He pointed to the backline stand-up mic, and pointed backstage. *She'd be up front the rest of the tour.*

Three hours and two encores later, the crowd still refused to release them. "We gotta go," Robiski said as Tom and Chester stood at the base of the stage stairs, contemplating. "The kids have a flash gig. The one Christine lined up. Remember?"

"A flash gig?" Chester asked. "Where?"

"The New Mnasidika. Down in the Mission."

The gig was spontaneously arranged during Christine's radio interview with Tonya Lee, the city's edgiest and most popular disc jockey. "It's nice to see a city that still has rock jocks," Tom said before dispatching her. "You could always count on them to spin your records and interview you when you came to town."

The originally brief interview mushroomed into two lively hours, with callers asking questions and Tonya going commercial-free the final half hour due to call volume. They covered the band's history, her background, and her thoughts about touring with a legendary father. "I know he's legendary, right? But he's my dad, same way on stage as off stage, although he directs me around a lot more on stage. I'm starting to feel and see how he's put the music together, where he goes to find all that excellence so many people have listened to."

"Where does he go?"

"A lot further in practice, and won't let go until it's the way he first heard it in his head . . . he hasn't slept much during rehearsals."

"He's done you an incredible solid by bringing you on tour," Tonya said.

"I didn't think that at first—I was the last-second substitute for Raylene Quarles, and you can't *really* substitute for Aunt Raylene—but yes, my dad has given me something I've decided to ride out to the max."

Tonya leaned over and stroked Christine's shoulder. "Speaking of which, I heard you, X, and Rogelio have been working your songs, on your own?"

"We have . . . where did you find that out?"

"Sources," Tonya chuckled. Then, into the live mic, she added, "How about a flash concert, one late night this week, The New Mnasidika? The three of you."

"I don't see how we can . . ."

"You've got the best road manager in Dudley. He'll sort you out."

As Christine replayed the conversation, Dudley and his roadies waited impatiently to load a minimal setup into a van coughing exhaust in the alley. Seconds later, Tom and Chester nodded at each other, Christine followed them onstage, and encore number three broke into an all-out jam, the group blowing away the delirious crowd with "West of the West," fronted by the dervish who sang her lungs out, her eyes gleaming from sparkly makeup and endless adrenaline.

Finally, the show had to end. "Good night!" she yelled, blowing kisses.

"Thank you for making this a great week for us," Tom shouted. "We look forward to coming back home in a few months."

Christine, X, and Rogelio raced upstairs to change while Dudley's crew packed. A half hour later, Dudley dispatched them crosstown, their driver the only person he knew crazy enough to make the twenty-minute ride on the roller-coaster streets in ten: his ex-wife. As motorists brandished middle fingers and wondered who escaped the cuckoo's nest, she sped by them, eighteen again, Neal Cassady driving Sal, Marylou, Carlo and the others on the road, or busing the Ken Kesey and his Merry Pranksters, loving every bit of the adventure.

When they arrived, Tonya wrapped her arms around Christine like they were besties. "You made it!"

"We're so stoked to be here! Sorry we're late."

Tonya nodded. "I think half the people here were at your show—or claimed they were. You guys were awesome! You're the stars of the city; everybody's talking about how fucking hot you guys are."

"Well, it's kind of my dad's hometown. Where he started."

Tonya glanced at Christine from bow to stern. Thanks to clubbing, mixed with feminine instinct and a brief experimental phase, Christine knew that look. While the thought was intriguing and Tonya adorable in a Goth way, it wasn't how she rolled . . . but beneath her angry militant, anarchist exterior, Tonya *was* the bomb.

While Christine introduced Tonya to Rogelio and X, Dudley caught up to his crew and walked inside with a monitor. He and the roadies launched into overdrive.

Soon, the world's newest trio took the stage. Fans crunched together up front, ready to unleash the steam from another week of punching someone else's time clock and enduring whatever grief came along with that. More people streamed inside, packing the club. The maximum number allowable by fire code came and passed like a minor suggestion. It was a coup for The New Mnasidika.

"Hello, everyone!" Christine gazed at the sea of faces, but the hairstyles caught her attention. They were across-the-board wild, West Hollywood and Venice wild, from peacock tails to purple mohawks, faux-hawks, shaved necks and sides of heads, and men with chest-length corn rows or USB code neck tattoos beneath their shaved heads. Colorful inks and piercings covered all parts of their bodies. They swayed back and forth in front of her, melting into each other, becoming a single organism.

She shook her hair out. Rogelio tuned a guitar while X fiddled with his barebones electric piano and bass organ setup. The rest of their gear was already crossing the Golden Gate Bridge, en route to Portland. "We've already played once tonight," Christine yelled, to cheers, "but Tonya asked us to come by."

Christine peeled off her scarf, revealing a spaghetti-strapped dress that clung to her lean torso and small, shapely breasts like a long-held breath.

As X and Rogelio kicked in, Chester, Tom, Will, Megan, and Chandra found the last reserved booth and slid inside, drawing annoyed stares from a half-dozen younger patrons who didn't like watching entitled people waltz into a booth, not after they'd waited an hour to get in, and another hour for the band, all while standing.

Christine worked all corners of the stage, leaning into the audience, delivering the tunes, dancing when she wasn't singing, her voice potent but scratchy. She pranced back and forth, rapping with the audience between numbers, holding court, the churned-up smoke in the room billowing around her, rising some more.

At the back table, Megan clasped her hands beneath her chin and beamed, a proud mother's smile. Tom leaned forward, hands on cheeks, jubilant that *both* daughters were alive. He closed his eyes as Christine covered a Pretenders classic with perfect pitch and bite. As the lyrics suggested, she was quickly becoming the talk of the town.

She finished to rousing cheers, and gazed at the crowd while catching her breath. "Want one more song?" She grabbed a towel from side stage, wiped her face, pushed her hair to one side and started twirling it.

"I love you! Come home with me! I love you! Come home with me!" a man screamed, over and over.

Christine stepped back. X eyed the man, his shaven dome half-covered by a tattoo of a hand palming a "basketball" . . . his head. The man leaned aggressively toward the stage. Christine turned and kissed X flush on the lips, making sure tattoo man saw every bit of it. "Keep your feet off the edge, baby," X told her. "Dude's off the reservation."

The man pounded his fist where Christine had stood seconds before. Two security guards roughly half the size of the Transatlantic Building dragged him off. "Thanks, boys!" Christine smiled broadly. "Girls, those bouncers hot, or what?"

Screams, whistles and cheers followed. "Before we wrap it up, ladies and gentlemen, let's give it up for Tonya—thank you for having us! You rock, girl!" She blew a kiss toward the hostess, who acknowledged Christine and the crowd before resuming an intense conversation in the back. Then they began.

Christine conceived "Holy Child Blues" in Tompkins Park, where poets like Allen Ginsberg and anarchists like Ed Sanders, the renowned poet, Fugs frontman, and raconteur, mimeographed chapbooks and broadsides to incite, inform, reveal or suggest. Pretty much the way education and street literature in the U.S. used to be. She thought of Gini, the girl, feeling her pain in her voice:

> *They say you're a menace to society*
> *A subject full of rage,*
> *You barely reach the judge's chest*
> *They're jailing you today*
> *For making a very big mistake*
> *How could you ever know?*
> *Your momma's sick, your daddy's dead*
> *You sold a little blow*
> *To feed yourself, to clothe your sis*
> *Your intentions all so pure*
> *For inside that twisted angry mask*
> *A soul shines bright and pure*

Rogelio and X held chords and notes until they started to snap from the tension, footsteps to an execution.

> *You're a holy child, brave holy child*
> *The new light of this age,*
> *Oh holy child, brave holy child,*
> *Just learn to trust your sacred heart,*
> *You'll find a whole new start*

Christine dropped her head as X slowly wound down the keyboard fill. The shocked applause told the story of a song that dotted you between the eyes.

While smacking his hands together, Chester turned to Tom. "That little girl is something very, very special. You can't teach that. One of these days, I'm gonna be saying, 'I knew her when she was a little girl just starting out.'"

Tom shook his head as he clapped. "Me, too. I had no idea."

"None of us did. But now we do."

Thirty minutes later, a still sweaty Christine stared at Tom slack-jawed, mascara seeping down her face. She sipped her beer slowly. Behind her, Dudley and his roadies tore down the skeletal setup, which his ex-wife offered to drive to

Portland; she'd always wanted to see Portland. When she popped in like this, after being invisible for months, he obliged her, enjoyed her company. . . but she'd head off again, her way of rekindling her gypsy past now that the boys had finished school. He'd long ago accepted her spirit for what it was—the same spirit that drove him on the road. He'd made the supreme sacrifice, leaving family to work on The Fever's tours, like she was doing in a way now.

Christine sat on the lip of the stage, swinging her legs back and forth like a child on a swing. "You're sure it's her, Dad? You talk to her?"

"No, but I will."

"Wow." Her eyes welled up. "I'm totally blown away. . . and she's been alive all along." She paused for a moment, shaking her head, sniffling. "Not to be a bitch or anything, Dad, but she couldn't let you know where she was during, like, the last forty years?"

He patted her hand, then squeezed it. "Honey, she was told I was dead. Just as I was told about her." He patted again, trying to find comfort, stripped to a naked nerve every time he thought about Maria's diabolical sleight of hand. It ran through his head, over and over, a hamster on a wheel: *I was told she's dead.*

Christine kissed his hand. "Well, Dad, I'm um . . . like, if it really is her, then I'm *so* happy for you."

She looked up, spotted Tonya, and held up her fingers. *Ten minutes.* She turned to Tom and faced the new thought of this phantom sister as a living, breathing being. "How you find all this out?"

"Robiski."

"How would he know?"

"Through some weird cosmic joke, he's her boyfriend."

"What?"

"Why he's been in Venice."

"Too weird." She pressed her palms toward the ground, arms locked, and pushed herself up. "Bat-shit weird."

20

"Annalisa?"

"*Si?*"

"This is . . . Tom. Your father."

A gasp. Silence, cocooned in forty years of time and space. "Hello?"

Sobs. "I do not know what to say . . . Papa . . ."

Papa. How deeply he had missed that sweetest of nicknames! *The nightmare without an end has just ended.* "How are you, Annalisa?"

"Wonderful. Now I am wonderful." She sniffled, went silent, composed herself. "I have wondered many times about you, but I am told you are . . ."

"So was I. I was told the same. Jason told me you watched our concert."

"*Si.* I saw you, and knew it was you." A nervous chuckle, tinged with sobs.

Tom held his breath, not a tough chore, since no air was seeping in or out. A million words fought on his tongue for release like agitated hornets. "Annalisa, not for one day did I stop thinking about you."

"*Miracolo.* I remember how much you loved me, Papa."

There it was again. Papa. *Pah-pah.* Her quiet tone, heavily accented, beautiful. He closed his eyes and returned to merry go-rounds and swings, below the stars and sky-high eucalyptus trees that opened radiantly to a father and his adoring daughter. "I have tried to find you, despite what your mother said."

"Mama told me the same. I never wanted to believe her, but when I never see you . . ."

"Let's not talk about her."

"I have nothing else to say about her," Annalisa said, "but I like your music very much. I remember you singing in the park, telling me stories. You always sing."

"Two of my favorite things to do."

"I liked your songs. My friends and I listened in school to the ones that get on our hits station, but I do not know it was you. My Paolo loved them when he was very young." A deep sigh.

He held the phone from his ear. "Paolo . . . my grandson?"

"*Si.*"

"How old?"

"*Ventiquattro.*"

'Twenty-four. Same as Christine."

Tom stared through the window, caught in a time bubble, talking to the middle-aged Annalisa while picturing her at five. "Now I know why these songs feel so good inside me," she continued., and then sighed. "It is a very bad thing, keeping a little girl away from her Papa."

More streetlights faded out in North Beach, replaced by morning light. Night owls, bar closers, city vampires, and lingering ghosts from the earthquakes and shipwrecks that rattled the city's bones finally called it quits. He rubbed his burning eyes. "I would like to visit, but we just started a tour."

"I know, Papa. My man is with you, remember?"

"How can I forget?" Tom marbled his next words on his tongue until he felt comfortable enough to release them. "Would you *like* to see us?"

"Very much, Papa, but something else . . ."

"Yes?"

"My Paolo has been sick, so I must make sure he is OK."

"Megan—my wife—and I can fly over when the tour ends."

"*Si.* So we will see each other."

A few minutes later, they hung up. The city swam in front of him, the buildings swaying and shapeshifting as though the San Andreas Fault was open for business. Their forms puddled and then ran down his cheeks.

21

PORTLAND . . . SEATTLE . . . VANCOUVER . . . SPOKANE . . . BOISE

TOM SUBMERGED INTO HUNDRED-DEGREE WATER THAT LAST felt the sun when Pliocene horses roamed Southern Idaho. He popped up between Megan's arms, the sun on his back, the water beading into tiny, phosphorescent bubbles on his chest. His muscles ached. His body ached. Five shows into the tour, and he could already feel it. What a difference a couple of decades makes. Three hours of rocking was enough, but to keep up with Christine? Rock and roll was never intended for anyone over, say, twenty-five; yet, here he was, deep in a hot spring, soaking out the aches and pains of playing a young person's game.

While halfway to Twin Falls after knocking the crowd dead on the blue turf of Boise State's football stadium, they stopped the caravan of buses and rental trucks. All twenty private pools quickly filled with musicians and roadies, their clothes tossed aside. You didn't have to tell this group twice. "Good move, honey," Megan said. "Close your eyes, let these minerals soak you, settle in."

She swept behind him, pressed her hips against the base of his spine, and rubbed his shoulders and lower back. He melted into her touch while rewinding the past ten days: visits from old friends, drop-in at after-hours "flash shows" at old haunts in Portland and Seattle, the Fillmore run that tightened them up . . . and the shocking news that trumped it all from halfway around the world. He had to admit it: they were playing tighter and more solidly than anticipated. Especially with three new faces.

They'd come close to nailing a perfect show in Seattle. Not bad for the second official concert of the summer. A few missed notes, a broken guitar string, and a tech's mistaken handoff of a detuned guitar to Chester messed up an otherwise spotless night. Twenty thousand screaming fans never noticed the little flaws. They were too busy bouncing up and down, dancing in the rafters, playing air guitar ferociously, singing until their throats ached. While Chester later gnawed on his tech like a chew toy for the slip-up, the audience headed home, their heads and hearts filled. Isn't that what mattered?

He slid further into the pool.

Megan kissed his ear. "My turn."

They switched places. Tom delivered her favorite hot springs massage, a full frontal, from the tips of her toes to the top of her head, moving slowly to all points in between, touching her with his fingertips, his sweeping hands, and finally his mouth. They slid under the water, only their noses, eyes and foreheads showing, the sight positively amphibious, her massage just getting started.

"Wade, you crazy-ass river running rock climbing fool!"

"Good to see you haven't rolled your kayak and killed yourself in those waves out there," Wade said, jabbing Will in the ribs and wrapping him in a bear hug. "Or getting mistaken for a seal sandwich by the great whites."

"Speak for yourself." Will turned to X and Christine, walking arm-in-arm up a dirt driveway shaded by a half-dozen massive cottonwoods. "This is the craziest man in a kayak you'll ever meet. One of the best I've ever ridden with, too."

Wade and Will had met on a Salmon River run. While staying in adjoining campgrounds, and after following each other's artistic exploits for years, they proclaimed themselves brothers from different wombs. During his ascension as Idaho's literary sensation, Wade made words bend, stretch, blossom, and tingle like Waterford crystal tapped by a feather. He and Will even resembled each other: sandy gray-blond hair, tanned, rugged outdoor faces, and lean, sinewy arms that steered them out of more holes, whirlpools, Class 5 rapids, chutes, flumes, and obstructions than either could count.

"Beginning to think you guys might not show," Wade said. "I'm sure you all found some fun on the open road, or in your case—" he glanced at Christine "—fending off half the men in the Western States."

Christine liked him already. He was brash, sassy, an outdoorsman . . . a brainy outdoorsman, too. What could be more appealing?

Wade poked at Will's shoulder as Rogelio walked up. "See those three young ladies over there?" A trio dressed in miniskirts and tight tops, all around thirty, all drop-dead gorgeous, leaned on his stoop amidst a small throng streaming out the door, curious about the commotion. "Two are mine; the other is their friend. So you know."

As Rogelio considered the not-too-subtle warning, Tom and Chester walked up with Megan and Chandra and embraced Regina. She dragged a case of beer out of the root cellar, the toils of being Wade's wife on party day. Chester looked over Regina's shoulder, to the masses milling at the door. "What the hell, Wade. Invite the cavalry?"

"You've shown up at my summer solstice party. My colleagues and former students in Boise called me all day today, raving about you guys. So now that you're here, what was it like playing on that eyesore of a football field?"

"Done a lot of things, Wade, I have." Chester sucked on the tobacco wad buried in his cheek. "But not play on a blue field. Cross that off the bucket list."

"Makes a great landing pad for aliens. Astronauts on the space station can probably see the damned thing."

Regina rolled her deep-set, fetching blue eyes, certain that Wade was about to launch into one of his weird tangents. "Only you would come up with that one." She turned to Megan and Chandra, and took their hands. "Writers and the bizarre connections they make . . . let's get you something to drink, and leave these silverbacks to scratch and sniff. So good to see you." She noticed Christine, who clung to X's arm, and squeezed Megan's hand. "You must be the proudest mother around."

"Besides you." Megan walked up to the porch and introduced herself to Regina's daughters, Karen and Samira.

In the yard, Wade turned to his guests. "I don't know what's going to happen tonight, but it's going to happen. These solstice shindigs can be as unpredictable as your third date."

"Don't you mean first date?" one of the men asked.

"Most predictable outcome there is, Dale . . . you're takin' her home and saying goodnight and hoping she picks up the phone next time you call, sharpshooter." He looked at the others. "As I was saying, have a good time."

Within an hour, another twenty people turned up, among them Jack Walden, just back from a three-month dig in Guatemala and Belize. "My idea of digging in the sandbox," he told Christine while regaling her with stories of Mayan royalty. In one hand, he held a glass hummingbird. In the other, he clasped a wooden flute, or huge straw. "This is an Amazon blow dart shooter. We'll try it later."

Will walked up, shaking his head and laughing. "Already boring the guests, Walden?" He turned to Christine. "Honey, gophers like Walden sometimes play in the dirt too long. There's a turning point . . ."

"Helping the world gain historical perspective and a sense of our long-held wisdom while these pricks try to keep ancient civilization out of school curricula and act like we started when a white-bearded dude flipped a switch a few thousand years ago," Walden said, eyeing the blow dart shooter. "Just like the assholes who say there's no climate or greenhouse gas issue. I'd say we gophers have a more important mission than ever: to thwart these deniers and give our kids some air and truth to breathe."

Music twanged loudly from the back corner. "Grab a beer and listen in!" Wade yelled, cranking up the volume and stomping around the room, spinning every woman he passed as though they belonged to his private square dance troupe. The song crackled and popped on the turntable like a cranky grandfather, the needle hitting every tiny scratch and pit. Chester heard a vaguely familiar voice. "Damn, Wade, it's good to hear some vinyl," he said. "Haven't had the pleasure in a couple months. Damned kids don't know how to listen to an album, cover to cover. Everything's a songlist or a shuffle."

"Where did kids come into it?" Wade asked. "Just enjoy the song."

Wade lifted his growler, a four-pint jug, which he produced after Regina insisted he limit himself to two beers for the sake of civility. *Fine.* He grabbed the growlers, met her fixed stare, and said, "You said two beers. One, two." She swatted him away like a petulant mosquito.

"Who's singing this song, everyone?" Wade turned to Chester and his wall-to-wall grin. "Chester?"

"Song was first played by WLS radio at the National Barn Dance, out of Chicago. About the time country was getting going, Jimmie Rodgers and Bob Wills and those boys." Chester glanced sideways at Wade. "Where the hell you get this?"

Wade chuckled. "You're done, Chester. Enough clues. Anyone know?"

Guests started shooting at fish. "Hoot Gibson?" "Hank Williams Senior?" "Roy Rogers? Old man Carter before he started the family? Has to be Roy Rogers."

"Wrong. Wrong. In the right direction, though."

The singer clip-clopped along, riding above a box canyon and onto a high mesa, guarding wagon trains filled with settlers, trunks, and provisions. He and the song rode into the final fading notes as Wade raised his bottle. "Bottom's up for Gene Autry. That's sometime around 1915, before he became the singing cowboy."

"No shit? Where'd you get it?" Tom asked.

"Library of Congress recording."

"Let me show you boys something else." Wade led Tom, Chester, and Will into his office, where the walls portrayed three men—a family man, a kayaker, and a poet. They all had the same face. Wade pointed to two large photos, newly framed and mounted, one of he and a younger man kayaking between two solid walls of white. In the other, he was careening down a forty-foot waterfall by bouncing off a side boulder. "You're nuttier than an stoned squirrel," Chester said.

Wade pointed to a broadside, framed next to the waterfall photo. Chandra walked up, grabbed Chester's hand, and read. It spoke of roses, sun, eyes, and other landscapes observed by the depth of love. She sighed deeply, leaned slightly away from Chester while still holding his hand, and hooked Wade's arm. "If anything ever happens between you and Regina, will you call me? I'll be right here. Chester or not." She kissed his cheek. "That might be the most beautiful love poem I've ever read from a living person."

Chester saw the fawning look on Chandra's face. "How am I supposed to top that? I'm just a guitar player."

"Play a solo just for me. Slow and sweet. In bed." Chandra released Wade's arm, slapped Chester's butt, and studied the pictures on the wall, unfamiliar with the ribbon of blue between two snowfields. Cold, foreboding. "Is that anywhere on this planet?" Wade hooked his growler and guarded it like smooth gin dragged out of a speakeasy. "Ah, my dear, we were having such a romantic moment . . . and the moment's gone." He pointed to the pictures. "My son and I kayaked in Greenland last year."

"Greenland." Chandra folded her arms, tucking them into her chest tightly.

"That's right. We kayaked in the fjords, found a couple of rivers, and floated down those. First time we could do that; all the melting ice opened it up."

"Colder'n a cadaver in a meat locker, I imagine," Chester said.

"Well, you don't want to roll your kayak, that's for sure." Wade looked up, his eyes dancing like celebrating leprechauns. "Let's get inside before someone tries to burn down my house."

They walked into quite a spectacle. Wade's two daughters and their friend were stretched across a Twister mat, arms and limbs intertwined with Rogelio's, planting hands and feet on the colors they'd just spun. The ladies laughed uproariously, one so hard she keeled over. She glanced over, found the spinner, flicked it again. "Red! Find the red, Rogelio! Samira! Deena! Karen—wait—that's me! Hahahaha!"

"Boy didn't get the memo," Wade chuckled.

Chandra shook her head. "Wade, Wade, Wade. You need to see it from their point of view. They're entangling limbs with a gorgeous guy, one of the best musicians you'll ever see . . ."

"That's the problem. Musicians."

". . . and totally harmless." She watched the human pretzels, how they moved in almost nothing, flexible and self-assured, her envy of once upon a time being *that* girl rising. She chuckled. "What a blast."

They crawled above, below and through each other, a tidal sea of limbs that constantly seemed to wrap around Rogelio. When he changed position, the leg-and-arm Hydra grabbed him, then made him the prize in a tug-of-war of sorts. "Mine!"

"Yeah right, honey!"

"See your name branded on his ass? Nooooo . . ."

"Can I see it?"

"Get your hands off *my man!*"

Wade glanced at Regina, her glare both light and challenging. "Things a dad don't need to see . . . over *your* bass player. I give up. I'm getting a beer."

"Just a hired gun," Chester said, winking at Chandra.

"You're done, Wade" Regina said, her face smiling more than her eyes.

"Only had one. Getting the other."

As he walked away, Regina turned to Chandra and Chester. "I don't want to be a bitch, especially at his party, but he's supposed to be watching it. Health reasons. He bruised his liver and kidneys a few months ago in a kayak accident, they're not healed, and alcohol doesn't help. Plus, he needs to think about slowing down."

Wade returned, tilted back the growler, and began draining its sixty-four ounces. Regina grew quiet, but flashed a subtle warning, a glint, imperceptible to all but the man who shared this silent language with her.

Then came a loud crash, followed by uproarious laughter. The Twister players collapsed on the mat, one at a time, the girls first, then the final domino, Rogelio. They looked at each other and laughed harder. The women carried on, rubbing Rogelio, their legs visible from hips to toenails. They drew closer, gazing long and hard at specific circles, specific colors, Karen and Samira whispering what two sisters could do to Rogelio, Deena giggling at the sight of her own wiggling toes.

Regina shook her head. "What is with you girls?"

Karen looked up, then turned to Deena. "If only she knew . . ."

"What?" Rogelio whispered.

"Acid. Really sweet acid," Deena said, kissing his lips flush.

After holding her kiss for a few seconds—it felt so good to be kissed again—Rogelio shook his head in disbelief. "You for real, ladies?"

They looked at each other and laughed. "OK."

"Watch out!"

Rogelio jumped. "What the hell?" Women and prey scrambled to their feet. "You're joking, right?"

"No joke at all, son." Jack Walden stood in the dining room, a flute-shaped blow dart shooter in his mouth. Fifteen feet away, Wade loaded. A dozen people assessed their escape plan as quickly as the inebriated can think and move. Wade used Chester for cover, popped out to his side, and smacked Walden with a small dart. Walden then blew a dart Wade's way, only to hit

Chester in the stomach. "That dart got that yellow frog poison on it, and you're dead!" Chester yelled, wagging his fist.

"I think *you'd* be dead," Walden said. He laughed and re-loaded.

They exchanged another round before Walden dipped into a back room and rolled out the heavy artillery—an eight-foot-long blower. For the next ten minutes, Walden and Wade used guests as human shields. "I pray I will wake up one morning and see an adult lying in bed next to me," Regina said. "It's been a longsuffering prayer."

"I know the feeling," Chandra said.

Long after midnight, Rogelio stumbled toward one of the guest rooms, following voices, quiet voices. He knocked, unsure of what or whom he would find, all possibilities open with the three amigas prowling the house, but wanting more than anything else an empty bed and a few hours of sleep. "Hey, it's Rogelio."

"Come in." X and Christine lay across the bed, comfortable in shorts and shirts, notebooks and sheet music strewn across the comforter, one of Christine's legs over X.

"You guys tired or something? You're missing an incredible party."

"We weren't into it," Christine said. "We've been playing around with lyrics and poems in my notebooks, seeing if there's anything we can work out . . . interested?"

Rogelio sat at the edge of the bed. "Always."

She grabbed her notebook, quickly read over the words, and turned to X. "I'll sing this one so you can see what we need to do to it."

She turned to Rogelio, leaned forward, and rubbed his back. "Have fun out there? Looked like those girls were having fun with you, dude. Twister mats . . ."

Rogelio glanced toward the other rooms, wondering if the women who fancied themselves as his maenads had fallen asleep, the only way to guarantee meaningful rest. "So you've been working out songs all night? Why didn't you come rescue me?"

"I didn't know you wanted or needed to be rescued." Christine noticed his tussled hair. "Mom came in and said you were *accounted for.* Who among the eligible wants to be rescued from that?" She chuckled and turned to X. "Think he'll sleep?"

X shook his head as he laughed. "Unless you sleep outside, dude, you're their play toy. Prey. Their mouse."

Their laughter trailed Rogelio as he loped back to his room, not bothering to turn on the light, not making a sound, yearning to tiptoe directly into a sound sleep.

No such luck. As he plopped on the bed, he felt something solid. Legs. A body. Nothing on.

No sleep.

22

SALT LAKE CITY . . . DENVER . . . TOPEKA . . . KANSAS CITY . . .
OMAHA . . . DES MOINES . . . CHICAGO

X LAY OVER CHRISTINE'S CURLED LEGS, FORMING A SOLID LAP desk as her fingers raced along the tiny tablet keyboard, firing off stories and prompts for the publicists to broadcast to the blogosphere. Once finished, she updated her corner of the website, and sent snapchats and Instagram messages of another flash concert with X and Rogelio. The New Mnaidiska had started something; they'd already added flash gigs in Portland, Spokane, and coming up, Chicago. For good measure, Robiski set up an acoustic Chicago gig just as quickly for Will, Chester, and Tom at the venerable Park West.

Tom watched her work while nursing a long-necked beverage of champions, a futile hair-of-the-dog effort following the after-show party in Des Moines that became a sunrise serenade. Megan curled against him, long gone in dreamless sleep. One cornfield after another raced past their souped-up RVs, leaving Christine to think not about waves of grain and the simple, hard-working greatness of rural America, but about shopping for the flash concert with Chandra and Megan when they rolled into town.

She glanced at Tom, smiled, and noticed the looks on her parents' faces, as illumined by love as she could remember. Tom's face glowed palpably, a glow that, essentially for the first time in his adulthood, was free of the pain of a loss that she couldn't begin to fathom. What do you do when you're suddenly liberated from a malignant force that burrowed into your bosom against the natural order of things? How do you mourn for so long only to learn your lost, dead child is neither of the above? She sighed. Annalisa . . . with Robiski. It was as weird as the most twisted reality show plot ever. . . but it was their reality.

Hopefully, this wouldn't change a thing. *Their* thing. The new thing where they talked openly almost every day, then got on stage and sang and danced together for three hours unless he had to "play some guitar"—which, she soon realized, was code for "breathe."

She chuckled to herself while rubbing X's smooth, hairless head as she looked at her screen, determined to get the messaging done before laying shopper's siege to the Windy City. Michelle would expect them when she opened Robiski's office. She was lightning fast, and just as efficient. Also a blast, as Christine found out when she and X partied with Michelle and her boyfriend, Lance, after the New Mnaidiskas gig, the four finally stumbling into Michelle's flat the next morning before all of them caught a midday flight to Portland in time for an evening soundcheck. Michelle had offered to ghostwrite the blogs, but Christine wanted fans to see their front-row seats from her eyes. She refocused, calling on the lords of discipline forged by countless 3 a.m. term paper scrambles, and more recently, lyric-writing sessions. She pecked away:

> *Dad & Chester have this thing about pulling up in small towns; it's more Chester than Dad. He loves hanging with country peeps—"Salt of the earth, little girl. They feed you." Uhhh . . . OK. When the bus pulled into Hays (where they filmed part of* Dances With Wolves, *one of my favorite old movies), people saw us walk into a café & invited us to pile in behind them and drive to a huge community picnic. Soon Dad, Chester, and Will were playing where buffalo used to stampede, while the rest of us are like "WTF?!" You can still see wagon wheel tracks in the hills, from when pioneers headed west and sang their gospels and campfire songs. We stuffed our faces big-time. Awesome barbecue, truck food, lots of nice people, the kind of nice where they will do anything for you, but never ask anything for it, the kind of nice that never seems to find its way to the city)—*
>
> *Dad, Chester, and Will are giving X, R, and this girl the stage for two or three songs a night. Crowds love it. Something else we do, change our set list—every night. Go on the website, and check the set lists. Can you guess what we'll play for you? Let's hear about it—and we'll see you on the next tour stop, or through your earbuds!*

Tom leaned across the aisle and read her computer.
"That's interesting . . ."
Christine shook her head in short, sharp jerks, her flow disrupted. "What?"
"Writing about that country picnic."
"Why not? The way we dropped into the café and got whisked out to a park? Totally ruled, Dad. Wild West stuff, like, my friends think it's *extinct*."
"Well, I don't think it happens enough. Seeing the road, hanging out with our fans. We race around and play, but all we see are hotel rooms, venues, and truck stops."

Christine chuckled. "All I have to do is write, 'Meet us so and so and set up a picnic, and we'll bring the music,' and hit 'send,' and you'll have picnics everywhere. The world's on my fingertips, right now."

"Would be nice if it happened more organically—like it just did in Hays, which is why you're inspired—but I hear you," Tom said.

"Dad, blogging, flashing, posting, message boards and IMing *is* doing things organically . . ."

"In the digital age."

"Is there any other?"

She thought of saying something about reaching into time, never letting go of Annalisa's hand, and how his life would have been different—how her life may have been different, or even non-existent. Instead, she smiled softly. "You really miss how carefree it used to be, don't you?"

He scooted next to her. She wrapped an arm around X, himself a deep breath or two from being comatose. "It's why we wanted to stay on the ground, at least to start with. Good food, good company, old friends, and jamming with good people. They love to see us, we're just as excited, and when we get together, the real music happens—the one language everyone understands." He paused for a moment. "But our RV days are about over. Jason just leased a jet. We'll fly after the Cumberland Festival, since he keeps adding dates and we've got back-to-backs coming."

"Works for me." Christine typed a reminder to finish one more story, then started to shut her laptop. "Hey, let me run something by you: What if I invited people online to request songs for each show, and we played one request per show—and then posted a video of it, that night? Like our own special song of the day, but instead of playing it at sound check or something, we do it live? I'd bet we'd go viral."

"We didn't hire anyone to do anything besides film for that documentary Robiski swears he's going to produce. And the streamcast."

Christine chuckled. "Sometimes, Dad, you really are your age. Michelle said people have emailed video clips they shot with their smartphones, camcorders . . . whatever. Some are streaming. My phone's pinging away. Trust me, if someone hears the song they requested, they'll send us a video, especially if I ask for it."

"How do you see us doing this?"

"X and I can go through the requests every day, push aside songs not on our master play list, and then have you, Chester, and Will weed it down further. If you like what's left, we draw one song—and play it."

Tom thought for a moment. "Great idea, honey. I'll talk to Chester. Let's do it."

She thought of the next entry, a story about the character of the band. "What was your best impromptu jam in one of these little towns, Dad, during one of these bus trips?"

"There were so many, everywhere . . . the San Juan Ridge in the Sierras, Northern Minnesota lakefronts, New York, the Smokies, farm festivals, a storytelling festival or two in Tennessee and Georgia . . ."

Christine wound her hand like a top, her patience stolen by both lack of sleep and the desire to sleep. "The best *one*, Dad."

Tom rubbed his hand through his lengthening gray-white locks, their curls flopping onto his neck. "Right before a big festival we played at Bull Island, on the Wabash River between Illinois and Indiana. We were driving from St. Louis, and pulled into a café in Southern Illinois. A barge worker recognized us, told us about a party for a friend who was dying of cancer, and said the cat was out of money for more treatment. Would we play, and could they pass the hat?

"An hour later, we were on a farm along the Wabash. It was a complete blowout, a thousand people, tons of food. The owner sent his sons to neighboring farms to find more extension cords, another generator, and a flatbed truck for us. We talked for a while with the guy who had cancer. He was in his thirties, had four kids, and always talked about beating it; he didn't have a word for 'giving up.' He was so brave, but you could see in his eyes— and his wife's—which direction it was going."

"That's really sad." Christine took a deep breath while glancing at her two healthy parents on the RV, something the man's four kids would never experience as adults.

The Northern Illinois landscape rolled past, field after field of head-high corn or ankle-high soybeans. "The farmer's boys returned with extension cords, many cases of beer, and three truckloads of neighbors," Tom continued. "We grabbed our amps and a couple of speakers from our rented U-Haul, set up, and played for almost two hours."

"That would've been a great thing to see."

"I was a couple years older than you are now when we played. That count?"

Christine rolled her eyes.

"All these people wanted their brother, friend, dad, husband to have a good time. And did he ever!" Tom continued. "Even with bone cancer, he gets up from his wheelchair and dances with his wife. He doesn't care how painful it is; he's going to dance with his bride! He even told Will, 'I don't give a shit if I drop dead; this is my barbecue.' You never stand in the way of a dying man's wish. We played 'I Know She's My Lady.' He and his wife kissed right through that song. Sweetest kiss I've ever seen."

Christine sniffled and rubbed her eyes. "You sure know how to make a grown woman cry, Dad . . ."

"Hopefully in the right away." He wrapped his arm around her, curled her head into his shoulders as her free hand palmed X's head like a basketball. "We raised three thousand bucks, a dollar here, five there, people dropping hard-earned dollars into the till. We took a quick vote and matched it. The man didn't want to take our money, but his friends saw to it that he did. We had Raylene give him the money, so he wouldn't even try to argue. Then they loaded our bus with leftovers. We had food for a week. I love Midwesterners and Southerners. Their idea of cooking a meal for you is to make you fat and happy. Their day isn't complete unless they somehow make yours better. Can't say enough about them."

Christine nodded. "That explains, at least to me, why you guys were folk heroes."

"Not folk heroes." Tom kissed her forehead as he chuckled, his stomach putting out its first plaintive grumble for caffeine. "Just musicians being good neighbors. The man's friends were the folk heroes." A convoy of speeding semis shook the RV as they roared past.

"What about the man?"

"He died a couple weeks later." Tom rubbed his day growth and peered out the window. The parade of cornfields continued, only occasionally interrupted by houses, silos, sheds, farm ponds, and barns. "His wife said they danced to 'I Know She's My Lady,' her twirling him over and over in his wheelchair, almost until his final breath."

"Wowww . . ." Christine leaned back, her heart plump and ripe, the walls of the past six years crumbling at her feet.

Tom grabbed a lock of her hair that had fallen into her face and moved it behind her ear. "Can I ask you something?"

"Sure . . . but I want to post what you just told me."

He nodded. "People would like that. So, how do you feel about having a sister? And the likelihood we're going to see each other sometime?"

"Majorly shocked . . . who isn't? But I'm totally down with it, Dad. What else would I be?" They shared a nervous laugh as she peeked out the window to gather her words from the waves of corn. "It makes the secret you kept from me less of a deal, like it all turned out to be a supposition. Though you didn't have any way to suppose anything else. I know you didn't know. A really bad thing happened to you and her, and now it's like you're getting the most incredible re-do I've ever heard of."

Tom stretched out, wondering how many more miraculous, bizarre moments a man could experience. "That's an interesting way to put it."

"Well . . ." Her eyes sharpened. "I've never seen you this happy. Nor will you ever see a woman more pissed than if you hold something major from me again . . ."

"I know that . . . have you thought about meeting her?"

"Yeah, a lot, but right now, Dad, I'm thirsty and have to pee." Christine stood up and stepped effortlessly over his legs, and then moved a pillow beneath X's head. He never knew the difference. "It's going to be weird," she laughed softly, her eyes softening. "But seeing you like this is so totally worth it." She wrapped her arms around his neck and met his eyes. "Thank you, again, for bringing me on tour."

"You're the jewel of my life." He kissed her forehead. "You always will be."

"I mean it, Dad. Thank you." She patted his heart.

"So do I."

Tom's phone screen lit up as the RV arrived at a packed United Center. "Hey man, it's Jason." His voice was frayed, scratchy, parched by another long overnight flight.

"All good? How was your flight? How is Annalisa?"

"Fine. Long. Dead asleep, like I should be. Hey man, something to know."

"What?"

"The Cumberland promoter just woke me up; don't Chester's people know how to tell time? Don't they know it's seven hours later in Italy?"

"I don't think Italy's a place they think about, Jason.."

"Couldn't understand his hills 'n' hollers accent at first; tell Chester I need an interpreter next time . . ."

"Yeah, yeah."

"You're headlining, Tom."

"Cumberland?" A jolt up his spine. "What?"

"They rearranged the lineup. You're headlining. A couple hundred thousand fans will be all yours. Tell everyone to bring their A games; this could make your summer." Robiski looked over at Annalisa curled against him: her closed eyes, her high cheeks and soft brown skin, thin lines delicately formed around her eyes, her full lips.

"I doubt anything can beat what has already made my summer," Tom said.

Robiski kissed Annalisa's cheek. "I hear you."

"What a show! "

"They ripped it up! Ever seen anything like that from a stoner hippie band *this* late in the game?"

"Keyboardist is off the hook!"

"Is that how you come back, or what?"

"Chester's solos with that bass player . . . yeahhhh!"

"I want to twirl with the girl!"

"Take me home, Christine!"

The co-eds hurled superlatives while running their hands down invisible fretboards, playing air progressions. The tallest of the group turned to his buddies. "You'd kick ass, too, if you had a chick that hot dancing and singing around you all night. I've just met the future Mrs. Marvorski."

"Well, lover boy, that line stretches to the other side of Lake Michigan," another said with a derisive chuckle. "Anyway, she's with the keyboard player. Not a chance."

The three DePaul frat buddies walked out of United Center while mashing "West of the West" and "Street Party" into the few hard-hitting words they could remember from "Holy Child Blues." They sang on and off key with their misspoken lyrics, like jamming to the car stereo when you're not quite in sync, but the song moves you to belt it out anyway. Concertgoers buzzed around like they'd inhaled jet fuel. "Who plays four hours anymore?" a fan yelled, hoarse and strained, his voice croaked.

They walked past the statue of His Airness, at the front of the building. The tall one tapped the bronze hand palming a basketball. "Sorry, Mike, but tonight, your house belonged to her."

23

ST. LOUIS . . . INDIANAPOLIS . . . EVANSVILLE . . . MEMPHIS . . . NASHVILLE

ROGELIO'S EYES JERKED LIKE A CHICKEN HAWK GONE BATTY during the sleepless slog along Highway 41, an alien landscape of cornfields, evergreen, oak, and sycamore forests, and shale cliffs fanning out in all directions. The sticky weather and abundant adrenaline from yet another great show made it impossible to sleep, but once they arrived at Chester's, they could unwind in a home rather than a hotel room or RV.

He closed his burning eyes to envision Ophelia, the on-call doctor who met him during soundcheck, made a date after the first show, talked all night, and showed up the next show with a night bag. They spent the day off between the Fever's second and third Chicago shows making love and cooking food, she a gourmet chef when not operating on broken bones, he breaking out half the Spanish romantic folk songbook. Late one night, they crawled out of bed, threw on some clothes and roamed the streets. She cajoled him into jumping onstage at Buddy Guy's, the legendary bluesman's club. Ophelia's curvy, athletic physique, eyes of dark pearls, and sophisticated surgeon's mind intrigued him in a way the Idaho sisters and their friend couldn't. Then she faded . . .

Hours later, he awoke in a room with guitars everywhere: guitars with necks and bellies of cherry, mahogany, ash, red maple, and a dozen other woods, and belly designs ranging from arrowheads, squares, and a treble clef to tear drops. There were a hundred acoustic and electric instruments in the room, the guitars joined by mandolins older than bluegrass, a dulcimer, a steel slide guitar, two dobros, and five- and six-string banjos that riverboaters once played. He eyed a five-necked contraption painted like a keyboard, its pear-shaped belly loaded with pick-up knobs. The tonal stories lodged within these bellies and fretboards! He picked up the cumbersome instrument and overlaid melody and rhythm until the room felt like a string section. He thought of his violocello, how he rocked up centuries-old pieces at the Chiesa di San Bartolomeo, Chiesa di Santa Teresa, Salzburg Residenz, or Schloss Nyphemburg so audiences could *feel* the rush composers felt when the music first graced them, aberrant rock stars of their day that they were. He cherished his resulting nickname among satisfied legions of German, Italian, and Austrian patrons: "Rockstar."

Chester walked into the room, clutching two cups of coffee. He inhaled the vapor of one and closed his eyes, ecstatic as a five-year-old watching *Frozen*. "Where did you get these guitars?" Rogelio asked.

"All sorts of places. A couple belonged to musicians I first heard on a Memphis black radio station as a boy. You could get the stations all the way up here if you spent half the night turnin' and tweakin' the sumbitch."

Chester grinned, his thinned cheeks reflecting the forty pounds he'd dropped since rehearsal boot camp began, helped along by playing live and Chandra's dogged attention to his diet. "I've acquired as I went along. Built some, too."

He walked to the far wall. Nearly every inch was covered with prints of the Fever's first, greatest, and final concerts (so they thought), alongside an acoustic show when June Carter trotted out as Chester's special guest. "Never would've imagined that," Rogelio said. "You and June Carter."

Chester cocked an eyebrow. "Never imagined you'd know who she was, New York. Why *you* so surprised?"

"She's the first lady of country. Didn't know you were into country."

"Not a helluva lot of difference between country and rock down here, son. Used to be, but now, it's like Tom Petty said about today's new country stars sometimes being rock and rollers who couldn't make it. Look outside, will you?"

Chester pointed through the bay window and its plant-covered sills toward a rolling meadow, with trees and hills behind it as far as Rogelio could see. "This *is* country, son," he continued. "We play country here, bluegrass, blues, some rockabilly. You'll meet some folks tonight."

Rogelio chuckled as Chester carried on, his lips vibrating from trying to force too many thoughts out. "But it's all about the blues for me, kid, down and dirty, river bottom, Memphis and Delta blues, cotton-picking traditionals and souped-up gospels. Love the blues. Most of the greats are dead now, but when one shows up at a gig, bet your ass I'm callin' him or her up for a song or two." Chester smiled. "Bet you never imagined this, either." He pressed a button; the framed prints disappeared. "My man cave."

They walked into a room of cushioned chairs, a wall-sized stereo with wireless speakers mounted in all corners, and audiophile headphones hanging on the antlers of a ten-point buck. Chairs of every ideal male stitch encircled the room—bean bags in one corner, an ancient sofa soft as a grandmother, loungers and rockers scattered throughout. One wall held nothing but albums.

"My workshop is to the left; invaluables to my right." Chester pointed with his half-empty coffee cup.

Rogelio remembered what he'd first asked on the RV while lightning bugs flashbulbed the Illinois countryside. "Can you fix the neck on my five-string before Cumberland?"

"Yeah. Let's get there, get situated. Have it fixed before sound check."

"Right on. So what's in your invaluables room?"

"My roots cellar."

"*Roots* cellar?"

They walked inside. Chester grabbed an instrument with a slightly longer neck than a mandolin, but a rounder belly. The wood looked old enough to be harvested by Romans during their slash-and-burn romp through the Germanic and Gallic forests. Chester lathered up with oil-extracting soap, dried his hands, and gingerly grabbed the instrument. He plucked tentatively, uncomfortable with the strings, but Rogelio recognized the riff. "Beautiful lute. An early version of 'Greensleeves,' right?"

Chester lifted his head, surprised. "Good ears. A version about a century older than the one we all sang in school."

"From the minstrel days, last of the Crusades."

"You know your shit, I'll grant you that." Chester swilled down the last of his coffee while cradling the instrument like a newborn. "Story is, the de'Medicis had a Florentine luthier build this instrument for that one tune."

Rogelio grimaced. "Damn, that's intense."

Chester chuckled. "Especially if it's true."

"No, the way you drink coffee."

A look of mock scorn ran across Chester's face. "Man's gotta have his campfire coffee. Chandra won't make it this strong; says it'll kill me. And she always washes out my cups; pisses me off. You ain't had coffee till you had it in a cup you never wash."

Rogelio stood over the basin and washed his hands like he was scrubbing off the plague, thinking how Ophelia washes before surgery, wondering how she managed to re-enter the frenzy of emergency medicine after their two-day romantic escapade away from the rest of their lives.

When he finished, Chester handed over the lute. "She speaks to you when you hold her. Like a Stradivarius. Let's hear a little sumpin' sumpin', *Rock Star.*"

He had only played a lute live once, in a Verona concert—a few rehearsals, and then five minutes of God's favorite instrument. He imagined the places the lute traveled, the hands it touched, the melodies it produced, how a pope or two might have liked "Greensleeves" on the one instrument specifically built to play that song.

Now, he plucked a tune he'd learned from the centenarian proprietor of a tiny Spanish vineyard while sipping wine with Consuela, his love, her life now a sad café ballad. Instead of joining him in New York after his European run ended, she left their relationship to tend full-time to her ailing parents. Despite the heartbreak, the decision worked out best for both. He sought to see more of the world through music, and she wanted family, home, kids, and to return to the fall harvest stomps in Spain she celebrated as a child. Now, Rogelio played the vineyard proprietor's tune, playing Consuela, her eyes, her touch, their love, his loss, the last note droning on.

"Where's *that* from?" Chester asked.

"His soul, sweetheart."

Chandra stood with Megan at the boundary of Chester's sanctuary. She walked up to Rogelio and kissed him on the cheek. "You are a lovely, lovely man."

"I kinda knew that," Chester said.

She chuckled. "Not you." Chester drew back a half-step. "Well, you too."

"We're fixing breakfast," Megan said. "Who's in?"

Chester's belly rumbled as he took the lute from Rogelio, rubbed it with an oil cloth, and gingerly slipped it into the glass case he'd specially built for the instrument. "Some fine playing, son. Real fine." He turned to Chandra. "Anyone else up?"

"Tom and Will are still sleeping. Christine and X went for a walk. Why don't you and Rogelio take a tractor and find them?" She headed for the kitchen, juggling a handful of eggs. "Or better yet, walk?"

"Eighteen hundred acres out there, baby. Too damned far to walk."

"You'll walk those hills in New Mexico all day, but walk two steps back home?" Chandra turned to Rogelio. "He's an old grump. I just try to laugh it off.. By the way, will we meet your new friend?"

"She's flying into Nashville tomorrow and driving up for the festival."

"Great. Another hen in the hen house." Chester shook his head. "Let's go find the other next-generation members of this band. And honey?" Chandra turned. "Could you call Robiski's assistant, Melissa, and have her hire a car to pick up Rogelio's lady at the airport and bring her up here?"

"You don't have to do that," Rogelio said.

"It's what we do 'round here, brother."

A fiesta for the senses. How else to describe the lingering scent of freshly mowed clover and alfalfa fields, stately sycamores and oaks rising into the milky, humid air, and jasmine and honeysuckle fencerow hedges emitting the last of their nocturnal perfume? All set to the persistent chants of a half-dozen whippoorwills? "You're in my country now, Rogelio, and here, there ain't nothing like right now—Fourth of July weekend. Hot dogs, tall cold ones, firecrackers, and *sweat*. Best party of the year."

He tapped Rogelio's arm and pointed toward a dilapidated structure. "See that worn-out barn?"

It was as gray as Manhattan overcast, its roof collapsed and frame slowly melted into the dark, fertilizer-enriched soil, its better days deep in Chester's childhood. Rogelio followed Chester's finger. "Yeah . . ."

"My forebears first put that up right before the Civil War." He rolled his eyes. "Worked cotton, sorghum, and tobacco before Ma Nature started taking her barn home. I worked dairy cows, crops, and some winter wheat for about ten years after we finished with the Fever. Got tired of that, leased the fields to a young couple down the road. Good kids, hard-working, know the value of a dollar, have a small boy, another in the oven. Love seeing kids work the land, understanding work, appreciating the land." He packed his cheek with tobacco. "Don't mind me. Chandra won't let me near the house with this."

"I don't blame her. Just spit off your side of the tractor."

A smirk stretched across Chester's face, mischief sparkling in eyes hovering at half-mast, a growing tiredness since the tour began, his return to the nocturnal life tougher than expected. "Could shoot you dead in the eye—or chest—or crotch—or your foot—from ten feet, son. Like fishin' on a stocked farm pond."

The things they do beneath the Mason-Dixon Line.

"Hey, Chester, you good with Ophelia joining us for a little bit?" Rogelio asked.

"Of course I am; everyone travels with their women, or men, these days.."

"It would be nice.."

"Well, then, here's our rule of the road: we pay for you, and you pay for her."

"Goes without saying."

Chester flashed a wry grin. "How does a busy doctor make time to skip town?"

"She just took a sabbatical, six months to rest, travel around, find adventures she's missed over the fifteen years or so since she last took a meaningful break—the summer after high school."

"Dedicated . . . and you're now part of her sabbatical. Good for you. You sure you want to toss her into this sack of nutcases?" The tobacco wad distended Chester's cheek as he spoke, spittle and words vying to spill out at the same time. "Leave it to you to find the smartest girl in Chicago. Hope she don't run once she sees what the rest of us are like."

They bounced along on the tractor, Rogelio thinking of romance, how long it had been since his heart jumped, a few years since he and Consuela felt that spark. Funny how it works. In Spokane, not ten days before, he'd told Christine he felt ready to date, maybe more. After the wild night at Wade's, backstage at the United Center, along came Ophelia Aguinigua, the daughter of lovers who escaped Castro after meeting at the Sans Souci in Trujillo's far more glamorous Cuban paradise, baby daughter in tow.

He then thought of Chester's life, how unaffected and unprejudiced he seemed, and how that could be possible for someone descended from the Southern plantation world—right down to the farm on which they stood. "Something I was wondering, Chester, and hope I don't offend you: Did your ancestors own slaves?"

"My kinfolk straddled the fence."

"Straddled the fence?"

Chester slung his arm on the steering wheel. "They claimed to be slaveowners, to keep the peace, and even had a few *hands* around to make a show of it. But they were paid cash money, and my kin owned none of them. That old barn I showed you? Underground railroad depot, so to speak. Escaping slaves used it on their way to the Cumberland, Tennessee, or Ohio Rivers."

"Really?"

He nodded. "People thought we were slaveowners. They all assumed we had tobacco or cotton in there. But us Cravens never owned nobody. Neighbors later called my forebears 'turncoat abolitionists,' 'Nigra lovers,' and worse, but it didn't matter. We helped people be free."

"You still do," he said. "How did the underground railroad work here?"

"Pretty quietly," Chester said. "Let's say I'm my great-great grandfather, I guess. I take someone in, hide 'em for a day or two, and drop 'em with the next keeper after the posse loses the scent. They take 'em somewhere—but never tell me where. Can't trace a trail that way."

So this is compassionate conservatism in the flesh, Rogelio thought, from mud-caked, boot-clad feet to scraggly silver hair and tobacco-swelled cheek. It really did exist, in the heart of this man who tended farm and family, and entertained millions with music written with hearts, feelings, and people squarely in mind. Chester loved his home, wife, music, people, Maker, and heritage. What more made a man? Wasn't that the prescription?

"When you were a kid, how did you get on with the workers?" Rogelio asked.

"Why these kind of questions?"

"I don't know. Maybe because this is a part of the country I've never been in, and I'm curious about separating fact from fiction."

"That one's tough," Chester said, "because we're storytellers down these parts. But I got along with 'em good. Real good. Word got 'round that we were good people, so hard-working families came here and worked." He wiped his sun-splashed eyes, proud to treat Rogelio to this sliver of family history. "We considered our workers family. It's what you do. When I was a little boy, they'd be singin' while chewing their hands to hell in cotton. Put your ear on the ground, and I swear, you can still hear them . . .

> *Children, we all shall be free*
> *When the Lord shall appear*
> *We want no cowards in our band*
> *That will their colors fly*
> *We call for valiant-hearted men*
> *That are not afraid to die*

Chester finished singing. "Didn't know you could sing," Rogelio said. "Not bad."

"Yeah . . . I'm underutilized." Chester's laugh rumbled through the heavy, still air. "My granddaddy Wilmer said the workers sang that since he was a young'un." Chester spat out his nicotine cud. "Hear of 'I've Been Workin' on the Railroad'?"

"Old railroad workers song. I remember the grandfather of one of my friends singing it all the time."

"Well, black minstrels, and not railroad workers, came up with 'I Been Wukkin on de Railroad.' Like nearly every other blues or gospel song . . . you go back and find the roots early in the last century, even before with the spirituals and field songs. Hell, if you *really* listen, you can probably hear moonshiners singin' 'When My Baby Smiles at Me' while brewing just over yonder."

Chester drove toward the end of the rolled alfalfa fields, a quarter-mile away. His stomach grumbled again for the eggs, fried potatoes, biscuits, gravy, and a half-slab of bacon frying on his stove. To hell with the rabbit and road food he'd eaten for two months: He was home, a God-fearing Southern man ready to *eat*.

They lurched onward, the rosy scent of Chandra and crisped bacon on his mind. He pointed toward a large, wide depression, flat as a pancake, bookended by two slight rises. "This is the Lick Skillet."

"Lick Skillet? Is that something you do when dinner's over?" Rogelio asked.

Chester chuckled. "Probably sounds that way, but it's a deer trace. They go after the salt deposits between the rocks. I wrote a lot of songs out there.

You live in a place long enough, it sings to you. Really does. It takes care of you much as you take care of it." He tapped his ear. "Can even catch some Cherokee right yonder: *'Hi Nv Ga La Ja Da Nv To / Ha Da Hv Si Ni Ja Du Li Sgai.'*

A glow crossed Chester's face as he chanted, now in English: "'Wash your spirit clean / Give away the things you don't need.' My first wife's favorite prayer-song."

Rogelio listened, mouth open, astonished. Just the idea of a Southern rocker singing a Native American *prayer* stretched the plausible. Had he not just heard it, he never would have believed it. "I know my place along *Athawomine,* what the Cherokee called this stretch of the Gap," Chester said, slipping his foot on the gas pedal. "I like to know what they sang and how they sang it. Good to know about where you live. Where my late wife Savannah came from. That sort of thing."

"X was right about you, man," Rogelio said softly. "Your get-up, your scruffy ways. All a disguise."

"I learned that from Savannah. You grow up Cherokee and black in the South, you dance carefully and hope people don't look at your skin alone in sorting you out. Goes for every day, everywhere. Stupidest thing we do in this country, fight over skin color. Can't believe we're still doing it."

"What was that?"

X's body stiffened as Christine's legs squeezed his lower back. "I don't know." She stifled her moans by biting into his shoulder. Then, "Probably someone shooting."

"Didn't sound like shooting. Sounded like a backfire."

"Whatever. Just keep doing what you were doing."

X gauged their distance from shore, maybe twenty feet from the nearest bank. He stood chest-deep in a small pond fed by a trio of artesian springs that flowed from the surrounding woods. "If I hear another sound, I'm out."

Christine wrapped her hands around his neck and leaned into his ear. With the sun at his back, he looked like an onyx statue. "Relax, baby. When will we get this chance again?" She kissed his ear. "As you were . . ."

"I'm down with that."

X tried to focus on Christine, but minnows nipped at his ankles. He hadn't noticed them before. He did now, along with every chirping cicada, cattails dancing in the slight breeze, and a bullfrog's mating calls, perhaps provoked by the pheromones rippling through his pond. Across the way, between two slate stones, a solitary snapper turtle lay in the sun, lost in serenity.

All the times they visited Chester and Chandra, she would walk to the pond and daydream, sing, skinny-dip, write, or draw while the sun dried her naked body. The pond was her sanctuary, her getaway. Now, she shared it with the man with whom she had spent the summer falling in love, against all common sense and convention.

X clasped his hands atop the dolphin tattoo on her lower back. She dipped backwards, her hair touching the water, light and cloud and sound of wind swirling into a dreamscape she wanted to occupy forever. She met the bullfrog at eye level while gnats stirred the surface, dragonflies cavorted, and a swallowtail floated past.

The pond reflected an approaching shape, a shadow. Only it wasn't a shadow.

Shit. She jerked her head up. A tractor.

A second later, laughter rip-roared towards them. "Y'all lovebirds come back when you're done doin' what you're doin'"—more guffaws—"and eat."

Chester's laughs echoed off the bluff as X and Christine plunged underwater, wishing they could drown.

24

THE PARTY RAGED ON. A DOZEN MUSICIANS JAMMED ON THE wraparound porch held up by three whitewashed Doric columns, some of its floorboards pried apart from the root system of the centuries-old oak alongside. Some musicians stood, while others sat on overturned buckets, chairs, and the porch swing. When a musician called out a song and key, the others layered down-home string playing with little solos, or blended songs into medleys. Out came bluegrass, Appalachian traditionals, old country, folk, Wobblie work songs, and blues from seemingly every inland port, and a host of pirate ports in between. Every song saluted bloody hands, aching backs, magnolia romances and flings alongside ponds, gains and losses, frontiers and hollows, songs that echoed real roots-of-the-land stories. The heart of the American Songbook ran through the people who surrounded him, Tom thought, calling and responding, singing and playing together, breaking bread. They were doing what musicians deep into national or world tours pine do, especially when beset with promotions, press, travel, meet-and-greets, recording, new deals, and the like: playing songs with old friends.

"What about you boys?" The musician, Deborah, tapped her fingers on her dobro, the steel guitar lying on a table next to her. "What do our returning legends have for us?"

Tom, Will, and Chester looked at each other. "We've got a little medley we've been working up," Tom said. "Come in when you're ready—see if you like."

"And if you do, we might drop it on everyone at the festival," Will added.

Chester tapped on the belly of his coal black guitar, setting the beat. They blended a half-dozen songs, a contained jam. Several musicians jumped in each time a song returned to a verse or refrain, leaping onto the merry-go-round, getting their feet set, catching the transition to the next song and keeping the jam going.

The thirty-minute segue left them noodle-armed and hungry. "That sounded like something you've done a hundred times," Deborah said. "I'd say polished, but you know better than taking all the edges of these songs, Chester."

"Well, Deborah, we've got a little sumpin' sumpin' brewing," Chester said.

"Always selling them tickets, aren't you?" Deborah laughed and swatted Chester's butt as he stood. "I heard you guys were playing acoustic, give you old farts a chance to catch a breath while the kids take care of business."

Within minutes, the screen door swung back and forth like a busy saloon, thirty people moving in and out of the sticky night. Musicians, family, and friends, and friends of friends, grabbed beers or sweet tea, and loaded their plates with beans, potatoes, and turnip greens to accompany the steaks, burgers, chicken, quail, dove, bass, catfish, frog legs, and ribs sizzling over three burn barrels converted to smokers.

Chester bit into a small, tender breast while flipping meat like a card dealer. ""Good dove there, Earl. Where did your gun run into them?"

Earl smiled, his prodigious belly jiggling. "Back of your land, over yonder by the pond. This mornin'. Whole flock of 'em. Until *someone* laughed 'em away." He shot a hard look at Chester.

Thought I heard gunshots at first . . . Chester thought back to how he fell into hysterics when X and Christine returned from their morning "walk," her hair soaking. "Can't tell the difference between a gunshot and a backfiring tractor?" he told X. "City boy." He started choking on his own guffaws.

"I jump when I hear gunshots, man," X said, "*because* I'm street. You do that. And there ain't tractors in Harlem. But I know gunshot, Chester. It was a gun."

Maybe he'd heard Earl, then the tractor, Chester thought. Not a good way to lose two bandmates, one his goddaughter, while enjoying what he and Chandra revisited now and again, a romp in a sunlit pond.

"Just be careful next couple of days with the gun, Earl. A couple of my bandmates were out there . . . 'walking,' while you was huntin'."

"Tell 'em to wear orange," Earl said.

Chester suppressed a laugh. "That would've been a sight."

He plopped half-charred steaks and dove breasts onto a pizza-sized platter. Earl worked the other barrel smokers with Jedediah Franklin, another lifelong neighbor. Meat smoke pumped into their faces like fog machines. Nothing so blinding smelled so good. Chester walked into the kitchen, where Chandra and Megan held court with assorted wives, girlfriends, daughters, and the men zipping in and out for beers. In the roughly forty seconds it took to cover the fifteen steps from door to kitchen counter, put the platter down, twist open a beer and walk back, he heard how someone's quilt won a blue ribbon, about the baby-faced teachers the high school just hired, Earl's complaints about washing dishes now that he was retired, and old Mrs. Gentry's latest run-in with the law. Seventy-five and still hitting that speed trap at 231A and Shiners. Never ceased to amaze him, the things you learn rapid-fire during kitchen talk.

Chester walked into the buzzsaw and kissed Chandra. "Grillin's about done, sweettheart." He made eye contact with everyone, from ninety-something Ethel Turnbull to Alyssa, Earl's teenage granddaughter, all swept up in the midsummer cabal. The crazy redhead among them, Callie, told her captive audience, "I love NASCAR races, 'cause the crowds, booze, and fuel make me *highhhh octane.*"

"That would literally be right," Chester cracked. He leaned into Chandra. "Next time, let me know when all these people are showin' up." .

"I invited the same fifteen we always invite. Word got around."

"Guess it did." *Feed 'em all.* The Southern way.

Chandra rubbed her hand across his back. He could grumble all he wanted, she thought, but he loved the outpouring. He always did. He was a simple man, really, and you could take away everything he owned and he'd be content, except for four things: his guitar, friends, stories . . . and her. She stroked his neck. "They miss you, honey. Their normal summer of jamming with you has been interrupted."

She flashed a lustrous "come hither" glance while noting the absence of his pear-shaped midsection. He'd done it. She never really minded the plump country boy—she was twenty pounds north of her beach girl prime herself—but *this* was the man she fell in love with and married. His chest looked like a barrel again, and he had more energy.

He walked into the guitar room and grabbed three of his finest collector's pieces: a fiddle once played by one of Bill Monroe's boys when bluegrass began, a mandolin he'd acquired from a player in West Virginia, and a Martin acoustic guitar like those played on porches since the Depression. The first one.

Earl limped to the porch. Within a few minutes, he launched into a mandolin and fiddle duet with Juanita, his wife and co-pilot in the area's best jug band. Faces gleamed from moonlight, music, food, camaraderie, and booze, the barbecue smoke a delicious reminder of the campfire jams most would join along the outer reaches of the Cumberland Festival.

"Them's some characters you tour with," Jedediah whispered to Chester while grabbing his finger slide. "Kind of like the Ringling Brothers rolled into town."

X and Christine walked up, arm-in-arm, Chester making eye contact. "Hey, want you to meet my old friends Jedediah and Earlene."

"We've met a couple times before," Christine said, firmly shaking Jedediah's hand. She leaned over and pecked Earlene's cheek.

"Child, you have grown into . . . damn, no wonder all them boys are going crazy over you."

"You still look amazing, Earlene." That she did, her lithe but solid frame strapping in blue jeans and a tied-off checkerboard shirt, her shoulder-length wavy gray hair and shiny green eyes practically jumping off the old *Hee Haw* show that Christine had to endure every week, only now appreciating what it meant that Earline played on many of those shows.

Earlene started chuckling. "I was the local beauty queen, big deal." She flipped her hand dismissively.

Earl strummed his mandolin, ending the conversation. "Hey Chester, Tom, Earlene. Give us something we ain't heard in a while."

Chester flashed a wry grin and turned to Tom. "Remember what our granddaddies played that day we hopped the train?"

Tom nodded. "When we were hoboes for a day."

Christine and X looked at each other. "Hoboes?" X started laughing.

Tom flicked his head. "Sure. What's the difference between being a hobo for a day, or an astronaut, or a baseball player, or a keyboard player?"

"I don't know . . . maybe what people are down with right now?"

Tom chuckled and thought of the hardest gap in history to bridge—the space between when you lived an event and when your conversation partner was born. "Well, to a couple of boys back then, jumping a train was pretty cool, X. And hoboes were fresh on everyone's memory."

"That makes sense now."

"Well then." He held up his bottle. "To hoboes."

Chester tuned his mandolin and slipped Tom the guitar. They plucked strings in search of a key stretching back to their boyhood. After finding it, Chester glanced back at Rogelio and X. "Get some guitars, boys. B minor. Easy switches, four chords. Catch us on the rebound."

The jam circle kicked in. Tom found the melody, the feeling, the day . . .

"Tommy, get your stuff in the bag!"

"Let's go, son," Wilmer Craven said, stroking his trim beard while practically strangling his banjo with his free hand. He handed the banjo to Neal Timoreaux, Wilmer's old field hand and partner in train-hopping, finding work on whatever field would have them, and cooking in old coffee cans. "Time to relive some past."

Grandfathers and grandsons walked to the railroad tracks, rucksacks on their backs. Tommy and Chester felt like the real deal, this adventure sure to put their Huck Finn trips down the Cumberland feel like put-ins at the lake by comparison. Behind them, Neal and Wilmer cupped their hand-rolled cigarettes, the hotboxes just above their palms, assessing which part of the train to hop.

A few minutes passed before the earth rumbled, followed by distant but closing whistles and puffs of smoke. Tommy laced up his sneakers, again, to make sure the laces wouldn't come undone and jam in the tracks. You didn't walk tracks all summer without that thought creeping in. Nor did you sit beneath the tracks without cupping your ears when passing trains shook the trestles overhead.

"Listen up, boys." Wilmer's impish playfulness had vanished. "Don't do anything till we tell you. We'll jump first. Then you. Neal or me will haul you in. Got it?"

Tommy and Chester nodded, their eyes glued to the approaching train.

Wilmer hoisted his rucksack. It was heavy, filled with enough lunch for a boxcar of cattle, far as he was concerned. The missus, Dorothea, didn't earn her local slogan, "If you're cravin', go to Mrs. Craven," by underfeeding the multitudes. Wilmer couldn't count the great meals he'd eaten since marrying her, nor those she'd served to folks who were needy, hungry, visiting the church. He wasn't going to argue over a swollen lunch for a schoolboy adventure. Took him a couple decades and scars to figure out when and when not to pick fights on the home front. It wasn't a fight he could win. Few were.

He turned to Neal. "Jump on first. You're the kid between us."

Neal moved down the track to a large bend. A minute later, the train arrived, and slowed for the curve. It was a half-mile long, a shorter freight. When the conductor and his four engines passed the bend, Neal popped out from a honeysuckle briar, grabbed the edge of a boxcar, and swung inside.

"Now boys—run alongside that train and get on it!" Wilmer yelled.

Tommy dashed ahead. Chester trailed by a couple of strides, with Wilmer bringing up the rear. Once Tommy reached the boxcar, he stretched out his arms and leapt at Neal. Chester and Wilmer did the same, but not before Wilmer fed Neal the banjos on his first pass.

Inside the boxcar, Neal broke up two hay bales for makeshift chairs while Wilmer rattled off train-hopping stories, how he lived a hobo's life from Kansas to West Virginia, first for the adventure, then out of necessity. The way he told stories, using "we" and "y'all" constantly, Tommy and Chester felt like they part of every train, jungle camp, and fire. "Few things more adventurous than hopping trains," Wilmer said. "Also necessary for simple folk if you wanted to eat during the Depression." What a life! What adventure! Banging tin cans and dead radiators, playing Jew's harps and banjos with missing strings while someone crooned into the night!

Neal pulled out a harmonica and played train songs—"Only a Hobo," "Waiting for a Train," "Nowhere to Sleep," and "Big Rock Candy Mountain," which had seeped into sing-a-longs at Chester's grade school. The boys swung their legs over the edge of the boxcar, watching the world go by, listening to their granddads' old journeys. "I hope we have adventures that boss," Tommy said. They mixed harmonica with banjo, then two banjoes. Wilmer's deep, soulful voice sang of sadness, mystery, the aches of hard, hard work, and the ultimate redeemer, hope. "How many songs do you know?" Tommy asked.

Chester's little chest puffed out. "My granddaddy knows every song played . . . colored folks' songs, too. Even the Indians. Don't you, granddaddy?"

Tommy and Chester loved the new music, from rabble-rousers like Jerry Lee and Elvis and Carl, a music *real* in their bones like these boxcar melodies, capturing lives carved on their granddads' foreheads, around their well-lined eyes. "Let's go around playing like them," Tommy said. "Only more rock 'n' roll."

"With what? We don't play anything."

"Yet." Tommy glanced at Neal, lost in the tune. "I can't remember seeing him like this since. . . ."

"Your granddaddy only stopped playing to tend to you, son, after your mama and Daddy left us a couple years ago to join our dear Lord," Wilmer said. "Day comes when a man has to sacrifice something big, something we really want for ourselves, but we need to sacrifice it for the sake of our families. Which your granddaddy understood. Which is why you ain't seen him play in a while."

Always so comforting, Wilmer, the way he handled the ultimate tragedy in a ten-year-old's world—losing your parents to a drunk driver on their anniversary dinner after the drunk smashed through the restaurant window and into their booth. "Your granddaddy kept many camps entertained," Wilmer said. "Outside of that Little Walter fella up in Chicago, your granddaddy might be the best I've heard on the harp."

Tommy stared at the floorboard slats and rubbed his hands in the straw, whirling with dreams and determination, wondering about his grandfather's sacrifice. *How do you give up something you love so much to raise . . . me?* As trees, bushes, and landscape rushed past, a thought hit: *I'm going to make his dream my dream. I want to make music.* Neal blew his harp, his endless mountain of responsibilities on hiatus on this, a true Godsend of an afternoon.

Wilmer peeked through the boxcar door. "Say, Neal, think we've gone, what, thirty miles or thereabouts?"

Neal spotted a familiar grove of sycamore, oak and cedar, speckled with fledgling pink and white dogwood blossoms. "About that."

"Train'll slow down about ten miles. We jump there." He tapped Chester on the shoulder. "Your nana'll be waitin' for us."

A few minutes later, Neal leaned over the edge and noticed a stand of trees that surrounded what looked like a dried bog. "Remember that place, Wilmer?"

"Sure do." He turned to Tom and Chester. "C'mon over here. See that clearing?"

"Sir . . ."

"Where we nearly got a recording contract," Neal said. "Closest camp to home."

"We were ridin' a train from Georgia to South Dakota for a harvest, picked up the smoke coming from this camp, and jumped off for some grub," Wilmer went on. "They fed us; we paid 'em with music. It's what you did. Camp was bangin' pots and pans all night. A couple people had harps, a banged-up guitar. We had about as much fun as two half-starvin' men trying to feed loved ones back home can have."

"How did you almost get a contract?" Chester asked.

"Well, one of the hoboes had started a record label after times got better. Word got around he was lookin' for two hoboes who once put on a show," Neal said.

"Did you get hold of him, sir?" Tommy asked.

Wilmer nodded. "Yes sirree." He recalled cranking the telephone dial, putting the wooden receiver to his ear, and resisting every frightened urge to hang up. "We had a good talk, but our music was a little bit past its time. Everyone wanted jazz, be-bop; hobo wanderin' songs were passé." He flashed his chip-toothed smile. "But I'll always remember what he told us: 'If I'd found you before, you'd have a contract.'"

"I'm sorry it didn't happen, Granddaddy," Chester said.

"Don't be. Good Lord didn't mean for it. He's content with me on the porch, playin' with the neighbors after Sunday worship. But you boys . . ." Wilmer glared at Chester, then Tommy. "You boys have a hankering for music. I see it in you. I know about the Blueberry Knob church, y'all sneaking up, listening to choirs, pastor not sure if it's a good or a bad thing."

Neal put the harmonica in his shirt pocket. "You want something to happen, you have to go and get it. You never know who's listening. Just like we didn't know a record man was in this camp we're coming up on. But I do know that if you don't give it a try, whether it's music or something else, you'll never know if someone would have been there to listen. And no one will ever know what you had to offer. You most of all."

When the train slowed again, they jumped, rolled down the embankment, dusted themselves off, and scurried to a nearby dirt lot.

"You boys have fun?" Dorothea Craven asked as she leaned from the Buick, her head covered in curlers, a scarf atop it. The sun glinted off the light-blue sedan's polished tail fins, temporarily blinding Chester.

"Much fun as I've had in a while," Wilmer said. He noticed Dorothea leaning from the passenger's seat. "You ain't drivin' us weary wanderers home?"

She rolled her eyes. "Your choice to wander, sonny boy. You drive."

Wilmer turned to Chester and Tommy. "Let you in on a little secret, boys: once the ring goes on, it never ends."

"What does end, Wilmer Craven, is you taking them boys train hoppin' and breakin' the law. Gives 'em the wrong idea. So does your marriage advice."

As Wilmer wrung his hands like a ten-year-old caught shoplifting, Dorothea got out, brassy and sure as Annie Oakley at dueling time. "Good then. No need for me to haul your tails out of jail. Now grab some fried chicken out of the back. Let's go home."

She handed Wilmer the keys.

Only two years after the train hop, Neal Timoreaux succumbed to lung cancer. He'd never smoked, but a life of coal-fed trains and radiator and asbestos factories got him. Also, while the doctors didn't say it, a grieving person is most susceptible to trouble in the lungs. In a one-year period, he'd lost a son and daughter-in-law, and then a wife; too much to bear. Tom found him in bed, lifeless and breathless, curled up as though he were cuddling Grandma Celine. Maybe he was.

An aunt offered to take guardianship and move into Neal's Southern California home, near Riverside, to finish tending to Tom. A year later, at sixteen, he lied about his age, enlisted in the U.S. Army, and was stationed at Fort Ord, a couple hours from San Francisco. While wandering aimlessly along Ocean Beach, the frigid ocean pushing broken sand dollars and crab shells onto the sand, the rough waves a junkyard for crustaceans, he closed his eyes. He envisioned Neal's harmonica, ocean spray, a melody within the steady breeze: Play *wherever you go. If you want it badly enough, make it your life, buddy.*

25

CUMBERLAND FESTIVAL, TENNESSEE

FLOODLIGHTS PANNED THE SEA OF HUMANITY AS HEAT LIGHTNING scrambled overhead. Roadies darted like fireflies to check wires and cables, tune instruments, set beers and water bottles on amp stacks, and fulfill any other pre-show tasks while scanning the stage through a checklist long ago embedded in their minds. The roadies lined up instruments in their racks and disappeared as the lights went down.

Backstage, Megan grabbed Christine's shoulders, tight as stones, and started kneading them. "Honey, this is your night. For both you and your dad." She ground her thumbs deeply into a pair of thick knots.

Christine, peering straight ahead, barely flinched. "I've come to love singing with him." She gave Megan a funny look. *Like, hello?* "He got on me about not syncing up my stage moves enough to the music, though."

"Well, try it his way and see what happens. He's not telling you to stop moving around; I think he probably wants you to move more—"

Christine shook her head. "That is so not what he said."

"Within the song, move more within what the song gives you."

"OK, I'm down with that."

A moment later, X walked onstage to loud applause, and dropped a few keyboard runs onto the sweaty, swaying masses, tying together bridges, hooks, and refrains from a half-dozen deep Fever tracks. Rogelio saddled the violin against his neck and shoulder and latched onto X's medley, switching from foot-stomping fiddle to loftier arcs, as though gigging for frogs with Vivaldi.

When Christine and Tom walked out, already singing, he hit a high note and then reeled it back to the original key.

> *They bail from their jobs, they travel far and wide,*
> *They take their music to the streets and meet the rising tide . . .*

"Christine! Yeahhhhh!"

"Tom!"

Tom jogged to center stage, guitar in hand. Christine skipped from one side to the other, her cowboy boots, Daisy Duke cut-offs, and sheer long-sleeved top suggesting that, here in the hills and hollows, angels descended to earth as farmer's daughters. Or dressed like them.

> *Just grab your girl, give her a twirl*
> *Let's party in the streets*
> *Let's GO!*

She kicked above her head like the air was a soccer ball. Younger fans jumped, older onlookers swayed, and others danced or bounced in place. No one sat, even after two days, even after thirty acts. Rogelio strutted from speaker stack to speaker stack with the bass Chester had just repaired in his shop, all cool attitude, long strides, and rippling runs, a tomcat on the prowl.

They gave the fans everything they'd stayed awake for: balls-out jamming, with Tom singing at full tilt and Christine perching a half-octave higher. She swung back and forth, hair flying from a barely visible headband. "I'll be a possum-eatin' sumbitch," Earl said to Juanita as they stood side-stage, abandoning their campfire jam to enjoy the stage passes Tom gave them. "Kid's got moxie. And lungs."

"Does she ever!" Juanita swung her hips into Earl, knocking him off balance. He groaned, never quite accustomed to her hip checks. Though he'd endured more than he could count.

Christine and Tom pranced back to the stage runway. They belted out the refrain in call-and-response, Christine bouncing on her haunches while toying with Tom, the straight man, her moves in perfect time to Will's beat. Fans converged front stage, pushing or holding each other, as celebrations broke out more than a quarter-mile into the meadow, fans and newcomers swept up by the vocalists playing off each other, conducting the night. Finally, Christine toed the edge of the stage and led the crowd in a clap-along.

Rogelio stepped onto Will's drum riser as he and Chester cut loose on a long riff, spurred by Tom's call. "What a night! What a crowd!" Rogelio yelled.

"Why I'm playing back here again—for nights like this." Will slammed his high hat cymbals, the towel on his shoulder doing nothing for the sweat already pouring into his eyes. He twirled his sticks, peered into a human sea now detonating into a pasture-wide frenzy, and closed with a snare sequence that squeezed the breath out of the night. The resulting screams could have drowned a jet at ten paces.

The set roared on. Christine danced and swayed and twirled and marched up and down like a majorette or clubber one moment, a dervish the next, reminiscent to some of Belinda Carlisle's and Gwen Stefani's rock-outs, to others Stevie Nicks's gypsy twirls, or even Zia McCabe, driving the alt crowd with her fellow Dandy Warhols with her mystery and moves while keeping one hand squarely on her keyboard. Smart phones and digital cameras burned up gigabytes, their owners already posting. One or more of these clips would explode, go viral; you just knew it. The night ripened.

"Street Party" rolled into "Cumberland Blues," which rolled into a forty-five-minute salvo of fire and fusillades. When they finished, Tom and Chester looked out to a crowd hundreds of yards deep. "We've been sitting on the porch at Chester's," Tom told the crowd, "trying to figure out what to throw at you that you haven't already heard . . . at least not from us."

Cheers. Loud screams. "West of the West!" "When I Become the President!"

"That you *haven't* heard!" Tom glanced over at Chester, who laughed. He pushed his palms down, to quiet the throng. "No, no, no; we'll get to those later." More cheers. "Let's switch gears and visit your roots, Chester's roots, our roots."

Chester grabbed the microphone. "We *originals* are gonna send these kids backstage for their nap." Cheers. "Ain't they awesome?" More cheers. "We're the luckiest sumbitches on earth to have these child stars up here.

"Now take five with us while we play some songs you older ones might've heard when you were young 'uns."

Chester took a chair Dudley had moved onto center stage. "I'm handing this to the other host of our shindig, Tommy T, but first, our special guests. Let's hear it for our First Ladies of rock 'n' roll, Megan Timoreaux and Chandra Craven, who are gonna do a little singing, and the sweetest fiddler you'll hear, our very own Juanita Kreps."

"Mystical Megan! Mystical Megan! Mystical Megan!"

Megan waved and hurried to the back line mics. Chandra glanced at Juanita, who was shaking. Standing next to them were Ophelia and Denise Halsey, both stunned by the massive crowd. Denise had just arrived from Shanghai to surprise Will after a month showing Chinese businesses the newest iteration of hybrid cloud computing. And not thirty hours before, Ophelia had been wrapping up rounds and going over case files with her replacement, one foot leaving Chicago Medical, the other stepping into Rogelio. Talk about a different world . . .

Juanita looked at Earl, her face frozen. "I don't have my fiddle!" A smile spread across Earl's face. "You're in on this, too . . ."

"Bet your honey-sweet ass."

"I'll tan your hide later. You and that Chester." She smiled through her tears, started to laugh, then choked up again. "Get my fiddle so I can play up there, will you?"

Unsatisfied with his tuning, Chester walked over to switch guitars. "It'll be just like the porch jam," he told her. "We'll play through once, then sweep in." He glanced at Ophelia. "Like the show so far, Doc?" He winked. "See Rogelio hit the lottery."

Ophelia's face flushed. "That was awfully sweet." And not something she'd hear at 11 p.m. on the south side of Chicago.

"Chester, I don't have my good fiddle," Juanita said, her hands shaking.

"Yeah you do. Re-strung it today before I fixed up Rogelio's bass." He located Dudley. "Brother, can you grab her fiddle?"

Thirty seconds later, Juanita fingered her prize, a late nineteenth-century fiddle she purchased in West Virginia after negotiating over day-old coffee and greasy eggs in a roadside diner, the town's lone streetlight flickering outside a window that read, "All You Can Eat Special." Radiance beamed from a face lined and furrowed by hard times, her wreck of a first marriage, a shard-covered road. They fell in love and forged lasting happiness from their pasts, which neither discussed.

"Knock 'em dead, honey," Earl said, kissing her lips.

"I'm gonna tap your ass for this. Lucky I love you."

Juanita wiped large teardrops off her high, rounded cheeks, genetic gifts from her Cherokee great-grandmother, Ayita. *First to Dance.* Ayita had survived the Walk of Tears as a little girl, knew the great-grandmother of Chester's late wife Savannah, given birth to Juanita's grandmother, and lived a simple life. Her cheekbones rode prominently on her great-granddaughter's face. "You'll do great, Miss Juanita," Christine said as she moved next to them.

Juanita marveled at the golden-voiced girl, her values apparently intact, living the dream Juanita coveted until her first husband denied her. One thing drove him: jealousy over her musical talent. When Earl entered her life, he brought his music along, reconnecting her with that side of her heart. "Honey, how am I ever going to repay Tom, Chester, y'all?"

"A loaf of your awesome cornbread from the other night will work," Christine said. She pointed to the stage. "Go live your dream."

For the next twenty minutes, the Cumberland Festival hosted a bygone era. Tom, Chester, Will, and Juanita wove together a medley out of Appalachia's hills, hollows, waterfalls, river bottoms, and juke joints. Tom and Chester swapped lead, with Will interjecting on jug bass and Nap Hayes's mandolin, and Juanita sweeping her fiddle high and low, arcs charged with joy. They picked, strummed and plucked through "Swanee," "Ol' River

Blues," "Tennessee Jed," and "Foggy Mountain Breakdown." "Half expectin'
Ma Rainey and Bill Monroe, maybe the Carter Family, to walk out of that
cornfield like those ballplayers did in the movie," Earl said to Christine.

"Who? What movie?"

"Another time . . ."

Tom and Chester dropped in "Catfishin' for a Ride," which Wilmer
Craven and Neal Timoreaux once sang to their two grandsons on a boxcar
when America liked Ike, then closed with "Statesboro Blues," once famously
covered by a juggernaut among Southern rock bands. Eat a peach. Revelers
marveled at the sass, attitude, and cut-to-the-bone fiddling Juanita brought
onstage.

Afterwards, she thanked the audience, giddy as a schoolgirl after her first
recital. *Who would ever believe . . .*

She didn't have to click her heels. A very real crowd kept cheering.

Christine took the stage with Rogelio and X, and then wrapped an arm
around Juanita's shaking shoulders. She turned and faced Tom. "Here's 'Ghost
Child.'"

> *Her lips kissed his every day,*
> *Beneath a sea of trees,*
> *Her dreams roosting within his heart,*
> *Then the howling winds came down*
> *And ripped their bond apart*
> *She was hustled so far away*
> *Death almost claimed his heart*
> *It hollowed him with deep despair*
> *That little voice that made his day*
> *Now a sad ghost in the air . . .*

She sang the mottled scream of a disembodied soul, hanging in limbo,
trying to stay, so frightened of passing over. Rogelio punctured the air with
his sax, tears and hardship coalescing in every note. She stood still as a stone,
imagining Tom's pain, his struggle to breathe, let alone sing, after Annalisa
was hijacked to Italy. When a soul hollows out until there's nothing left to
take, it can refill with a cold-heartedness and insatiable temper, a pair of lethal
demons. Or, the person can rise beyond it, try to help someone, give to them.
The choices are very clear when everything in your life is swept away and you
must figure out how to start over. Christine knew that in his own suffering,
Tom came up with an approach that, she felt, was the coolest thing about him,
something she'd begun to emulate: "Always look for one person in the crowd

who is hurting. Perform for that one person, give it up for that one, and every gig will feel fresh, no matter how many times we play the same songs."

After she finished, the Fever dove into a half-dozen hits, playing them with the most sustained power of the tour. Chester and Tom glanced at each other, eyebrows raised, *on,* in the zone, which every fan imagines their heroes occupying every night, but in reality, you're lucky to get there a few times per tour. Now they had it. Magical. Powerful. Beautiful. Perfect.

Once they wrapped the non-stop half-hour with a keyboard-guitar duet in which Chester and X took the crowd to within an ounce of its collective sanity, Tom asked for quiet. "We've been sharing old stories on this tour," he said, perspiration dripping, "but tonight, you're the story of how a band came back from the dead." More deafening cheers. "You know our new vocalist. She's made it clear all summer, along with our newest aces, Rogelio and X, that they're the story." More cheers as each took a bow.

Rogelio kicked into his contribution to Chester's porch jam, a violin-keyboard duet with X, a centuries-old tune he'd first heard in an ensemble, then again at a concert at Schloss von Nyphemburg, a castle outside Munich, performed by a great Renaissance-themed band with a legendary guitarist. Christine morphed into a ghost dancer, swinging from side to side, her voice blazing like fire at midnight, on the verge of losing control—until she noticed Chester's raised eyebrows and Rogelio's bow wiggling in the air. *Time to bring it home. Stay within the song.*

They transitioned into "Gypsy's Prayer," now exploding across airwaves and mobile devices, thanks to a sped-up release by Robiski. She twirled around Tom as if he were a Maypole, singing of love, joy, devotion, beauty, vision, feeling, and power at the intersection of heart and divinity, where the seven chords of heaven are reputed to dwell:

> *I'll offer a little prayer,*
> *My little gypsy's prayer*
> *That we all find bliss tonight,*
> *It's what our world so needs,*
> *A little tenderness*
> *Found in a prayer and a kiss,*
> *Tastes of divinity we share . . .*

Deep in the sweltering night punctuated by screams, whistles, hoots, cheers, and a shouted-out marriage proposal, she laid fullest claim to the stage. *It has always been my place,* she thought as she danced. She'd eschewed Tom's career path to find her purpose, her art, her way. She looked over to find the world's proudest and happiest father smiling at her while strumming away. Shivers fishtailed down her spine.

Time to bring my little girl home. This night, this moment, possibly the band's best outdoor gig ever. He twirled his hand through the air, sad to have to close:

> *So climb with me*
> *Oh won't you climb with me,*
> *Your love is my gypsy's prayer,*
> *Your love is my gypsy's prayer*
> *Your love is my gypsy's praaaaaayyyyyyer*

Five minutes of raucous cheers later, the band returned for its encore. "OK people!" Tom yelled. "Where we going?" The answer, "West of the West," left the crowd delirious.

Finally, Chester tapped his echoplex and shot the final note into reverb heaven. The band stood arm-in-arm, towels over sweat-drenched bodies, the crowd trying hard to keep them at 2:30 a.m., wanting more of what they'd just witnessed for three hours:

The perfect concert.

PART THREE

"I come from a time when artists didn't just sell their soul to the highest bidder, when musicians took a stand, when the message of songs was 'feed your head,' not 'feed your wallet.'"

—Grace Slick

26

VENICE STRUTTED HER MOST SEDUCTIVE WILES. SWATHS OF yellow, pink, and bright orange light slid like dancers' legs around the marble columns, fountains, statues, gilded buildings, churches, towers, and alleys. She might be sinking, but Venezia flashed the same alluring style that seduced the Romans, Goths, Longobards, Tartars, Persians, Turks, and a host of Dogen and popes into calling the lagoons, islands, and mysteries of the seaport between East and West home. The *carnevale* city floated on the edge of the wild, pickled by the lagoon, as it had for a long, long time.

Violin notes rose from the alley, soft and vaporous. Annalisa hummed while watching cobblestoned walkways already gridlocked with tourists. The violinist, a kid sitting in a neighboring third-floor nook, drew her bow back and forth quickly, the piece robust. She imagined Vivaldi's red-orange hair flying like it did when he presided as choirmaster at the Chiesa di Santa Maria, the ornate church maybe ten bridges, piazzas, turns, and twisting paths away.

She glanced at her watch and stuffed her skirt and sandals into a leather handbag, blue with red patterns that looked like the footprints of prehistoric bird, maybe a Pterodactyl. She'd procured the bag at one of Milan's countless boutiques, where the Parisian bag designer showed up the first day the store carried her line. "Italian Dawn," it was called. Perfect name for life today, she thought.

She scanned the flat. After work, she would buy flowers and clean the place up. She tingled with anticipation, Jason's arrival only a day away. After years of emptiness, she was growing used to this feeling . . . but not too used to it. How can you take for granted a feeling you pined for, one you never thought you would feel again? Every time they dropped into her bed after he sloughed his bags into a corner, she wanted to spin a cocoon around them, never let the world ruin her life again.

She reveled in the delicious agony, envisioning his lips on her, as she grabbed her bag and sunglasses and skittered down two flights to Maurizio's shop. He was bent over his workbench, a thick oak slab on which, rumor had it, the great Renaissance painter Caravaggio ate Sunday dinner for many years. Maybe Maurizio created the rumor, storyteller that he was. Maybe he knew because he sat at Caravaggio's table, which sometimes seemed possible, his eyebrows bushing out like hedges beneath his thick glasses. His face was a worthy topographical map of a century lived simply, family first, his craft and love the only things on his mind when he awoke each morning, rolled over, and kissed his beloved Clara. With her gone, he prayed at bedside, drank a stiff double-espresso, waddled into his shop, and plunged his gnarled fingers into someone else's broken, scuffed, or scarred shoes. He took such loving care with each pair that Stradivari would have hired him, Annalisa thought. Maurizio not only preserved the family business, but thoroughly regenerated it.

Shortly after Maurizio's ninetieth birthday, a raucous, festive celebration many locals still recalled, Clara died. As his world collapsed, he asked Annalisa to move back to Venice from Verona, where she'd taken Paolo for schooling. He offered her half of everything—the business, the flat, and the building, once a secretive inn for mariners, offering respite while half the city-states in Italy were crumbling from the Plague. Its arched side entrance was so low that Annalisa had to duck. It was built for short, squat men like Maurizio, not tall women with tall American fathers.

Her move proved to be a right choice in a life badly needing one. Paolo had been tethered to her side for eighteen years, mother and son leaning on each other, battling one tempest after another. When Maurizio's offer came, she knew it was time to give Paolo his independence, and to wean herself from her emotional dependence on him. Their recent fights had left her weary, searching for answers that, as a woman, she didn't feel she held for him. Welcome to life with a fatherless teenage boy. She didn't want him becoming *mammoni*, depending on *her* for everything. Dependent sons led to dependent, needy and authoritarian husbands and boyfriends. She had fallen for two such *mammoni*, only to coddle their frayed emotions and enable them until something happened and they left or she left and she had to deal with more wreckage. Paolo would not be that way. When she moved, he took three years to travel throughout Europe, get an education, fall in love, trek in the Alps, and visit twice a year.

When he got sick, everything changed.

Maurizio heard the doorbell and peered above his glasses. "*Buon Giorno, Nipote.*" He stood up, labored around the table, and held his granddaughter's cheeks in his hands, kissing both as he looked upward into her eyes. "Every day I see you, you look happier. And more beautiful. *Bellissima.*"

Annalisa returned his kisses. "*Gracie,* Poppa Maurizio. Ever the charmer, *si?*"

"The day I cannot charm a lady, I will ride in my funeral boat." Maurizio noticed the smile, so rare in her earlier years, which returned when the American came into her life. Now, it was a constant. "Jason arrives?"

"Tomorrow. I have to take Paolo's shift again, then I will return and call the customers whose shoes we'll finish."

Maurizio's eyebrows bushed together. "What do the doctors say?"

She shook her head. "Not much. Paolo wants to work; he says he feels better. But he doesn't look better. Since I might go to America with Jason, I told Paolo to rest."

Maurizio glanced at a calendar above his workbench. "You leave in one week?"

Joy flushed her cheeks. "It will be very strange. If I go."

"My girl, do not expect much from Tomas." Maurizio lifted his glasses from his whiskered face. His deep-set eyes reminded her of an owl. "I spent years scolding your mama about running from a good man, but it was her choice and what am I to do?" He frowned, his face dark and defined by its thick, well-worked lines. "I cannot figure out what we did wrong, but she is my daughter, and I will always love her. I will never agree. Your Papa was kind to your mama. Not all the time—they fought, they were very young, he could have taken a job instead of playing music all the time—but he was kind."

"But he is one of the biggest rock musicians in history," Annalisa protested. "Why would he need a job?"

"He was not a star at all when you were a baby. He was just starting." Maurizio winked and patted her arm, his touch soft, yet strong. "You will know what to do, and so will he. But also keep in mind, nothing may happen. Do not let your hopes take flight, my girl, until you know for sure."

Annalisa rummaged through orders and receipts on the front desk, not wanting to heed his words, but realizing he was right. She needed to protect her heart, much as the thought soured her. "Can I ask you something?"

Mauricio smiled. "*Si.*"

"If Papa was so kind, why did we come back here?"

"I asked your mama. Many times." Maurizio closed his eyes to an old, bitter frustration. "At first, she told me he was dead. I wanted to believe her, but her eyes tell me differently. She was not sad; she did not mourn. 'Tell me the truth, girl, or I will not spare the rod,' I told her. 'I do not care how old you are.'

"'He is a hippie,' she told me. 'He only wants to lay around, play music. Doesn't work. What man would make their family suffer to play music?'

"'Does he work hard at his music?' I ask her.

"'All the time. Why can't he get a career job like every other man?'

"'Is he a good musician?'

"'People say he is, but this does not matter.'

"'It matters if that good musician can feed his family. And will work other jobs—is he at least looking?'

"'He finds day jobs sometimes, but mostly it's the music.'

"'He can work and he can play. What is wrong with that? Music is in his soul; he has to play. Just like an artist has to paint. Or I have to make shoes.'

"'It does not matter.'"

Maurizio frowned. "'It does matter, child. It matters for the little girl.'

"'Not if the father cannot provide.'

"'Maria, I would die if your mama told me I had to stop with shoes. That is part of my soul. Just like music is to Tomas.'

"'I do not care. I will not live with a filthy musician.'"

Maurizio's eyes gazed past Annalisa. "'He is anything but filthy,' I tell her. 'Tomas is good to you! He is good to you, to the little girl. This is all wrong.'

"'I do not want to be in America. He is dead to us. His friends use drugs.'

"'And him?'

"'Never saw him do anything but smoke, but he must sneak.'

"'If you never saw him, how do you know he sneaks?' She made no sense.

"'Because his friends do. So he does, *si*?'

"'You do not know that.'

"'Call it a lucky guess, Papa,' she said. I give up then." Maurizio shook his head. "I forgive her for saying this because the Good Lord tells me to. She is my daughter."

Annalisa shook her head. "When I saw her last week, she said I was dreaming old dreams when I told her what Papa was doing now. Even when I showed her on the computer, she wouldn't believe it."

"She believes it," Maurizio nodded slowly. "She now faces her lies. I tell her that a time will come when she has to face her lies about him. It is here."

"*La femmina muta, ignorante.*" Annalisa's words felt like bile.

"Yes, she is troubled," Maurizio said. "I wonder, did I shelter her too much? When your nonna Clara and I met Tomas, we saw that he was a fine boy." He brushed her hand, and then took it in his. "Your mother was jealous because you and he were very close. Your nonna thought she broke the two of you apart so you would not be able to stay close to him."

Maurizio threw up his arm, disgusted with himself. "You will see your Papa." He shook his head repeatedly. "We will not revisit this madness again."

Annalisa patted his arm. "Thank you for telling me."

"You were your Papa's world.."

"That makes me very happy."

"*Si*. And God blesses me that I am alive to see this." He brought his hands together and gazed at the ceiling. "*Grazie, o Dio, per aver risposto alle mie preghiere.*"

Vaporetto 82 and its stand-in skipper sputtered along the Canal Grande. She studied the façades of the shops, churches, palazzos, apartments, and hotels, the decaying palazzos once crowned jewels of the dinner party set, thinking of what Maria put her through. Every time Maria brought home a man, the early honeymoon disintegrated into a dark tale that ended one of two ways: the man took advantage and/or beat her up; or, he skulked away when he fell into her emotional pit, always at her fingertips, the first time the man paid less than rapt attention to her.

She puttered forward. She thought of her darkest year, age twenty-five, when she briefly became her Mama. There was Alan, "the bloke from Ipswich," he called himself, swooping into Padua and whisking her away on another tryst, never longer than a week, always somewhere different—Amsterdam. Madrid. Provence. Munich. Prague. Brest. But never Ipswich. Or England. They frequented four- and five-star hotels, fulfilling her dream of being a pampered princess. Then she realized his stories didn't match up, and his eyes roamed when she tried to make sense of them aloud. Still, he treated her like a queen. Who wouldn't welcome it after a string of *mammoni* who saw her as a replacement for their mothers?

The clock struck twelve when Alan circled back to his wife, spurred on no doubt by Annalisa's pregnancy with Paolo. He packed his bag, and left their suite in the Hotel du Louvre. She tearfully boarded the train to Verona, where Maurizio picked her up.

A month later, she drowned the heartache, the broken promises, with Fritz, a banker she met in Padua. He asked her to move to his home in Salzburg. Then, in her fifth month of her pregnancy from Alan, as the baby started to show, he said she would only need to do one thing to secure their life together.

"Anything, *mi amore*," she said, her heart racing.

"Get rid of the baby."

She thought he was joking. He was not. "I do not even *think* about abortions," she protested. "That is taking a life. A soul. I could not live with myself."

"*I* will be your family. And so will the children we make *together*." His stance reminded her of male lions that take over herds, kill the existing cubs, and create new offspring with their lionesses.

It didn't take her long to reply. "*Arrivederci.*"

She kept up her search for the perfect man, the most futile search on earth. After many errant tries, she grew skittish to the point where, at the first sight of trouble, she ended it. Snap of the fingers. Just like that. Until it hurt no more. "Be ready to leave everything behind and go in thirty seconds," Robert DeNiro uttered in one of her favorite American movies. Those words formed her quick trigger. Still, she returned for the fix, the rush, the dulling of pain, the brief physical and emotional contact with a feeling, love, that had all but deserted her. The downward spiral only stopped when Paolo told her, when he was ten, "If you bring any more mean men home, I leave."

She abstained for three years. Then she met Kalan, a Ghanian art dealer who traveled regularly to Venice and drew her in with dark skin, large eyes, soft voice, meticulous grooming, and kindness. For one dreamy year, Kalan took her places within herself she didn't know existed. He also liked Paolo. He showed love in the way he held her, talked to her, made love to her. Maybe the mirage of love could be real.

It turned out to be a mirage. After a weekend spent professing their growing love, Annalisa returned to Venice and Kalan flew back to Ghana.

She never heard from him again. That was a very long decade ago, one devoid of men and romance until Jason landed on the Adriatic shore.

She parked at the marble base of Rialto Bridge and took on passengers while awaiting relief, her shift over. She marveled at the marbled bridge, the project Michelangelo didn't win, all because Pope Julius II, his Vatican "benefactor," kept him on a tight leash of statues. So it is with those who use their power to quash creativity and genius; they appear in every generation. The weak crumble and settle, their creativity gone forever; the strong fight like hell, like Michelangelo.

She glanced at her watch, grabbed her thermos, shoulder bag, and hat, and entered the check station. She changed into sandals and shorts, unfolded a canvas shopping bag, and glanced at the market across the bridge, where shoppers milled around open-walled stalls. The sun loped across the sky, enjoying the perfect day it threw itself. After chatting for a few minutes, she signed out on Paolo's time sheet, distracted by thoughts of Jason boarding a plane in Los Angeles. She laughed at feeling like a teenager thirty years late, then took a deep breath, suddenly not giving a damn how silly her face looked when she glowed. Isn't that how we all want to feel?

After an hour of choosing, picking, bargaining and cajoling with a dozen different stall owners, she headed home, bags bursting. She kicked off her sandals, spread vegetables, cheeses, and fruits on a kitchen counter whose tiles she'd painted by hand, slipped a dozen tiger lilies into an urn, and put on music. She would spend this last night alone preparing a two-lover feast . . .

The shoe orders! *Are you dizzy? Merda!* She slapped her forehead as her brain fast-cut to thoughts of Norvagese welt, Tramazzas, stilettos, heels, and boots. She looked at the clock—"How did I forget this? Jason, quit making me dizzy!" she said aloud. She left the food on the counter, grabbed her sandals, flung the door open—

"My God! You are here already!"

Robiski held the door open. "Just visiting with Maurizio," he said, his voice weary. "I had a meeting in Rome this morning, so I decided to surprise you."

She pulled Robiski's face close. "So surprised!" She kissed him deeply and started burrowing into his chest, then remembered why she'd opened the door. "Come with me quickly. I have to help Poppa finish his shoe orders. Then the night is ours."

They stumbled down the stairs, arm-in-arm, banging into the wall for quick, rabid embraces. When they walked into the shop, her smile lit up the room. "Can we take care of the immediate orders now, Poppa, and the rest tomorrow?"

"I looked through the orders. We will do them all tomorrow." Maurizio leaned on his cane, patted Robiski firmly, winked, and smiled. "Go upstairs and *acquaint,* what your nonna and I did all four times we were apart for more than two days. In seventy years. One of those times, I fought in the war."

"Really?" Robiski asked. "Four times apart in seventy years? Impossible."

"But true," Annalisa said. She grabbed Robiski's arm. "They were inseparable. That is becoming my hope for us, too."

27

THEY SOAKED IN A CENTURY-OLD BATHTUB THREE STORIES ABOVE the alleys, reminding Robiski of a luxury treehouse, the new rage in off-the-grid living. "So this is what you've raved about," he said.

"And?"

"Better than I imagined."

She sat atop him, her curls falling below her breasts, her hair now longer than at any time since Paolo was born, the smile on her face unyielding. "You just lay there and . . . how do you say it? Space . . ."

". . . Out. Space out." He chuckled softly. "Your dad's generation, and mine, had a very intimate relationship with those two words."

"Then you space out, Jason Robiski, and I will make you feel very good." She stroked his cheek and dragged her fingernails down to his chest, then rocked back and forth slowly, her eyes closing with the bliss of feeling him, everything she saw and felt and wanted and loved, wanted for all these years, now moving in delicate waves of joy through her body. "You make me feel so beautiful," she whispered.

Afterwards, he ran his hands on her smooth legs, caressing her skin above muscle lines that had become more defined in the few weeks since his last visit. "*Sei radiosa*. Sexy. Very sexy," he mumbled, fighting to keep his eyes open.

Annalisa placed her finger on his lips. "*Vero amore*. Listen to my heart."

He was already asleep. *Men.* She lay awake, considering a decision she'd made, one many would not have chosen: to trust one more time. Sure enough, love appeared from the other side of the world. She ran her fingers through his short, thick hair, his face already in tender repose. He let her feelings grow naturally, without prodding or pressuring or overstating what he liked about her (though who *really* gets tired of a regular stream of endearing comments?). That helped her shed the steel and chains binding her heart. She made a few changes she liked more and more—losing weight, growing her hair, and dressing like she used to dress on her best nights out. She felt again the vibrant, inquisitive, adventurous little girl she'd lost in San Francisco, a girl she deeply wanted to love because of the way she embraced everything good that mattered in life, all things possible in her world. And who better to share it with?

She leaned over him and blew out the candles, offering a tiny prayer for each flame. She curled into his side and pulled a thin sheet over her shoulder. The nearly full moon lit their *love nest*. Jason's term. *Bellezza*. A stage all their own.

"*Dormi, amore mio,*" she whispered. "Sleep, my love."

Robiski grabbed an envelope from his briefcase as he inhaled the espresso aroma rising from his cup. *Annalisa*, it read, the handwriting ragged but legible.

She wrapped herself in a sarong, and held the letter to her heart. "You read while I drink this and close my eyes again," he said.

Her lips slowly curled into a smile. "Did you know you woke up in the night talking about walking on the moon when you were a little boy?"

Robiski grimaced. "That's . . . embarrassing. Where did I leave off?"

"Trying to land here. The place between asleep and awake."

Annalisa rubbed Robiski's whiskers, grabbed the envelope, and retired to the terrace. She lounged in a bubble of sunlight, protected from roaming eyes by the jasmine-covered lattice, which also obscured the sagging backside of a building Marco Polo would have recognized. A handful of cats rustled through the creeping vines, part of Venice's fleet of feral felines. Tom and Megan's aloof, imperious Steppenwolf would fit in perfectly, Robiski thought as he watched two cats take their chase onto the adjacent rooftop, a couple feet away.

She opened her robe to feel the sun and slowly peeled apart the envelope, her heart skipping beats. When she unfolded the note, a photograph of a sharp-looking man fell out, his gray hair nearly touching his shoulders, every bit a venerable rock star. *Papa*. Her eyes filled as she stared at his photo. This man clearly was happy, and so were the women next to him. She peered through his eyes and into her deepest past. When your deepest past is the most stable part of your life, how do you go on without trying to reconnect with that magic?

She opened the letter. The words were handwritten, neater than the envelope:

> *Dear Annalisa:*
> *I have spent every day wishing I would see you again. I have dreamed; I have prayed. Even when others told me it wouldn't matter. And now, by the grace of God (and Robiski), I write a letter I had all but given up hope of writing. My wife and I tried to find you in Italy—several times—but never succeeded. We thought we saw you about twenty years ago in Venice*

... but how to know? We tried to follow you—if it was you—but it was a crowded day.

She thought of waking Robiski, but decided not to. His words triggered a strange memory: *A man standing in a gondola, an obvious tourist, yelling at me ... while I was kissing my boyfriend at the Hotel Bellini stop. The way he spoke, his tone.* The letter shook in her hand. She'd seen him — right in Venice! — but thought him a leering middle-aged tourist.

Her tears dropped onto the paper, smudging the ink. *That close! If it was him.* She stared over the rooftops at the lagoon, shimmering in the distance, and then looked down:

I figured you forgot about me. That is OK. You were just a little girl. How could you remember? Now, this miracle of miracles.

After talking to him, she'd found thousands of web pages, photo galleries, video and concert clips, and ten albums she downloaded. She would have tunneled to the center of time and back to find out more about Tom's past. About her own past.

I cannot get away until later, when we may add a few European dates. I hope we do not have to wait so long to see each other.

You don't, Papa. His letter was a deep, warm embrace, written by the strong hands she now imagined holding her.

I have never stopped loving you or thinking about you, Annie. I tried to make her stay. I tried hard. I looked hard for you, too. I can understand that she wanted to go back to Italy, I think, but not to act like I was dead.

She'd never had the strength to confront Maria, instead cowering inside a thick wall of numbness. *Never again.* She would confront her, burn away lingering pockets of abandonment that could derail she and Jason, she and Tom, and move forward.

Jason says you are a wonderful woman—I've never seen him so happy. I still think it's crazy, you and he, out of seven billion people on the planet ...

Very crazy, she thought. Laughter bubbled through her tears.

You and your son have a home here. Megan and I would also like to visit after this tour. Can we do that?

With all my love,
Dad

28

ROBISKI CLICKED HIS HEADSET, WONDERING HOW A SIMPLE discussion about dates in Europe could become a negotiation on which country and its particular legion of fans had the most right to host the Fever. He glanced at his computer and looked over at Annalisa, his irritation at Francois dissipating as soon as his eyes landed on her. *What did I do to win the lottery?* He leaned over to kiss her as Francois finished speaking.

"Get back to me with dates and places . . . yeah, pack them together, we can set up a satellite city, Paris or Munich," Robiski said. "Four gigs in five days is fine . . . no, not ten in ten days; we're hard-working rock musicians, not marathon runners . . . no, we can't do it 'just this once'. . . Yes, I understand you could book fifty shows, but we're booking ten here. Not eleven, not fifteen. *Ten* . . . no, they won't see it your way . . . Call me with dates . . . Yeah, yeah, February. Maybe we can play *carnevale* somewhere."

The show requests piled up again after videos from the Cumberland Festival went viral. The tidy, forty-stop tour now numbered fifty confirmed shows, with two dozen other venues making offers and inquiries. That was just in the U.S. and Canada. Now, European promoters like Francois Duprisson were throwing in castles, palaces, and outrageous contract riders designed to entice—backstage meals prepared by five-star chefs, thousand-dollar wine, dinners with sons and daughters of heads of state—or heads of state themselves, in a few cases—massage therapists, the works.

The Cumberland Festival pushed the buzz through the roof. It reminded Robiski of his dad's favorite story, when the ascending queen in the San Francisco scene walked into a Jaguar dealership one morning. She was barefoot and disheveled, fresh off a night of partying in the Airplane house, where Enrico Caruso and his golden voice had ridden out the Great Earthquake. The flat-topped, bespectacled, square-backed salesman fingered the slide rule in his shirt pocket, not knowing that two of this disheveled hippie's songs were the hottest in America. She wanted to buy a car. He told her to get out. She repeated her intention. He threatened to call the police. She repeated her request once more. He started dialing. *Is he clueless?* she wondered. You didn't mess with two things in San Francisco in '67—Governor Reagan, or the music queen.

She pressed the salesman again. He looked outside, phone receiver to his ear, hoping potential customers wouldn't see the stringy-haired bohemian standing on his showroom floor. She reached into her pocket and pulled out one hundred crisp portraits of Ben Franklin. *Ten grand.* "I'm buying a car—now!" she said, minus the vibrato.

He hung up the phone and grabbed the paperwork. A few minutes later, she drove off with her new Jaguar.

Robiski chuckled. You could take all the great Sixties stories you want, and let's face it, many have been teased, repurposed, and elevated far beyond their original scope, to mythical status. That's what happens when a conscious dawning descends on millions at seemingly the same time; the stories become experience now, history later. But for his money, his take on the second half of that decade, he'd take the story of the psychedelic rocker who drove off with a Jaguar, leaving a flabberghasted salesman behind.

Now, adding to the whole screwball comedy, his love of Tom's lost daughter deepened by the day. He didn't want to rehash the unlikely sequence of events in his life the past year; it would probably flip him out. One thought filled his mind as Annalisa lay in the sun, head and breasts tilted to the sky, his mood improving just by watching her.

He had never felt love like this.

Later, as Annalisa rummaged for espresso beans, Robiski swore at his computer from a nook Maurizio built into a corner. She turned her head while rubbing an eye. "Do you have much work, love? We have dinner guests, and the festival tonight."

He closed his computer. "Done for now. I have to keep my phone with me, but otherwise, the world can wait."

He stood up and opened his arms. She curled into him as if they'd been doing it for thirty years. A new feeling. When it came to women, any moment besides the present was cause for concern. He preferred to never get that close, that intimate, that influential in another's life to cross over into the world of commitment . . . but Annalisa retired that saddle-worn playbook. He was madly in love with a woman who endured pain he couldn't fathom and only wanted to be loved. He felt it in her pleading eyes, the hungry way she sometimes kissed, the way he had to pry her arms apart to get out of bed. In the past, he would've been out before daybreak, throwing on his shirt while running down the driveway. With her, he wanted to see how it would go.

While in the States, he found himself missing her more and more, her absence a subtle but visceral ache in his chest. Who would have imagined finding a woman who could settle him? Let alone one who appeared with a vaporetto, a water taxi, to transport him from airport to hotel—after which she accepted his invitation for a glass of wine?

There was no place for the old Robiski playbook here. No place at all.

"Would you like some fruits and bread?" she asked.

"Definitely. I'm starving."

She turned the corner and watched him. "You are busy in your mind, *si?*"

He nodded. "It's all good."

"*Buono.*" She poured two espressos, sliced two chunks of olive bread, and grabbed a hunk of mozzarella. Working swiftly, she poured olive oil onto a plate, slid the squeezer from its corner, and juiced a half-dozen oranges. Then she reached into the cupboard, pulled out a circular tray, plopped down a fruit bowl, bread, and cheese, and rimmed the edge with cheese slices. His stomach growled for mercy. Most Italian women carried along a delicious, dangerous accomplice: the skills to make great food.

Annalisa's eyes sparkled through their lightly swollen lids. She grabbed a small fork and plucked a huge blackberry, sank her teeth into it, and kissed Robiski as the berry exploded. After a quick chuckle, she peered onto the rooftop terrace. Emilio, her favorite stray cat, lay beneath the vine-entangled canopy, not giving a damn what they or anyone else thought about it. "Reminds me of another cat I know," Robiski said. "Incorrigible."

He ran his fingers through her hair, losing them in her thickening locks. A thought crept into his mind, not as fearfully as when it first edged the surface, now a little louder, a little more comfortable telling its story: *I could walk away from the Fever and the label and live here, no problem.* Maybe he could become a glassblower, fisherman, or furniture maker. Or run a little studio for local musicians. Anything but driving the funeral boats. He closed his eyes and felt the thrill of the chase, of sending bands into stardom, of watching fans go crazy. Of calling it quits and living in a place where cultures have percolated for almost two thousand years.

Annalisa backed into Robiski's chest, rubbing against him. She mentally clicked off the list of heels, blown glass pieces, and silk scarves she wanted to give to her new family, along with her own wardrobe. She thought of the responsibilities she'd shouldered, both for Paolo and Maurizio, and how this was her first chance in years to let everything go, fly to California, revisit her happiest memories.

He'd confirmed it the day before: "I want you to fly back to L.A. with me," he said. "It's the only chance you might have to see him for a long time, as hot as they are."

Her eyes moistened as his words flowed through her mind, then her heart. Time for the little bird to return.

29

WHAT A DINNER. WHAT A FEAST. ROBISKI STARED AT THE thin ribbon of remaining dusk from the stern of Maurizio's boat. Other vessels gathered off San Marco Piazza as the Campanile bell clanged the passing of the hour, its signature act for six centuries. Robiski licked his lips, re-tasting the best seafood he'd ever eaten, the meal triggering memories of father-son fishing trips he and Don took to the Sequoias, or on deep sea boats around the Farallons, where great white sharks were ready to snatch a halibut or salmon off the hook—or you, if you fell in. Don Robiski cleared his schedule for two weeks each summer to enjoy what fathers and sons enjoy—simple outings, tough hikes, playing catch, little talks, and grilling fish over a campfire. Those times, a boy never forgets. Then Don would run another blockbuster Fever tour.

Now Robiski stood at the helm of the Fever's *blitzkrieg*, which had soared far beyond anyone's expectations. Tom, Chester & Co. had blown away the Cumberland Festival. Newly added shows sold out the same day tickets went on sale, sometimes within an hour. For nearly a month, the Fever owned the Billboard charts, running 1-3-10 in album sales, and taking two spots each in the Top 10 for rock/pop and alternative singles. They hadn't charted like this since the Seventies. They were hitting on all cylinders, making such an impact onto fans' minds, hearts, and memory banks, downloads spiked in the day following each show. Hard to believe half the band consisted of pinch-hitters for original members, Robiski thought.

He thought again of the dinner, the way Maurizio fashioned a Venetian merchant's fiesta. Maurizio brushed aside a frozen hip to lord over a grill inlaid into a stack of bricks—his handiwork, like most of the touches in Annalisa's flat. While leaning on his cane, he lathered a dozen giant shrimp mantises with a sauce Annalisa whipped from garlic, rosemary, paprika, thyme, and red pepper. Elephant garlic cloves sizzled alongside. Maurizio waved a long fork that held a skewered prawn. "My friend, could you bring the vegetables?" he asked.

"Of course." Robiski walked into a kitchen that looked like the aftermath of a tornado, with spices, vegetables, garnishes, knives, bowls, and seafood strewn everywhere. Annalisa moved with arms in constant motion, running knives and stirring spoons, wiping her hands on her apron, chopping and tossing pears, walnuts, creamy mountain cheeses, fennel seeds, purple onions, olives, arugula, white lettuce, pea pods, and artichoke hearts into a Murano bowl, its blown glass swirls a rainbow unto itself.

He looked down at the stereo between the kitchen and main room. "What you have on here?" *A stereo. With a turntable.*

"The spirit of this night, *mi amore.* 'Carnevale di Venezia.'"

He gazed at Christine's half-sister. Even the words of the song felt surreal, like someone else's miracle. "Vivaldi?"

"Tchaikovsky. Could you carry out the *mozzarella e pomodore e basilicum,* and this?" She handed him a dish of sardines, tiny fried octopus, chopped dogfish, and thumb-sized baby artichokes drenched in olive oil and garlic. "How is Poppa doing?"

Robiski grabbed the two dishes. "I can't even imagine living to be his age, let alone running the grill for something like this."

"This is Maurizio." She said it with fortitude and pride, a touch of defiance. *What do you expect?* If that wasn't a statement of respect and honor, what was?

Robiski left the kitchen, nearly colliding with Paolo. *If Tom was an inch or two shorter, had a dark tan and black hair . . .* He shook his head, trying to shake the weirdness of it all. A dark-haired girl with purple streaks joined him. "*Buona sera,* Paolo."

Paolo pulled him in. "*Buona sera, signore Jason.*" He turned to his girlfriend. "*Cara mia, Leticia.*"

Annalisa walked into the foyer, cheese cleaver in hand. She hugged and kissed Paolo on both cheeks. "How are you feeling?"

"Ready to get back to work, Mama."

No. Annalisa's stern look needed no translation.

"Really, Mama, I must drive the vaporetto," he argued. "I am tired of sitting around."

Her frown crept into her voice. "You go too far. It would not be so bad if you allow Letitia to take care of you, but she tells me that is impossible, too." She punctuated with choice words in rapid-fire Italian, in a tone Robiski had never heard, one that left him happy he wasn't on the receiving end.

Annalisa and Paolo argued for a few minutes, points and counterpoints rising and falling like a churned-up sea. Or two seas converging. Robiski glanced over at Letitia, who watched with interest. The girl's opaline eyes and thick eyebrows reminded him of the post-punk, *Flashdance,* Go-Go's L.A.

scene . . . with more edge. Her wild, curly hair spilled beneath her white derby, while her legs glimmered like fine alabaster carvings beneath a tiny mini-skirt and three-inch heels. Then it hit him, who she reminded him of: the sultry three-girl horn section on Guns N' Roses' last great tour. Right down to the black skirt that looked painted on. With a single coat.

After dealing with Annalisa's withering stare, Paolo walked over to Robiski. "You make Mama happy, this talk of California. *Gracie.* Though she is not so happy with me," he said.

Leticia kissed Paolo and joined Annalisa in the kitchen. A light-blue opal with diamond insets sparkled from her ring finger, the opal matching her eyes. "You will be staying here with him, when he watches the flat for me?" Annalisa asked.

"*Si, signora.*"

Annalisa switched to Italian, to speed up the conversation and leave Robiski clear of it. "He is doing better? I have not spoken to him since Jason arrives."

"Yes, Mama. He eats. His white blood count is lower. There is life in his eyes, and color in his cheeks. I told him that I will not be a young widow. If he tries to leave, I will drag him back from the other side. I mean it."

Annalisa laughed through tears that sprouted from onions she was cutting . . . so she chose to believe. Letitia tied on an apron and slung her arm over her future mother-in-law's shoulder. "Do not worry about us, about Paolo. Make your life with Jason. See this other family Paolo tells me about." She paused. "Try not to think about us too much." A frown crossed Annalisa's face. "Well, who am I fooling? You are his mother."

Where did this girl develop such capacity to love so early in her life? Annalisa blinked away tears while giving silent thanks for this girl, who gave Paolo the romantic stability she never knew at that age, or really any age, what with her choices of men. *If only I'd had this girl's grasp* . . .

She clasped Letitia's hand and raised it to her lips. "I will leave Paolo to you. But tell me everything when I call, because he will not. And I will call."

Letitia squeezed her hand. "And I will tell you all."

"I am going to the Feast," Maurizio insisted, his eyes as fiery as the seafood spices.

"*Sei pazza?* You crazy? You are not walking well, you need to save your energy."

"For what, child? Tomorrow? Why do I need to save energy?"

"You have been so many times . . ."

"Annalisa, *Abbastanza!* Enough! You and Jason will join me on my boat." Maurizio swept his arm around the candlelit table. "Will anyone else tell me why I cannot go to my favorite festival, that I like even more than Carnevale?"

Robiski shook his head. *No way in hell.* Annalisa patted his hand. "He is stubborn."

"I see his point. It's probably the highlight of his year."

"Don't say that too loudly," she chuckled.

Paolo leaned across the table, two olives on his fork, his large green eyes a foot from her. "Mama, he is right. He lives the best way." He waved the fork rhythmically. "You are doing the same with Jason, *no?* Living your life in your way? Finally?"

"Your mama is protecting me in her own way, son." Maurizio turned to Annalisa. "My girl, I will rest when I die. But . . ." his eyes cast a wider view. "When I see your nonna again, maybe no rest at all. She told me when I get there, she will not leave me alone. I hope not!" Stars twinkled on his face.

"Let us see how you get up tomorrow to fill the busy shoe orders," Annalisa said.

"I will help him if he needs it," Letitia said.

"Then it is settled. I am ready for the festival," Maurizio said.

Annalisa nodded. "You can carry on with the other ancient mariners, the Dogen."

Maurizio opened two Cuban cigars and smacked his lips. "One for you, Jason?"

An hour later, the dark, cured pride of the Pinar del Rio between his lips and Paolo's protest quashed, Maurizio steered into the heart of the lagoon. He grinned over his latest hard-won dinner argument—the right to captain his own boat. It brought up one of the few riddles of parenthood that still puzzled him: Why do they argue as teens to leave the house, and then argue years later for their elders to sit home and wait to die? He shook his head. Some riddles cannot be answered.

They cruised past the twin Piazza lions, the stone sentries to Venice. Maurizio turned to starboard and headed out another two hundred meters, picking through speedboats, vaporettos, rowboats, gondolas, motonaves, and traghettos. More vessels streamed into the lagoon, draped in flowers and flags, the colors the greens and reds of Italy, the blues and whites of Venice, and plenty of others; the lagoon looked like a starry night reflecting onto itself. "That is how we decorate boats," Annalisa said, holding Robiski's forearms against her stomach. "Poppa wanted to decorate this boat, too. I would not allow it."

"Why not?" Robiski asked. "He uses his hands. It keeps him alive. Busy. He has to be in motion."

"There is more *Marmor* in that man than in the Apuane mountains. Stubborn, stubborn man." She laid her head against his shoulder. "He has taken on this family's problems for so many years. He does not have to be our rock anymore."

"Being anything less would hurt his spirit. He knows no other way, sweetheart. And Tom—your dad—is the same way, so get used to it." He paused. "What does this feast we're at commemorate, anyway?"

"*Redentore*. Our liberation from the plague.*"

Robiski nodded slowly, reminded of his amazement over the Old World's litany of festivals and celebration, once and still the very stuff from which communities were built. "That's worth celebrating . . . six hundred years ago."

"It is still worth celebrating. None of us are here if they do not stop the plague. Venice is not here."

"OK, but still, six hundred years . . ."

She kissed Robiski's cheek. "Americans. So young. Your sense of history."

"You're an American too, don't forget."

She smiled broadly. "I never think like that, but I guess I am."

After settling into place, the boats and vessels transformed into floating cafes of flowers, candles, and small dining tables. Old doors or boards connected some boats, allowing people to walk from one to the other. Baskets of food opened, candles glowed, the revelers' volume increased, and the sky blossomed with explosions of every color as Annalisa turned to the bow. She dipped into the basket at her feet and grabbed a bottle of cabernet, along with four stemmed glasses from the side pockets.

Maurizio wobbled to the stern, flanked by Paolo and Letitia, Paolo also moving slowly. Whistles erupted from a boat filled with coeds, their prosecco-infused hormones focused on Letitia and Paolo. "Let them whistle. Let them call. Let them dream. Who sleeps with her tonight?" Paolo asked.

Robiski nodded. "A great way to look at it."

"And I live their dreams."

"Serves them right." Maurizio wrapped his arm around Paolo's shoulder. "They did the same when I first brought your nonna to this feast. The summer before Mussolini spread his war disease. When they made noises and calls, I kissed my Clara in front of them. They whistled louder, and when I kissed her more, they whistled louder." He winked at Paolo, and then Letitia, while handing a bottle to Annalisa. "I want us to drink this tonight. A very special wine from our sixtieth anniversary."

She read the label: *Giacomo Contero 2000 Barolo Monfortino*. The ruby reserve was rare. Unseen for years. Vintage. "I thought you said you would only open this . . ."

". . . at my last Feast of the Redentore."

Fireworks lit up Venice, the smoke riding light easterlies towards the Lido, and from there, the Adriatic Sea and Dubrovnik. Maurizio turned to his floating party. "*Mi familia*. Everyone is in love. Everyone is happy. Annalisa is going to see her Papa. Let us open this bottle. It cannot be any better."

Maurizio filled the glasses, his hand shaking. Unlike so many other revelers, he would walk away on his own terms, while still vital to his town, his town, his society. He sipped from his glass and lifted it higher. "*Brindisi, mi familia*. A toast to our lives, our happiness." He looked up at the sky. "And you, *mi amore*."

They drank quietly. After they finished, Annalisa poured her bottle. On they went, sipping and watching fireworks, yelling to friends, sharing jokes and laughs until, sometime around 2 a.m., they concentrated on the grand finale—a ten-minute explosion of shapes, sizes, colors, and music filling the lagoon, drums and horns and cymbals wrapping the celebration, the smoke settling into a quiet fog atop the lagoon.

The boats dispersed slowly. Maurizio steered to port, Paolo threw the anchor, and Robiski tied it up. "I am tired now," Maurizio said.

A thought struck Annalisa: the opera singer she'd seen floating with tourists on the Grande Canale. She turned to Paolo. "Can you and Letitia take him home?"

"*Si*, Mama."

Thirty minutes later, Annalisa and Robiski drifted on a side canal. The open backsides of old depots, boat builders, and various artisan stalls were draped in soft, velvet light. She closed her eyes, tucked into Robiski, California rolling through her mind. He held her close as he opened his eyes to the sinking city, revealing her deepest hidden beauty. Just like the woman now sleeping on his chest.

30

CINCINNATI . . . COLUMBUS . . . CLEVELAND . . . PITTSBURGH . . .
PROVIDENCE . . . PHILADELPHIA . . . BALTIMORE . . .
RICHMOND . . . CHARLESTON . . . CHARLOTTE . . . LOS ANGELES

T HE FEVER ARRIVED IN L.A. AS THE HOTTEST BAND OF THE
summer, drawing Angelenos from their Los Feliz, Silverlake, Malibu,
Hollywood, Brentwood, Laurel Canyon, and La Tuna homes,
playhouses, and mansions to be seen with them. *We know you! We love you! We*
want our picture with you!

Adulation and fame are funny, elusive plays of light and shadow, Tom
thought as he walked past another flurry of fans, smiling and quickly
bumping fists or shaking hands. Everyone clamors for the front of the rope
line. Everyone wants to share the red carpet. *Thank you! Glad to see you! Thanks*
for listening! Problem is, what if you don't know any of them? They approach
you as if you're best friends, but to you, they are strange, blurred faces in a
summer-long tempest. Maybe they would be great friends; how could you
know? You appreciate them for attending and buying your music, but are they
friends? How will they act? He thought of an old guitarist friend who returned
to the town where he'd played backyard parties a year earlier, this time as lead
guitarist for a major national headliner, and a lifelong friend standing in front
of the stage yelled out "Hero!" "My idol!" "Take me home!"—disrupting the
show until the headliner danced over and asked what the problem was. He
said to the guitarist, "You need some new friends." Not what you want the
bossman to say to you in the middle of a live concert with fifty thousand on
hand. You never really know. Strange days, indeed.

More fans hovered around their limos, though their attention was
increasingly directed toward the car behind him. He grinned. Christine's turn
to deal with it.

Christine's world couldn't be more different. She'd left L.A. not three
months before as a new graduate and budding muralist, and returned home
the rock world's emerging sweetheart. As her limo inched past Tom's car and
sped off, the fans screamed, delirious. *We saw her!* She and X, along with
Trish and two other sorority sisters, raced off to meet Melissa at a round of
press interviews she and Robiski arranged. They lasted two hours. They parted

ways so X could drop off their bags at Will's beach house in Venice. The girls directed the limo driver west, by way of slithery, scenic Sunset Boulevard. Rogelio and Ophelia met them in Santa Monica, followed by X. They danced, drank shots, and paid back the house band's shout-outs by joining them for two Fever tunes. They signed autographs on napkins, arms, and ball caps. "Welcome to the bigs, baby," X laughed.

After closing the bar down, they stumbled into the limo with Rogelio and Ophelia, and sped off to Mulholland Drive to view the City of Angels from the Hollywood Hills. They finally found their way back to Venice and spilled into Will's beach house as dawn peeked over the San Bernardino Mountains.

Christine collapsed and went black.

A few minutes later, she opened her eyes and peered at the nightstand: 1 p.m. *Where did seven hours just go?* Her head throbbed in a defibrillated fog. She remembered something about jumping onstage, singing, drinking, drinking more . . . then something about Rogelio and X subduing a crazy drunk boy who tried to whisk her away.

Tom looked down at his sprawled-out daughter and chuckled. "Sweetheart, you'll learned not to get smashed when you're not used to getting smashed. Hope you had fun."

"Uhhhhhhhhh . . ." She plastered the pillow over her head.

He rubbed her shoulder until she fell back asleep, his concern beginning to grow over her increased drinking and anxiety. It was pressure, rising to stardom and dealing with the parties, events, and temptations that awaited at every stop. You had to be a super being to stay clear of it, and besides, who would opt out of a social scene now beginning to shape up around you? Christine was now in the spotlight, living the dream, her moves and movements tracked by fans and pararazzi. Could she handle it? Could she keep her focus? So far, so good, he thought, but her drinking troubled him. Not as much, though, as a question:

What have I unleashed?

The Cumberland Festival offered quite an answer. The following three weeks turned into a blur of interviews, reviews, radio spots, and guest DJ gigs—live promotion, always worth it—and standing room-only shows at every port. Their performances had grown strong, mistakes and missed notes dwindling to almost nothing. Their sound and stage choreography was equally tight. "Perfect night," Tom said after Philadelphia, an extended three-and-a-half-hour set.

"Feel like we've been saying that a lot, but all y'all were on top of your games," Chester added.

They also averted trouble in Philadelphia. Authorities threatened to fine the band under a noise ordinance seemingly invoked only when rock bands came to town. So much for brotherly love. "No way we're stopping," Tom told the supervisor, who confronted him after the second of what became four encores. "The people want us, the people paid considerable money—more than I want them to pay, the way they run ticket sales these days so re-sellers can make bank. So our solution is to play longer." He stared at the supervisor whose fingers fidgeted on a two-way radio, clearly not used to musicians arguing with him as he debated whether to call in the police. "Fine us. I don't give a shit. But you pull the plug, everyone in this building's going to riot, and they're going to be coming for you."

The supervisor relented. Robiski received a bill for the fine, which he paid, but fans got the music they wanted.

More and more, they also wanted Christine.

Tom dragged her out of bed, whipped up tomato soup to soothe her stomach, and returned to the next radio interview on his list. After wrapping up the phone interviews, and after Christine stirred to show proof-of-life, he and Megan escorted her to see Twyla Partinson, a premier entertainment and modeling agent in L.A. and an old friend. They asked her to handle requests for Christine to appear in shoots in New York, TV commercials, and talk and live show spots. After chatting with Christine for thirty minutes, Twyla signed her.

At the satellite radio interview that followed, the general manager, Martin Jammer, asked Tom following a lively run through the Fever's musical history, "Would you and/or Chester consider hosting a weekly program after the tour? We'll fly a technician to your home to set up one studio, and another to Chester's farm."

Tom glanced over at Megan, whose smile reflected her feelings. "What's the format?" he asked.

Jammer leaned across the table, smiling as he rolled up his sleeves. A large guitar tattoo rode from one wrist to an armpit. "Here's the format I see: An hour of anything you choose, roughly three parts music with one part storytelling. We want you and Chester to banter about your best shows, history, musicians, bands, one-hit wonders, and local legends that would blow you two away, but are unknown outside their regions."

Tom chuckled. "We've run into a couple over the years."

"In other words, share your experiences."

Awesome. It never ceased to amaze him, the opportunities that opened out of nowhere once you pushed the ball forward and invited the universe to jump into the game. And these days, with a million and one ways that a well-penned and well-turned song can reach its audience . . . Just move that ball forward. A satellite radio show of their own? What a coup, an honor for their body of work. "Chester'll love it," Tom said. "The man has more musical knowledge than the internet. How about he, Robiski, and I meet you in the next day or two? We're in L.A. for a few days."

"Done and done." Martin Jammer shook Megan's hand, then Tom's and Christine's. "Bring Chester and Robiski, and we'll discuss a multiple-year contract for you boys, maybe thirty-five, forty weekly shows per year. Figure out the split between you two."

"No need." Tom shook his hand firmly. "We'll split it fifty-fifty."

"Really?" Jammer peered over his bifocals. "No one in this town knows what the hell fifty-fifty is. Know how many great ideas run off into Santa Monica Bay because people can't do simple math, like realizing they had an equal amount to do with the initiative, so you split the proceeds?"

"Well, we roll differently. Sometimes, old school is good school."

"What are we looking at, dollars wise?" Megan asked.

Jammer wrote down a figure, and handed it to Megan as Christine glanced over her shoulder. "Holy shit," Christine whispered.

"What we pay someone that comes along once or twice in the twenty years satellite radio's been around," Jammer said. "Especially when it's Gandalf and Merlin."

Megan handed the note to Tom, who looked at it and smiled. "Consider us agreed, Martin. Run the contract through Robiski. He's flying in later."

"Baby, wake up. Time to go."

Song lists . . . where's my song list . . . are the tunes cued up . . . is the satellite working? . . . heavy blankets. Megan sprawled atop him. He cracked open an eye, rubbed her shoulder, smelled her overheated, lavender-spritzed skin, and wished they could never leave Will's little paradise.

However, duty called. He kissed her head, rubbed her back, and then stood up, stretched out, walked to the edge of the balcony, and watched the sun sink slowly toward its Pacific cradle. "What time is it?"

"Six-thirty."

"Good thing the show's at eight."

Megan fiddled with the pendant on her chest. "Don't forget the warm-up band. You've got a little longer."

He looked down at the beach. Inline skaters raced along the boardwalk in their bikini tops and headphones, high on adrenaline and youth. He caught the eyes of a woman staring at him from the beach, pointing to her husband, excited. He laughed and waved. What a trip, being a rock star, a trip that always seemed to have new twists.

He showered, changed into jeans and a shirt, and grabbed extra clothes for the launch party . . . another long night. The Southwest swing now included ten concerts and only four days off, thanks to added dates in San Diego, Vegas, and Reno. Consequently, Robiski turned the launch party into a post-concert soiree, to be hosted by Daphne at her spacious gallery. Press, recording artists, paparazzi, friends, and celebrity wannabes would likely show up in droves. The glitterazi would arrive with enough bling to boost a third-world nation's GDP, along with smiles and stories, some genuine, others empty, most exaggerated in some way. You've got to love an L.A. music bash, Tom thought.

Megan wrapped her arms around his neck. "Daphne called and asked if I could help her set up. Would be great to catch up with her; it's been ages. Chandra's going with me. We'll see you after the show."

"When did you talk to Daphne?"

"A couple of hours ago, while you were sleeping. Ran into her on the boardwalk."

"Tell her I said hello."

"Tell her yourself later."

31

TOM WALKED OFFSTAGE, MICROPHONE IN POCKET, THEN FLEXED his arms, returned with his guitar and swayed back and forth behind Christine's final pass through "Gypsy's Prayer." He grabbed the mic as she swayed in front of him, singing along, feeling the love of the fans, the love twenty thousand happy souls can bring to any moment when connected by a song. A man reached for her feet, coming up with air instead of toes as she deftly skip-stepped away. Tom eyed him closely, singing yet ready to pounce, something singers had done to protect band members since Jim Morrison and Marty Balin went flying into throngs in the Sixties. When the man backed off, he settled back into the feeling of recaptured youth, a sense of belonging, his daughter on stage, the band his family, the crowd part of it. He was the ringmaster for the greatest rock show on earth this night. Euphoria mixed with excellence, a mighty combination, a nectar not unlike that gods and goddesses drank in their sandstone and polychrome mugs before they performed their godly feats.

He sat back on one leg and fired off guitar volleys as Christine commanded center stage, the fans at her mercy, moving as she moved. The set was even more musically crisp than Cumberland, though social media buzz and a few music journalists were already comparing Cumberland to the best festivals of all time. They'd spent weeks building off each other, finding new wrinkles in songs that, you'd think, were gassed after being played live hundreds of times. Then, in that sweaty meadow, they hit their sweet spot, the songs performed with originality and improvisation, cohesiveness, and joint purpose. So much for what "The Fever's Greatest Hits Tour," that weary aphorism for "cashing in." Now, that very same press was proclaiming that all along, they'd predicted the Fever would take the summer by storm. He could only chuckle.

Christine kept pumping her fist up and down, leading a small revolution in the seats. Chester stepped on his echoplex and blasted his final chord into the night. As he waddled offstage, shaking his guitar by the neck as he passed his amp to intensify the echoing, a familiar face blocked his path toward the coveted backstage beers. "You made it," he said to Robiski.

"Finally. L.A. traffic sucks. Always has, always will." Robiski glanced at the delirious crowd. "Looks like you boys have stirred up the Hollywood stars and starlets." He and Tom shook hands as Tom stepped off stage, and then he slapped Chester's shoulder.

Chester grabbed a towel from a roadie and wiped his face. "How was Italy? She turning you into a romantic spoutin' Hallmark card sayings?"

A huge smile flashed through Robiski's half-lidded, burning eyes. "How was Italy? Well, last night or the night before, not sure what night it is, I joined Venetians in a big boat festival, then floated down a canal with my lady. Now, after flying for God knows how many hours, my driver played chicken on the freeway and somehow didn't kill us both, and now I'm standing here with sweaty musicians." He chuckled. "Yeah, Chester, Italy works for me."

Tom toweled off his face. "You know you'd rather be here keeping *us* company."

"Yeah, *that's* it." Robiski rolled his eyes and handed Tom a beer. He saw the bandage on Chester's strumming hand. "How did that happen?"

"A fan in Cleveland."

"A fan . . ."

Chester nodded. "Got excited, threw a firecracker onstage, my hand was the landing pad." He glanced over to Tom. "Led to a little moment."

Did it ever. As Chester doubled over, Tom stopped the song. "You people see a chicken cage up here? Don't throw shit!" Next to him, Christine attended to Chester as she spotted the perpetrator, pointed, and summoned a pair of refrigerator-sized defensive linemen, the yellow-shirted security. "Can you get that dick?"

Less than thirty seconds later, the assailant left the building, his arm pinned by one lineman, the other popping him in the head with the heel of his hand. The show stopped for nearly an hour while Chester received medical treatment and the house announcer lambasted the crowd. The Fever then returned and finished, with Tom playing lead and Chester acoustic guitar to relieve the pain.

Tom grabbed another towel. "You've missed quite a bit, Jason." He looked down the corridor. A phalanx of yellow shirts and suited men with walkie-talkies stood by, part of the beefed-up security since Cleveland. One was chatting up a woman with dark graying hair, and dark-framed glasses. He hadn't seen her backstage before, but that didn't mean anything. Probably a roadie's lady. Or press.

Christine waved while skip-stepping above the outstretched arms of fans. "So, I'm curious: when did the kids start running the playground?" Robiski asked. "Looks like the center is moving stage left. Not sure if that's how you planned it, Tommy, at least right now, but the press is noticing."

"Been that way since Cumberland," Tom said while yanking out his earpiece and unhooking the transmitter from his belt. "I agree with Chester—I hate this damned thing. I'm not using it again. It's old school from here on out—monitors, eye cues, hear the songs like I want to hear them." A roadie bundled earpiece and transmitter into Tom's sweaty towel and took it away.

Robiski cleared his throat. "So, at our launch party tonight, I'm announcing that four of *their* songs"—he pointed to Christine, X, and Rogelio, waving to fans with Will—"will become an EP."

"How did that come about?" Tom asked.

"You gave me the songs on rough tracks in New Mexico. Remember?"

Tom tugged at his narrow rockabilly tie, a little added dress-up for the gig and party. "Yeah," he chuckled, "but I didn't say anything about an EP. And those were rough tracks."

"Christine wanted to surprise you. We worked it out. She insisted you get a co-credit on all of them, along with X and Rogelio. Kid's cutting you in on the publishing—you raised her well, Tom." Robiski threw his palms out. "I'd like to look out for her interests along with yours. You good with that?"

He thought for a moment. "Yeah . . . yeah I am, Jason. She just signed with an entertainment and modeling agency today, but you handle her music. And, speaking of interests, Chester and I are getting a satellite show. Can you call Martin Jammer and wrap that up?"

"He already called me. Gotta say, Tommy, that's the best possible way for a musician to head to pasture. You and Chester'll be doing shows until you're a hundred."

A smile crossed Tom's lips, growing larger as the impact of what Robiski said hit him. "I'm glad you want to look out for Christine. She's going to need it."

Whenever a business type in the industry told Tom, "I'm looking out for your interests," his response was often the same: run for the hills. How many times over the years had he and others been swindled by sharks ready to take advantage of young musicians with infinite creative and sales potential, but zero financial sense or career vision? So many gold and platinum bands ended up going toes-up in bankruptcy because their handlers considered them *their* meal tickets to early retirement. The Beatles, Jefferson Airplane, Elvis, Tom Petty, Grand Funk . . . everyone knew someone who was screwed.

He and the band were the lucky ones. Don Robiski corralled them just three years into their career. His son was the same protective way. Christine was in good hands.

"Be right back, Dad," Christine yelled. "Nature's calling." She ran down the corridor. The others joined Tom, Chester, and Robiski, while twenty thousand ecstatic fans erupted: "Fever!" "More!" "Fever!" "More!"

Christine nearly collided with the bespectacled woman as she talked with security guards while stealing glances at Robiski. "Sounds like they want you back onstage, Tom," Robiski said while watching the near-collision. "But . . ." The smile faded from his face. "You need to know something."

"Can't it wait?" Chester asked.

"No."

"Has to," Tom said. "We've got to get back up there."

"Can't wait. Sorry."

Robiski turned toward the corridor. The woman excused herself from the guards and walked toward them, sleek and chic in a dark summer dress and pumps, a glass of wine trembling in hand, her smile tentative, shaky. She pushed her glasses further up her nose, but they slid down a thin sheen of perspiration.

As she approached, her eyes moistened. "Damn, honey, you don't have to cry over me," Chester mumbled. "I'll take care of you. If my wife lets me."

Robiski threw his arm around the woman. "That's what you call a Chester Craven redneck greeting." He chuckled.

The woman blinked rapidly when hearing Chester's name, as though trying to decide if he was a mirage or real. Tom watched, Robiski's arm around her . . . no, no fucking way . . . can't be . . . has to be just another backstage guest. He glanced at the woman, nodded, looked down, tried to fight off his surging belly, glanced at her again—

Her eyes. Inside the thin lines and wrinkles, the deep sockets and prominent cheekbones, there they were: *her eyes.* They peered back from faded black and white photographs, from the other side of the darkest night of his soul . . . now five feet away. Beads of sweat burst across his forehead. His next breath refused to come out.

She extended her arms, tears beginning to creep past her eyes. *"Buona sera, Papa."*

32

ANNALISA CLUNG TO HIM FOR ONE MINUTE, THEN TWO, HER tears drawing out his own, decades of tears.

He tried to breathe. He tried to speak. Nothing. "Dad, we've got to get back onstage," Christine said softly.

When Tom and Annalisa turned, Christine saw their faces, the similarities in their cheeks, their eyes. She caught her breath and covered her mouth. "Oh—my—God . . ."

The crowd grew borderline riotous in its pleas for more music, unaware the most improbable father and child reunion was happening backstage. After all the stomping, screaming, and shouting, they wanted their encore. *House lights are still down! Get back out here!*

Annalisa cupped Tom's cheeks. "My whole life, I pray for this. Even when I am told you are gone. I never forgot you, Papa."

"Sweetheart, I just . . ." He didn't even try brushing the tears away.

Annalisa looked slightly upward to Christine. "What a beautiful lady you are. More beautiful than the pictures," she said.

"Hello, miracle woman." Christine wanted to say "Annalisa," or "sister," but both skidded on her tongue. What do you say to someone who's biologically your sister, but you've never seen before and have thought dead—for the few years you actually knew of her existence? She wrapped an arm around Tom. "Dad, you want us to handle the encore?" she asked.

"No, I've got it." Tom slipped away from Annalisa and, for the first time, took in the exquisite sight of his daughters together. He smiled as Annalisa and Christine exchanged quick words and nervous chuckles. "We're going to lay these people out, girls. One of you needs to join me up there," he said.

"You're on, Annalisa," Christine joked.

She playfully pushed Christine toward the stage.

Fans would talk for years about the twenty minutes that followed, twenty minutes in which the Fever threw the City of Angels on its shoulders and played on the emotional high that rippled through its founder. They ended boldly, triumphantly, Chester's final power chord reverberating into the night, X playing cut-throat keyboards, Will tying it together with a machine-gun blast that hit the crowd flush, along with the strobe lights firing out of his kick drums.

The twenty-minute ride to Daphne's gallery moved faster than breath on the run, a cacophony of talking, clothes changing, drinking, and toweling off faces—and sneaking looks at Annalisa and she at them. It was like peering into a trick mirror, only both the mirror and carnival were real. Due to the launch party, the band took a flyer after the show, running into the loading tunnel and awaiting limos after their extended encore, the fans screaming for more while SUVs whisked them down Manchester Boulevard. toward Venice Beach.

Christine's legs bounced up and down, as did Tom's, decelerating from the three-and-a-half-hour show. They laughed about a comical moment, a soccer mom up front shrieking, "You went *off!* *Off!* *Yahhhhhhhhhhhhh!*" As the woman was busting off kisses at Tom, she flung her arms in the air and trance danced. "You see her poor little twelve-year-olds?" The moment rushed through her in a huge laugh, rendering it difficult to talk. "Rolling their eyes, visibly disturbed, texting . . ." Which they did. *Mom's finally lost it*, the daughter posted, attaching a picture of her life guide in full trance dance. While the daughter seemed embarrassed, Christine thought, the mother undoubtedly ruled her office the next day, attracting a sort of celebrity status among her colleagues.

The front of Daphne's gallery looked like an overrun nightclub or the crashing a Sweet Sixteen party. Security fought to restrain hundreds who'd gotten word of what was supposed to be a private affair. As with all launch parties, every other person seemed to think that knowing an invited guest or band member was enough to ensure admittance, or rattling off completely unrelated credentials as if *that* created enough celebrity to let you into *this* party. At the Fever launch, security stuck to the names on the list, disappointing many.

Inside, cuts from the new album and the Christine-X-Rogelio EP looped from ten speakers spread overhead on walls, in corners, and between sculptures and paintings. The gallery was packed. The band members and guests walked up to and through the front door, through the crowds, shaking hands, accepting kisses, Annalisa and Robiski soon standing between Tom and Christine, Megan and Chandra joining Daphne to greet them.

Once inside, Robiski brushed off his edge with vodka on the rocks, stepped to the mic, introduced the band, and announced the big news Michelle texted while he and Annalisa were landing: a quarter-million pre-orders for the Fever's new live album, to be released as soon as the tour ended, and another fifty thousand for the Christine-Rogelio-X EP debut. Tom spoke about touring again, the new songs, and how Rogelio, X, and Christine made them a better band in many ways. He kept glancing at Annalisa, making sure she didn't disappear like she had one horrible afternoon. And in twenty thousand dreams that followed. She stood with Megan, Chandra, Ophelia, and Robiski, equally proud and amazed that this same man who once sang her to sleep was a star—or, to be fair, one of the greatest musicians America and the world had ever known.

After a few minutes, Christine and Chester regaled the audience with backstories and tidbits from the tour, stories that never tire real fans, because they connect and relate to the musician through the songs and melodies, some songs growing lives of their own, making ours feel better. Music stories carry the sticking power of heart and memory; they become part of us. Committed fans always come back for more.

As Chester finished, Tom felt two arms wrap around his stomach. "If it isn't Tommy T paying a visit to our fine little beach town. Hello, beautiful man."

He turned to drink in her rosy cheeks, lips, and eyes, her sly, dark outfit, beautiful and black as her hair, electric. "It's been a long time, Daphne . . ."

Their embrace was warm and tender, a reminder of the one bright spot in his lost year away from Megan, of the love they held for each other, the love of friends, a love that remains forever deep but can never again grow into physical form. It wasn't about being the third wheel, Daphne thought as they held each other, the odd woman out. It was about loving and being loved, and now loving Christine as her most interesting young friend in L.A. She would hold the love for all of them, a person out there in the world to whom they could turn, the type that makes every life and relationship better just by being present, somewhere on the earth.

As she broke Tom's embrace, she glanced at Annalisa, turned to speak to Megan, glanced again at Annalisa's eyes—

And stopped. "I don't believe we've met."

Annalisa stuck out her hand and grinned nervously. "I am Annalisa, *signora.*"

"So pleased to meet you." Daphne held Annalisa's hand between hers. "I'm glad your friends brought you to our little soir—"

She stopped, the Italian accent freezing her in place. "Annalisa . . ." *Same name as Tommy's other daughter. Heard she never died, she was in Italy. Wasn't the mother Italian? Gone since . . . well, this woman would be the right age.* She glared into Annalisa's eyes and turned to Tom. "*The* Annalisa?"

Annalisa stifled a chuckle as shock seized Daphne's face. "You know about me?"

"Oh dear God, of course I know about you, honey!"

They looked at each other. "Where did you come from? Christine never said anything about you when she and I saw each other before she went home to rehearse."

"She did not know," Annalisa said.

"Please forgive my surprise, but this old girl is *stunned*." She shook her head, wondering who drip-dropped acid in the punchbowls. All of it was so surreal: Through Tom, she knew a five-year-old girl, never pictured her any other way. The woman before her was maybe ten years younger than herself, no more, though she looked a few years younger than that. She quickly eyed her arms, upper torso, legs, all sleek, defined, shapely, only a few wrinkles. Fitness and light sun can turn the clock back quickly.

Daphne turned to Tom and Megan, a scowl crossing her face. "You two have just walked my last nerve. Why didn't you tell me, Megan?"

Megan shook her head. "I didn't know."

"Come on, honey. You were with Tommy all day, he goes to the show and you come here, and then she just shows up?" She motioned to Annalisa.

"Robiski didn't even tell Tom about her flying here with him," Megan said, pleading her case. "I don't think he knew, either. I met her five minutes before you did."

"And Christine?"

"They met before our encore," Tom said.

Daphne nervously twirled a golden half-note earring, scratched the diamond stud in her nose. "*Bellisima*," Annalisa said. "Your gallery is so beautiful; the black-and-white styling is very classy. Your paintings—are they your paintings?" Daphne nodded. "Their power, the emotion they show: I see you want people to feel the power of the love with the bold strokes you have painted for their faces and bodies, the thin lines in between them."

Daphne nodded. "Bless you, child." She turned to Tom. "That's how you win someone over, Tommy: you dial right into their art and don't give a damn about that artist's former life."

"She wasn't here during your playing years," he said.

"Exactly. Nice that she only knows what I do now." She squeezed Annalisa's hand. "Would you like a private walk through the gallery while you are in town?"

"I would love this."

She flashed Tom a sideways glance, then turned back to Annalisa. "Well, since I've gone from being the host of the party to the last to know of its most special guest, when did you get into L.A.?"

"Just a few hours ago."

"You must be half-dead, flying across the pond, being dragged to a concert, then a party that doesn't start until midnight because these guys can't tell time on stage."

Annalisa smiled. "*Si, Signora.* I am very tired, yes, but so very happy."

"I'm sure you are." A wry smile crossed Daphne's face as the final piece of this crazy puzzle dropped in front of her, as Robiski wrapped his arm around Annalisa. Leave it to Robiski, the sly fox, to find and pluck this jewel out of Venice. She watched Annalisa walk with him, her loping stride very much Tom's stride, her joy radiating from her face to light up every group they visited.

Daphne double-checked the catering table, filled with far too much food for a midnight bash, then spotted Tom as he chatted with Martin Jammer and his satellite team. Earlier, they'd asked Daphne for Fever tracks that spurred on her career, as well as a couple stories about the band. That led to an offer for her to guest host a program or two if Tom and Chester supported it, which, guessing from the way Tom kept looking back, was in the process of happening.

She watched for another moment, then turned to Annalisa. "That man there has kept you right here"—she tapped her heart—"every minute of every day."

"I tried to do the same."

"Somehow, even though you were very young, I believe that. I hope you can stay for a while."

Annalisa smiled, her eyes smaller, weary. "Two weeks, maybe one month."

Tom walked up. "Really?"

"As long as I am welcome, Papa, and everything is OK at home. I will stay with Jason, but I would like to see your concerts, and come to your home if that is OK?"

Papa . . . papa . . . it rolled off her tired lips like liquid smoke. *Papa.* Though his heart melted inside, he played the gracious rock star for the next two hours, the label's triumphant launch party suddenly the last place he wanted to be.

33

THE SAND DESCENDED TO THE SHORELINE, WHERE ABOUT FIFTY people scattered beneath a blazing moon, hunched over, mixing rapt concentration and sidesplitting laughter. An older couple curled into a nearby berm, listening to a wireless speaker synced to a smartphone. *Let's swim to the moon uh huh* . . . written on this beach a half-century before, probably during a similar king tide. Nearby, two co-eds tumbled into the ocean. Others focused on what the waves pushed onto shore—sardine-sized silver fish squirming around others that stuck out of the sand, their lower halves buried like inverted mermaids, their mating and egg-laying alive and well.

Annalisa pointed. "What are they doing?"

"A grunion run." Half-drunk or otherwise affected bystanders scurried after the fish, diving headfirst into the sand. Their slippery quarry squirted through their fingers, leaving them with only more squeals and uproarious laughs. "They lay their eggs on the beach on full-moon summer nights," he explained. "People go crazy trying to catch them."

He gazed down the beach. Pursuers waddled with garbage bags and buckets, some even showing good timing, gauging the incoming water and catching a few grunion. Many more escaped. Annalisa curled her knees to her chest and rested her chin, *just like she used to do*. He cleared his throat. "Isn't it funny? I spent years thinking what I would say if we saw each other again, and now . . ."

"I remember we made buildings with pails, our hands, sandcastles. Do you?"

The words spilled from her like she was describing another person. She talked about how little Annie ran into and just as fast out of the frigid Ocean Beach water, singing to a sandpiper as it drilled for clams, racing back with handfuls of sand, then slowly squeezing each handful out the bottom of her hands and dripping it onto the growing towers. Eventually, the tide rose to claim the castle, usually after she and Tom created royal characters to live there, saddening her. Until they built another.

She ran the warm, dry sand through her hands like an hourglass. "One of my happiest memories. We were so happy on the beach. Even Momma was."

Even in this exquisite moment, hearing her say "Momma" cleaved him. Take a child from a loving parent, and the wound never recedes. You deal by trying to build a gate around the loss, but it swings open whenever something is said, or implied, or a girl walks by that looks like her. Every dangerous emotion rushes forward, from violent anger to seething malice to words you want to say, even to thoughts of finishing off the other parent . . . or yourself. When you lose a kid, you find how far and wide the extremes of your emotions and feelings can go. Not a place he wanted to see again.

At long last, he could release the torment.

Her resemblance to Maria was strong. Like her mother, she was darkly beautiful, mysterious in a way quiet, exotic way, her skin olive and smooth, her lips rosy to near plumpness. Her face was rounder than Christine's, her cheeks fuller, her eyes darker, though their deep setting beneath her full brows was very much a Timoreaux trait. "Did your momma ever become happy?" he asked.

She leaned into his shoulder. *Just like little Annie used to do.* "No, Papa. She has many demons."

"Still?"

She nodded.

"That's too bad." She gave him a mildly suspicious look. "No matter what happened between me and her, you never want someone to live their life unhappy."

"I saw her two weeks ago, but not for one year until that. When I tell her I may come to see you, she screams at me—after she understands I know you are not really dead. She says I remind her of you. She sees in me the love she once had for you, especially since Jason is here. I think it makes her crazy."

"Do you think she regrets leaving America?"

"Now that she knows who you have become? Maybe for that reason, but . . . I can already see she is not right for you." Annalisa clamped down on her words, a frosty bitterness tightening her lips. "I ask one time why you are not right for her. She screamed at me. She screamed every time I said your name." She took a deep breath to still the blood percolating on anger and exhaustion. "She screamed again two weeks ago. You would think we get past these things."

"Not when one person lies and then has to face those lies."

She took his face into her hands, feeling comfortable, moving closer until their noses nearly touched. "There is one other thing, Papa. I never believed Momma when she told me the drugs made you dead."

"Did you believe I was dead?"

"For some time, yes, I think so. How do I know you are not? But I never believed the drugs."

"I tried a couple, like everyone else in San Francisco did, but I quit before we became famous. Drugs were not a problem. Not when we were all there, either."

His heart balled into a fist, recalling one of Maria's machine-gun accusations, one you'd expect to see from someone whose bipolar disorder was unmoored . . . which, come to think of it, explained a few things:

"You drink and take pot and acid and mescaline and pills and hash and DMT and speed and mushrooms and . . ." It sounded like a psychedelic emporium, though only beer, whiskey, pot, a couple of pills, and two acid trips ever applied to him. She then took off, placating her demons, controlling her narrative, maybe even running away from the horror of what she was doing to try to forget about it. A "geographic" it's called in anonymity programs. However, her mania and rage resurfaced, delivered in slaps and beatings and countless insults to Annalisa.

What people do to destroy each other. Son of a bitch.

Maria never chose to know him past a certain point. He wasn't digging deeply, either. They loved the street life, parties, and art nouveau scene, fueled by psychedelia and its cast of thousands. However, in the big picture, the one that shapes a life, what were the chances of an unproven musician and a walking time bomb to make it as teen parents? None at all.

Annalisa noted his pained expression. "Do not worry. That is over. We are here now. And Christine is a beautiful girl, Papa. She makes you very proud."

He nodded. "I wish I could have given you the same chances that Christine had."

"We each had our lives. We cannot change that."

"I was part of the problem, too. She is right in saying that, Annalisa. I did not know what I wanted, besides music. She didn't have it easy in California." He told her the pre-Annalisa story, how his parents—her grandparents—died in a car crash, how he lived with his grandparents until they died, too, then losing her, the feelings of abandonment.

She curled her toes until the sand covered them, and watched a boisterous teen smack into a wave while chasing a retreating grunion. "How did you meet Momma?"

"At a Beau Brummels show. The first San Francisco folk rock band to get a contract, before the whole scene really started jumping; they showed all of us the way. Your Momma was so beautiful; we had so much fun. She came to San Francisco the summer before graduating from high school and convinced her parents to let her stay with friends in North Beach, be an exchange student. Then we met, and she became pregnant with you."

"*That* fast?" Annalisa chuckled.

"Yes, you were a love child, as we called them. You wanted to be alive so much that you arrived quickly.

She smiled. "I can see Poppa Maurizio allowing her to learn in California."

Tom grinned. "Maurizio . . . what happened with him? He was such a nice man."

"He still is."

"*Still?* He must be a hundred."

"In two months, yes. We celebrate the Festival of the Redentore with him before we come here. His thoughts of you are very good."

"Please tell him I said hello, and how great to know he's—"

"Maybe you tell him yourself. In Venezia."

He shook his head. "I tried to imagine what your life might be like," he said softly. "I thought many, many times about it. Now, it would be easy. Google search you, get on FaceTime, talk to each other."

"But maybe if you raise me like the Papa I can tell that you are with Christine, maybe you stay home with Mama and me and not become a rock star? I watch tonight, and these people *love you,* Papa. You give them something that makes them feel happy inside."

Her point made sense. After all, the Fever's earlier ballads referred directly or indirectly to either Megan or his torment. "Maybe so, sweetheart, but I still would have raised my daughter, and you would have had your father."

"So do you really know why Momma did these things?"

Tom shook his head. How could he answer a question he'd spent his entire adult life trying to sort out? "I wanted your momma to not feel jealous about our closeness, yours and mine. I tried to get her to see it as a good thing, a daughter who loved both parents *that much.* But I was a threat to her. And music was a bigger threat. She was angry all the time after we started playing."

A ghost moved through him, an old feeling, a memory. "You came to me sometimes in my dreams. Once, years ago, you came to me, looking a little like you look now, though I saw you more as a little girl . . . that's all I knew." He paused as she smiled, drinking his every word like a desert lapping up rainfall. "You told me, in the dream, I was a grandfather . . ."

She lifted her head, astonished. "I remember such a dream, very well, I held out a boy and you held him and . . ."

"That sounds like the dream I had—"

"And the boy I am holding is my Paolo. I was pregnant; that is the last great dream I remember when we were together, somewhere else. But I believe you would be to Paolo as Poppa Maurizio is me."

She faced him now, her eyes glowing. "I want my son to have that . . . if you are comfortable meeting him."

"I would love that. As soon as we can get off this tour." The urge that had begun building after Cumberland continued to grow within, an edgy change of focus from the next stops to life after the tour.

The beach began to empty. Grunion hunters and bystanders brushed off and walked away, the receding tide and dying waves lulling the ocean to sleep. Nearby, twenty people hovered in a drumming circle, chanting and banging. In the middle, riding lead drum, was Will. Right next to him was Christine, playing tinksha bells, her eyes closed, fully immersed. "I remember those circles, in the big park," Annalisa said, cupping her arm inside his. "It is a very beautiful thing, how music feels so good, how you can feel very close, just by a song."

Tom nodded. "It does do that."

Annalisa kissed his cheek, then his lips. "*Si*, Papa. It makes this miracle."

34

OR TWO YEARS OF WINTERS AND SPRINGS, SHE WALKED INSIDE the meditation center's white walls while Danny surfed. The sweet, palpable energy enthralled her, divine and permeating, like dipping her nose into a nectar-infused flower that never stopped giving. The visits inspired her journey into deeper yoga, an inner world of ever-growing devotion, wisdom, and perception to which Danny objected, out of abject fear of losing his woman to Eastern woo-woo. "You want something spiritual? Get on a board, paddle out, and ride atop the world," he said. "Better yet, get slotted. Tube rides are what religion's all about. Like going to the womb and heaven in the same wave."

Amazing, she thought, how a man who presented himself as strong, stoic, and Southern California cool could be so none of the above. When he began leaving her home from surf trips, she found solace in the gardens. She started distancing herself, just enough to give her a little safety net, but as it turned out, not enough: when he left on the final surfing trip he told her, "You never were my type. I want a woman who stands by me and my surfing, loves me, loves my surfing. Not sure what you've got going for you."

Well, asshole, how about buying a seat to the next show and finding out? She imagined the astonishment in his face. Had she been able to peer deep into the loge level at the last L.A. show, to the seat where a stunned Danny shook his head over and over, she would have loved what one of his friends busted him down with: "Good on you, Dan, leaving her for that other girl, dumb ass. Dumping the hottest new rock star . . ."

She and Annalisa walked past a koi pond and its stepladder waterfalls, tropical plants from several rainforests, and a couple meditating together on a redwood bench beneath an overhanging palm. "That is what I'm beginning to think makes relationships last forever," Christine said. "Touching divinity. X and I work on that. In our special way." She winked.

Annalisa chuckled. "That is beautiful," she whispered as she looked around. "This reminds me of two different gardens in Venezia, only this has a greater feeling."

They passed an empty concrete swimming pool atop the bluff, ruined decades before in a "pineapple express" storm that flooded California before regenerating into a blizzard that killed thousands during the winter Hitler was beginning to march on Europe. They walked along a bluff of sandstone, ice plant, coastal sage, bamboo, plumeria, and salted breezes, an open view of the beach thirty feet below. She told Annalisa of the yoga master who taught Americans to meditate, how the cliffside gardens became his first beach retreat, the monastery of adobe buildings with red-tiled tops harkening the state's classic Spanish architecture era.

"You share your soul, Christine. You share it in your songs. You thrill and deeply touch the people; I see how they look at you," Annalisa said, rubbing her legs. "You lift spirits, make people feel better. That is a gift. A great gift."

Annalisa admired her gleaming fingernails, part of a girl's day in which each slapped down a credit card for the other's pedicure, manicure, and makeup. They left the Dadtourage to business with Robiski in L.A. after a lively group breakfast at Daphne's house, and drove towards San Diego. A tern etched circles in the cloudless sky while, two feet above the ocean, a long line of pelicans caught dinner, one and then another plunging into the sea, stuffing perch and bass into their regal beaks. "That is how you are," Annalisa said. "Free to fly."

They walked down the garden steps, hand in hand. Near the bottom, two young couples approached, their skin the approximate color of lobsters. "They might feel their sunburns tonight," Annalisa whispered, chuckling.

The couples grew more animated as they saw Christine. *There she is! The star! The most amazing singer! We love you!* "Could we get a photo or two with you?" one of the women asked. She quickly grabbed her smartphone.

A monk picked up his garden rake, walked over, smiled, and reminded the woman to refrain from shooting photos and texting inside. His friendliness and almost ethereal demeanor surprised the couples. "Thank you," he said. "Many blessings on your day." Why couldn't we send each other along like that regularly? Christine thought.

Christine winked at the girl and nodded at the monk. "Annalisa, this is Brother Sumundra. Sumundra, meet my sister."

"Sumundra . . . what a beautiful name," Annalisa said. "Ocean, *si?*"

"It is the Sanskrit for ocean," he said as she drank in eyes that made you feel better just by looking into them. "You know the language?"

"Just some words, but you have a perfect name for this place," she said, also recalling the sign across the garden's arched entrance: *The Guest is God.* Warm chills shimmered through her.

"Miss Christine, forgive me for intrudin'," the fan said, clutching her phone like a child's hand, "but we saw y'all's show last night and we're there tonight . . ." She blushed through already reddened cheeks. "To run into you here . . ."

"I'll leave all of you to your day," Brother Sumundra said. He smiled, walked to a nearby cluster of bursting flowers, and raked the soil while chanting, each stroke as metered and tranquil as the song flowing through him. "*Bellezzo,*" Annalisa said.

The texter turned to Annalisa. "You are sisters?"

"We are."

"Uh, didn't know you had a sister, Christ—" The fan choked back her sentence, trying to remain respectful, appropriate, and brush off her ignorance.

Angst brushed across Annalisa's face. "We did not know we were sisters until not long ago." She smiled at Christine. "But here we are."

"I cannot imagine . . ." The girl looked to her friends, reluctant to join in.

"You never have to, I hope," Annalisa said.

The fan was engaged and spry in an ingratiating Southern sense, her spirit bubbling up from honeysuckle, biscuits and gravy, sweet tea, sweltering summers, hopping neighbors' fences routinely—if they even saw the need for fences—and playing hide-and-seek in cornfields and church pews. Like Chester. "Would y'all sign something? And take a picture?"

"Of course," Christine said. "Let's go outside the garden."

Two minutes later, the tourist returned with the Fever's final live DVD. Christine smiled, her comfort for the visitors growing. "Hey, why don't you guys come to a little flash gig Rogelio, X, and I are playing tomorrow night like five miles from here. At the Belly Up. I'll have passes at the door."

"We're there, Christine!" She flipped her flowing hair to drape down the other side of her face. "My family's huge Chester fans, I guess 'cause he's from the South, too." Her eyes turned into moons. "Tell me: Is Rogelio married?"

Christine laughed softly. "Newly taken."

"As of when?"

"The Cumberland Festival. You just missed him." Christine glanced at the man who stood impassively next to her. "What about this good-looking dude?"

"I love him to death. Treats me right. But a girl can always fantasize." She looked at her husband, whom she married a year out of high school. "Just like he does . . . we saw you at the Cumberland."

"Really? That's like the other side of the country."

"It was the best festival I've ever seen."

Christine nodded, realizing she wasn't speaking to a girl who stumbled into their music, but one who followed them. "How many of our gigs have you seen?"

"Seven. Last night was eight. We'll catch y'all back on the East Coast, too. You're kind of our dream vacation. We've been on the road since Cumberland."

"Well, I can understand how you feel about Rogelio," Christine chuckled. "I've had a glance or a hundred at him myself."

The fan laughed and folded her arms. "Aren't you X's girl now?"

"He doesn't own my eyes." She winked and grabbed the DVD and pen. "We've been standing here talking, and I don't even know your name to sign."

"Desiree. Desiree and Scooter." She quickly scribbled their names, a brief inscription, and then her own.

As Christine signed, Annalisa waved the others over. "If you give me your mobile, I make a picture."

Ten minutes later, photos taken and visitors thrilled, Christine whipped the rented convertible onto Coast Highway, peeled off her shawl, retracted the roof, and let the sun bake her shoulders. Annalisa planted her freshly pedicured toenails on the dashboard, red and shiny. In the next lane, a car whisked past, the passenger's foot sticking outside the window. Annalisa shook her head. "If you do that on the highway near Roma, near Napoli, you lose your foot."

Skateboarders, surfers, woodies, vans, campgrounds, and smoothie stands dotted the coast highway in both directions. Annalisa took in the scene, overwhelmed and thrilled alike, sitting next to her sister with the top down, being girls, cruising to a Fever concert along the greatest sun-kissed highway in the land, old California 101, just like countless other California girls over the years. As they passed by, some busted their brakes, recognizing Christine, even gawking at her older sister, too. "We're gonna have fun with this," Christine said, slowing and accelerating, flirting back.

"It amazes me, how they bother you. Like movie stars."

"We *are* movie stars, Annalisa. Rock stars replaced the great movie stars as cultural heroes, a long time ago."

Christine continued to play chicken with motorists, entertaining herself as the guitar-on-steroids surf, trumpet, and saxophone licks of Dick Dale rippled through the speakers. What's better than cruising the coast with the King of the Surf Guitar, your dad's first guitar hero, your older sister in tow, with an afternoon of sunshine, breezes, and surfer boys ahead of you?

Annalisa tilted her head back, her hair billowing. *This is being free.* Free as a little girl in San Francisco, once upon a time.

Late that night, in a sandstone cave fifty feet beneath a five-million-dollar beach home a storm or two from sliding into driftwood, down the beach from the throng roasting fish after performing in San Diego, Annalisa clenched Jason. Her legs were wrapped around his waist, resuming the love they initiated in the ocean, her pleasure fed by a feeling to which her body, heart, and soul yielded as much as they did his touch: *I am Californian. As Californian as this beach. As this ocean.*

35

_H_OME. The word, like the sound, reflected its root, the Latin for both hearth and fire. Go back further, to the Sanskrit root, _Aum—Om._ The cradle of life. The middle two letters of home.

He maneuvered various root words of home in his head like magnetic poetry as he sprawled in the vibrating double recliner, his remnant chair from the Victorian and sole piece of furniture remaining from San Francisco. After almost four months of touring, hotels, RVs, planes, guest houses, restaurants, call-in deliveries, press, overnight transport, avoiding groupie scenes backstage and in lobbies, and more meet-and-greets than he could count, the buzz had worn off. Now it felt like a grind, an exhilarating grind, but a grind nonetheless. The grind that's buried deepest in the bones, never forgotten, the grind that twenty years of being away can't quite shake. What could be easier or luckier than playing sold-out arenas and stadiums for work? What about the constant travel that far exceeds actual time on stage? Annalisa's return had prompted him to retrieve the recliner from its shrink-wrapped tomb, make it part of the studio, part of home.

Part of sorting out what to do next.

Sierra Blanca filled the window, the old glacial jewel now a stoic brown cone after baking all summer. Golden eagles scanned the earth for four-legged food, the thunderbird, the Native people's equivalent of a Leo. He couldn't decide which he liked better, thunderbird or lion, both commanding beings that protected fiercely, operated with vision, and minded their own.

An eagle broke from its companions and rose toward the sun. He thought of the bird's sense of earth and sky, every day a miracle for even daring to dawn, to exist, majestic and noble as the chiefs and medicine men who roamed the Sacramentos for millennia before becoming the Mescalero Apache, some of whom remained, depending on the thriving casino on the other side of the mountain ridge. A few still carried the old stories, wove the old ways into their very modern lives. One day, Tom thought, we will realize how precious these last protectors of the old ways are, and record their languages and stories.

He tried to immerse further, but thoughts of upcoming dates overtook him. Whatever happened to the thirty-gig limit that became forty? Now, it was at fifty. As the nights piled up, and Robiski kept peppering away with new offers, the party began to feel like a grind.

At least for him. By the time the tour reached California, he found himself waning despite their performances being, as one online reviewer put it, "the most dynamic in decades," even calling him "effusive," "the consummate frontman," and "the luckiest vocalist in the world today, with his highly talented daughter singing alongside." One reporter wrote, "Christine's the luckiest vocalist on earth, too, because she has the ultimate mentor and starmaker in Tom." It might feel like a grind, but this grind was coming home to roost with great reviews and more fans than ever, including many in their teens and twenties. *Thank you, Christine.*

Now that Annalisa was back, it felt like enough. How do you top the top of the show? He used to spend sleepless nights trying to make a great show even greater. He felt no need now, only the responsibility of how to keep it going. Or whether to even bother. He remembered what it felt like twenty years before, raising Christine the primary factor, but that evasive apparition, *the rest of life,* also calling him off stage.

He watched Annalisa make herself at home as though she'd always lived at the house, her comfort and graciousness more noticeable by the day. She prepared meals with him and Megan, hiked with Christine and X, spent hours discussing outfits, styles, and Greek archaeology. Then, every night, she came to the studio, or he went to her guest room, and they shared events from their lives, telling stories. Just like before, only with their experiences rather than picture books.

The thought of more gigs, more time away from family, growled inside. But didn't he owe Robiski a few more gigs for pulling off this miracle? Maybe he could do the Europe swing if everyone else in the band felt like continuing past the current tour, come back for the ten-show circuit Robiski was in the process of nailing down for the spring. Maybe.

This break was short—ten days. Then they were off to New York for the final gut-check: twelve shows and who knew how many flash concerts in twenty days, ending with the "Back-to-Back-to-Back-in-the-Bay" swing, as Robiski called it—Silicon Valley, San Francisco, and Oakland. There was no more Candlestick Park, where the Beatles bade farewell to live concerts; its long, windy run as a ball stadium and concert venue ended in an implosion. The other classic big venue, Cow Palace, was an old, creaky alternative. Earlier in the day, Robiski had lobbied for a swing across college campuses, a notion picking up steam thanks to a deft stroke of genius that gave the Fever headline billing on college campuses hosting big Saturday football games for the final two months of the season. That meant eight big Saturday gigs after the current schedule. Who could imagine college kids freaking over a band with three members who played for and possibly broke bread, wine, and honey oil with their grandparents?

Tom rubbed his eyes. He thought of how Sierra Blanca presided over the white sands since the eon she emerged from the primordial tropical sea that birthed her. Likewise, he yearned to plant himself again. Fall was coming, the season of football, cutting wood and harvesting the garden, a time to slow down and draw inward, bring the neighbors over for some house concerts and parties, stay home.

Stay home. Well, then. He replayed the best moments, the best nights, noting how his energy level tended to wane the final hour of every show. He couldn't keep up anymore. He played gamely, but this was a young person's sport.

Time to stay home.

Christine poked her head in the studio. "Dad, what's up?"

"The newest satellite radio network on earth, here in our own home."

X folded his arms, surprised. "Aren't satellite studios located in . . . what's the word I'm looking for? *Cities?*"

"Only when I'm in L.A. or New York." Tom chuckled. "Chester's home right now with his own station techs, hooking up. The marvels of modern technology. Besides, our recordings are here. Even the downloads of our shows, which I've been listening to."

The radio setup reminded X of a scene from a movie with a great soundtrack, *American Graffiti*. In it, the greatest of the Saturday night DJs, Wolfman Jack, transmits overhead as though his voice spans the skies from New Guinea to New England, a proto- satellite radio, come to think of it. "Great setup, dude. I'm really impressed."

"Tell the techs that flew out," Tom said.

"And busted their caps to get here."

Tom and Christine stared at him. "Say what, baby?" she asked.

"Knocking their teeth out on your bouncy road."

Tom laughed. "Time for me to figure out all these contraptions."

"Want to save some time and have me walk you through it?"

Tom looked at the board and control panels, feeling almost as lost as a balsa wood model plane pilot examining a jet's instrument board. "You'd think a guy who's produced as much as me could do a lateral shift, but yeah, X, I'd really appreciate that."

They sat down in front of the soundboard, CD, and digital tape racks, and tested levels. X then walked Tom through the setup. Within an hour, a few days quicker than if he'd tried to master the equipment himself, Tom was set to broadcast, reminded again of the optimal way to learn new technology—find the nearest kid to show you.

Christine's watched X and Tom fiddle. "How are you going to do your show while touring, Dad?"

"We'll record some in their New York office. Plus, we recorded a few test shows in L.A. after our San Diego gig, while you, Rogelio, and X played the Belly Up and Tucson. We'll be fine, me and Chester, like kids in a candy mall. If we can put up with each other on a stage, we can handle doing shows a thousand miles apart."

Christine led Tom, Megan, and Annalisa to her rocky perch, recalling how she brought X out, seemingly forever ago, which kindled exactly what she vowed would not happen: a relationship. No complaints now, though. She loved how he sought things that lasted in music and life, things to which he could affix his strong, comforting sense of loyalty. He was proving to be a rock, as well advertised by his physique.

"What are you smiling so smugly about?" Megan asked. "Daydream?"

"You could say that."

A minute later, Annalisa huffed and puffed to the perch, trailed by Tom. She doubled over, gasping for breath. "It is very hard to breathe," she panted. "I think I am in a good shape until I hike this trail."

"Honey, it takes weeks to get used to this altitude," Megan said. "You're over two thousand meters up. You have to go to the Dolomites to get up this high back home. Hold your hands over your head and breathe deeply."

She did so, and a few rounds later, her breath returned. "Much better. *Bellezza*. Beautiful."

"Yes it is."

Annalisa seized another breath as her distress diminished. "Did you love this place from the first time you came here, Megan?" she asked.

"Loved it. This place reminded your dad and I of what really mattered between us. Now it's hard to imagine anything else." Megan brushed her hair over her shoulder. "This place still makes me feel like a kid sometimes."

Christine's eyebrows arched. "Sometimes?"

They all laughed. "I have a hard time feeling like a kid as I become older," Annalisa said, "though Jason makes me feel things that remind me of it."

"It's hard for me to associate you with a woman getting older," Megan said, "because, well, we will need some time to see you as being other than the little girl. . ."

"Then I will take this time to feel younger," Annalisa laughed.

Megan rubbed Annalisa's cheek with her hand. "Trust me, you can do it. Your face tells a different story than the calendar."

Annalisa bowed her head, mildly embarrassed, entirely unaccustomed to compliments from motherly figures. "I am not sure I agree about my face, the same thing I tell Jason, but yes, I feel younger." She sighed and breathed deeply, drawing the air into her lungs, her chest rising, all effects of the ridge climb vanishing. "Megan, what was going through your forties like?"

"First of all, I felt *young*, like I'd lived the right way, sticking to what mattered and staying away from bad habits. When I compared myself with my parents, I felt *really* young."

"How's that?" Annalisa asked.

"Well, their generation rarely worked until they dropped. Why grow old like *that? But I learned later, that is a question my generation was the first to ask— because our parents gave us more than other kids had gotten in history.* They got us through the Depression, so they knew no other way; they were not going to let their kids suffer through their hardships. But when they got older, it's as if they *wanted* to be old; my mother even said she liked being older more than being younger. I think that's why our generation, mine, your dad's, tries to retain something from its youth. For us, it's the music. Now that you've been in America for a couple of weeks, have you ever seen more grandmothers with long hair, leggings and yoga outfits, or better toned bodies than many of their daughters have?"

"Never, although there are many beautiful women in Italy, in Europe. We are making our youth older, too."

"I get jealous when I see the way Mediterranean women age. Your beauty becomes even more profound. But this is more about an attitude, an approach to life—and most in my generation refuse to think they're old. In this family, we have the perfect denier of age—a rock-and-roll band."

Megan flipped her hair like a flirtatious teenager. Yet, Annalisa thought, one thing seemed antithetical to her carefree baby boomer talk. "How did you and Papa make a marriage work while you tour with a band and your friends enjoy, how you say it, *free love?*" she asked. "Musicians are what you call bad boys, bad at relationships, *si?*"

"That depends on the musician. I got lucky." Megan glanced out at Sierra Blanca. "We decided we would stick together, no matter what. We found what worked for both of us, and got rid of things that didn't." Picking through words to answer Annalisa resembled a barefoot walk through the cactus garden. "Your dad's grief over losing you created our only separation, but we made it through that, too."

"Just as I hope Jason and I will do. I am in love with this man, Megan."

Megan grabbed Annalisa's hand and rubbed her long, turquoise-and-silver ring-covered fingers. "Honey, he's in love with you, too. I have known Jason since he was a boy, and I have never seen him like this before. He's always wanted someone who loves him for himself, not for his money, the bands he manages, or who he knows. But he's never found the person. It takes a strong woman with a lot of understanding when money, resorts, luxury, and girls are massive temptations, always right there. The nice thing about knowing Jason now, and him knowing you now, is that you know what you want."

"I wonder what it would have been like to meet him ten years ago . . ."

Megan waved her hand, brushing away a thousand images Annalisa would never want to see. "No you don't. You met him at the right time. For both of you."

They walked back to the outcropping, where Christine and Tom spread out a picnic blanket and topped it with enough food for a small buffet line. Christine poured wine for everyone but Tom, who opened a longneck beer.

After they ate, Tom took a knee on the rock like a football coach in training camp. "Ladies, I've made a decision. I'm done after the Bay Area concerts, no matter anything else Robiski is stirring up. If the band decides it wants to go on without me, I'll do the Europe gigs with you next spring, but that's it." He turned his attention to Christine. "Chester said he'll stay on through the college gigs and Europe, then help you transition into another guitarist if you want to keep performing, which I suspect you do. You'd be crazy not to."

"We're just getting going, Dad . . ." Christine protested. "Why?"

"I signed up for thirty gigs and three months. I had no idea we would blow up like this. I've had a great time seeing friends, playing great venues, hearing the cheers, playing with bandmates old and new, and especially performing with you." He smiled. "This has been a dream come true, to rock with my own kid. But it's not my thing anymore. You want to go out on top, not like a dried-up husk of what you once were. I want to free up some time for the next thing that comes around."

Christine cocked an eye. "Which would be?"

"Satellite shows and . . . I don't know. It hasn't come around yet."

Christine glanced at Annalisa. "Well, it has."

Tom followed her eyes. "Yes, I agree."

She fought back tears as they rolled in. "But Dad, Jason keeps wanting to add to the schedule. Annalisa told me he spent almost every morning in Venice arguing with promoters over there who wanted us."

"And for which we agreed to ten gigs there, which I'll play. Then maybe you, X, Rogelio, and Will can fly on your own. You're ready."

"Why, Dad? With the band we have, we could stay out there for the next two years if we wanted to." Her eyes sharpened into diamond points as Tom's words sank in. "Well, to answer your little hint-question, I'm going to want to keep doing it, and so will X and Rogelio."

Tom grinned. "If you don't want to go back to painting your commissions for a while, well, there's a shitload of fans who will be very happy with your decision. And Will and Chester will stay until you find replacements."

He tugged on his beer, alternately happy and concerned with the entry point he'd provided this emerging superstar who happened to be his daughter. He stroked her shoulder. "Make sure you know what you're getting into."

"I've just had a four-month preview."

"You're talking frontwoman now, the focal point."

Her frown deepened. "It's not much different . . . except you won't be standing alongside me."

"Well, honey, me not standing up there with you makes it completely different." Tom finished his beer, grabbed a chip, and chomped on it. "As the center of attention, you cannot have an off-night. Or at least one that's obvious. People need to feel you're connecting like you're their best friend or lover, and the band needs to feed off your energy. Then there's the press, meet-and-greets, and shoots." He paused, a gather-the-forces pause. "It's an entirely different scene when you're the big girl on campus."

The weight of determination deepened across her face. "Dad, I've thought about it." Her eyes were unwavering, committed lasers.

He nodded and grinned. She could go far as a frontwoman. She possessed the right skill set of equal parts vocal talent, performance instincts, and toughness to handle off-stage issues. She also had a standing relationship with a bouncer-sized keyboard player, a huge point of relief, Tom thought. "If you come back and tell me the same thing by our final gig in the Bay Area, then I'll ask Robiski to call all those promoters we've declined, and those we worked with this summer, and put together a tour for you."

He stroked her wind-blown hair as Annalisa walked over and sat. Christine followed an impulse she'd never felt before, and laid her head on her older sister's shoulder. Tom drank in a sight he would never get used to. "You're right," he said. "It's your time, Christine. You're who the people want to see."

Christine shook her head. "No, Dad, you're the reason there *is* a tour."

"True, but my tour is over soon."

She fought off tears. Why did this have to end right now, when she finally trusted him again? *If only people knew.* She wanted to see more of him, play more with him, be around him more, after this remarkable Summer of Turning Twenty-Five. A new calling, a new love . . . a new parent. "Thank you, Dad," she said softly.

"For?"

"Being amazing."

Annalisa grinned broadly. "That is such a nice thing to say."

Christine looked over. "Now you're seeing why for yourself. But how do you *really* know it's over, Dad? Can't you keep an open mind about it?"

Tom thought for a moment. "Let me tell you about a concert I was lucky enough to attend, along with half the rock world, it seemed. Might be the greatest performance ever by a vocalist, especially under circumstances only he knew at the time." He went on:

"Wembley Stadium, London, July 1986: Freddie Mercury contracts HIV and it will become AIDS—a death sentence. He and his doctor are the only people who know. He and Queen play in front of a hundred thousand wild, rowdy fans. The band was unnerved when they saw the sea of humanity. Not Freddie. He takes the stage, squeezes the crowd into his hand, and then delivers the show of his life, waving his mic stand like a conductor, swinging on the scaffolding, running wind sprints, his voice mighty and powerful and lovely and plaintive, the crowd exploding.

"Why?" Tom asked rhetorically. "Why, while staring into that diagnosis, did Freddie deliver the performance of his life?"

"I have no idea, Dad."

"Because he already knew Wembley was his final live performance. He was too vain to perform at less than a hundred percent, and he wanted to say goodbye to his beauties, his fans, while at his best. He loved the crowd, they loved him, and it was the fondest farewell an entertainer could ever give."

"What about our little bow?"

"That was beautiful, and a nice photo, touched a lot of people, for sure, but honestly, not close to the same gravity as Freddie's final gig."

Christine exchanged glances with Annalisa, and sat quietly for a moment. Then, "That would've rocked. Tricia and my girls and I like a lot of their songs, and Freddie of course, but . . . what does it have to do with me?"

Annalisa took her hand. "You can be famous and loved by your people like him if you love the crowd, love singing to them, make it your passion."

Tom smiled and nodded. "Spoken like the daughter of a singer."

Christine squeezed Tom's hand. "When are you going to announce this?"

"Soon. Or maybe not at all. You'll know."

36

MONTREAL...TORONTO...HARTFORD...PROVIDENCE... NEW YORK CITY

THE UNION SQUARE FARMER'S MARKET BUSTLED WITH students, residents, neighbors, leashed bulldogs and pugs, tourists, and dressed-down celebrities passing or stopping at tables of flowers, vegetables, and summer fruits. Conversations were fast and laughter loud, though countless pairs of eyes were still locked in the iron-clad intensity that enabled them to navigate the noisy, packed streets. "Two thousand story subjects passing by every fifteen minutes," Tom chuckled.

The people always hit like a runaway train. Broadway and the Theatre District might have served as New York's symbols of entertainment since the Civil War ended, but for Tom's money, the Village, East Village, Chelsea, and NYU did it. All four neighborhoods converged in one square block that felt like the human vortex it was, especially when dropping in from the mountain ridge.

They walked past a young couple watching a movie trailer on a nearby bench. A cute, bespectacled public relations type waited to retrieve their feedback, as well as the tablet on which they viewed the three-minute clip. The man glared at Christine, then Tom, and stopped them. "Can we get a picture with you? We're seeing you in the Garden tomorrow night." He extended his hand. "My dad thinks he's found the missing link to bonding with me. He played all your old albums for me."

"And?" Tom asked.

"First time I liked any of his music. It worked."

Megan smiled, taken in by the man's crisp London East End accent. "We keep circling back to our earlier years," she said, "but this may be the first generation where our kids love our music, too."

The man grinned. "Mystical Megan?"

Megan fanned her eyes and cocked her leg like she was riding the nose of a World War II bomber. "A long time ago, sweetie."

Christine laughed and rolled her eyes as she shook the man's hand. "We'll never hear the end of it now."

Megan nudged Christine in the ribs. "I'm not washed up yet, girl."

"To use Jason's words, 'smoking hot,'" Annalisa said.

Megan's eyes opened wide. "*Jason* said that?"

Annalisa moved her hands like a crossing guard, suddenly frantic. "Yes, those words. *Mi dispiace.* I am sorry; my English, I am still getting back."

"Every one of you is hot. Bloody hell." The man turned to his wife, whose eyes had long since left the tablet, now focused on the trio diverting her husband's attention. "Love, this is Tom and Christine from the Fever, Mystical Megan"—who chuckled and rolled her eyes—"and . . . you are?"

"Annalisa. Tom's other daughter."

"I didn't know . . ."

"Listen to 'She Flew Away.' Then you know."

"But that song's about a child gone forever." He shook his head, befuddled. "What do you mean?"

"Well, I am that person."

The couple exchanged glances. He shook his head. "Nooo . . . really?"

"*Si.*"

His wife grabbed his arm and held it. She rubbed his wedding band and then her own in plain sight. "May I?"

She pulled her camera from an overloaded purse, and made eye contact with Annalisa. "Would you be so kind?"

"Of course." Annalisa shot photos of the others. She handed the camera to the woman, who immediately inspected the photos, clicking backward, trashing one, zooming another, hoping for something to launch into social network orbit. What a difference, Megan thought, from all-nighters in the lab, souping film, and creating great prints. Now, everything was so instantaneous and disposable. The concept of using a darkroom was as alien to Millennials as smart phones and digital cameras were to kids growing up when Kennedy launched the space race.

"The photos are spot-on," the woman said, her accent lilting and polished, her nerves yielding to a cheeky smile. "What a fantastic cape you're wearing above that dress. I'm gobsmacked by your dress, like the minis you wore as a girl, only a few centimeters longer."

"That I wore as a girl?" Megan stared, astonished. "Pardon me? How would you know what I wore?"

"You modeled in London a bit during the Swinging Sixties, right?"

"Two or three fun little shoots, high school dares maybe . . ."

"A photo of you still hangs in the London Fashion Institute for Girls, and a couple in King's Road boutiques; they brought in those photos and some others when Sixties retro came back. My auntie did it; she was one of your friends at the Fashion Institute."

Christine nudged Megan. "You never told me you modeled."

"Ancient history, sunshine. Goes with the saber-tooths that make up your next tank of gas."

The woman smiled, her admiration obvious. "They are beautiful photographs."

"I've never seen those photos," Tom said, his expression souring.

"I made a little money for boutiques a couple times, that's all." Megan grinned at the woman. Her husband, the Fever fan, pawed the ground impatiently, apparently not enough music in the conversation. "But that was it, except shots for class."

"The photograph of you curling on a leopard-skin rug, wearing the Judy Quant scarf, is sublime. Fabulous."

Horror rode through Megan's face like the Four Horsemen. "I hope to God it isn't the photograph I'm thinking of."

"The scarf covers you *there*, but you are otherwise just as God made you."

"You posed *nude*, Mom?" Christine asked, her tone shifting between awe for her daring and shock over . . . well, she had to admit, she would do it if asked, too, but we're *talking about Mom here.*

"*Semi*-nude, darling." She smiled meekly, a smile of both being freshly busted and feeling ecstatic. She turned to the woman. "Aren't there laws against pictures of teens like that? I was maybe seventeen. Not even of age."

"In 1967, that *was* of age. And the scarf wore . . . well on you."

"Do you have it on your phone?" Christine asked.

"Here."

Christine inspected the photo with Megan and Annalisa over each shoulder. "A very elegant photo," Annalisa said.

"It is," Christine nodded begrudgingly.

Megan exhaled the breath she'd been holding for the daughterly inquisition, which fizzled before it could move further. "Moving on, who is your auntie?"

"Fiona Otter."

"Fiona? My girl? In that case, even more of a pleasure to meet you . . ."

"Jocelyn. The one-man admiration society next to me is my husband, Simon."

Christine chuckled. "I guess that means you know stories, Jocelyn. First a racy photo, then a girl you ran with. Do tell, mother."

"Best served on another table, on another day, love," Jocelyn said.

Megan grabbed Jocelyn's hands and squeezed. "Your auntie was the talk of Londontown, the finest in our class, her long legs always in black tights, short black hair, great scarves and boots, the most beautiful arching eyebrows in the world. She was a sight; she moved around London like she owned it."

"A way she carried through her life," Jocelyn said. "Every time I saw her, she wore great earrings and beautiful scarves, and talked about the city like it was a lover who would never stop pleasing her. She talked even more like that when it became necessary to wear those scarves around her head."

Annalisa's eyes dropped to the ground, thinking of Paolo, his battle, where such battles usually lead. She'd only called twice, her mind occupied with her new family and creating and strengthening a relationship for which there was no guidebook, none at all.

Now, suddenly, he swept through her consciousness, and not in a comfortable way. *Something wasn't right.* Both he and Letitia said on the phone that everything was great, he was driving the vaporetto, and he was eating more, all signs he was finally getting healthier. However, her rumbling stomach spoke otherwise. *What was it?* She'd call after the press conference.

"Fiona isn't with us anymore?" Megan asked.

"I'm sorry to say, no. She passed a few years ago. She talked about you quite a bit. I think she felt you were too famous and inaccessible, although she never said it."

"Honey, that's ridiculous. I would have flown to London same-day to spend time with her. I just never knew where she went."

"The London Museum of Art, curating for thirty years."

"That's impressive. Me? I've mainly been a housewife and a touring wife."

"A housewife known to millions," Jocelyn said.

Megan chuckled. "I thought she'd either be a curator or fashion or museum designer of some kind. She accomplished far more than me, Jocelyn; I just rode some long coattails." Megan turned to Tom. "Tomorrow, can you play 'I Know She's My Lady'? It always reminded me of how Fiona walked down the street, for some reason."

"I wrote it for you, but sure," Tom said.

"That is so kind," Jocelyn said. "I trust she will be listening, wherever her soul is voyaging right now."

"Can I tell you a bit to show you how fun your auntie was in high school?" Megan asked.

"Sure!" Simon grabbed and squeezed Jocelyn's hand, a signal that they needed to continue their day, but promptly stopped when he realized he wasn't going anywhere.

Megan turned to Christine. "Remember I told you about that week we spent following Jimi Hendrix around when he first hit London?"

She nodded.

"Fiona set that up." Megan exchanged warm smiles with Jocelyn. "She was one kick-ass girl, if you'll excuse my slang."

"My *Auntie*? We talking about the same person? The one who cared for paintings and then tended to her flower and vegetable gardens? Always so prim, measured, everything in its place. The one who never married and spent time with only two men I know of, both barristers? She told me some of her past, but never hinted at anything wild."

"Well, in respect to her," she caught Christine's inquiring look, "and my daughter, we'll leave those stories be. I *will* tell you this; she loved Jimi, worshipped the ground he walked on, and gave us an incredible week of clubbing, which Jimi turned into an historic week indeed."

Tom nodded at Jocelyn. "I only heard about it later, from the Cream guys, when they came to San Francisco and blew *our* doors off."

"I have a little surprise for you, Ms. Timoreaux." Jocelyn rifled through her purse, emerging with a vintage scarf, vaguely familiar. "This was in Fiona's possessions. I brought it here to wear to your show, but . . . here. Fiona and Judy Quant are gone, so here."

She handed the scarf to Megan. It was the same as the one in which she was photographed for the Fashion Institute of London. "My God." Tears pooled in her eyes.

Christine felt the need for some quick cultural context, a recurring feeling during a summer that, at times, felt like walking into a history lesson. Or a diorama. "Who is Judy Quant?" she asked.

Megan smiled as she wrapped the scarf around her shoulders. "The goddess of Swinging Sixties fashion, baby. My inspiration as a fashion designer, my polestar, my heroine."

Jocelyn smiled at Christine. "How did you become such a good singer so fast?"

"Genetics, I guess." Christine glimpsed at Tom. "I sang a lot of these songs around the house when I was a little kid, too."

"I'd go with talent and hard work," he said.

"I told Simon that the way you sing and perform would give him thoughts of leaving me." A delicious impishness crossed her lips, borne by one of those fleeting notions that will never see the light of day, pure brain candy. "Or make me consider it myself." She looked down, suddenly embarrassed. "And here you are."

"Well, the good news is that he's married and you're married and I'm taken by our keyboard player, so everyone is safe," Christine laughed.

Christine looked at her watch, and nudged Tom. "We've gotta go," she said, "but you two said you were coming tomorrow?"

"One of the reasons why we're in New York," Simon said.

She glanced at Tom. "Well then, let's get together, yes? We'll leave backstage passes at will-call. Hang after the concert if you'd like. We'll either kick it backstage, or hook up with X's and Rogelio's friends and go somewhere. Either way, you're invited." She pulled out her phone. "I'll text our people right now."

Within a minute, her phone pinged from Melissa, confirming that Simon and Jocelyn Rooney would be backstage at the Fever's return to the Garden after beginning the day as two tourists watching a movie trailer for a focus study. Not a bad turn of events. The Brits shook their heads, astonished by the unintended consequences of their chance meeting.

They parted with hugs and handshakes. The film distributor's hired gun glanced at her watch, annoyed, grabbed the unstudied tablet from Simon, and left.

They passed Tammany Hall, where America's first labor union met, then walked a half-dozen blocks to Gramercy Park. Tom's love of literary history kicked in, like it always did when he walked certain neighborhoods . . . North Beach, the Boston and Concord of Emerson and Thoreau, the Sierra foothills where Gary Snyder protects an environment while writing the finest we-are-nature-is-us poetry since Whitman, or the Lower East Side and Greenwich Village, where creative activity and familiar faces rivaled Paris. "Within a six-block radius, Washington Irving dreamed his shadowy dreams of Ichabod Crane, Henry James and his fellow *literateurs* filled the bars with stories . . ."

"Here we go," Megan said, rolling her eyes, thinking of her favorite literary nest, the Big Sur of Jeffers, Miller, and Steinbeck. But her love had far more to do with redwoods, beaches, Esalen, and rock-hopping the Big Sur River than specific authors.

". . . Dylan Thomas also hung out in the neighborhood sometimes," Tom continued. "Just up the street a few blocks, little Teddy Roosevelt, a future author among other things, charged up and down fire escape ladders and ran across the rooftops, driving his mother and neighbors crazy. Even then, he was a thrill-seeker."

He turned to Annalisa, who asked, "Henry James wrote something very famous with Venice, yes?" she asked. "About lovers? Three lovers?"

"*The Wings of the Dove.* A great Venice story."

"It is very good, true."

They walked down the tree-lined street, past garden-level coffee houses and around the corner to Irving Plaza, part of an informal cluster of small- and mid-sized venues with distinctive décor and atmosphere and kingly reputations, rock's version of off-Broadway. Inside, the press conference had just started. Robiski briefed fifty members of the traditional and online press on the tour, the new album's platinum status after just two weeks, and Tom and Chester's satellite radio show.

Then came the reason for a press conference: to share the big *news.* Tom held his breath, hoping Robiski would refrain from mentioning his near future. Robiski announced the Fever Anthology, which combined five CDs of re-mixes, three CDs of archival, previously unpublished music, and a Cumberland Festival mini-DVD. "There's also a photo collection, actual ticket stubs, coupon codes for discounts on Fever t-shirts and caps, and other goodies. Including, in fifty copies, free tickets to future shows. Our version of the Golden Tickets, without the chocolate tour." That drew a laugh. "We'll have it out for holiday season."

"That's what we've become: a band in a box," Tom quipped.

A white-bearded man moved among the reporters. "Sure you made enough *good* music to fill that box, son?"

Tom didn't even have to turn. *Ulysses.* "The old man of Harlem . . ."

"I'm just a crazy Fever fan tracking your every move." Ulysses uncorked a barrel roll laugh, the kind that adjusts a room's attitude upward. Several reporters laughed with him, having no idea why.

Tom took the stage. "Folks, before I start, we have among us the blues legend, Ulysses Washington."

Ulysses tipped his derby cap, a relic from his days as a young Beat struggling through Columbia University. Reporters knew a legend when they saw one. His cool-as-a-cat demeanor and lined face, deep-set eyes, shock-white hair, and slight stoop, the effect of thousands of days and nights hunched over pianos on the world's stages, screamed it. When you play for sixty years, you've earned the designation.

"Thank you, Tommy," Ulysses said. "And this beautiful woman who just wheeled up ain't no back porch plodder, neither."

Robiski stepped behind Christine, who had taken the stage with Tom. "Can we get on with this?"

"Raylene!" Christine exclaimed.

Tom shook his head. "No way."

"Sugar, I told you that I would find you. I ain't missing out on anything I don't have to miss out on."

"Then don't miss out." He chuckled and shook his head. "Get up here and join your band. Unbelievable."

A few rows in the audience, Annalisa walked up to Megan. "Who is that?"

"Their original bass guitarist, the lady Christine and Rogelio replaced."

"Two people for one?"

"She needed two replacements—a bass guitarist and a singer. She couldn't tour because of her health. She has trouble walking." Megan patted Annalisa's shoulder. "Let's say a quick hello before she wheels up there."

In a few steps, they reached Raylene. Megan knelt down and wrapped her in a sweeping hug. "It's so good to see you, sweetie. We were planning to get together before one of the shows, but you beat us to it."

"You're a sight for an old girl's eyes." Megan kissed her cheek, then held her face at arm's length. "Girl, when you gonna start aging with the rest of us?"

Megan laughed loudly. "Put your glasses on, Raylene. But thanks for the thought." She grabbed Raylene's hands and rubbed them, every caressing stroke an elixir to Raylene's ravaged body, now adorned with silver necklaces, bracelets, and bangles over a long dress. "Dressed for a day on the town?"

"And a couple of nights, from what I hear." Raylene turned to Annalisa. "Who might you be?"

"Annalisa." She extended her hand.

"Nice to—" Raylene stopped in mid-breath, held it, then turned to Megan and dropped to a whisper. "Say what? Ain't that the same name as Tom's lost and presumably... gone little girl?"

Megan grinned broadly and nodded, then glimpsed at Annalisa and back to Raylene. "One and the same," she whispered. "Long story, which we'll tell you when we have a minute, but yes, a miracle walked into our lives."

Raylene looked at Megan, and then back to Annalisa, peering in search of the precocious toddler that used to dance rhythmic, almost tribal circles when she practiced bass runs in Tom and Maria's flat. "You messin' with me? You for real?"

Annalisa chuckled. "She is. *Buon giorno*, Aunt Raylene."

"This ain't just a miracle. It's the miracle of miracles," Raylene said, shaking her head, tears rapidly filling her eyes. "Dear Sweet Jesus. Hmm, hmm, hmm. I cannot believe it. I used to tell your daddy you've got the eyes of an angel." She studied Annalisa. "You still do. How in our Almighty Lord's name did you find each other?"

Robiski walked over. "Hi Raylene, thanks so much for being here, you look great, I see you've met Annalisa, now we have to get on with it." Though locked in press conference mode, he kissed her cheek, winked at Annalisa, and leaned over and kissed her quickly.

"Well, *that's* a twist," Raylene whispered, glancing sideways. "Robiski, you tappin' the boss's—"

"—We were together months before we realized this."

Raylene smirked and shook her head. "Uh huh." She leaned over to Annalisa. "Keep that man on a short leash."

"*Scusi?*" Some metaphors she couldn't translate.

She looked up at Robiski. "Why don't you wheel me up there now, lover boy?" Then, to Annalisa, "You and I have some catching up to do. I don't even have words now; this is the most astonishing thing I've ever seen! You and me later. A talk."

Robiski wheeled her to the stage, Raylene barking at him the entire short journey about both the perils of dating the boss's daughter and not being told about Annalisa.

Jeremiah Denton watched the conversation, one of thousands he held, observed, and commented on during his long, award-winning journalistic career. He heard snippets, enough for him to focus on the Italian woman talking with Raylene and Megan. The lead writer of music's largest website and blogging collective, a group of more than three hundred blogs—the wire service of music blogs—was renowned for his encyclopedic knowledge of conversations past and present. He rimmed his three-bedroom apartment in Gramercy Park with fifteen thousand albums, as well as CDs with more than a thousand recorded interviews. Industry executives nicknamed him "The Fisherman" for his ability to cast feelers from hunches and reel in eye-popping exclusives and stories, again and again. The man could dig through charcoal and find prize-cut diamonds as a moving character within his own pieces, part of the New Journalism laid down by Capote, Thompson, and Wolfe for a generation of young reporters, himself included.

The rock world's most hardboiled gumshoe reporter walked over to Annalisa. "He's a good man, that Robiski," he said. "Heard he's found a woman in Italy who, word is, has ties to Tommy T. One that fits your description."

Robiski watched the exchange, not thrilled with the bulldog dropping in on his lady. Tom followed his eyes to the subject. "Any questions today, Jeremiah?" he asked.

"Good to see you, Tommy. Been awhile."

"You too, man."

Not one for idle chatter, Denton jumped in. "Your re-releases are selling like bonkers, there's this mega-set of your basement tapes Robiski just announced, Raylene shows up . . . any other surprises for us?" He looked at Annalisa. Nice to see an elegant, chic Mediterranean woman in the mix of rock-and-roll reporter types. "How are you adjusting to Christine fronting the band with you?"

Tom glanced at Christine. "Besides the fact that she, along with Rogelio and X, has made our crowd just as young on average as it was when we last played, thanks to all the twenty- and thirty-somethings coming out? I'd say we're adjusting well."

However, Denton had another story on his mind. He turned to Annalisa. "Let me reset. I know the sad part of Tommy's—your dad's—story. I met him around that time. All kinds of people started writing about it when the Fever got big, but I took the time to actually talk to *him* about it." He extended his hand. "I must say, young lady, that I am honored to meet you."

"You know who I am?" Annalisa took his hand and grinned slightly, not sure how to read the man. "*Gracie.*"

"I heard you met your dad again in L.A. The little bird returns," Denton continued. "Finally, this universe decided to give Tom something back for all he's given with his music and generosity . . . you. I am so happy for both of you." He smiled, revealing two missing lower teeth, and tapped his heart with his digital recorder. "Would you mind if I wrote something about . . . this? About you?"

Annalisa looked into bespectacled eyes ringed and lidded from a lifetime of parties, deadlines, concerts, bars, and sleep deprivation. "Yes, I think we can make a story, *signore.* Have you talked to my Papa?" "I certainly will," Denton said.

Robiski returned to the mic, his ears ringing from Raylene's quick upbraiding, the whoosh of her voice rushing like a backhanded slap from a hurricane. He glanced at Tom, and broke down the remaining tour schedule: "We're playing the Garden for two nights, Radio City Music Hall for spillover Garden fans who were shut out, Jones Beach on Thursday, then we're going split-squad—Tom, Will, and Chester at The Beacon Theater, the younger three at Webster Hall. On Saturday, we've got a free concert in Central Park, a fundraiser for diabetes that our legendary founding member Raylene Quarles—who is with us today—so generously co-chairs, then we close out Sunday with a private party at an old friend's on Long Island."

Denton turned to Annalisa. "They keep busy, don't they?"

"It has been a very busy time, yes."

Denton flashed his impish, time-to-dig grin. "It's great to meet you, Annalisa. Here is my card. We will do this. I have in mind something that will make you very happy." She sent him off with an affectionate European peck on his cheeks.

Robiski handed the mic to Tom. "We've got a couple of new songs to give you a taste of our newer material, which we're slowly breaking out."

"What about some real news?" one of the younger journalists yelled.

"New songs? That's news, when it's been twenty years," Tom said. "But, on another note, joining us for a couple of shows will be this beautiful woman to my right, our founding bass player, Raylene Quarles."

Just four months had passed since they'd reported on the debilitating reason for Raylene's absence. Doctors said they were hopeful she would survive the year. As for playing again? *Fahgedaboutit.*

Raylene wheeled up and hugged Tom, who handed the mic to her. "I just want to thank Tommy, Chester, Will, and these three incredible kids for letting me come back to play a little," she said, beaming as lights of appreciation, of gratitude even, began rising in the eyes of the older reporters.

"Have you been practicing? Which songs will be more of a challenge for you?" asked an intense Oriental woman whose angular face, sharp voice, endless fidgeting, and hard-wired build suggested a flaming arrow. She seemed like the Berklee or Juilliard type; you could see it in the way she bent her fingers, though hovering over the piano.

Raylene tapped her chest. "I know the songs right here, sugar. That's where they came from, and that's where they'll always be." She looked at Tom and chuckled as he rolled his eyes playfully. "But seriously, my rehearsal starts right after this event."

"How is your health?" Denton asked.

Annalisa looked over her shoulder as she walked to the side of the stage. What would it be like, to stay in one career for longer than she has been alive? After bouncing through dozens of jobs, maube hundreds of jobs, the concept of sitting in one career for almost fifty years was confounding. Not to mention beyond her realm of possibility. There was plenty to admire about the man with a face and manner of speaking carved from a hard, rugged life.

Raylene smirked. "Wanna take it outside for a moment and see, Jeremiah?"

No love lost there, Tom thought, remembering the argument that led to Denton and Raylene not speaking for ten years. Denton publicly accused Raylene of overstepping her bounds (as if he dictated what the Fever did) by singing vocal leads, and repeated it when they met later at an MTV Awards party. When the Fever carted off three awards, including best album for "Backroad Melodies" and best video for "Quantrill's Revenge," Raylene snatched Denton's arm. "Guess the rest of the world feels differently, bitch."

"Well, there's the rest of the world, and then there's me, who knows and understands what he sees up there. And I see you shaking right into Tommy's space."

Thirty years later, Irving Place erupted not in fisticuffs, but in laughter. "Seriously, Jeremiah, you ask a good question . . . this time." Some things just couldn't be forgotten. "I'm doin' fine, just slowed down. Better than I've felt in a while. But you know, I'd roll off the slab in the morgue for one more chance to play."

Denton nodded. "I'll take that as a 'good enough.'"

Raylene folded her hands on her lap and smiled. "Well put, Jeremiah. Good enough."

"I have a question for Christine," a photojournalist piped in, camera at his side, backpack on his shoulders. "You've become a rock star almost instantly. How did you develop so quickly?"

She twirled her hair, her nerves rising as the New York media awaited her answer. "Having my dad next to you makes you learn fast." A few nods from the press. "I've always loved to sing, dance, and perform, but just haven't done it like this."

"What about replacing legends like Raylene?"

She rolled her hair through her fingers like straining spaghetti. "That's the thing. I'm being made out to be a star—I'm not complaining!—but X, Rogelio, and I are really hired guns. The three stars are over there." She pointed at Tom, Chester, and Will, now gathered beside Raylene. "Make that four. No one replaces Raylene, or Treg, but we've tried to fit in and add our own little styles, or interpretations of songs, as Dad, Chester, and Will have urged us to."

"She makes a good point," Tom added. "I think the biggest mistake legacy bands make when they reform is to stick to the script—the songs as they sounded when they recorded them. Just about every band has at least one or two replacement members, so why not see what they can add? They've got their own styles, experiences, ways of working songs, bending notes. We've taken a wide-open approach with our new members, and as you've seen and heard, it has really served us well. And it makes us three old-timers— make that four," he looked at Raylene, "feel like we're playing new music and our people are hearing it for the first time. That's why it's so important to recognize how much we've evolved as musicians, and what great gifts these younger folks bring to the table."

A journalist in his early thirties followed up with Christine, moving his digital recorder atop his notebook so the mic would pick up her response better. "Do you feel your dad showed favoritism in selecting you over a more experienced vocalist?"

That surprised her. She started to stumble through an answer, but Raylene leaned into the mic. "Ain't no favoritism at all. Creighton Page, right?"

"That's right, ma'am. Good memory."

"You covered my music school here ten years ago when you were a cub music reporter. 'Course I'm gonna remember you; that was a great story."

"And I remember you. That story advanced my career. Thank you so much."

"Good for you, son, but you need to understand how it went down for Christine. I recommended her, simple as that. Tommy was reluctant to hire her due to exactly what you asked—he didn't want to play favorites or pressure his kid. But I had an inkling what this girl could bring."

"Bring it she has," Page said.

Raylene winked. "That's my girl."

Denton moved alongside Megan. "I miss her sassiness. Such a nice change from these sanitized Pop-Tart stars and their cookie-cutter answers these days. You know a lot of them get schooled by media coaches before they ever meet a reporter now, let alone cut a single?"

"I did not," Megan said. "What happened to speaking your mind and turning it into art? Isn't rock the musical version of saying what you want to say?"

Denton chuckled. "Yes and yes, but corporately, that ship sailed long ago. We made rock mainstream, then commoditized it into part of everything. Just like everything else that starts off cool. Where's the edge? Breaks my crusty heart. This alone is why I'm glad Tom, Chester, and Will got off their recliners to play and—I heard—even toss their earpieces."

"More than once."

"Going old school. And I'm glad Tommy hired your kid." Denton waved his notebook at Christine as continued talking. To Megan, he said, "Smart move. Ballsy, and smart."

"Thank Raylene. She all but hammered it home to Tom the day before she had to go to the hospital to see if her leg was going to be amputated . . . thankfully, they found a way for her to keep it." She stepped back, taken by Denton's consideration. "Do I know you, Jeremiah? Where did the gruff old bastard go?"

"Grandkids."

"They'll always get you . . . though I'm still waiting my turn."

After fifteen more minutes of questions, and whispers from two front-row reporters that Tom might be stepping off the tour—which Robiski answered with "every band evaluates their next step after every tour; nothing's different here," he closed down the conference. "The Fever will be back in twenty minutes."

As soon as the curtain crossed the stage, Tom found Rogelio tinkering with the hookups and knobs on a second bass amp. "How we going to work with Raylene?"

"I've got her covered," Rogelio said. "She can use my bass and play through my amp today, then tomorrow, let's turn the sound check into a rehearsal, so my tech and I can fine-tune her rig."

Tom motioned to Dudley, just walking through the door, accompanied by an assistant roadie who took notes feverishly. "Dudley, we need an extra bass amp, extra monitor, and a comfortable stool by tomorrow's sound check. Make sure it roughly matches the stage color-wise."

"Can do, Tommy." He turned to the girl, who pulled her phone out of her purse, and started calling equipment suppliers. "What we doing this for?"

"You'll see in a second . . . who's the catchy helper?"

"You and I both had girls around the same time."

"I recall."

"Well, she's mine." As surprise overcame Tom, Dudley added, "She's in graduate school at NYU, and wanted to help for the week. Her boyfriend's that wiry kid over there who's checking Will's drums; their version of couples' week, I guess. We needed two more bodies; worked out perfectly."

"Very cool . . . but can't believe your baby is a grad student."

"And I can't believe your little girl owns the U.S. of A. right now, but what do we know? They do what they want. All we have to do is get them there, and hopefully they learn the errors of our ways and make theirs different. We've done good."

Dudley walked away, and turned the corner. He stopped, stunned. "Some faces a man can only pray he'll see again."

"Hello, you lovable grizzly," Raylene said softly.

"I thought you were too sick to . . ."

"Jump in on a gig, here at home? Not a chance, honey."

"Then you're why Tommy's sending me and my daughter on a wild goose chase for equipment."

Dudley lifted Raylene a few inches off the wheelchair seat, kissing her lips. She cupped his neck, holding him in place. Twenty seconds later, she released. "Your mouth is as sweet as the last time I kissed it," she said.

"A wife and a kid ago." He held her tight. "How's your old man?"

"We've been separated a long while."

"Sorry to hear that."

"But I see that spark in your eyes." Raylene smiled as he slid her back into the wheelchair. "It's been a long time for us, before your wife, before my old man, but I can be persuaded to take up old acquaintances." She turned to him. "You're just gonna have to carry me a little more, is all."

"You two can reprise old times later," Tom said. "Can we get three hours for a long sound check at the Garden tomorrow, Dudley?"

Dudley stood behind Raylene and rubbed her shoulders, his fingers instantly recalling a body he hadn't touched in more than a quarter-century, but one that comforted him for several years prior. "I'll call them as soon as you guys start this mini-set."

Chester and Tom began tuning their guitars as Raylene patted Dudley's hand and wheeled over to Rogelio. Next to them, X hurried onto the stage. "How did the studio go?" Christine asked.

"Laid down piano for two tracks. Felt like old times, a bunch of dudes trying to drop something besides hip-hop. Like real music."

"What tracks?" Rogelio asked.

"Grind-your-booty blues. Bottleneck guitar, a little organ, bass until your ass is dragging the ground. Best kind." He smiled and stroked Christine's cheek. "My boys are playing in the Village and Williamsburg this week."

"We've got concerts," she said.

"These are late-late shows. Don't start till twelve, one. Let's check them out."

"Right on," Christine said. As she'd learned, clubbing was entirely different when your face was plastered on newsstands, concert stages, videos, and streams. All drinks are on the house, the energy rises when you arrive, management escorts you to the back of the club, and the house band invariably invites you onstage. Not hard to get used to.

The Fever closed the press conference by playing two songs off the upcoming album, along with "Holy Child Blues," penned not two miles from where they stood. Raylene leaned against Rogelio's amp and accompanied the final number, "When I Become the President," as Rogelio switched to his sax. The younger reporters could only dance in place and shake their heads, their perceptions of the Fever as washed-up oldies shattered. Someone still trusted their work enough to let the results create the story. Then they backed it by being every bit as good as the legend—and as current as Christine's latest outfit.

37

NEW YORK . . . CENTRAL PARK . . . LONG ISLAND

THE EXPLOSION OF CHEERS AND APPLAUSE REMINDED TOM OF A time when the Knicks and Rangers were champions and the Garden was *the Garden. Going to a Garden party . . .* could Ricky Nelson have written a truer lyric?

He peered into the raucous black din, blinded by the stage lights, hearing but not seeing the twenty thousand ready to spend as much of the night as they could with the Fever. Christine danced back and forth across the stage, apparently in feral recklessness but in perfect time with every song, the most photogenic new front woman in the business. Tom, Chester, X, and Rogelio wove every solo, bridge and fill into their funky, hard-charging melodic precision, every note plucking some screaming fan's heart string, summoning joy, sadness, an old memory, a smooth glow inside. Christine filled eyes with her short dress and floor-length cape, headband, and bare feet with a row of anklets. She could've carried the night by herself, easily, but often yielded the spotlight to Tom in the garden of the rock gods.

What fans didn't see before was Tom vomiting backstage, the thrill and anxiety of playing the Garden sweeping through his stomach like a scirocco. Most musicians struggled to keep it together when they played the Garden, even new stars who grew up in a now-is-the-only-history culture. Something was wrong if you didn't get nervous, Tom thought. No matter how cool, every musician felt jittery at the Garden.

Pandemonium erupted after the regular set, when Rogelio and Tom led Raylene onstage. She played the encores, singing three-part harmonies with Tom and Christine, jamming from her chair. Now freed from the bass, Rogelio strode from one end of the stage to the other, blowing pure fire from his sax, swaying back and forth. Then he walked offstage, his riff thick and mighty, bending and swaying, filled up with Charlie Parker attitude, channeling The Bird himself.

One song later, Raylene raced along to "Cumberland Blues," Chester's rockabilly-on-steroids, so popular a live favorite since the festival that the band moved "West of the West" to the earlier encore. She anchored the beat as the stage lights fell to black. A second later, two spotlights announced Christine and Rogelio twenty feet above the stage on opposite speaker stacks, she twisting in place, he be-bopping, the go-go dancer and the horn man, the fans delirious. Tom looked up, driving power chords as though their vibration could push her further away from the speaker lip with his instrument, hoping to still have two daughters when the show ended.

Sidestage, Megan turned to Annalisa. "I'm going to kick her ass if she falls."

Annalisa smiled. "It will already be hurt." She danced with abandon, hips swaying, hair flying, feeling like a young girl again. What a thrill to have musicians for a dad and sister! She grabbed Megan's hand and they danced side by side, at home in a world that, a month before, never existed for her. Now, she was part of rock royalty.

Chester walked to the backline. "Let's send these midtown yahoos into orbit!" he yelled. X drove his piano like a nitro-turbocharged engine for an amped-up ragtime riff that Scott Joplin and Nap Hayes would have appreciated. Chester, Tom, and X drove "Cumberland Blues" home. As the band bowed to the frenetic crowd, Christine, back at center stage, noticed her newest guest, Jocelyn, standing near a speaker stack. She danced over, grabbed Jocelyn's hands, and shared a couple of twirls under an ever-pursuing Super Trouper floodlight. Jocelyn folded her hands reverentially and tipped them toward the stage, then erupted into tears.

They kept the night alive. X, Christine, Jocelyn, and Simon hit the Cellar Club, once the basement of a mansion. The guitarist spotted X, and within two songs, called him and Christine up. They played a catted-up, slowed-down version of "Gypsy's Prayer," Christine doing her best burlesque imitation while stretched across the top of the piano, pawing the air and stretching, reprising something she saw on an *American Idol* finale, the great Billy Preston on his almighty Hammond, growling and grooving in what would be his last live appearance. *Goodbye, Jo-Jo.* When they finished, she said, "We'll give you the band now, but go out and find love, give it, make it the driving force in whatever you do," she said.

Jocelyn and Simon sat at the reserved table, guzzling free drinks, nearly undone by two days that, Jocelyn imagined, would have thrilled Auntie Fiona. She tossed the curls that cascaded down her chest like Van Gogh's starry night, her ordinarily straight hair banished like a shadow. She ran her ring-covered hand along Simon's thigh and squeezed softly, her new pink manicure part of the gift of an afternoon with Christine's makeup girl. "Let's get to our room, love, and transform Christine's lovely suggestion into the rest of our night."

He smiled and tipped his drink to X. "I never thought you'd ask."

Four days later, the band turned an hour-long Central Park hit-and-run set into a three-hour extravaganza, delighting fans who pumped nearly a half-million dollars into the diabetes fundraiser. Raylene, the face though not the beneficiary of the fundraiser, played every song in the set, with the exception of a three-song break for an insulin shot. "You sure about going all the way, honey?" Chester asked mid-set as he strummed.

"This is how I'm rollin'. With the band. Quit your country fussing. I'm good. Just move those fingers and try to keep up."

He nodded, the glare in her eyes all he needed to know. Her heart was overflowing, not just from playing, but also spending late nights and early mornings in Dudley's arms at The Plaza, reprising their on-again, off-again decade before each met their spouses. This gave her the impetus to finally kick the reliance on her ex and send him on his way. Dudley and his burly arms were the only loving she wanted. Or needed. A funny little circle of life, that, but circles of life came in all shapes and forms.

She leaned toward Chester as she settled into the next riff. "What more can a sister want? If the good Lord takes me away while playin' with my boys, doing what I love more than anything on God's green earth, then he truly *is* a good Lord."

As the weekend neared its finish, Megan stretched across the back of the limousine. Her eyes cast into another world, beyond the buildings and billboards whisking past them on the Long Island Expressway. "I have a surprise."

Tom stroked her hair. "A surprise . . ."

"You'll see after Boston."

He rubbed her stomach, his fingertip touch leaving her purring like a dreaming kitten. "Unfair to leave me hanging, but I know better than to ask for a clue."

She smiled, eyes still closed, her stomach lifting softly to receive more of his hand. "Wise man," she whispered. "After Boston, let's go away for your days off."

"So it's a trip."

"Sort of. You know where."

"I do?"

"Mmmm." Within seconds, she was asleep.

The front grounds of the Westhampton mansion, its porch as big as a house and lined with meticulously carved Doric columns, reminded Tom of Jay Gatsby's mythical place. Or life as a Greek god. Three white canopy tents stood near the entrance, a catering truck backed up to each. Dozens of cars rimmed the long, circular driveway as others streamed in, all guests of East Coast financier, investor extraordinaire, and philanthropist Jeanette Dos Santos, who decided to throw a huge benefit to celebrate her favorite band and musician. She made it a fundraiser for the domestic violence organization she spent a decade turning into a primary source of supplies, counseling, and the expensive piece, clandestine operations often as harrowing as the Underground Railroad. The special event took shape just as Jeanette liked, with none of the media or corporate machinations that could blow or misconstrue her intent—to get women safe anonymously, get them help, and get them empowered so we'd hear about their great accomplishments, not the mess in which they currently found themselves. She might have made her millions in the corporate world, with the media her friend more often than not, but this was not a media event. Not at all.

As she surveyed the grounds, Jeanette eagerly awaited hearing the band fronted by the man she loved for a precious short time before the Fever hit its stride. They shared two weeks of hot Village nights during the Fever's final run as a small band, stretching Tom's thirty to fifty bucks per gig, dreaming openly of bigger lives, and ignoring the stuffiness of the rented brownstone room across from Electric Lady, Hendrix's studio. The only TV they watched turned out to be consequential: coverage of an enormous human jam in upstate New York caused by a massive rock concert on a farm near Woodstock, where The Band hung out. They made dinner and love every day and night, while she appealed to his collapsed heart by convincing him to pour his agony over losing Annalisa into his music, and learn to trust love again. *I'd be the ideal place to start*, she thought. She should've said it. She'd dated enough musicians and artists who could love physically like there was no tomorrow. There wasn't; when tomorrow came, they often left. He was different. He focused on her more than himself, maybe to deflect the pain cutting his heart, but, perhaps, also because he, too, felt what she was feeling.

Their two weeks opened the floodgates. Tom left for a week of shows at the Boston Tea Party to start a fall swing of warm-up gigs. "I'll be back down when we're finished," he'd said, kissing her at the door.

"No, lovely man, you see where it goes. I'm not really going your way, and you're not really going mine. I wish we could, but we'd hold each other back."

Tom's smile twisted into a quizzical frown. "What about the last two weeks?"

"Beautiful. I will never forget it. But you have your life, I have mine, and intersecting the two is going to be hard. The way we look at things and feel is so similar, though . . . you certainly know how to make me feel special, beautiful, and important."

She said it with tears in her eyes. She'd fallen in love, against her own wishes, knowing the best to do with a deeply, recently wounded man is to comfort him, give space. That uncertainty, and road touring, added up to a lifestyle that interested her not at all. Which made the moment at the door harder.

"I hope we see each other again . . . someday," Tom said. "You helped me feel again. I will always love you for that."

"We will see each other." Jeanette kissed him, letting her lips linger a few extra seconds, the ties of her nightie undone. "Every day when you wake up, you'll know there's someone out there who loves you for you—regardless of who's looking at you in bed. Make sure the woman in that bed loves *you*, because Tommy, with that voice and those songs, you are going places."

Nostradamus couldn't have forecast it better. On the final night of the blistering Boston Tea Party stand, the Fever had its first record deal, part of a band-signing frenzy in the weeks and months that followed Three Days of Peace, Love, and Music. And Tom spotted Megan sitting in the front row, shooting photos.

Jeanette's life took off, too. She financed her Ph.D. from one of the Seven Sisters schools by flying to Tampa on weekends and dancing in the classier men's clubs, her ample curves drawing many eyes and fat tips, but never anything further. She was not about to ruin her dreams to feed a fling. She took her four hundred dollars for two nights' work, astonishing money, and headed home. Within two weeks of earning her Ph.D., she landed her first job on Wall Street and ditched the weekenders to Tampa. After forming a trusting client base, she started rolling the investment dice above the pass line, again and again, for those same trusting clients. Her calls were almost always lucky sevens, until clients realized there was little luck involved. After all, who intuited that computers, software, and cellular telephones would change the world? She did. She had fifty combined positions when the companies went public, many now Dow Jones and NASDAQ leaders. She also steered clear of commitment, not marrying until forty-five.

She thought of the disarming line she once gave lecherous executives after they painted her body with their eyes at yet another convention. "You guys think you're swordsmen? Well, I had a rock-and-roll friend." It almost always did the trick; how could they match a rocker in a fight for the girl? For good measure, and a dash of unattainability, she casually mentioned that he became one of rock's biggest stars.

Jeanette descended the porch chairs as the limo reached the head of the turnaround driveway where porch, columns, and house intersected. She opened the door and leaned into the back seat. "Two of the most beautiful souls alive. Welcome."

Tom stepped out first. She pulled him into her large body for an engulfing hug she gave no other men but her husband. She then stepped over and took Megan into her arms. Megan squeezed her hand while surveying the grounds, the benefits of her short nap kicking in as every manicured plant, lawn, and tree snapped into sharp focus. "What a magnificent place, Jeanette."

"Have a moment to see it?"

She patted Jeanette's hand. "Of course. I'm not the type to set up speakers and amps, that I can assure you. Especially when there's a palace to check out."

"But first . . ." She called the chief attendant, who was instructing a half-dozen groundskeepers on plant placement on the porch. "Is the east wing master bedroom ready, Randy?"

"Yes ma'am."

"Thank you." She turned to Tom. "That'll be the dressing room for you boys . . . Christine can use my room."

She returned to the attendant. "Randy, could you pull the doors to the west wing? I don't want them seeing our little restaurant, yet." She nodded cordially to Annalisa, who had walked up.

"Restaurant?" Megan asked.

Jeanette flipped her hands up. "Flash food, as opposed to fast food . . . a Hamptons thing. I hear you guys have even been doing little flash or pop-up concerts . . . this is our version. Once or twice a year, we neighbors turn our kitchens and dining rooms into restaurants. We bring in four- or five-star chefs, offer two or three prix fixe menus, invite guests. We eat and drink, talk, party, talk and eat more. It's fun."

"You can do this? Legally?"

"Good God, no," she laughed. "We don't have food or beverage licenses. And liquor licenses? We're talking bring back the speakeasies, girlfriend. That's how off-paper we are. But since some around here are connected to government or law enforcement in some administrative way, don't think we're in any danger. Plus, a girl's gotta have fun, right?"

Tom tapped Megan's shoulder. "Don't mean to cut this short, sweetie, but we need to set up."

Jeanette laughed and rubbed her hand across Tom's back. "They're all set up, Tommy. They've been out back all day."

"Out back . . ."

"The back portico is your stage. I wanted the beach, but we're still recovering from winter. What a mess. Storms ate the shoreline like it was a bowl of ice cream. They were grinders, like hurricanes, only it happens a lot more often now than the odd hurricane hooking this far north."

As Tom walked away, nodding, Jeanette turned to Annalisa. "On that lovely note, I don't believe we've met."

"I am Annalisa. Tom's daughter." She smiled. "The one who doesn't sing."

Jeannette sized her up, the dark summer dress, beautiful skin as richly olive as a Tuscan hillside, the soft wrinkles, deep, dark eyes. "You're not the one who was, um, *lost* to him way back when . . ."

"*Si, signora.*"

"I'd heard you had reconnected, but to see you in the flesh?" She glanced at Annalisa's lapis lazuli butterfly necklace, surrounded with pearls, inlaid in gold. If she didn't know any better, she thought, it's Ancient Greek. Annalisa seemed to wear her beauty naturally, without added cosmetic touch-ups, a statement of elegance, sophistication, attitude, grace. "You're gorgeous, sweetheart. What a pleasure to meet you. Your dad and I had a lot of talks when . . ." *how do I say this?* "—you were a little girl."

She thought of lying in bed, stroking Tom's hair, how he would gaze into space, hoping someone would see him, the story in his eyes the saddest she'd ever seen. "Join us. I'll show you the house."

"*Gracie,* I would like that very much."

They walked through a lower floor filled with Jeanette's classic taste, walls covered with original paintings, sculptures on sconces, and wall-to-wall windows facing south toward the Atlantic, and west towards sunset. A glass case caught Annalisa's eye, filled with Greek, Etruscan, and near eastern urns and vases, some chipped and cracked, others pristine. "Do you know about these, *Signora* Jeanette?" she asked.

"I know what they're called, but not much else, except that they're quite old. And, I believe, you are wearing an antiquated beauty."

"Then you know." Annalisa grabbed her necklace. "This is from sixth century BCE. I found it on a dig my son and I go on. The Plains of Marathon."

For the next fifteen minutes, Annalisa educated her about the vases, made easier when they switched to Italian, Jeanette's second language. "Now I feel like I know these vases in homes, temples, amphitheaters," Jeanette said. "Where did you learn this?"

"After my Paolo—my son—and I went on a holiday to Greece, I took a job helping make exhibits at the Accademia in Venezia. Later, they invited us onto digs to the Plains of Marathon, Smyrna, Delphi . . ."

"I'm utterly jealous." Jeanette grabbed a small vase, a sandstone *lekythos* of four Amazon warrior-priestesses colored in polychrome, the finish of choice. It was also sixth century BC, Annalisa guessed. "When you were describing my urns and vases, you said you did not have this at home. Now, you do. Thank you so much."

The urn was just over a foot tall, but worth a year of *vaporetto* wages. "You do not have to do this, *signora*."

"No, I don't." Jeanette's teal eyes widened and brightened, their roundness accentuated by her arched brows. "But I just did."

As they chatted about the Plains of Marathon dig in the hallway, Annalisa's purse buzzed. She let it go. It buzzed again. "*Merda!*" Her purse buzzed a third time.

She unzipped the pocket, grabbed her mobile phone, and looked at the screen. "*Scusi,* Jeannette. Megan. It is my son. I must take this."

She walked to the foyer, talking slowly, then a little faster. Within thirty seconds, her hand flew through the air, her mouth open, her eyes frantically combing the walls and floor, as though searching for something, her calmness gone. "No, no, no," she said, shock leeching her face, speaking rapid Italian. "Do not tell me this. It cannot be true. How do you know? How do you know for sure?"

"Mama, it is true," Letitia said, her sobs and sniffles bungling her words. "We are going into hospital tomorrow morning. We are home to grab some things."

"I am coming home."

"*Si, Mama, we have everything under control right now, bu*t *si*, I think you need to come home soon if possible."

Megan opened the door to the makeshift men's dressing room, a walk-in closet larger than their guest bedrooms and filled with enough clothing to outfit all of them. Or a sizable boutique. "Honey, you need to talk to Annalisa."

Tom finished buckling his belt. "For?"

"Right now."

"Why?"

Megan fought back tears. "Don't ask. She's in the foyer."

Tom saw the look in her eye and walked out. He found Annalisa sobbing, her head on Jeanette's shoulder. The hostess stroked her face lightly, soothing her. He clenched his teeth. "What's going on?"

She lifted her head, her cheeks and puffy eyes smeared by mascara. "My Paolo. His cancer. It is back. It is very bad. I must leave immediately."

"Oh, no." He pulled her into his arms. "Where is Jason?" He already knew: on his way to San Francisco, sent by Megan, Christine, and Annalisa to make early preparations for the final stops of the tour.

"I just talk to him. He can come to Venezia in some days, but I cannot wait. I must go to the airport in the next day, maybe two days."

Tom and Megan tried to console her as Jeanette walked into the foyer. They told her of Annalisa's dilemma. Within moments, she summoned her executive assistant, a beautiful, smart, caffeine-breathing whorl of efficiency and sass built with class and professionalism. She reminded Megan of Melissa.

Jeanette and her assistant talked quickly, during which the assistant glanced at Annalisa, her ultra-focused eyes softening into vessels of compassion. "I am so sorry," she mouthed to Annalisa before disappearing into a side office.

A minute later, she returned. "Did you reach him?" Jeanette asked.

"They're packing up right now."

Jeanette nodded, turned to Annalisa, and took her hand. "My lovely assistant, Samira, will make sure you get out of Islip, the airport closest to here, after the show," she said. "My husband is flying back from the Bahamas in our private plane. They're racing to the airport now; they'll be wheels-up in thirty minutes, forty-five max." She smiled at Tom, an old lover bringing all her love—and influence—into play. "He's been bonefishing long enough in those sweaty mangrove swamps, anyway. Enough time fighting mosquitoes the size of alligators with the boys." She smiled again. "This princess needs her man time, right?"

Annalisa tried to say something, convey her thanks over this random act of immense generosity . . . but nothing came out. Why was this complete stranger being so generous? Why did she always hear about the wealthy in America being concerned with nothing but themselves or their immediate family, and yet, everywhere she turned, they made it easier for her? And how, after leading a life just a shade above a pauper's, does she becomes a queen because of meeting Jason Robiski? And get her father back?

Yet, amidst such a radiant moment, God was threatening to take her Paolo . . . *Perchi, cari Dio?* She rubbed her stomach, calming it, trying to hold her guts inside. What kind of cruelty was this?

"They told us that, if this came back," she said, tears garbling her speech, "this would be probably . . . it." Tears garbled her accent, her words tough to understand.

Tom shook his head, knowing this feeling too well to ever wish for it to resurface in any person—let alone his daughter. "Go home, sweetheart, and find Paolo the best care. Don't worry about the cost. We'll get you whatever you need."

"I cannot ask for that, Papa. This is something for Paolo, and me."

"You didn't ask." Tom grinned and patted her head. "We insist. Jeanette, can you have Samira call Robiski so he can transfer funds into Annalisa's account?"

"Done, honey." Jeanette walked to Samira, who re-entered the room and whispered. Samira opened her phone, turned and walked outdoors, already talking, her own energy surging. Like all top-grade assistants, she relished the challenge of having to put something together on a moment's notice. The more disparate and apparently difficult the logistics, the better. But a sadness gripped her chest . . . she couldn't imagine the torment going on inside the Italian woman.

"Does he already know?" Annalisa asked.

A minute later, her phone buzzed again. A text: *Baby, need your bank information. Call me. Wiring 100K Euros. Will be available when you arrive in Venice. I love you. Jason.*

She looked up through flooded eyes. "You are so generous, Papa. Jeanette." Hope lifted its head anew, only to be leveled by the next wave sweeping through her chest. "I'm afraid Paolo may die this time . . ."

"You don't know," Tom said. How many more losses could this family take?

Five hours and a successful concert later, a concert that collected a quarter-million dollars to help abused women, Annalisa boarded Jeanette's private jet. So did Tom, Megan, Christine, and X, having decided to use their four-day break to zip to Venice and back.

38

ANNALISA RUBBED HER EYES AND FOLDED HER ARMS TIGHT against her chest. "Paolo, please accept this offer. This is about your life."

She sighed, weary from both the journey and Paolo's stubbornness. How could she convince him to come to America for treatment? The thought superseded a thousand others that gobbled all ten sleepless hours of flying, spurred on by Robiski's texts and Tom's comments. Then again, why would he leave? "Paolo, we will get the very best treatment," she said, her voice more commanding. "This is your chance. There is a great place in America. City of Angels."

"Momma, he is *your* family and America is *your* country." Paolo turned to Tom. "With all respect, *signore,* this cancer comes when I want to stay here, for my Letitia, for my life. This is home. I must stay."

While Tom tried to find an answer, Letitia said, "Going to America for your treatment might be our one chance to grow in that happiness, Paolo. To have a future to grow into."

Letitia was still stunned by Annalisa and her American family, these emissaries dropped into their lives by angels. Maybe they were *angels.* Who extended these kinds of offers anymore? Who even cared enough? When Paolo's cancer returned, she didn't know what to believe: her own optimistic words, or the oncologist's dark outlook, honed and hardened by a lifetime of cases that began from thousands of different causes, but customarily ended in one way. "Whether you are here or in America, we will do this together, Paolo. Your mama has invited me to America to join you." She looked at Tom. "So has your poppa."

Tom noticed the fear dancing in the boy's eyes. He may have *felt* like dying when he was twenty-four, but real death was creeping onto Paolo's doorstep—a much different story. His forehead furrowed. "Do whatever makes you comfortable, Paolo, here or in America, but let us help you get the best care. OK?" He patted Paolo's shoulder. "You will have every Euro you need."

Annalisa unfolded her arms and grabbed Paolo's hand. The last thing he ever wanted, she knew, was to depend on another person, for anything. Especially this strange man. "The money is already in my account, Paolo," she said softly.

"*Gracie,*" Paolo said weakly, yielding to a fight he would not win. His ashen skin tone and the dark circles beneath his eyes felt like a sordid lie; hadn't he been in remission? What happened?

Soon, the rooftop filled with his light snores. Megan turned to Letitia. "What are the hospitals like?"

Letitia adjusted her short-billed cap. In her black dress, knee-high boots, and alabaster skin, a gift of her homeland, the Dolomite Alps, she could pass for the cover girl of Transylvanian chic. "*Molto buono.* Very good. The best is in Basel. But the doctors are not so confident anymore."

Paolo stirred, opened an eye and turned to Tom. "Thank you so much for helping me. I will grow healthy here, with my Letitia, with my life. And when I am healthy, maybe I come to America to see where you live?"

As Paolo came to grips with the blank check he'd just received, Christine and Maurizio walked out of the kitchen and onto the rooftop patio arm in arm, a conqueror's grin on Maurizio's stubbled face. "Poppa Maurizio has a thing for beautiful girls," Annalisa chuckled through her tears. "My Nonna had to listen to him talk about girls. A lot."

"There is a reason." He winked at Christine. "My dream comes true today."

"How did you not . . . suit every girl in Venice, Poppa Maurizio?" Christine asked.

"Well, my Clara would have killed me. With a tool the Doge used after the prisoner walked over the Bridge of Sighs; you don't want to know." Maurizio wagged his finger. He squeezed Christine closer, then released her with a pat on the shoulder. He turned to Tom. "May I speak a few words?"

"Of course."

"Tomas Timoreaux, of all the miracles my eyes have seen, this miracle is the best. My Annalisa now has her whole life, and I have never seen her so happy, with Jason and now you. But now, we have one more miracle to pray for."

He sat on the lounge, and urged Paolo to join him. Then, "Son, you need to accept this gift. If you don't go to America, then I expect you to be in Basel or Roma. This is your decision, but Poppa Maurizio is telling you to do this now. Your mama raised a man who makes strong decisions that a man makes, not a *Mammoni.* You and Letitia decide, but you make a strong decision. And do it while these people are here, please." He looked up at Tom, who nodded in assent. "Do it soon, please."

Christine studied Letitia's hair as she curled into Paolo's side. The girl definitely knew style and fashion, the blended highlights, Goth get-up, gorgeous half-sleeve of a mermaid swimming up one arm. Daphne would love her, too. *My kind of cousin.*

"*Mi amore,* if the treatment does not work here, and the doctors say you can fly, we fly to America. Can we agree to that?" Letitia asked.

Paolo looked at Maurizio and Annalisa, then the other family, this new family, this family that never existed in his life until now—and with a rock star for a cousin. How cool was that? It all felt like a crazy movie: who wakes up one day and finds out they have a cousin for a rock star? Or a poppa who is a living legend? "*Si.*"

Letitia turned to Tom and Maurizio. "You heard it. As did you," she said, looking at one and then the other.

"Then it is settled." Maurizio looked at Tom, who nodded.

Paolo nodded and sensed Annalisa's resolve to stay in Venice, knowing that, when on highest alert, her maternal instincts and protectiveness were the strongest forces on earth. He also noticed her reluctance at having to stay. How could he convince her to move forward and spend more time in America with Jason, who really loved her, not like those *Mammoni* who gave a million promises and ended up hurting them? He hoped she would feel free to go, free to be with Jason. Not to mention her long-lost family. No one deserved greater. But with this cancer, the way she was . . . "Momma, I hope you know I am fine with Letitia if you go back to America."

"I want to go to America; I want it more than anything now, Paolo, and I will go back as soon as possible," she said, tears molting in her eyes. "But it is not possible now. You are not well, I am your momma, and I belong here." Her words were firm.

Megan noticed the puzzled look on Tom's face, like an encounter with the twilight zone, the reality far different than the images of a little girl still fighting for space in his perception of her after having his brain to themselves for so long. "Strange hearing your daughter being a mother, isn't it honey?"

"Very."

"She's good. That's obvious."

Paolo looked around the concerned faces, and then turned to Tom. "I have no way to repay you, *signore.*"

"Repay me by getting better and giving this beautiful girl as much of you, and the world, as you can." Letitia's grin suggested a deep, calm wisdom. "She will carry you through this difficult time. We all will."

Maurizio slapped his hands together. "Enough sad hearts. Let us celebrate."

With that, he took Christine's arm, and his California girl for a day escorted him into the kitchen, where he pulled a blood-red cabernet from Annalisa's small wine cabinet. "Excellent vintage. Let us drink to this opportunity to be together, and to Paolo's health. Christine, will you give us the pleasure of tasting it?"

"You are like such a total stud, Poppa Maurizio." Christine kissed his cheek. "If I were a little older, I would tell every woman in Venice to back well off. You'd be mine."

He smiled. "To be almost one hundred . . . to be called this . . . yes, my life is complete."

Annalisa shook her head. "Italians. Blondes. *Penso che anche lei lo scarico si.*"

"One can only dream," Christine replied, winking at Maurizio. She pecked his cracked lips. "Now I know why Annalisa loves you so much."

"And why she loves you," he said. A devilish smile crossed his lips. "I can tell Venezia about an old cobbler who kissed the most popular girl in America."

"And, he will." Annalisa rolled her eyes. "Poppa, you will need another hundred years to tell this story, because you will try to tell everyone, won't you? And then you'll get on the vaporettos and tell the *turistas.*"

"It is my story, child," Maurizio grumbled. "I tell it as I please."

Annalisa chuckled. "As I said . . ."

Christine hooked her arm into Maurizio's, and looked into eyes so deep she felt she could dive into them and never touch bottom. "Tell our story well."

39

HARTFORD, PROVIDENCE, BOSTON, PHILADELPHIA,
BALTIMORE, VIRGINIA BEACH, COLUMBIA, CHARLOTTE,
ATLANTA, NEW ORLEANS, GAINESVILLE, JACKSONVILLE,
TAMPA . . .

MEGAN ROSE FROM THE BLANKET, HER EYES SCANNING TALL grasses plump from a summer-long feast of sun and rain. The meadow seemed as wide and verdant as before, even though the hike from the deep-forest spur of the Franconia Notch Railroad, now an access trail, seemed shorter. Though, how could you trust any measures after not seeing the place for so long?

"We're definitely alone," Tom mumbled, talking into the blanket.

"We definitely are." Megan peeled off her blouse, straightened her bikini top, rolled her shorts to her thighs, and lay back down. "Perfect."

He turned over and lay against her chest, brushing her breast with his hand. "Just like I would imagine you as a kid . . . half-naked and free, soaking up the beauty."

She squeezed his leg and moved her hand higher. "I have to say, Mr. Timoreaux, that you have some of the most tender come-on lines around."

"I'm just a music freak in mad, everlasting love with the foxiest chick around," he said, turning over, removing her top, and running his mouth over her breasts. "Isn't it interesting how we look back on the things that made us happiest when we were kids, and then start doing them again? Like lying in a meadow?"

"And what should we do now that we're here?"

He smiled. "I was just getting to that."

They'd hiked all morning before reaching a cluster of large table rocks in the middle of the shallow river, its current swiftened by an overnight downpour. They walked gingerly over slippery, moss-covered stones, arrived at two car-sized table rocks, and laid themselves out, absorbing the sun. They dove into the cool waters, the residual snowmelt and runoff from the White Mountains soothing bones achy from touring, traveling, and scampering to Venice and back. What an emotional whirlwind.

Megan turned her head, one eye open, wet hair sprawled across the rock, cupping her hand over her face. "We always said we would get back. We never did."

"That's why it feels so good."

"Among other things."

After soaking for a half-hour, they climbed a steep trail of protruding tree roots and mushroom clusters. It looked like a boulevard for a gnome. When they reached the top, the trailhead spidered into a half-dozen directions. They scouted the surrounding trees and granite formations, seeing little they remembered . . . but what to expect? Last time, they were caught in the rapture of being smitten, their surroundings only a beautiful backdrop to the swirl of feelings and desires. Not to mention the passing of time. Tom shook his head. "I don't remember any of these . . . only the trail we just climbed."

"That's because you were getting to know *my* trails and landmarks," she laughed. She pointed to a pair of boulders leaning into each other, painting themselves onto the landscape where Robert Frost lived and wrote their story, the story of the northern forests, the poems that filled her literature books. Few things create more appreciation than going to the nooks, crannies, hills, and shorelines where your favorite poet, musician, or writer did their thing, and dropping into their world. Live poets, dead poets, poets she didn't really care for in a sterile classroom . . . didn't matter once you came to the place where they lived their lives, she thought, her inner Frost channel defrosting as verses began threading from her memory, triggered by the day.

"Let's go left." She pointed to two boulders leaning into each other, hugging giants fossilized by the last ice age. "Remember these? What I called them?"

He kicked mud off his boot, took an ascending breath. "The Lovers."

"After us."

Later, in the meadow, she rolled onto her stomach and stroked his chest. "Do you remember what you wrote when we first came here?"

"I remember the way your parents freaked about a San Francisco hippie without a 'real' job taking their little girl into the mountains."

She laughed softly. "They just wanted to be sure."

He chuckled and cupped one of her breasts. "Judging from your dad's scowl? I made a strong first impression."

"But they liked you deep-down and never chased you away."

"You were nineteen."

"Not too old for parents to chase a boy away in that day and age. You know they only wanted the best for me, which in their world, meant a Seven Sisters degree followed by a great job or a Mrs. Degree. Or in my case, a fashion career. Thankfully, unlike most every one of their friends, they didn't push me on the Mrs. As the only option. Or even the first."

"Mrs. Degree . . . ?"

"Find the right man to marry, he supports you, you raise the kids and take care of him. A Mrs. Degree."

"They got that," Tom laughed.

"That's one way to put it." Megan kissed his forehead. "What I remember, though, is how you sang your heart out for a week at the Boston Tea Party and we made love in this meadow after we found out how much we liked each other. Then, when "I Know She's My Lady" broke, and put you on the radio, everyone decided it must be the theme song of this new couple called Tommy T and Mystical Megan."

"Only in the movies." Tom smiled and stroked her face. "Don't forget, the song and nickname were about a year apart."

Megan knelt in front of him and kissed him fully, her face filled with fresh sun, her spirit feeling some space again. She rubbed her hands over his arms and legs, and settled them on his thighs. "Sing to me, Tommy, like you did when you won me over."

> *I know that she's my lady*
> *So warm her transfused grace.*
> *Her eyes caress the sky, her hair*
> *Takes flight upon the breeze,*
> *She peers inside and grabs my soul*
> *Her love contains my life,*
> *My lady love, my life*

"As beautiful as the day you wrote it," Megan said.

"Is this where I say, 'every day is Valentine's Day with us'?"

"Sure, if you're into cheese . . . but it's true. And every couple should be so lucky to revisit the place where they consummated their love," she said. "It should be their sacred place, one that, as we've just proven, rekindles desires . . . or offers a most sumptuous excuse." She pinched his side. "Even Mom and Dad did it."

"Really? What?"

"Revisited their sacred place," Megan laughed. "They were not as stiff and stuffy as they showed you most of the time. Their place is pretty special; they conceived me on a beach in San Diego, during one of Daddy's investment seminars."

Tom sat up. "I never knew that."

"You never asked. So you, Christine, and Annalisa, and even Chandra, can go on and on about how Californian you are, but I *began* on a California beach."

"I have a hard time picturing your dad taking off his black shoes and plopping his feet in wet sand. Not to mention undressing on it. I never saw him *not* wear those shoes."

She shrugged her shoulders. "Maybe he didn't." They both laughed. "Remember when they went back, a few years before Daddy died?"

"Sure."

"They relived their moment. Almost got busted, too. Cops drove down the beach, and they had to duck behind a sea wall. Back when they first visited that beach, you could tuck under a blanket, light a bonfire and spend as many nights on the beach as you wanted. Now you have to be off that beach early at night, when the bar bands are just starting to play. Such a shame, another freedom taken away."

He chuckled and looked around. "We only have blades of grass to duck behind."

She rolled atop him again. "Why duck?"

The getaway recharged him. He and the Fever powered through three strong late-summer weeks in Philly, Baltimore, Virginia Beach, Charlotte, Atlanta, and Tampa, peppered with a handful of flash split-band shows and add-on dates in Jacksonville and New Orleans. They added wrinkles and surprises every night, the band now a choreographed force. Christine combed through daily requests online and presented the four or five most requested songs at sound check, where they would pick one not on the set list, and rotate it into the night's set. Beginning in Philadelphia, fans also walked into something new at arena and stadium lobbies—donation boxes. Tom asked fans not for money, but for notes of encouragement to Paolo, whose situation he shared each night. Megan shipped notes to Paolo every few days while wiring Annalisa thousands of dollars in ones, fives, tens, and twenties fans pitched into those boxes in defiance of Tom's requests.

Every time he took the stage, Tom thought a little more of Annalisa and Paolo, Christine's huge leap of faith in coming home, his full, reconnected family together. He played for them. He played for Paolo. He played for Chester, Will, Rogelio, and X. He played for his daughters, the one singing with him, the other facing every parent's most gripping horror—losing and then surviving your child.

He knew that feeling all too well.

Night after night, he left every note of every song on the stage and in the ears of the audience. Older fans compared the shows to their favorite Fever concerts of all time, many in letters and posts on social media, now hitting view numbers a small country would appreciate. DJs, journalists, bloggers, and reviewers wondered, in print and broadcast, how the Fever could sound better than ever. Weren't they old? Washed up? Leaning on young musicians? Yet, the articles invariably boiled down to how well Tom, Chester, and Will played.

The satellite radio shows also took root. While recording at local stations grateful for the visit, Tom and Chester took listeners backstage with prime-cut tales, shared tunes from promising local bands, or obscure or classic old groups, and aired a different live Fever cut from the tour each show. Their song lists, available online, gave musicians new and retired alike a new berth for fans to download their songs, in some cases changing the fans' perspective of the song or performer, in others prompting them to mentally revise what they thought they knew as the history of a song, or performer, or body of music. "That's part of the point," Tom told one station manager. After each show, they put down their headphones, broke out their guitars and played for fans who gathered outside the studios, then shared food and drink before joining the rest of the band for sound check.

As the Southern run wound down, Tom, Will, and Chester played a house concert outside Tampa. House concerts provided great ways for family-bound folkies and other acoustically oriented groups and artists to perform to small, enthusiastic gatherings in the intimacy of a home. Some groups played a dozen house gigs a year; it was like a secret society, little known to the general public outside of respective house mailing lists, but always available to musicians. The intimate gig was hosted by Dave and Elisa, venerable folkies they'd met at the big springtime folk festivals, where swamp alligators, bearded oaks, cypress hammocks, and some of the nation's most treasured pieces of music intermingled. During their acoustic set, Tom and Chester regaled the packed house with stories, thrilled by the intimacy of the venue, eighty friends, community, food, and good tunes. It was fine home cooking in all its forms.

"I'm really lookin' forward to getting back on the farm," Chester said near the end of the show. "Plucking my guitar on the porch, watching the leaves fall, howling at the moon with my dogs."

"You guys *are* going to keep touring, right?" a silver-haired fan asked.

Chester gulped softly. *Shit.* "That's the plan, Sadie," he said quickly.

"But my daughters told me your tour ends next week, in California."

Afterwards, Tom grabbed her arm and led her to a quieter spot. "Don't say anything to your daughters, Sadie. Or anyone else. But we've been friends since . . . I'll tell you that my grandson is not well. I need to help him out after the tour."

"I didn't know you had a grandson. Until I heard about the donation boxes."

"I just found out myself."

"Big news in your life, for sure." She started humming "Little Bird."

"Yes, she's back."

"I've heard. And?"

"We're making up for lost time. Not sure it's possible, but . . ."

Sadie smiled and rubbed Tom's back.

40

THE FEVER'S TRIPTYCH FESTIVAL: 8-15 TO 8-17
3 SHOWS • 3 SITES • FINAL SHOWS OF TOUR!
PALO ALTO • SAN FRANCISCO • OAKLAND
CATCH IT!

T HE STREET LOOKED LIKE A GHOST SHIP EMERGING FROM A LONG, dark night. Annalisa stared at the roof, eaves, and bay windows of the three-story Victorian, the shape triggering a foggy image from deep within that sharpened as the ghost ship sailed slowly into the dim light of memory. "So this is where I spent my *bambini* years," she said.

Tom wrapped his arm around her. "Your first home, sweetheart."

Tears filled her eyes, which she did nothing to stop. "I remember the three floors—like a cake with layers. We lived on the top floor. What was its color?"

"Light blue with all sorts of psychedelic designs when we lived here. We even painted clouds and birds on the walls."

"I think I remember the feeling, the food, always incense burning. Everyone happy so much, singing, laughing, dancing, clapping when we *bambini piccoli,* how do you say—"

"—small children . . ."

"*Si.* You know Italian now?" She slapped his shoulder playfully.

"I've been there enough . . . and your mother spoke it when we lived here. As you were saying . . ."

"I remember the mamas made a little school and made it fun. They really cared." She sighed and wiped her eyes. "All those smiles, joyful hearts. My first five years." She peered into his eyes. "I was very blessed. I could not feel that way after."

He froze, unable to respond. There was nothing else to say, anyway. Then, "Let me show you something else."

They walked along Haight Street, a daily ritual in her early childhood. She rubbed her arms as fog rolled into and out of the district from Golden Gate Park like an indecisive teen. "You must be very happy to play the last show," she said. "It is a long summer for you, playing as much as you have played, and so many new things."

Tom nodded as he peered down the street, took her hand, and tucked it inside his arm. "Starting with you? Yeah, I'd say so," he said. "But there is something I wanted to ask. It's about the final show—no one is bothering to tell me. You know anything?"

She stifled a grin. "No."

"If you knew, you would tell me, right?"

"About?" She leaned into his shoulder. "Enjoy this day, Papa."

"Forgive me, sweetheart, but once upon a time, I knew what was happening with this band, since I was its *leader*."

"Allow today to happen. No leading, just enjoying."

"So you do know."

"I know this will be a very special evening for you. I fly from Paolo's treatments in Basel to be here for you. I am not the only one. You will love it."

"Who else is coming?"

"I do not know these people . . . but you will love it."

"What I will love is flying back to Venice for you and Paolo, and then getting snowed in on top of the Ridge so I can't go anywhere. How is he?"

"A little better. He looks better. His spirits are positive. The doctors give him good treatment. I think he can make it through this; I just hope that he never again gets a visit from cancer, because this is three times, all bad. I know he is very grateful to you."

They walked to the end of the Haight and passed five homeless veterans on the sidewalk. Tom acknowledged them with quick greetings and five-dollar bills, insisting they spend it on their next meals. Then he thanked them for their service, a gesture he made to all veterans, since it never happened when he and others finished their Vietnam tours and came home to the turbulent second half of the decade. In his case, the turbulence fed the music that fed the rock and roll masses, but he would never pretend how brutal and rude the "welcome homes" were for many returning soldiers. They'd had absolutely nothing to do with the terrible decisions and lies politicians made and their superior officers followed.

It was doubly brutal for Tom, who took flak for openly supporting the troops while decrying the government. You just didn't do in the sixties what became the politically correct flavor *de rigeur* a few decades later: rail on the government's decision to go to war, but support every soldier over there. The soldiers, fresh off their high school prom nights (or younger if they lied about their age, as he did) had to fly into the theater and take fire ordered by others thousands of miles and a safe air-conditioned office away, suffer the deaths, injuries, PTSD, and other horrors of war. A different world, for sure, yet what was different? Some things never stop being screwed up, because to reverse that mentality, you have to erase the biggest factor: the primal instinct for going to war and the geopolitical or financial excuses for doing so. Tom and the others thought their voices, songs, loving, and community-based approach to life, the Flower Power Generation, the greatest expression of a new, communal way of living the world had ever seen (if you don't count thousands of years of Native American life, of course), could turn the tide. Sadly, though, this tide always came down to whether the decision makers started storms. Or muted them and the voices of the unwitting citizens who voted them into their power.

It was perfect cannon fodder for an artistic explosion, the Sixties, all the forces fighting for control of society, to feed impressionable minds ready to be the exact opposite of their parents. Some of those young minds took charge of their own destinies, which is part of why the era became a benchmark for the concept of peace, freedom, love, spirit, community, and self-expression, a benchmark sparking all sorts of commemorations as time rendered the Summer of Love a certain age itself.

Tom riffed on mentally as he and Annalisa entered a tunnel covered in graffiti, emerging at the base of Hippie Hill, the eastern edge of Golden Gate Park, scents of eucalyptus and mint filling the central gathering place. People milled around, catching up on the week's gossip, just as they had since the park was conceived during Reconstruction. "Do you remember this place?"

"*Si.* I rolled down this hill many times." Annalisa turned in a slow circle, inhaling the meadow, playground, and hill that formed a natural amphitheater. A half dozen silver-haired women walked slowly ahead of them, conversing about grandchildren and great-grandchildren, walking in and out of the fog as it crept around the towering eucalyptus, oaks, sycamores, and redwoods.

She rubbed her hands on several trees, a smile crossing her face, wide as time, her eyes closed, trying to picture faces. Nothing. Only cheers. Cheers building onto cheers, laughter, shouts of joy, singing together . . . *people in the park. Cheering inside my baby heart, always. My baby heart, always cheering.* "We came here, I talked or played music, and you played with other kids on the playground over there," he said softly.

Annalisa smiled, blinked, and studied the trees. The air was large, open, charged with the sharp light of late summer. Up ahead, two children slid, climbed, and swung through a large playground, a carousel behind them. "Let us visit," she said. They moved slowly, the lush fragrance of grass, trees, salted air, and coffee triggering something just out of reach, a life experience once held before it got away. She tried to grab it inside, couldn't quite reach it, the scents remembered but not specific moments.

A girl rode the carousel, her mother watching her with one eye as she shared a muffin with her husband. "Mom! Look! No hands!" the girl squealed, squeezing her legs against the rainbow-colored horse, throwing out her arms as the calliope pumped out canned popcorn music.

Music. Calliope. *No hands! Look, Daddy! My horse is so happy I'm here! What's her name?*

Delight! Hanging on, one arm out, spinning around, treetops swirling, the joy of riding Delight . . . jumping off dizzy, excited, jumping into open arms. His mighty arms.

"Coming back?"

Her eyes filled with wonderment. "Yes. We were here many times."

"Almost every weekend. These were your horses." He patted the rainbow-colored horse on which she now sat. "Especially this one."

Delight. "Still here? After all these years?"

"Looks like it."

She felt five again. "Let us ride the carousel."

She turned to the operator. His sour, pained but youthful face, cap turned sideways over his dark eyes, and the way he clung to a quart of steaming coffee like a lifeline, left little doubt about his previous night. She gave him a dollar. Two girls paid their money and joined her a few horses away, wondering why someone older than their mothers wanted to ride—but thinking it oddly cool just the same. "Do you like riding?" one asked, her smile covered in braces.

"Very much."

"I've never seen you here."

"I have not ridden in a very long time."

The girl was puzzled. "Then how do you know if you like it or not?"

"I do this when I was young, like you."

The girls looked at Tom, raised their eyebrows, and chirped to each other. "Your accent totally rules, ma'am," one said, pushing her glasses into place. "I like how people from different places talk. We're boring."

Annalisa chuckled. She held onto Delight, her rainbow mare. The operator rousted himself from his wicked hangover long enough to flip the switch.

With every revolution, images seemed to form within the trees and buildings, spun from her innermost places. Running, smearing ice cream, flying kites . . . colorful clothes, feather boas, headbands, necklaces, bangles, beads, painted faces, goofy sunglasses . . . tag and keep-away, laughing and screaming, drum and dance circles, laying on the grass, telling cloud stories . . . always children, always playmates, but Daddy nearby, always right there . . .

"What stories do you see in the clouds, sweetheart?" She rode atop his hands, above his extended arms, as he lay face-up on the grass, his hands cradling her back.

The clouds bloomed into two ovals, the smaller attached to the larger, the belly of the larger flecked with sunlight, releasing that light into the smaller clouds. Once they joined, they flew through the sky as one. "Casper the Friendly Ghost!" *she exclaimed.* "He's here to sing and dance with us."

"He might even take our songs into the sky . . ."

"Where people in heaven can sing them . . ."

A chuckle. "That would be nice."

"Casper is going to fly around, take the best songs, and sprinkle the clouds with them. When it rains again, it will rain songs . . ." *She smiled and stared at the clouds.* "Casper is laughing."

"Why?"

"Because he knows what makes you happy. Singing."

"No, honey, *you* make me happy."

Casper laughed again. He would always laugh . . .

She stepped off the carousel and walked down the ramp. Tom pointed to a nearby kiosk. "I'm getting a couple of coffees."

Two half-asleep women slid open the corrugated security door, one wrecked from an all-night study session for a medical school exam, the other looping through the ascendant moments of a date that, her rising eyebrows suggested, rose to where all great dates summit—with the promise of more.

Annalisa exchanged goodbyes with the girls on the carousel. As they skipped away, Tom heard one say, "She's old, but totally nice. I want to talk like her!"

"I remember more," she said when she reached him.

"It's a lot easier to remember when you're standing in the place itself. This place really made an impact on you, didn't it?"

"It kept my spirit alive. Poppa Maurizio did, also."

Tom pointed toward Hippie Hill. "Do you remember what we used to do there?"

"Besides rolling down the hill?"

A half-dozen young men and women sat in a circle, drumming and chanting to Kali, Saraswati, Aham Cara, Parvati, Kuan Yin, Divine Mother . . . "Invoking deities, goddesses," Tom said. "Love hearing music played for the reason it was first played tens of thousands of years ago—to invoke spirits in the night, something the shamans did with their drums."

Annalisa slowly scanned the perimeter of the hill. The droning beat of the drums moved deeper into her body, dislodging another cache . . .

Adults dancing in circles, adults grabbing her hand, she dancing, too . . . drums, drums everywhere, the ever-present sweet scent rising from hand-rolled cigarettes and pipes, making people happy . . . sharing food, flowers, beads, scarves . . . a girl with flowers woven into her waist-length hair, reading . . . "love" and "peace," the greatest words . . . one huge family, me and Daddy and Mama and Uncle Chester and everyone . . . more drums.

Later, in bed, the ceiling painted in stars, rainbows, and mist from which dreams and visions grow. On the other side, the grown-ups talk and play. Some crash out, some leave, some watch sunrise . . . them reading stories in bed, no matter how big the party, Babar the Elephant, Make Way for Ducklings, Winnie the Pooh, Island of the Blue Dolphins— *her books. The fight to keep the eyes open . . . he tucks her in, sings her favorite story, now a radio song, about little Alice who feeds her head . . . can I be Alice?*

They're fighting again! Daddy trying to get Mama to talk to him, Mama going back to bed, screaming at him, him screaming back, Daddy saying everything is all right and holding me even tighter and telling me he loves me even more, and Mama saying she's taking me away and if she takes me away where will my daddy be?

And what is wrong with Mama?

Tom nudged her shoulder. "Where did you go, sweetheart?"

"A good place. Then a bad place. No need to speak of it." She sat up and wiped the grass from her hair. "How long have I been away?"

"You've been sleeping about a half-hour."

She opened her eyes and closed them just as quickly. The sun had taken charge, the fog bank vacating like a fleeing sprinter. More people walked past her, chatting, finding seats on the hill. The drumming circle grew louder. "Looks like they're going to have a little shindig here," Tom said.

Merda! She sat up and brushed off the grass. "Papa, let us walk now."

She glanced at a wide swatch of greenery bordered by old mansions of the Pacific District, a magnificent thousand-acre park of gardens, conservatories, museums, ponds, dunes, meadows, wilds, and paths that stretched to the sea. She remembered a day when she sat at her easel in the back of the flat, and merged ten plants into a watercolor. The kindergarten teacher, a matronly woman hired by the mothers for their experiment in schooling at home, asked Tom and Maria if they had subjected Annalisa to any "funny medicine."

"Why? Because she's creative?" he asked, perturbed. "Have you seen or smelled it when you've come here, ever?"

"Can't say that I have." The teacher shook her head. "But I ask because she is gifted, and I don't want her adversely affected."

"By . . . we don't do that."

The teacher put her hand on her ample hip. "Mr. Timoreaux, *everyone* smokes here. I don't care what you do, but please not in front of your daughter.

I tell this to every parent, more in your case, because you need to help your daughter develop her gift, or she will be frustrated in life. Take it from one who stopped writing far too young."

She may have looked like a refugee from the Hoover administration, but she bore wisdom, the same degree of insight that, come to think of it, the increasing hordes pouring into the Haight were trying to grasp and spread.

With a brisk walk, they could reach Ocean Beach in less than an hour. After sitting in the sand and eating a bite, they could catch a cab and be back for sound check.

The final check.

They took the northern route to the beach along John F. Kennedy Drive, a spectacular walk past waterfalls and creeks still flowing, a wet winter and spring burdening the Sierra snowpack like an overloaded burrow. It had to flow somewhere. "Can you sing 'She Flew Away'?"

"*Si.*"

They walked past the stream and catch ponds, his voice soft as his lyrics told the agony of a child disappearing, those same lyrics moving through her as she walked, as though she were ripped from her moors, tears falling, a little girl screaming hard inside . . . and now, a final release from everything about the song.

> *"I told you I leave! Now!" Pans and knives across the kitchen. A rock through a window. Overstuffed suitcases sitting like pregnant prunes near the door.*
>
> *Maria snarled. "Pack,* bambini! *Now!" She slapped her forward.*
>
> *"There's no reason to go." His voice was hard, his tone low. "I can easily get a job until Chester and I figure out how to make this band work."*
>
> *"I will not live this way! You will never make it! You music people say the same. I did not stay in America to live with weird people, weird music and wild dreams, drugs . . ."*
>
> *"What drugs? I haven't done anything you haven't done. What about Annalisa? She loves it here—"*
>
> *"She now will see what I love."*
>
> *"Where are you taking her? Italy?"*
>
> *"It does not matter, but no, not Italy. Why would I do that?"*
>
> *"Because you are from there."*
>
> *"I do not know."*
>
> *He started to say something, bit his top lip down, spun in a circle, raked his hair until he felt his roots straining. "I'm her dad. Our baby doesn't deserve this.."*
>
> *"From now on, she is my baby!"*

He tried to calm and reason with her, brush off her barks and bites as heat of the moment brimstone. It wasn't.

Annalisa pressed her ear to the wall. "Don't take me from Daddy!" she screamed, beating her tiny fists into the wall.

"If you were such a great father, you would throw away the music," Maria said, her voice venomous, coiled to strike again. "Annalisa deserves more."

"Than love? She deserves more than love? What is more than love, Maria? My music will never be as important as Annalisa—or you. Never." He paused. "When I make it, and we're set, I'll get off the road and be at home. You watch."

"You have never been on the road! How do you stop something you never started? Give up the music! What difference, quitting now or later? It is only music."

"I will always play music, and I will always keep food on our table."

"That is easy now. You feed one person. Play all the music you want!"

Then, Annalisa's final memory: Her Papa running down the street, bare-chested and barefooted, yelling for her. Her palms slapped the cab's rear window, trying to escape, coughing from all the congestion her screams and cries stirred up. Maria smacked her back into the seat.

"You will have to change the ending, Papa," she said softly.

"Yes I will. Tonight."

41

"Ready, Dad?"

"As I'll ever be."

Tom wiped his eyes as images from the best shows threaded through his mind like an end-of-life montage. On the other end of the hallway and corridor, twenty thousand fans threatened to tear the roof off the coliseum. The show was thirty minutes behind, the crowd stomping and screaming for the whole time.

Christine brushed her hair, checked her makeup, twirled into the mirror once more to make sure everything was in place, and canvassed the dressing room. "Everyone ready? You, Aunt Raylene? I still can't believe you flew out here."

"Against doctor's orders," Chester said. "Damned rebel."

"Well, Chester, put that little red neck of yours away . . . last thing a black girl from Louisiana's gonna be is a damned *rebel*." She peered at Chester, an eyebrow cocked, her face awash in a smile. "Honey, I'm walking out on that stage, you guys helping me, and I'm gonna be a part of this." She rubbed her fingers and started playing the chord progressions for "United Our State" into thin air.

Christine and Annalisa walked over to Tom. Christine stifled a yawn after a full day with Megan, coordinating the elaborate stage setup with Dudley and his crew, while Chester and Will discussed songs being added with the light and sound team. "This is both the happiest and saddest moment of my life," she said. "Happy that we had this summer on stage together, Dad. I still can't believe you went for this, and I went for this—and now it's almost over. Sad because you're saying goodbye."

"With an asterisk," Tom said.

"But you're done here."

"It has been a summer filled with miracles," Annalisa added.

"That it has." Tom wrapped his arms around them. "I am a lucky man and father." He kissed their cheeks, and then looked at Christine. "Let's kick their asses, honey, one verse at a time, be that father and daughter who took the stage one night and left everyone with their mouths hanging open."

She hip checked him into Megan. "You bet your ass, Dad."

He turned to the rest of the band. "Boys? Raylene? Everyone ready? Tonight's the night we ride."

WAS TOMMY T'S FINAL SHOW THE FEVER'S FINEST HOUR?

BY JEREMIAH DENTON
EDITOR EMERITUS

WHEN RECORD EXECUTIVE JASON ROBISKI URGED ME TO FLY to the San Francisco Bay area, I had no idea why, though I suspected Tommy Timoreaux might be contemplating his final exit during a recent press conference in New York. "You've got to catch the Fever's show in Oakland," Robiski told me. "Not one to miss."

Really? What's so special about Oakland? Besides getting skipped out on by their beloved Raiders and a decent alt-rock and hip-hop scene? "Robiski," I told him, "I've seen forty, fifty Fever shows. Three this tour alone. I've got grandkids bouncing on my knee, the wife all but making me drink protein smoothies instead of a frosty mug every day. Not sure I'll miss anything."

"Oh, you will," he said. "You'll never see them in this shape and form again."

Tommy T? Chester? Gotta be Tommy T.

As noted, this intrepid music scribe had felt that Tommy T was working to hand the mantle to Christine Timoreaux, his daughter and star of this legendary band's summer run. In this case, triumphant's a small word: These veteran rockers redefined how to play a reunion tour. You can shuck together your greatest hits, and book halls and smaller arenas with devout fans, like most legacy bands or a myopic politician. Or you can retool half the band with dynamic, charismatic musicians who could lead bands on their own, and let them play a couple of *their* songs, thus securing another generation of fans and turning their show into one for the ages.

The Fever made a believer out of me, that's for sure, a believer that legendary bands could tour on something beyond nostalgic fumes. They did it twenty years ago, when yours truly scoffed at Tommy's desire to play an eighty-show extravaganza to close out, their long-blazing star finally waning as hip-hop, over-dubbed pop, and sappy vocalists kicked the rock can down the road. He showed me just good these musicians are when in their element, the live stage.

Still, when drummer Will Halsey told me right before the tour started, "This isn't a nostalgia tour. This is the new Fever's first tour," I almost laughed. Know how many legacy bands claim that?

Funny thing, though: Will was right. I've covered this business for forty years, and liked and sometimes loved the Fever, at times writing I'd never seen a better band. That sentiment comes and goes, like it does for all hardcore music fans, but one thing's for sure: I've *never* seen a night like the one they laid on twenty thousand ecstatic guests in Oakland. It was a monumental three and a half hours of great music, even by the Fever's lofty standards. They are so tight that an errant note or chord bounces off the stage like a soccer ball off a roadie's noggin when Rod Stewart gets in the kicking mood mid-show, a moment's distraction, quickly forgotten.

This band and its show still revolves around Tommy T, the man whose voice and words beat inside the hearts of two generations. How a low tenor can project as powerfully as James Earl Jones in a Darth Vader moment is, well, part of his wizardry. Was Tommy T at his finest? Outside of a lost half-octave (or a little more) from his range, you bet, and Christine made him better. Did they take advantage of the styles and talents of new keyboardist Ulysses "X" Washington and instrumentalist extraordinare Rogelio Matias? C'mon, Einsteins, throw me a real question. Did they reach into their archives and drag out some real treasures instead of settling for a greatest hits show? On each of their fifty gigs, , they switched out at least two or three songs. Every time. Let's look at how that works in today's ridiculously choreographed stage setups. Bands tour with two set lists, four at the most. Because of how tightly shows choreograph lighting, sound, stage, earpieces, pre-recorded overlays (usually on keyboards), and performers, bands don't vary much. Even if they wanted to, it's very difficult. If you play by today's rules, that is. But Tommy T and the Fever dialed back the clock to remind us of what summers used to be like, a series of spontaneous, free-flowing concerts, incense and more in the air, every set a creation unto itself, every concert floor exploding with dancing and rocking out, all of which were becoming extinct art forms.

Spotlights hit the twin speaker stacks about thirty minutes after the scheduled start. Twenty feet up, Tom stood on one stack, Christine on the other, the band beneath them. A few times this summer, they opened on a mellow note, and did it again with quite a surprise, pure ear candy to anyone from the Bay Area: the sweet Jefferson Airplane ballad, "Comin' Back to Me." They followed with Tommy's own masterpiece ballads, "Mystical Dreamer" and "Her Heart Was Something New."

Let's step on the gas, boys! And girl . . . Will Halsey kick-drummed them into a rousing four-song medley, Chester, Rogelio, and X trading leads with power and precision. Chester's mini-solos reminded me of George Harrison or Mike Campbell, the captain of Tom Petty's merry ship, in the way he jumped in and out of solos in sixty seconds or less throughout the medley, firing off ridiculous licks every time. He's not as likely to go after the ten-minute monster solos as before, but he did treat us to a half-dozen long solos during the night.

Tom and Christine descended the speakers and strode onto center stage, Tom in a shirt, bolo tie, and jeans, and Christine in a white cape, short black skirt, long-sleeved half-top, and adornments fit for a gypsy or Bedouin dancer. Or a flower child. They made me feel like I was again standing in the Sixties. You can call me a chauvinist and file a complaint, but barefoot singers remind me of Polynesian dancers, very alluring and lithe, only a hundred decibels louder. Something about it feels so organic, rooted, innocent as walking in flower-covered meadows. Sounds corny as hell, I know, but think of Jewel, Joss Stone, Samantha Fish burning up that blues guitar, Kelly Clarkson, and before them, Belinda Carlisle, Debbie Harry, Cherie Currie, Janis . . .

The band busted the crowd in the chops with "Street Party" and "United Our State," and kept it coming with time-honored standards, rearrangements, an extended Chester solo or two, and two numbers off the new album.

Midway through the set, the Fever broke for "the Zeppelin moment," slowing it down, taking their seats, trotting out acoustic instruments, showing off their mellow side a little more, always the "yin" to this band's "yang." Will, Tommy, and Chester plucked out "the same couple of tunes we played at our first rehearsal," Tommy told the crowd. When they finished, Tommy and Chester stepped backstage, Will moved back to his kit, and the youthful half rolled out *their* hits, including "Holy Child Blues," a tune any hard-nosed urbanite like myself would appreciate.

Seamless onstage communication, Rogelio's virtuosity on horns and four- and six-string bass, and the nifty back-and-forth between Chester, Tommy, and X made this a show for the ages. Christine spun it all together, the dancing gypsy rocking each note like it was her last. How a band can move so seamlessly between funk, prog, psychedelic, dirty blues, straight-up hard rock and these sweet, tender mellow songs, with two singers, I'll never know. That's why we will always love the Fever. It's also why, thanks to the sheer fortitude of Tommy, Chester, and Will coming out of a long retirement with great new songs, our grandkids may one day listen to the Fever with *their* grandkids.

Finally, we arrived at the point when many a classic rocker looks at his or her watch, sees that the contracted ninety minutes have elapsed, grabs the

Evian bottle, bows and says "I love you!" and takes a runner into the awaiting limo, while people who paid $150 to $250 a pop chant, "One more song! One more song!"

But that's not how the Fever rolls. Ninety minutes? That's halftime. They busted out for three hours . . . and they weren't done. On this night, three hours may as well have been a long sound check.

For the encore, a truly wonderful scene unfurled, one I'm pretty sure I'll never see again. (Trust me, when you've covered a scene for forty years, very little gives you pause or reason to think you'll see anything different.) Two dozen of your favorite rock and rollers (and mine) stretched across the stage. Before they began, Tommy reprised a staple of the shows that started indoor rock, shows at the Winterland, Avalon, Fillmore, Longshoreman's Hall, Fillmore East, Café A Go Go, or Academy of Music. He brought out a poet. Back in the day, a poet, wordsmith, or legend like Dizzy Gillespie or Sam Cooke would often open. Remember Michael McClure taking the stage in *The Last Waltz*, The Band's final concert, to recite Chaucerian English . . . as in, English that Shakespeare thought ancient? *Whan that Aprille with his shoures soote/The droghte 2 of Marche hath perced to the roote . . .*

We got the idea, you say. Moving on…

After Tommy's guest poet was finished with a much more understandable paean to the ethereal beauty and wisdom of music, a large projection screen dropped behind Will's drum riser. Smoke poured onto the stage, followed by psychedelic light show blobs, with raw 8mm footage from an early Fever show. In the cramped Boston Tea Party scene, Raylene and Chester jammed next to Tommy, beaming because, unknown to everyone else at the time, he'd just met Mystical Megan. The speed and efficiency of their early shows was obvious and breathtaking. It was like watching early Santana at the Fillmore before Woodstock shot them into the stratosphere; you could see the superstardom coming. The film piece offered a wonderful juxtaposition of both ends of this band's career, the hungry tigers zipping around the screen, the wise legends they became playing in front of their black-and-white youth. Put it together, and you have one of the greatest countercultural experiences in American music history.

Within this feast of music and memories, Tommy's older daughter, Annalisa, took the stage. If Fellini had ever wanted to cast a brunette in a sequel to *La Dolce Vita*, Annalisa would have been a good choice. Sadly, her formerly fractured life would've suited Fellini's twisted vision, too. "My sister and I honor our father and make his final performance special for all of us," she said in her endearing Italian accent, with Christine standing alongside.

Annalisa could've brought the house down by stating that she was the unintended early inspiration for Tommy T, sheer grief being the great creative driver that it is, but safe to say, she and her father are happy with leaving "She Flew Away" where it belongs from this point forward—away.

Two of Christine's words did cause a collective gasp: "Final performance." You didn't get the memo? Well, ladies and gentlemen, I didn't get the memo, either, because in typical Tommy fashion, he never sent one! How he and the gang kept this night under wraps in today's 24/7 social digital instant-grat-anything-goes texting-I'm-your-Facebook-Friend Instagram world, I'll never know.

Chester refocused the stunned crowd with musical machine-gun fire from his vintage Les Paul Reverseburst on "When I Become the President." All guest musicians played on this one. A half-dozen sang along with Tom and Christine, the microphone stands looking like a grove of naked aspens. Christine then performed her hit, "Gypsy's Prayer," with the power and finesse befitting a rising star. She's the full package. She turned to the rock-and-roll royalty on stage, which incanted, "You'll be my gypsy's prayer; you'll be my gypsy's prayer," for another minute as she danced side to side, lost in her world, which must feel awfully abundant and open to possibility right now. If that hookline isn't looping through your brain, and looping back for another tantalizing replay, then you didn't see a Fever show the second half of the tour. Or turn on or log onto an alt or rock radio station anytime in the last two months.

After the guests exited to wild cheers, another wrinkle arrived: legendary bassist/vocalist Raylene Quarles, who missed the tour for health reasons. Fans danced in the aisles, others stomped in place, and I suspect a few more babies than normal will be born in the Bay Area in nine months. Kind of like the winning Super Bowl team's fan base. I digress, but point is, it was a love and music explosion, just as Tommy and Chester sought when they formed the band. And again when they shocked the music world by returning after twenty years with a dynamo of a band that set fans and promoters ablaze with delight.

What made the Fever tour so memorable and successful? The way they presented themselves and their music. They threw the clock back to a more innocent, pure era, when everything was about the performance and experience, about jamming together, about talking to your fans through the music, about letting that music expand our hearts and minds as we explore the melodies and lyrics, singing them over and over to feed our minds, our hearts, to maybe look at things a different way. Everyone was in it together, fans and musicians alike, a community, a musical family. They reminded us of the best of those times, beautiful people yearning for adventure, knowledge, insight, and greater consciousness, filling an emptiness left inside by the vacuous late Fifties and early Sixties (unless they read the Beat writers). They turned to their musicians, poets, and artists for words and depictions of wisdom, love, and new possibility, the creatives serving as our heralds and priests while we married hearts to minds and tried to express our deepest, mightiest, most loving selves. Damn, I miss that era. But that was the Haight-Ashbury dream, the so-called Summer of Love (so named not by an actual resident, but by *Life* magazine). It later spread to rural communes and then went mainstream, got conflated and gentrified at the same time . . . and now we feel halfway underground again.

The Fever also reminded us of the spontaneity of early rock shows. If musicians didn't want to play a song on a given night, they just skipped it and moved on, often with an impromptu jam. In this far more programmed era, where predictability is preferred and everything has a branding label, corporate imprint, and stiff price tag attached, simplicity seems to be a crime. A rocker can't just go play a show without half a dozen interests being involved. Money, money, money . . . Tommy, Chester, and the others did a huge favor by reminding us of what it's about, why music came into existence in the first place: touching the hearts, imaginations, and spirits of a fan or two with the notes and words. You never know: the right song, delivered at the right time to the right person, can literally transform a life. Tommy taught me that. I'm pretty certain lives were transformed during this glorious summer of marathon shows.

Sometime around one a.m., four hours after they took the stage, Chester fired off his final riff, the Super Trouper spotlights swaying back and forth like a belly dancer's hips, with Tommy and Christine crooning, "Going to the West of the Wessssst . . ." As Chester held his guitar like a tommy gun, backed by Will's thunderous kick drums, a roadie walked out with a white oak rocking chair, handmade by an Amish woodworker from a community near Chester's Tennessee spread. He motioned for Tommy to sit in it.

A rose petal dropped from the rafters. Then another. Then thousands more. I looked up into this petalstorm, a fabulous touch, this reverential send-off moment typically reserved for sacred ceremonies. In India, at that. And apparently, brilliant shows. George Harrison's friends added this touch to the phenomenal tribute concert of his music the year after he died. So nice to see it done again, properly.

When the music was over, they turned out the lights, as one James Douglas Morrison sang. Except for the light focused on Tom. "Thank you so much for all these years," he said. "You have given us so much, for all of our lives. We've had a great summer, I've had a great summer, but truth be told, it was always going to only be this summer, for me at least. But the band will keep on keeping on."

"Tommy T! Tommy T! Tommy T!"

As the rose petals turned the increasingly smoky arena into a haze of flowers, one of my favorite photos filled the projection screen: Tommy and Christine, then a toddler, bowing after the Fever's 1997 finale. Annalisa and Megan joined them onstage. He then did something that, in this once inconceivable tour, might have been the most inconceivable part of it: he wrapped his arms around his oldest daughter, lost to him for decades, and her younger sister, the newest front woman in the business.

Tommy, Megan, Christine, and Annalisa threw kisses, and bowed as one.

The Fever European Tour
BACKSTAGE PASS:
San Marco Piazza, Venice, Italy
a benefit for Paolo Frantazzi
featuring Tom Timoreaux
Coming in Winter 2018 . . .

THE END

ACKNOWLEDGMENTS

FOR THE MENTORING, ENCOURAGEMENT, AND FRIENDSHIP THAT prepared me to tell this story, my thanks to: Tom Robertson, Don Eulert, Gary Snyder, Kemal Gekic, Charles Redner, Jeff Kleinman, Regina Merrick, Barbara Stahura, Brian Wilkes, Felicia Poe, Charles Warner, Christine Fowler, and to the musicians whose helpful tips and words added plenty of insight to this story: my fellow author and North San Diego County local Stevie Salas (Rod Stewart, Mick Jagger, Terence Trent d'Arby); Michael Shrieve (Santana); Brian May (Queen); Florida folk/roots virtuosos Ellie Schwartz and Doug Travers; John Doe (X), Robert Munger (Seraphim, The Neat); Lita Ford (The Runaways); and Toni Tennille (The Captain and Tennille). Thanks to my colleagues at FX Group, Kristian Krempel, Jim Denny, Adam Longaker, Lilly Salas, and the team at Dick Clark Productions, especially Jennifer Hiraga, with whom I work on the Billboard Music Awards and American Music Awards event publications. Also, to my favorites in good times from five years at *American Idol Magazine:* Ace Young (*Joseph and the Technicolor Dreamcoat*), Bo Bice, Constantine Maroulis (*Rock of Ages*), Katharine McPhee (*Scorpion*), Taylor Hicks, Chris Daughtry (Daughtry), Kellie Pickler, Bucky Covington, and musical director Rickey Minor.

To my high school classmate, Rick McConaghey, for our first-ever trip backstage—to hang with his old neighbor, Kansas violinist/vocalist Robby Steinhardt, as they toured *Leftoverture.* That remains my favorite rock album design and title.

A special thank you to Danielle Webster for your thoughtful comments on an earlier version of this manuscript, insight on music and Millennials—and for offering up a perfect example of how cool Christine Timoreaux would be in real life.

Another special thanks to my friend and colleague of almost twenty years, Shane Brisson, for a great cover design, your work on the promotional side of the book—and great times seeing Black Sabbath together on its fare-thee-well tour in 2016.

To my beautiful sweetheart and friend of many years, Martha Halda, for your selfless love and patience in putting up with the writing process—and having to deal with a "wannabe" rock-and-roll musician and a lot of loud tunes.

Finally, to the very real muses behind *Voices:* Rock & Roll Hall of Famer Marty Balin, the original Voice of San Francisco's psychedelic era, whose many conversations with me (including a memorable walk on Haight Street, reprised in *Voices*) hatched this book; Carrie Underwood, every bit as wholesome as her image and the most down-to-earth superstar I've ever known; guitarist-songwriter-producer and *Rumble* executive producer Stevie Salas, with whom I wrote *When We Were The Boys* about his time touring with the Rod Stewart Band; and my daughter, Jessica Yehling Dutton, who turned a kindergartner's night of banging on bongos in perfect asynchronous time to a David Byrne song—not easy—into a lifetime of musicianship. Jessica, pass our love of music onto Keira.

ABOUT THE AUTHOR

ROBERT YEHLING HAS WRITTEN ABOUT MUSIC, ALBUMS, musicians, and their relationships to society, culture, fans, and entertainment for four decades. The author or co-author of twenty books, Yehling is the co-author of *Full Flight*, the memoir of Jefferson Airplane leader and Rock & Roll Hall of Famer Marty Balin; and *When We Were The Boys*, the memoir of former Rod Stewart Group lead guitarist Stevie Salas. He was also the editor of *American Idol Magazine* during the iconic show's peak seasons (2004–2008). Currently, he edits the Billboard Music Awards and American Music Awards event publications. Yehling lives in Southern California, where, as a young boy, he became fascinated with something cross-country called Woodstock. The music has played ever since.

ALSO FROM OPEN BOOKS PRESS:

Writes of Life: Using Personal Experiences in Everything You Write by Robert Yehling

The Write Time: 366 Exercises to Fulfill Your Writing Life by Robert Yehling

Wide as the Wind by Edward Stanton (young adult & literary fiction)

Resting Places by Michael C. White (inspirational fiction)

The Fragrance of Angels: An Accident, a Taste of Eternity, and a New Life by Martha Brookhart Halda (memoir)

Through the Eyes of a Young Physician Assistant by Sean Conroy (memoir)

OTHER TITLES BY ROBERT YEHLING INCLUDE:

Beyond ADHD, with Jeff Emmerson (publishing in August 2017: Rowman-Littlefield)

When We Were The Boys, with Stevie Salas (Taylor Trade)

Just Add Water (Houghton Mifflin Harcourt)

Full Flight, with Marty Balin (SAP Press)

The Champion's Way, with Dr. Steve Victorson (SwymFit Publishing)

Backroad Melodies, poetry and essays (Tuscany Global)